Summer of Speculation

2022 Edition: Villains

Published by:
Cloaked Press, LLC
P. O. Box 341
Suring, WI 54174
https://www.cloakedpress.com

Cover Design by:
Fantasy & Coffee Design
http://www.fantasyandcoffee.com/SPDesign

ASIN: B09ZSK8MWR
Paperback ISBN: 978-1-952796-13-5

With Stories From:

Benjamin DeHaan
Laura J. Campbell
Linda M. Crate
Nicole Walsh
Alex Minns
MR Wells
Eve Morton
Andrew P. McGregor
Melissa Ferguson
Glenda Thompson
Lyra Meurer
Sarah Lapalme
Helen Obermeier
Jordan Davidson
Steven E. Scribner
Erin Swann

Contents

Scalevolution

by Benjamin DeHaan

This was a different kind of heat.

Not a bubbling simmer in the back of the throat, nor the hot after taste of post meal belch fumes. This was under the scale searing and ripping and I couldn't remember the last time I had suffered as I did now.

It happened so fast.

I had been torching a small band of pale skinned Chadlits; bottom of the barrel greasy slave laborers that worked the northwest Haselyst mines. They are consumables to the Yula Empire and discarded once their backs give or nature calls them back to earth.

I heard rumors from my brothers that despite their low status, their aged meat is of the highest sweetness and their weathered tough hide shouldn't be judged by observation. Once their life water soaks the tongue, you'll understand the bliss we speak, Pawla, they had said.

But hate beat hunger tonight. My saliva steamed out from my cheeks as the blaze exploded from my mouth and across the Chadlits sending an aroma of absolute wonder into the night air. In a normal world I would have taken them in whole one at a time when smoke billowed out from their lungs, but the screams excited me and compounded my building hunger.

The more they screamed the more I lit up the night sky, the brighter the world got, the more I realized that this was all but play in a world devoid of any Ryunalan save myself.

And that fact tore me to my reptilian core.

I had been looking at my painting, a masterpiece of charred flesh and fused bone upon the canyon wall in front of me when the feeling came. I was at my weakest. My ganja sacs were completely empty and my legs felt like I had just climbed Mt. Opa.

It was at that moment with my back pressed up against a father Yoon tree and enjoying its rough bark biting into a beetle fungus outbreak when I heard the whispers that rode the wind.

The cold of the voices seeped under my skin and gripped tight on my hide. As if the world flipped upside down the cold transformed into a sickening heat that would have surpassed that of the annual Ryunalan fire breath trials winners.

And here I was. The last of my kind, dragging my giant pathetic burning body through thick vegetation and endless tree groves.

Scales ripped from back. My claws which could scratch the hardest Uni diamond in all of Lancasta, were now but filed down to useless Yulan sheepra nails. My face itched and I fell into fits of coughing. Strings of black bile hanged from the sides of my mouth.

The first thing that came to my mind through it all was simply water. Luckily my sense of smell still functioned and I caught the fresh cool scent of a river on the wind. I began to crawl to its calling.

The forest and foliage around must have blocked the scent because I could no longer taste it on the air. I knew the general direction however and I would not be shaken by the extremity of the emergency that wrapped my spirits in a compressive snake tail coil.

The more I pulled ahead, the more my body felt as if it were being stripped of all the power I had accumulated over the three hundred years as commanding chief of the Ryunalan army.

I didn't want to believe what was happening to me. I wouldn't, I believed, until I saw him standing high above.

I came upon the water that waited patiently. Not a river, but a lake. To the west, endless water and a smear of orange and pinks of a setting sun on the horizon. To the east, a red canyon wall that shot straight down into the water. On the cliff of this canyon, he stood, the whisper on the wind.

"Blackthread," I said, knowing that he couldn't hear my voice. But I wanted to say the sorcerer's name out loud. I wanted to assure myself that I would not waver nor tremble under the sound of the ones responsible for the down fall of my brothers and sisters. "I knew it was you all this time."

Black robes flailed in the wind. I pulled my focus lens down and could see his sickly burnt face looking out on the water. His lips were threaded closed, his eyes blackened around the sockets, and nose concaved into a triangular opening so that you could see his wet nasal workings.

He turned his head to me and nodded so that all I could see was his bald scarred scalp.

I felt my heart sink to the bottom of the world. The whisper on the wind was the last Blackthread Sorcerer and I was the last Ryunalan. With my death would come the defeat of a two hundred-thousand-year race.

I tried to get up. I imagined myself flying at the pace of a Cloudwither hawk, sending my claws deep into the sorcerer's chest, erasing the Blackthreads, the Yulan Empire, and their dreams of dominance over Lancasta. I must stay alive. There has to be more Ryunalans. I would search every rock if I must to prove I am not alone. How lonely, I am now, I thought as I dragged myself to the edge of the lake water.

Moonlight spilt across the face of that abomination on the cliff. A bony hand projected from his robe and clenched tight.

My scales burnt hotter than the core of Lancasta.

Water. Survival.

I screamed at the water's edge.

Muscles fatigued to the bone and mind wrung dry, I couldn't drag myself forward anymore. It was as if a thousand dull-bladed pikes pierced my hide.

I refused to become one of them.

Was this it, Blackthread?

Well, was it?

#

My eyes cracked open to blinding morning light.

White Twitla birds danced on the lake beach and hopped merrily across my arms that felt boulder dense and weighted me down. I spit up sand and rock that had made its way into my mouth during my slumber and the little things of innocence darted away into the nearby forest.

The lake was still and my face reflected into the darkish gray water. For the first time in what seemed like half a Ryunalan life I see my complexion.

My father's orange blazed iris and mother's vertical slit pupil with a purple overglow. Grandpa Yinla's thick heavy ridged brows. Great Grandma Balyamja's blessing of smaller than average sized scales and their soft elegant light green hue. The feminine soft coloration and pigmentation was contrasted by my masculine overhanging fangs.

How fast would I change? I wondered. It was unknown because any Ryunalan touched by Blackthread was too abashed to stay around once inflicted by the curse. No one knew where they went. I only assumed they assimilated with the other Yulans.

How dreadful it must have been to mix in with such vile Lancasta plague. How disgusting to be stripped of your own armor and lowered to such fermenting bile. I would never be a part of it. I would find a way. I would make the Blackthread demon return me to my former self, to my former glory, to Chief Military General Pawla of the Ryunalan Army.

I would find him, yes.

I tried to get up but I still couldn't move. My energy had totally been drained. Bloated Hina fish corpses floated in to shore and I swallowed them up so fast I didn't give my tongue a chance to taste.

The water again felt so very close. I wondered if it would swallow me up and take me to the bottom, I wondered a lot of things, but I just remained silent and still and stared at my face, right underneath my eye where my cheek bone protruded sharply. My body trembled and my back ached when I saw it.

Missing scales.

Where the scales had been I could see the softest pink color.

Over the next three days of thunderstorm and biting rain, I searched every pebble of rock and every grain of sand for the Blackthread heathen that took away my chance to find any remaining Ryunalan survivors.

He was too quick and the curse too thick in enchantment. At full capacity, I could have ended him within the beat of my heart, but the bones in my right wing had retracted so far into the side of my chest that I couldn't make the full flap cycle of my wings to go airborne. I tried pulling at it, thinking that maybe I could stretch it and it would just magically pop out of its little cocoon, but the pain was excruciating, and in fact, it appeared within five minutes after that that my arm had been sucked even deeper inside than before.

Vulnerable, weak, ugly, and slowly decaying I gave up on Blackthread and the idea that I would ever be able to fly again. I needed to travel fast. The scent of water on the air gave me an idea. Travel by river.

Sure enough, after trudging through sharp Thang thickets and poisonous Biter ferns over the past hour, I came to the edge of a great river dotted in mossy boulders. Perfect.

A Ryunalan in itself seen by a Yulan would have caused a fuss but who knew what they would they would do with me if they saw the mangled half evolved creature that I was now. The boulders would make adequate cover during the night.

And so I went, with two rotten tree logs underneath each armpit, I floated down the Myiantra river and it took me south. I traveled for what seemed like days eating any fish and river bottom dwellers I could to maintain dwindling energy levels.

During the night I sat on top of the logs and prayed to all the Ryunalan's that have passed on to the bright kingdom above. I asked them to show me the way, prove to me that I am not the last one of our kind. If I am not the last, then bring them all back, I had said towards the great void above peppered in white twinkling dots, the kingdoms of past fathers. By day I was under the water save my head positioned between dead floating trees.

The days seemed to be consumed faster than a herd of Yulan farm pigs at a Ryunalan banquet. I looked at my arms and realized that the size had decreased now by almost two times and was deathly itchy. Trying to scratch gently, with a chunk of the floating wood, but I applied too much force and scales and skin ripped and peeled away. The midday sun beamed on the scales as they danced in a rainbow array of colors and sunk away to the bottom of the river. Skin exposed on my arm, I had begun to feel hot, uncomfortable, and completely panicked. My arm was now the pink and white shade of Yulan skin. I rubbed the skin on my newly formed arm and looked to the sky in disappointment. Even a newborn Ryunalan had tougher skin.

#

Time passed away for who knows how long. I've been defeated in battle. Civil wars have drove talons and fire into my hide so deep I wish I had been put out of my misery. But the pain and suffering of this new body, this new existence was beyond anything. There was nothing left of my former self. I was a Yulan. And it felt as if the world itself came unhinged and wandered into some endless abyss in the blackness of the cosmic void.

Here I was naked and washing out a blackened eye with mid-summer swamp water. I had approached the men with care and warmth and even offered fresh rock trout and sweet fruit but their hearts were cold, and they batted it away.

One of the men looked me in the eye and said, "You're not one of us." He spat on my lips. "Don't care about the Emperor's agenda with the Blackthreads. You should all be dead."

As I floated down river, eye puffy and stingy, mouth full of sand grit and blood, and determination to live shattered, I came upon a particular Yulan, a careless Yulan that whistled some tune. She had long brown hair and was wearing a blue dress.

She was hanging her hide, what they called clothes, on a line between two trees as she went back and forth to the river for washing.

I would have called out to her as I've done to the other Yulans, but today will be the last day. There will be no more ridicule, there will be no more taking beatings nor taking the sharp blade of a vile tongue.

She came down to the riverside and began to clean the clothes. I kept my head low behind the pair of logs that I had tied together.

I peered out from the backside my contraption. In that moment I wasn't sure but I believe her gaze was fixed tight on me. I would have cursed but that would have given me away for sure.

"Hello," she called out. "Don't be shy."

I returned nothing. No need to. I wasn't about to start another scene of rejection.

The logs and I continued our journey south, not far however, because all I required now was a solid tall tree, and a good distance between me and the she Yulan.

Clouds grew blacker than cave beetles as it swallowed the sun, and winds lashed out at my face stinging my eyes. It would be a perfect night. A night fit for the last Ryunalan.

It was not hard to find my resting place. Lightning guided me through shrubs and groves so thick I almost felt gratitude towards the Blackthread that cursed me to wither away into this small fragile hide.

I climbed.

A perfect Yip tree. Two hundred years old and taller than the length of four fully grown Ryunalans. I climbed branch by branch ignoring the cracks of lightning that threatened me from above. Do what you must my thunder gods, but the door to my brothers and sisters will be open. That I can guarantee.

Do what you must.

At the top of the canopy, sliding the threaded Himla tree skin noose around my neck, I looked up towards the grumbling skies and angry Ryunalan gods.

I belonged up there. With all of them, not here where everything hurts and doesn't fit, where I am now but a displaced fool to carry out the rest of my life in a prison of rejection.

I tightened the noose.

Thirsty. One last drink. I closed my eyes and let the biting rain fill my hands. I drank. I filled again. My reflection stared back at me. Its eyes were still Ryunalan, save my left knee, it is the only part of my past life that made it past the Blackthread's curse.

A thin slice of pupil from top of eyelid to eyelid. And iris so bursting with shades of oranges and reds you would have sworn that the lava of Mt. Uila itself flowed within.

I filled my mouth, swallowed, and looked out at my plank; a thick branch that appeared suffice in holding my weight. Step by step, I made my way to the edge of the limb.

Steady now, Pawla.

I closed my eyes. I checked the noose. I breathed in deep, imagining the air feeding some great fire within.

We may not rule the lands my family, but we will rule the heavens.

As if some great spirit from above controlled all of nature, the rain subsided and the crack of the thunder was now but a low grumble on the horizon. Birds chirped. Small Inla squirrels scurried from their hiding places. A small breeze brought yellow Grassa butterflies fluttering playfully around the canopy. Blackened clouds grayed, then whitened, and split open spilling rays of light across the scene bathing me in its brilliance.

The stage has been set. And it was now my time to play the part in the scene. It was time to play the main character of this great tragedy, the fall of the Ryunalans.

I looked down through the canopy floor. Just as I leaned forward a woman scurried forth from thick brush. It was the lady from the riverside. Same long brown hair, same long dress. For sure it was her and she began to saw violently at my rope's knot tied at the bottom of the tree.

I tried to lean back but it was too late, I was already going over the edge and there was no turning back.

Air rushed past me as the rope wormed and fluttered about.

"Stop," I screamed.

She didn't flinch.

I felt a quick tug at my neck, then there was a snap, the choke on my throat released, and my back drove into earth.

#

Standing on the cliff, bathing in the sunlight of a fresh morning rise, I opened my wings and let the thermals take me up into her grasp. The southern air brought warmth and comfort to the membranes that had iced over during the night deep in the hideout.

Three Ryunalans flew behind me. On the horizon, the Yulan Empire, sixty thousand strong marched over marsh fields and ripped through thickets with their metal trinketry. Ahead of them, the land was green. Behind them, the land laid to a browning wasteland.

Ganja sacs filled from a feast of lava rock and mountain goatsalas, we flamed hundreds of them, but were overcome by the thousands of projectiles that bit into us one scale at a time. Hyalan took a spear to the right jugular. Pyanya was roped down as his flames blackened a group of cavalrymen. But forces came from their flank and they drove needle pointed glass blades deep into the soft tissue of his arm pits. To see a Ryunalan before my time, who had won countless battles go down like that drove me mad.

I dove through blinding white clouds, my wings screaming down towards earth as they cut through calm winds. When my talons slammed into the ground, in front of the thousands, I flamed, tore, roared, split, ripped, cracked, and rammed anything that had a heartbeat.

My ganja sacs were emptied, but they were still thousands strong. My muscles ached and it all seemed that the world would no longer belong to us.

Mulayan, my only other companion on the battlefield, the youngest of all us battle Ryunalans, was sprayed in a vile black soup. I had heard rumors of this new Yulan tactic but there wasn't enough evidence to be concerned until now, until the fires spread across him and he collapsed and crumbled in on himself and lay wasted on the battlefield.

The three commanders of the Ryunalan east, west, and south empires were gone. The Ryunalans they had protected for centuries were now exposed and ready for the taking. Yulans would become the new lords of Lancasta.

My soul burning and my mind aching, I flew to an overhanging cliff and surveyed the canyon valley below. Millions of Yulan soldiers marched, their footsteps rumbling the rocky floor as they headed north to Mulayan's district. It would soon fall and there wouldn't be a trace of Ryunalans after their thunderous conquest.

I took to the ash gray skies and burnt my remaining ganja at the biting arrows that followed my tail. I pumped my wings down and up climbing through thick rain and strong winds. The air crackled along my scales and lightning sprawled all around me.

Flashes of light.

Darkness.

Flashes of light again. Winds ground my cheeks and I could hear something whistling through the air. It was approaching.

I pumped my wings, again and again, almost snapping the tendons in my arms and ripping the membranes against the turbulence of angry air.

The whistle became a high pitch.

A metal harpoon exploded from my abdomen.

Rope ripped my down.

And , I fell. I fell, plummeting through thick clouds.

I fell through rain and ripped at the air in despair.

Nothing was going to save me.

Earth swallowed me whole, bone crunched under bone and there was a great pinch…

But, I awakened.

A woman's face backed away, her mouth quivering and eyebrow twitching.

"You...you," she began, but she tripped on a rock and tumbled down to the dirt floor.

It was the Yulan girl from the river save the clothes that she had worn. These Yulan beasts had always been bashful whenever sliding out of their own hides. She dressed quickly pulling up new hide from a basket and went dashing across the room to shut the small circle windows in the walls. It was pouring outside.

She looked at me as if something precious had been hidden behind my eyeballs. What was it that she was looking for? And more importantly, why did she have to cut me down at such a critical moment in my life? The moment to end it.

I tried to sit up, but the pain in my ribs kept me down firm and tight against the grass mattress.

The girl pulled up a wooden chair next to the bed.

"You are lu—"

"You shouldn't have cut the rope."

Her eyes did not waver. A dark ocean awaited in her gaze. I've never met someone so fixed on me.

"I want nothing to do with you and your people. What you have done to us all can't be forgotten. In this life or the next, we will come back."

She remained still and her eyes didn't move.

Her hand slowly moved to her mouth and her eyes widened.

"It's true..."

"What is true? What is it you talk of?" I hardly cared, but the opportunity to talk to a Yulan doesn't come around often.

"The rumor."

"The ru—"

"Blackthread."

So even the Yulans from the southern continent knew of the Blackthread sorcery.

She took my hands into hers and rested her elbows on the mattress.

"You poor thing," she said, and she looked at me one eye to the next, moving back and forth. "To have your very identity stripped from you like this. Once a great Ryunalan, now, a Yulan."

She began to pet my head.

"I just want you to know. I don't hate you, nor your kind. I've often dreamt of a Lancasta where all beings coexisted and worked together. Do you ever think a world like that could be?"

I turned away and faced the room's sweating mud wall.

"Did I say something?"

I was the last Ryunalan. There was no doubt about that. Lancasta belonged to the Yulans and all the thousands of years of memories would be forgotten and the histories burnt. Coexistence?

"There will be no more Ryunalans." The northern Ryunalan hemisphere is now a land that has been conquered and rebuilt to suit the needs of those vile creatures.

"You were the last one then?"

The bitter bite of reality keeps my mouth closed.

"And your name?"

"Does it matter?"

"My name is Claythra. And when you are ready, come to the other room."

"Yeah, we'll see. I'll maybe give it a thought."

She shuffled away.

I looked over my shoulder and she was gone. I rolled on my back, looking up into the underside of the grass roof. There was a spiderweb in the top right corner glistening in its wetness as low grumbles of thunder made its way through the thick mud walls.

A white moth flew around the room, its wings flailing up and down in a sporadic manner. It bounced into the walls and then began to dance around a candle lit on top of a small table across the room. It lost interest in the flame and then began to ascend to the ceiling, towards its enemy.

The spider sat at the edge of the web, motionless and emotionless.

The moth's right wing grazed the web. Then the lower left leg sunk into the soft silk and was wrapped thickly. Both wings now. The spider dashed to the moth and sunk its fangs in the soft belly.

I wondered what was going through the spider's mind as its many eyeballs stared at me. Did it too think that I was some unfortunate trapped in the big web of things? Did it see me as someone else's prey?

I closed my eyes, feeling just as trapped as the moth.

Moonlight spilt in through the windows glazing me in a blue hue.

As soon as I heal and get out of here, I'll go to them. I will scream through the clouds and trek across the dark depths of space, the vast room that separates heaven and Lancasta.

I looked at my eyes in the reflection of a metal plate hanging on the wall, and rubbed my left knee.

But will they remember me?

#

"Pawla. My name." I stumbled and almost fell to the ground.

Claytra turned around. She smiled but then came rushing to my side in a fit of worry.

"Are you ok?" she said, taking my arm and wrapping it around her hot neck. There was a warm aurora about here that I'd never felt before.

"It's this body."

Ashamed I needed help from such a girl I unraveled her arm and winced at the pain in my knee as her support was now gone.

I sat on a block of wood and pulled up the cloth that she had put on me while unconscious.

The joint was vibrating.

Claythra gave a look of pity and her brown eyes seemed to well with tears. Another trait that I could never understand. Another form of Yulan weakness. Instead of controlling their emotions properly and containing them, they leaked them out from the soft eyes in their head.

I wanted nothing to do with them, I thought, as I watched the Blackthread curse snap bone and rearrange ligaments in my leg. Something bulged against the skin on the back of my leg and then slowly crawled its way to the knee joint. It stopped in position with a click.

I tested the new leg swinging it back and forth. The leg bended back now like a proper Yulan limb. I was only one step away now from becoming my own enemy. How much longer would it take? I thought as I stared at my reflection on the metal plate. Would the Ryunalan eyes stay? Would my soul just float away to the clouds and fizz away into nothingness?

To be one with their kind physically, but to be far from their world spiritually is what kept me up on the first night in Claythra's mud house as I tried to fall asleep under a sliver of gray moon.

I would leave in the morning. There was no point in spending another second here.

I began to search the house for things that I could use for the journey back north to search for my lost brothers and sisters.

Claythra's hand pulled me away from the dresser I had been rummaging through. I was shocked at first, but she showed no anger or disappointment.

I let her drag me into the backroom I have not searched as of yet.

The walls were full of wooden shelves from floor to ceiling and there was only enough space for Claythra and I to stand and turn around comfortably. She tugged at a piece of pink cloth and revealed a Ryunalan skull, a juvenile one.

Savages. I instantly regretted the situation I had been pushed into. I could have just crushed the skull.

Dead was dead. I wanted to see my Ryunalans alive and well.

"So, your people here are barbarians just like the northerners."

Claythra turned to me, I swayed back and forth, and then she pushed me down on a chair and gave a great sigh.

"Settle down and let me explain."

She rested her pale hand on the skull and petted the top of the snout up and down as if it had still been alive.

"During the Eastern Burn, this little guy was injured badly. It had flown south and landed in our yard half dead and bleeding from the abdomen. We thought we had taken care of the injuries, but overtime his internal injuries didn't mend well. Though our time was short, we bonded well. We, two different species, looked past the conflicts that plague the Yulans and Ryunalans of the northern hemisphere. We looked passed the things that separated us and focused on the things that meld us together into one strong unit. Do you understand?"

I couldn't understand. Surely the people from her village were just as vile as the northern Yulans.

"I wish, I could. But I have been on Lancasta for too long. The ways of the lands, the rule of all things have been burnt into me."

The next morning, Claythra took me through the forest until we reached open highlands and could see the ocean on the horizon. Destroyed buildings, under construction buildings, and structures in pristine shape littered the coastline. A small network of roads snaked in and out and wiggled their way beyond what the eye could see. On the roads carts full of goods and people on foot traveled from all directions. I stopped in my tracks and just stared for a moment at Claythra.

"Is this your idea of a joke? I can't go there."

"But you can't stay in my little house forever."

"You can't drag me out there."

Claythra drove her thumb in my chest and then dragged the same hand up to my chin and forced my eyes into hers.

"Pawla, come with me. It's ok."

I grabbed her arm. I was about to swing it away, when a thump in my heart stopped me from doing so. The firmness in her demeanor, the softness of her touch all but melted the thick walls I had built between us. Is it wrong for me to feel this way? I thought, and then looked up at fat clouds slowly marching across the sky.

"Ok," I said plainly, and gave in.

And we made our way to the town.

Claytha first took me to a half-charred building. A group of workers tore down the burnt structure and loaded horse wagons with the blackened wood. Even a body had been pulled from the wreckage and was lying next to the wagon.

One of the men from the worker team approached Claythra and I. When our eyes met, I expected to be ridiculed and ordered to leave immediately. I listened carefully for the words of rejection, always.

The man stabbed the ground with a shovel and waved and arm at the smoking structure.

He looked at me in the eyes.

I was still waiting for the words that would give me a reason to leave Claythra and her assertion that everything was going to be ok. Here they come.

The words.

"Nice to see a Ryunalan around here. In these parts of the woods, anyone who helps is a friend. Anyone who believes in rebuilding a great life for themselves and others is family."

There was a pause in the air. Hammering of nails, sawing of wood, those were the only things that my mind could concentrate on.

"Are you one of those people?"

I didn't know why and I didn't know how, but my head nodded up and down. It was clear that he knew I was Ryunalan, but why was it so clear that I didn't mind being entangled in such a Yulan affair.

Claythra took my hand and we continued to walk the road. She explained about the civil war between her clan and the Eastern barbarians. A never-ending conflict over sea territory. Land sourced food was scarce in these parts and it had drove both sides to take arms against one another.

I heard cries from a mud hut. A woman was screaming and perhaps growling and rasping for air. I couldn't see her but I could see the image in my mind that she was being murdered. Did they kill their own? A Ryunalan wouldn't touch a scale of one of their own.

Claythra nodded her head at the window.

"Go ahead. Go on now."

I peeked inside the window.

From the lower parts of the woman that was clenching at blankets and screaming at the top of her lungs came forth the smallest Yulan I've had ever witnessed with these Ryunalan eyes.

An elderly Yulan woman took the screaming baby into her arms and rested it on the new mother's chest and she wrapped her arms around her creation.

Her half crying, half smiling wet face sent a bolt of lightning to my heart and ripped a fragment from an already crumbling shell. How dare her get to me like this? How dare I allow such softness to entire this Ryunalan spirit?

"Ok," I said to Claythra. "I think it's time that I get going. My journey to find my own needs to continue, I need it to continue."

Her expression grew into something of Yulan discomfort and disappointment.

"But why? The agenda has been fulfilled. Complete. This news has already been spread from every crack and stone of Lancasta."

"And I don't believe it."

"Don't go."

"The journey always needs to go on."

I walked away in the opposite direction. It was evening and I could already make my way North following the stars.

"Just stay tonight," she called after me. "I'll take you as far as I can tomorrow morning. We can spare a horse cart for a while. But please just stay tonight."

Horse cart. Yes, that would save a considerable amount of time and plus my left leg wasn't in the best shape after the morning's bout with the Blackthread curse.

"Ok, just tonight."

She grabbed my hand and took me to a place I would never have dreamed of. The night grew blacker than coal and we arrived upon a small plaza surrounded by buildings made from gray wood and pale, yellow rock. In the middle of the circular plaza was a giant bonfire and sitting on half-charred logs were Yulans with glowing faces of orange.

Without a warning, without any cue, three men and three women stood up, formed pairs, and began to spin wildly and shout around the fire to the low hymn of a flute.

I stood mesmerized.

In all my years I thought I would never see this, never hear this, but before me now is the very thing us Ryunalans have no concept of.

"Dancing," I muttered to myself.

A hand grabbed mine.

"Yeah, dancing," Claythra whispered into my ear. "And that is exactly what we need right now in this town."

She pulled me into the chaos of arms and legs that swayed this way and that. A sound of beauty came from the long wooden devices covered in holes as they blew into them. What was this warm magnificence in my heart?

Claythra grabbed me by the waist and brought me close to the fire. She insisted not to worry and just follow her lead as we revolved around the orange glow like the planets in heaven go around our sun.

Along with the flutes came a singing voice from a woman. It was the woman who had given birth to the young Yulan. She had it wrapped in her arms as her voice caressed the scene with her words.

The words talked of this town's fall and how they would never give up and one day they would talk the barbarians out of war and they would all be happy and live together in complete harmony.

And the words continued and continued.

And finally, my heart shattered. For the words danced in the air and swam in the darkness of the night and promised that anyone could be a part of the life they were rebuilding. Up high they would build. High to the skies.

Like a juvenile Ryunalan at first flight, I too would go high with them.

Up as far as I could go, as anyone I wanted to be.

Benjamin DeHaan is a speculative fiction writer and creator/editor-in-chief of the science fiction horror magazine, Dark Void. His fiction can be found in Novel Noctule Magazine, Lovecraftiana, Write Ahead The Future Looms, The Dark Corner Zine and other various venues.

The Omong Sri

by Laura J. Campbell

"Well, well, well," Mary Osprey asked. "What have going on here, then?"

Mary was addressing an older woman; the two women shared similar features, with reddish-blond hair and a broad forehead. Even although the women were from different planets, they could easily have been mistaken for mother and daughter.

"I am going to investigate why my ship is not responding to me," the older woman proclaimed.

"It is not your ship," Mary reminded her.

"I am the Queen Mother of Sri'Quis; it is a Sri'Quisian ship. Therefore, it is my ship."

"You are no longer on Sri'Quis, and you are no longer in power. You command no ships. You are in exile here on Lough Dergh, to protect you from the person who *is* in power on Sri'Quis – your son, King Torin. You should recollect that Torin is quite intent upon from killing you, to prevent you from seizing power. Fortunately for you, I am equally intent on keeping you alive."

Mary then turned to a young man in a brocaded suit, who stood next to the exiled Queen Mother. "You were actually going to let her go up to that ship?"

"She is a member of the royal family," the young man, Othello Amberjack, replied. "I am the Earth Foreign Service Officer here on Lough Dergh. Lough Dergh is an Earth colony planet. Therefore, I have the authority to authorize Queen Rigel to take a shuttle to wherever she pleases, including to the orbiting *Omong Sri*."

"I am Earth Secret Service, Martian Agent Registry," Mary Osprey reminded him, pulling rank. "I have superior jurisdiction in *all* matters and events on or near this planet. What on Earth, Mars, or Sri'Quis made you think that transporting Rigel to a non-responsive ship loitering in passive orbit was a *good* idea?"

"The ship is transporting Queen Rigel's lady-in-waiting. Her loyal subject."

"She has no power; she has no subjects," Mary reaffirmed.

The Queen Mother unzipped her off-world excursion jacket, resigning herself to Osprey's jurisdictional superiority. "If I am not going to see what has happened up there, then who is?" she asked. "My lady-in-waiting and a trusted pilot from Sri'Quis are aboard that ship. It looks like a ghost ship now, mindlessly circling this watery grave of a planet."

"Situation report, Othello," Mary Osprey demanded of the Foreign Service Officer.

"We lost contact with the *Omong Sri* as it approached Lough Dergh," Othello Amberjack replied. He ran his hands nervously through his long black silken hair. "We have attempted contact numerous times but have received no response. The ship settled into geosynchronous orbit."

"My lady-in-waiting, Lady Bianca Aircia, and the pilot, Captain Padi Amnata, are aboard." Rigel stated. "The purpose of the trip is to transport Lady Bianca there. And bring me supplies."

"Who approved the transport?" Mary asked. She wanted to observe the response. If Rigel replied, it would indicate that she was pulling royal rank on an impressionable Earth agent who was not bound to obey her; if Othello replied, he at least had the balls to own up to the mistake of being swayed by Rigel's title and personality.

"I approved," Othello replied. He was very nervous now; he yanked on his hair so hard that Mary wondered if he would pull his hair out of his scalp. Othello Amberjack knew that Mary Osprey could have him removed from the planet and his post within the hour.

"We go through proper channels, Mr. Amberjack" Mary stated. "Proper channels is me. *Always* me. When was this transport arranged?"

That was something that Mary Osprey did not know, and she considered it a personal failure that Rigel and Amberjack had evaded Mary's detection while they arranged for this transport. It was not a mistake she would allow again. That much she silently promised all of them.

"Very recently," Othello answered. "We had a briefing prepared for you. For when *Omong Sri* arrived. Lady Bianca and Captain Amnata would have been brought to you for your interview and inspection prior to being sent to the palace."

"You are new to your position," Mary allowed Amberjack, "But let us make one thing clear. Every ship, every person, every object, coming to or out of Lough Dergh is cleared through me long before the transport. *Every* time. A silent ship could be a weapon, designed to assassinate the Queen Mother. I will reiterate the protocol, for your benefit: Rigel stays in the palace, unless I personally clear her journeys. Torin IX is a very ambitious man. He knows that he is surrounded by those secretly loyal to his mother. She is of the Bovsliver Dynasty. Notwithstanding Sri'Quis's archaic practice of male primogeniture succession, she has as claim to the throne. Perhaps a more persuasive claim. Her husband, Torin's father, was only of the Forndraishin Family. A far less imperial lineage. Torin's surname is Forndraishin, not

Bovsliver. That distinction alone feeds all sorts of nefarious plots."

Amberjack breathed in deeply; he had been holding his breath the entire time she was talking.

"Thus, endeth your history lesson for today," Mary said. "Go back to your office, Earth Foreign Service Officer Amberjack. I am done with you for now."

He stood still, swaying just a little.

"Go!" Mary Osprey commanded with a sharp wave of her hand.

The young man scampered away.

"And you," Mary sighed at the Queen. "What were *you* thinking? A lapse of reason from a rookie bureaucrat is one thing, but you are savvier than this. Putting on an excursion suit, preparing to be transported to a ship idling dead in orbit."

"Lady Bianca has been with me for decades," Queen Mother Rigel replied. She pressed her thin lips together. "Her welfare, as my subject, is my concern."

"You have *no* subjects," Mary reminded her again. "That sort of statement is exactly why Torin wants you dead. I will have you escorted back to your palace."

"And the ship? It looks like a ghost ship now."

"There are no such things as ghost ships," Mary replied.

"Yes, there are," Rigel objected. "They drift in space. Some with dead crews aboard them. Everyone has heard about them. Like the Earth ship *Mena*. The ship went silent seven years ago, coming off a run in the Gestalt System. It is occasionally caught up in planetary orbits, but always mysteriously breaks free. Everyone aboard is dead, looking at the ship's portal in terror. They say that even the ship's cat has its eyes transfixed on the portal in horror."

"There are no ghost ships," Mary emphasized. "You'll just have to trust me on that."

#

Dr. Nabu, like Mary, was a Martian. He was shorter than Mary, but his vibrant personality projected ebullience that made him appear much larger.

"Any and every little thing might be important on board the *Omong Sri*," Mary told him, as they donned their excursion suits. "Keep your eyes open."

"There is no evidence the *Omong Sri* lost hull integrity," Nabu reminded her. "The ship should still be habitable. Why must we get dressed up in this awkward garb?"

"We do not know what occurred on that ship. So, we wear the protective suits. And before you ask: yes, that includes the weapon shielding. Just in case."

"You are such a see-the-glass-as-half-empty type of person," Nabu complained.

"A glass filled to 50% capacity with water is half-filled with water, half-filled with air," she replied. "It is, in totality, always full. It is our perception of what matters to us that dictates how we describe the glass and its contents."

"You really need to develop a sense of humor," he advised.

"I have a sense of humor," she replied. "It only requires that something actually amusing be said to me in order to engage it."

"Well, you got me suited up," Nabu said, securing hoses and belts. "Body armor and all. It's hot and itchy as hell in this mess of an outfit. Time to go visit the ghost ship before I go crazy with the itching."

Mary sighed, refraining from objecting to the term 'ghost ship' yet again.

#

The small shuttle joined the *Omong Sri* in orbit, pulling alongside. The shuttle connected an airlock assembly between it and the idle ship, creating a short safe bridge between the vessels.

Even although the *Omong Sri* was a small ten-person capacity ship, it was designed for interstellar travel. That meant is was much bigger than the shuttle. The shuttle looked like a newborn Humpback Whale calf keeping close to its full-grown mother.

"Your having a personal shuttle is handy," Nabu said, referring to Mary's personal near-space craft. "A nice perk of being Earth Secret Service."

"A necessary piece of equipment," Mary replied. "I need to be able to travel freely and undetected. This shuttle enables me to get to and from places without having to log flight plans or being observed by surveillance systems."

"And your ship's hold is substantial for a vessel this size," Nabu nodded in approval. "Good for our current mission. There is apparently quite a manifest of supplies aboard the *Omong Sri.* Items that Queen Rigel ordered transported from Sri'Quis. In addition to her Lady-in-Waiting."

"Rigel seems intent upon making her palace here a little Sri'Quis," Mary noted disapprovingly. "That woman is not content to leave danger behind her. It is exhausting protecting her." She flipped switches on her shuttle's operations panel. "We're ready to board. Is your suit atmosphere on?"

Dr. Nabu pressed a button and gave her a thumb's up. "Activated. Ladies first?"

"Earth Secret Service first," she answered.

They traversed the airlocks, boarding the *Omong Sri* and securing the portal for their return.

"Life support and anti-gravity are still operational and activated," Dr. Nabu noted, hoping they could at least take their suit helmets off.

"Keep the full suit on," Mary ordered. "A few layers of defense is better than no layers of defense. We don't know why this ship is silent."

"It's silent because it's a ghost ship."

"There are no such things as ghost ships." She remembered a line from a Martian lullaby, the tune weaving though her thoughts: *Hush little baby, the moons are setting in the sky…* She hoped that Nabu would be quieter.

Instead he continued talking: "Where are Lady Bianca and Captain Amnata?" he demanded.

"Crew quarters forward, hold amidships, engines in the aft," Mary noted. "We go forward first."

They walked in silence.

"I have heard that the Martian Agent Registry has never lost a guarded target," Nabu said, not liking walking in silence.

"That it true," Mary replied. "Even when the target seems determined to circumvent our protections."

"Is that a reference to anyone we know?"

Mary replied with silence.

"You don't like talking? Or are you concerned we might be overheard and detected?" Nabu asked.

"Anything hostile would have heard our airlock assembly docking and assaulted us as we boarded."

"You're so much fun to be around," Nabu shook his head.

"Everything appears operational," Mary said, checking on displays and logs, as they passed through the silent hallways.

The two investigators inspected the crew and passenger quarters thoroughly. There was no one in anyone of the small two-room apartments. There was no one in the galley, the mess deck, the heads, the gymnasium, the brig, or sick bay.

They entered the bridge. "Auto-pilot," Mary noted. "This ship navigated itself into orbit."

"Where are Lady Bianca and Captain Padi?"

"We'll search the hold. Maybe Rigel's cargo will give us a clue."

"I remember the Queen had quite the manifest of goods being delivered."

"She's not the Queen," Mary corrected. "But she does have quite a manifest, I will agree. Supplies, equipment. Produce, fancy cakes. Raw ingredients. Things from Sri'Quis that she misses. Lots of cookies."

"Cookies?"

"Every culture has a special affection for its own cookies. Don't ask me why. Maybe something about the air they are baked in."

They arrived at the hold; Mary unlocked the door to the hold and opened it.

The hold was in complete disarray, barrels turned over, boxes strewn about, and containers broken.

In the middle of the disarray, there were two unmoving bodies.

"Lady Bianca Aircia and Captain Padi Amnata, I presume," Mary said. She turned to Nabu. "I will approach first, do a scan, and assess the scene. They could have been attacked *en route*; their bodies sabotaged. Our armor is only rated so high."

"If they are still alive, I need to attend to their medical needs stat. If they are dead, then the sooner I can begin my duties as coroner, the better." He watched her. "And sabotaged bodies? Who thinks of things like that – other than you?"

Mary waved a handheld scanner over the Captain, analyzing his body and clothing. She removed a lanyard from around his neck. "I have his identification and transponder," she said, placing the items in a bag and sealing it. "And the Captain is already dead," she added. "Not much saving for you to do with this one, Doctor."

Mary moved to Lady Bianca, conducting the scan and search, retrieving Bianca's identification and transponder lanyard and an envelope from her pocket. "She is also deceased."

Mary stepped aside, to allow Dr. Nabu access. He waved a palm-held medical device over the bodies. "Initial external examinations are unremarkable. I need to get them to the morgue."

Mary consulted at a series of recorders on the wall. "Look for carbon dioxide," she said. "The air quality tapes show a recent spike to 25% CO_2 and decrease of oxygen levels to 4.2%. The event lasted about an hour. The levels have since corrected." She downloaded the data.

"Good thing we didn't come in here during the event without the suits," Nabu commented. "We could have been rendered unconscious ourselves. Possibly worse."

"That is why we take precautions," Mary noted.

"Well," Dr. Nabu replied. "Time to make your shuttle a hearse."

"I remind you that this mission is top secret," Mary commanded Nabu. "No one but you and I is to know what we have seen. We will discreetly transport the bodies and the salvageable goods to your lab, for autopsies and screening. All inquiries are to be directed to me. Is that understood?"

Dr. Nabu nodded. "Yes, ma'am," he replied.

He knew better than to disobey; the Martian Agent Registry did not only have a reputation for keeping those under their care alive. The Registry also had a reputation for eliminating anyone or anything that threatened their mission.

#

"Report," Mary demanded.

Dr. Nabu sat across from her at a clean glass conference table. "As you guessed, both died as a result of carbon dioxide intoxication. Not always the easiest thing to diagnose – CO_2 levels rise in the blood after death, so detecting CO_2 as an intoxicant can be difficult to distinguish by blood gas analysis. Both exhibited pleural petechiae and moderate lung congestion, consistent with the cause of death." He paused. "One interesting finding was bruising and lacerations on both of the bodies – notably the knuckles and palms of Captain Amnata and the forearms and neck of Lady Bianca. Her wounds were defensive wounds, his offensive. There was a struggle between them."

"Due to the carbon dioxide intoxication?"

"Difficult to tell. It appears they were involved in the conflict as they died, based on the position of the bodies. I will send you my report with all of the data."

"Thank you," Mary stated.

"One more thing," Nabu mentioned. "Queen Rigel is asking about Bianca and Captain Amnata."

"Tell her that we did not find them. Tell her the ship was abandoned when we boarded."

"And Bianca and Amnata's bodies? What do we do with those?"

"Quietly cremate their remains." Mary replied. "Give Rigel their identification badges and the transponders. Tell her that's all we found; and instruct her to contact me for additional information."

"Queen Rigel does not trust you," Nabu commented.

"Quite the contrary, Dr. Nabu. Rigel trusts me completely. That's why she doesn't like me."

#

The Queen Mother looked at Nabu. "Their clothes and effects?' she asked, standing in the antiseptically clean laboratory. "Where are those?"

"On board the *Omong Sri*. We did not find the Captain or Lady Bianca. No sense in bringing their clothing with us. We had just enough space in our own hold to carry the supplies we could gather," Nabu replied. "Some supplies were damaged; we left those aboard. The items that we salvaged were cleared and forwarded to your Master Chef."

Mary Osprey sat in a chair by a lab bench, looking over the inventory of the ship. "There were numerous supplies from Sri'Quis on board the ship. Flour, baking soda, baking powder, spices, vinegar, Sri'Quisian goat milk, butter, salt, sugar, dried fruits, and truffles. Frozen desserts. Your precious cookies. Dried egg powder. We have chickens here that lay eggs – why import dried egg when you can have fresh?"

"Lough Dergh eggs are Earth chicken eggs. The dried egg I ordered is from a Sri'Quisian fowl known as the mulmute. You cannot bake a Sri'Quisian cake without cracking a Sri'Quisian egg. For some reason, Mulmute eggs don't travel well in space. They get tough. But their dried egg powder is still superior to Earth eggs. I cannot speak to the Martian eggs you might have grown up on. Do they even have eggs on Mars?"

"Of course, we have eggs on Mars," Mary Osprey replied. She couldn't suppress all the incredulity in her tone. "Mars is an Earth colony. We have free range chickens on Mars. Earth eggs are nowhere near as good as real Martian Chicken eggs."

"Then you understand the importance of quality when it comes to eggs," Rigel noted. "At least we have that much in common. Thank you for forwarding my supplies. My chefs have been planning my menu for an upcoming feast. A celebration you have already approved, Dr. Osprey." Rigel seemed disturbed.

"And the rest of the ship? Are there any other items that should come into my custody?"

"No," Nabu replied.

"Who did the actual collection and cataloging?" Queen Rigel pressed.

"Dr. Osprey," Nabu replied.

"You relinquished all property to Dr. Nabu?" Rigel asked Mary.

"He has everything he asked for," Mary replied.

Queen Mother Rigel stiffened her back. "I will conduct a personal inventory of what supplies and effects were recovered when I get back to the palace." She left with a regal twirl.

"A lot of kerfuffle for eggs and making cakes," Dr. Nabu noted, after Rigel had departed.

Mary frowned. "They say if you can bake a cake, you can make a bomb. It will be interesting to see who she invites to future soirées."

#

Mary Osprey entered the royal household's kitchen. Rigel's chief chef, a tall, pale man with a greenish pallor, no eyebrows, and a round belly smiled to see her.

"Dr. Osprey!" he greeted, embracing her warmly.

She hugged him back, diplomatically. "Master Chef Dto," she greeted. "I saw you had quite a collection of items arrive for Rigel's little dinner party."

"So many wonderful things," he beamed. "Has Her Majesty invited you to the royal event?"

"Not so much 'invited' as she has begrudgingly accepted that I must be there, and she doesn't want to look ungracious by having me standing around her guests. Better to have me sitting at the table, where she can pass me off as a subject and not a reminder that she requires a bodyguard."

"Good," the Master Chef nodded enthusiastically. "If she had not, I would have invited you as *my* guest. The meal will start off with Mulmute Drop, a delicate soup…"

"Made with Mulmute dried egg powder," Osprey guessed.

"It is delicious," he promised.

"Tell me, is there anything else you need?" Mary prodded. "I can arrange for a shipment of replacement supplies from the nearest Earth colony, if you need. To replace the items lost on board the *Omong Sri*." Mary kept herself embedded within the inner circle of the chefs, to guard the Queen Mother's food and prevent poisoning attempts, as wells as to keep an eye out for any other activities they might be engaged in.

"We lost a number of items," Dto lamented. "We lost barrels of Sri'Quis cider vinegar. *All* the frozen desserts. I suppose that we can make the desserts from scratch, as best we can, with Lough Dergh supplies. We also lost Sri'Quisian baking soda and some spices. Most of the spices have Earth equivalents. Never fear. I am a Master Chef – I can work with what I have. But thank you for your kind offer. You always make difficult situations more palatable."

"It's your job to make things palatable," Mary smiled. "You sure about those desserts? They sound like they can't be replicated."

"Special Sri'Quisian delicacies. They were packed in dry ice, to keep them very cold throughout the transport."

"Dry ice?"

"Fluctuations in the freezing cycles of mechanical freezers negatively affect their full flavor. For the upcoming feast I can work with what we have in stock and locally sourced ingredients. As you are attending the feast, do you have a favorite dessert, Dr. Osprey?"

Mary was surprised by the gesture. Few people ever asked her what she liked. "Martian trifle," she answered.

"Hmmm," Dto thought, bringing the recipe up on a small tablet he carried with him. "Martian egg custard, almond liqueur and sherry drenched pound cake, poached pears, raspberries, slivered almonds, fresh cream, Martian vanilla beans. I think I can make this for you, as a symbol of our gratitude to you for protecting our household. Raspberries are not in season here, but I can use Sri'Quisian Xinmea berries. They are like hairless raspberries."

"Thank you, Master Chef," Mary replied. "You are most kind."

It served her purposes for the Master Chef to think that she was somehow in his debt.

#

Dr. Nabu contacted Mary at her home on the palace grounds. She was taking time off to recharge. She assigned her bodyguard duties temporarily to a trusted ESS agent she had personally selected for the job.

"Yes?" Mary answered.

"Queen Rigel contacted me," he reported. "She seemed … odd."

"Odd?"

"A mixture of irritation, concern, anger, panic," he replied. "It's difficult to put a finger on the exact emotion. She demands to see you. In my lab, of all places."

"Tell her to come and see me at my home," Mary replied. "I am off-duty and I am only a short distance from her apartments in the Exile Palace."

"She may not like that."

"I am her bodyguard, not her pet," Mary asserted. "I do not come running obediently to her side just because she whistles."

#

There was a twist of the locked doorknob. A moment later, a knock.

Mary unlocked the door and opened it. Rigel was not accustomed to encountering locked doors. She was used to entering any room she pleased, whenever she pleased.

"Please, come in," Mary invited.

Rigel entered. Mary nodded to the Earth Secret Service guarding Rigel during Mary's time off. "Take a short break," Mary ordered. "We will call if we need you."

"Plural 'we,'" Rigel noted, as Mary closed the door. "As in you and me or a royal 'we'?"

"Does it matter?"

"Yes. You treat me as if I am your equal, not as your better."

"Please, sit down," Mary gestured, ignoring the temptation to say things that would neither serve her nor Rigel well. "I have fresh brewed iced tea. Would you like a glass?"

"I would, thank you," Rigel said. She looked around Mary's residence, music playing in the background, a full-sized harp sitting by a chair, an easel on her patio. Books. True old-fashioned page-and-spine books.

Mary turned the volume of the music down and handed Rigel a glass of iced tea. "You look concerned. I assure you, the only place safer than my home are your apartments at the palace."

"I am not used to being a guest." Rigel answered. "In fact, this is the first time I have ever been someone else's guest. People to come to have an audience with me, not the other way around."

"You're doing a fine job of being a guest," Mary noted.

"The music you're playing is very unusual."

"The genre is twenty-first century Earth rock-and-roll," Mary replied. "Very popular on Mars. We like very old tunes."

"And very old secrets."

"Very new secretes, in your case. It makes my job more difficult to have to protect you from yourself."

Rigel did not reply. She sipped the tea and watched the ocean through Mary's bay window.

Mary handed Rigel the piece of paper she found in the envelope she took from Lady Bianca's body. "This piece of paper could result in Earth terminating their protection of you," Mary admonished. "I found this letter on board the *Omong Sri*. It is from a group of dissident Sri'Quisian aristocrats, addressed to you. A pen-and-paper letter. Very low tech, but low tech evades technological tracing, doesn't it? Before we discuss the letter, let's make a solemn oath that you are *never* to engage in this type of tomfoolery ever again. I may not always be able to save you."

"Tomfoolery?" Rigel did not look at the letter; she already knew its contents.

"A Martian term meaning frivolous stupidity," Mary replied sternly. "Like that letter. A communication to you, asking for your signature. Your supporters are seeking your authorization, your engagement in a plot to kill your son. If Torin had that letter presented to him – especially after you had signed it, he would have no other alternative but to issue a death warrant for you. Your acquiescing to an assassination plot would place you squarely under Sri'Quisian jurisdiction and Earth would have no alternative but to hand you over to Torin. You have value to Earth as a bargaining chip, Rigel, but not infinite value. They support an exiled queen at their discretion but will not harbor a fugitive and assassin. You were nervous when you did not know where that letter was. You knew that it couldn't be found by the wrong people. That is why you were so anxious to get on board the *Omong Sri*. You didn't care about Lady Bianca or Mulmute eggs."

"Does Earth know?"

"If they did, you would be on Sri'Quis right now. Disavowed by Earth."

Rigel handed the letter back to Mary. "Then I have no knowledge of this. Destroy it." She sat regally in the chair, then relaxed her posture. She knew that she needed Mary's protection, now more than ever. "Please."

"You said the magic word," Mary noted. "See - being an equal isn't so difficult after all."

#

"Lady Bianca was loyal to Queen Rigel," Nabu said. He handed two small boxes of ashes reverently to Mary Osprey. "May she and Captain Amnata rest in peace."

"You said that you had a theory about what happened aboard the *Omong Sri*?" Mary wanted to know if Nabu had any idea about the letter. If he did, she would have to kill him.

"From my autopsy, I think I can guess the order of events. Lady Bianca seems to have run to the hold for some reason, apparently evading Amnata? Lady Bianca turned off the air handlers and oxygenated air supply. She dumped the dry ice out of the dessert boxes. There were dry ice burns on her hands, and her body indicated longer exposure to the carbon dioxide than Amnata's. Meaning that she was in that room longer. Then she turned over the barrels of vinegar and baking soda. I found grains of the baking powder and dried residue of the vinegar under her nails and on her hands. Amnata's body demonstrated no evidence of handling the dry ice, vinegar, or baking soda."

"And?"

"Sri'Quis vinegar is transported as a concentrated liquid. When Lady Bianca turned over the barrels, she did so in such a way that the acetic acid mixed with the sodium bicarbonate from the baking soda. Producing carbon dioxide gas, liquid water, sodium ions, and acetate ions. Amnata got into the hold shortly after Lady Bianca caused her commotion; Bianca locked the door, confining them to the hold. The atmosphere in that small space was already toxic with sublimated carbon dioxide from the dry ice. They struggled for some reason, and the added exertion of their fight caused them to succumb even more quickly than they would have. Eventually the automatic air handling controls took over, readjusting the climate. But it was too late. They were already dead. A murder-suicide. I have no clue as to the motivation. But people have been known to have panic attacks in space."

"And the *Omong Sri*?"

"The *Omong Sri* guided itself here under auto-pilot. Amnata must have activated the automatic systems when he went to the hold."

"You are better at mysteries than humor," Mary noted.

"Why do you think they fought? It makes little sense."

"We will probably never know," Mary replied. "I suspect it will all remain a mystery."

#

There was something about a quiet ship in space. Even with the lights on, it was highly unnatural. A creature of metal, born to carry people and goods through the near emptiness of space. Now quiet. Now without purpose. It was beyond death.

Mary hummed an old nursery rhyme of as placed two plates on the table, partially filled with food, the forks laid on them, as if the diners had reacted in haste to some mysterious event. She put down two cups, one appearing to have been drunk from more than the other. That was the secret: it couldn't be too uniform.

Hush little baby, the moons ate setting in the sky… Mommy will be back, by and by. Mary sung as she approved of the scene.

Mary then programmed music to play over the ship's sound system, giving it an eerie sense of normalcy. One of Captain Amnata's playlists, stored in the computer. *Soft space jazz mix,* he had called it. It had mournful horns and wandering piano, against a fluid drumbeat.

Mars needs Mommy, as do you… she'll be back when her work is through.

Then she erased the ship's recent data recordings to hide the carbon dioxide spike in the hold and removed the last few entries from the Captain's log, erasing Amnata's orders from Torin's ministers to confront Bianca and wrestle the incriminating letter from her possession.

And if the Earthlings attack today, never forget you're a Martian baby.

Mary Osprey programmed a drifting course for the *Omong Sri.*

She stood back, evaluating her work. It needed something else, she decided. Something to give it an unattractive mystique.

She sat down at the communications consul and programmed it to automatically respond to any inquiry with a simple message: *I die.*

She left the hold in its existing state of disarray. Rigel and Dto knew the hold had been disturbed. That part of the story had to remain sacrosanct.

Mary had experience doing this sort of thing; she had done it before. One of the reasons she didn't believe in ghosts ships was that she knew that she had staged more than half of them to appear that way. Myth was an important tool in helping hide truths she knew could not be revealed.

Mary nodded; her work done. She departed the vessel and returned to Lough Dergh undetected.

#

Mr. Amberjack was frantic. He burst into Mary's official office at the palace.

"The *Omong Sri* is gone!" he exclaimed. "It escaped orbit – just like they say the ghost ship *Mena* does. Just like that! No captain at the helm, no port to call home."

"Explain what has happened," Mary asked.

"It just started off on its own," Amberjack babbled on excitedly. "It is drifting into deep space. *A ghost ship*." Amberjack's eyes were wide with excitement. "See -- I told you – ghost ships do exist!"

"Hmm," Mary replied. She settled into her chair, looking directly at the impressionable Foreign Service agent.

"*A ghost ship*," Amberjack echoed. He left, as quickly as he had arrived, feeling satisfied with himself.

"Food fills the belly, knowledge fills the mind, myth fills the void," Mary said to herself, after he had left. It was a Martian saying. Just like another: *Spirits only talk to wise, for fools have no credibility*.

But Amberjack was a good spreader of myths; he would be useful in spreading this one.

Mary sat alone in her office, thinking of all the ghosts she had created. All the myths she had authored.

Distrusting the universe just a little more than she had the day before.

Hush little baby, the moons ate setting in the sky…she sung to herself. *I will guard you, with stealth and with lies.*

Laura Campbell writes, runs, weight trains, and attends rock concerts in Houston, Texas. Many of her more recent works are available on-line. Her children, Alexander and Samantha, encourage her in her pursuits. Her stories "From the Garden" and "416175" can be heard on Spotify's *Scare You to Sleep* podcast.

Queen Amalia

by Linda M. Crate

I refused to be a pawn in the chess game of my father. This was the first strike against me. They say that you ought to honor your mother and father, but what if they don't honor you? I suppose you would expect me to turn the other cheek. You're wrong. I wouldn't, I couldn't, and I am not sorry for what I did.

It was either my father died or I would be a pawn in gaining the support of some kingdom that he wanted to have an alliance for because he told me once when I was a child that all women were good for were mothers. They had no talents, no ambitions, and no truths worth discovering or exploring.

He was a disgusting man, and I don't understand why my mother stood by his side.

It disgusted me to see her honoring her husband as if he were some hero. Many would praise him as such. He rode into wars and fought beside his men, he fed and clothed the poor, he made sure every orphan of war was given a good family and even checked up on them to ensure that they were okay.

Yet he never once hugged me or comforted me in my darkest hour. He was only emotionally available to my brothers, always telling them how one day they might be kings of the Kingdom of Sylvan - the Autumn Faerie Court.

Instead they got me, an evil queen.

They should've seen this coming. They gave me no choice but to become the villain. Seeing someone as only someone's future wife and/or a pawn for a political alliance or gain was absolutely disgusting. So many men were mediocre and were praised for the most mundane of things, and yet they held women to an impossible and ever changing standard where they were would never measure up or be good enough. Where they were always criticized and critiqued for their every move, as if a woman's only place in society was to be a pawn men could use for their own entertainment or enjoyment.

Well, I was going to put that standard to rest and put the nail in that coffin as if it were the one that belonged to my father.

Just knowing he would be rolling in his grave knowing what I was doing to his precious Sylvan made even my wings flutter and flap with excitement.

I was dismantling the patriarchy and installing a matriarchy. However, unlike most matriarchies that didn't embody the same principles of the patriarchy - I was out for blood and for revenge. I was going to make women superior to men. I was done with being inferior. I was done watching feminists fight for equality, and seeing the way men laughed at them and belittled them and insisted they were wrong and their opinions were superior.

I had fired every single person that had held court for my father when I was a young girl, and every advisor I appointed was non-binary or a woman.

I would not allow men to hold any sort of office in any part of my country. This kingdom was going to realize every mistake that they had ever made against a woman, and I wasn't going to feel bad for it even if I should.

My little sister died trying to prove her loyalty and devotion for my father in one of his wars, and he didn't even utter her name after she had died. My mother had died from the heartbreak of losing her youngest child shortly thereafter. Did she roll in her grave knowing that my father never spoke her name after she had died?

I had killed him the morning of what was supposed to be his second marriage.

I also killed his to be wife with such utter and unhinged joy. She had threatened to marry me off to some prince in some land that would treat me horribly because she didn't like that I was unmarried nor did she like how disrespectful I was to my father.

Yet, now here I stood in the role of queen undisputed.

I remembered how warm her blood was when it left her body, and the defiantly sweet taste of it against my tongue. It made me smirk as I thought of her helpless in my arms, pleading for a mercy that I would never give her. Disrespect came with consequences, and that was a lesson she learned well.

My brothers were furious, of course, but they could do nothing. I had become queen as they were sleeping in their beds dreaming of whatever fancy my father had told them about was theirs.

My advisors were all the women that either grew up agreeing with me and my rants against my father and the men of this kingdom, his scorned mistresses, or those that my father had disrespected who saw me and my power.

I had the strongest magic of all my siblings, and I thanked the gods for that.

Because I had lofty ambitions for this country mine.

It was going to be a better place for women. It was going to be a place where men feared to go, a place were men would finally shut their insufferable and collective mouths and allow women their space to speak.

I knew that I could go about this a different way. I knew that I could've been more peaceful about it, but why should I be expected to keep peace just because I'm a woman? I have always been a feral, wild creature and for that I will make no apology.

They couldn't appreciate my magic, my worth, or my truths and so I would bury them beneath my ambition and my strength instead.

One of my father's old advisors spat at me as I walked past him in the dungeons. "You won't get away with this, Amalia."

"Queen Amalia," I amended. "And I already have, I'm afraid," I sighed.

"You're a demon from hell."

"Why, thank you!" I twisted around him, my garments wrapping around my long legs and my deceptively thin ankles which were very strong. "It's very few men who know how to appreciate a woman's true beauty," I told him, winking.

"Your father would be absolutely disgusted with what you've done."

"That's the plan," I smirked.

"Don't you have any shame?" he demanded of me.

"No," I crooned. "Because whilst a single man breathes audacity into any universe in any realm in any kingdom, all I shall ever have for them is rage." I patted him on the head. "Nice try, though. Got anything else for me?" I asked, arching a brow.

"This isn't a joke, Amalia. You will fail. No man will ever want to marry you, and what is a queen without her king?"

Ah, yes the moment I had been born for. I was waiting for him to say something like this.

"Historically they were more powerful," I told him. "Besides who needs a king? Why should I waste all this beauty on a man who wouldn't know how to appreciate it? I might find myself a wife and we'll be two powerful queens together."

"Disgusting," he spat.

"What's disgusting, darling?" I demanded. "The rats that will feast on you until there's nothing left or the fact that you cannot respect women?"

"What do you even mean?" he asked, blinking.

"I saw the way you looked at my mother and sister like they were nothing more than pieces of meat," I scoffed, glaring at him.

"Well, they were real women! They behaved as a woman should."

"Not all women are doormats for you to walk over, and I certainly will never be," I informed him. "I will never be anyone's doormat. Some women may be meek and submissive, some may not wish to upset the status quo; but I am a woman who will make every woman proud. I am a woman who will fight for every woman, and I will win!" I growled.

"We shouldn't be at war," he insisted, blinking at me.

"We shouldn't, and yet you men never learned how to respect us so it's come to this. I will be the villain that you'll all love to hate. I'll be the one you rally around in agreement should die, but I will be the wicked queen that outlives you all." With that, I swept past him and walked out of his cell; locking it behind him.

"You're going about this the wrong way!" another man that used to advise my father shouted.

"Perhaps, I am," I agreed, shrugging my shoulders, nonchalant. "However, some of you only respond to violence so violence is what I will give you."

They couldn't say that they didn't ask for this.

With that, I took my leave of the dungeons. It was hilarious how they thought they could talk me down, as if talking would do them any good. I had killed my father when he had begged me for mercy, I had also killed the woman who was arrogant enough to assume that she could be my mother or ever take her place.

I may have not liked my mother much, but the way my father had forgotten her was simply unforgiveable.

If that was the type of person that was going to be lauded as a hero, then I would gladly be the villain; every single time.

My brothers were all in the room I asked my advisors to prepare them for me in. They all glared at me from their seats, and I swept in; uncaring and unheeding of their nasty looks.

They could hate me all they wanted, I was their queen. There was nothing they could do about it.

"What is the meaning of this, Amalia?"

"Respect your queen," one of my advisors snapped, digging her nails deep into my brother's back. He was the second oldest, the one born six months after me.

He let out a squeal of pain that sounded like a dying pig.

"Surely it could not have hurt you that badly," I smirked. "Surely, a war hero has more strength than that, or were those stories of your valor overestimated by father?"

He glared at me, spitting at my feet.

I turned around so quickly that he blinked his surprise that I didn't have whiplash before I slapped him hard enough across the face that his face was left with a giant red mark that covered his face. "Don't be so disrespectful," I growled. "Like it or not, I am the queen."

"What do you want of us?" my youngest brother asked, looking scared.

I had to admit that the fear in his eyes gave me such a thrill.

"Don't be scared," I remarked. "I won't hurt you unless you give me reason to. I have brought you here today because I have arranged marriages for all of you. Our alliances with these princesses will strengthen our alliances with these kingdoms."

"You're joking, right?" one of my brothers asked.

"Absolutely not," I responded. "I've never joked about anything serious, Amos. You should know that about me by now," I snorted, rolling my eyes. "You said nothing when father wanted to marry off Azaria and I off to some foreign princes in lands we had never heard of so this is your punishment and your fate for not standing up for your sisters, as you should have!"

"Amalia, father was just doing what he thought was good for our country!"

"Then you should have allowed yourself to be one of his pawns! The pawn that he never so much as embraces when they are in times of need, the ones that he is willing to murder in his wars and then forget the names of! You should have bid your own life and not mine! So you're going to get what you deserve."

"When are we to meet these princesses?" my oldest brother asked.

"Tonight," I answered. "After the ball tonight, you will be going home with them; so do your best to pack everything that's needed before the celebratory ball tonight."

"Tonight?"

"Do you hate us so much?"

"I do," I answered. "Because you saw me as nothing more than a pawn just as father did. Not once did any of you treat me like your sister. Just an inconvenience or annoyance. So tonight you will feel the same."

"Amalia, please!" one of my brother's called, but I had already left the room.

It was too late for heartfelt apologies or protests that they truly did care about me or any such nonsense. I would not be moved by any lie or plea they had to issue to me. They had made their beds and now they were going to sleep with their bad decisions, and reflect on how they could be better faeries and brothers in the future should they ever be born to royalty again.

The celebratory ball was something I knew my subjects were looking forward to. They didn't know that I had murdered my father or his wife to be, they just knew they were going to glance upon the face of their new queen. I wondered when the clapping would turn to a silence where you could hear a pin drop when I entered.

I was going to be wearing the red dress that my father had always was too immodest for me to wear.

I had long legs that went on for days, and this dress had a slit that went all the way up to my right thigh. The sleeves went all the way down to my wrist but they were see through gauze, only the very bottom being a solid trim for about an inch. He also didn't like it because it showed some of my cleavage, but it was no fault of my own that I was better endowed than my mother had been.

I would relish all the chaos this dress may cause when I walked into the room.

Of course, it wouldn't only be the dress. It would be me assuming my father's throne without anyone else's prior knowledge. It would be the knowledge that my brothers were being the ones sent off to form alliances for my country instead of me. It would be the knowledge that my father was dead that probably would rattle some of them to their core, and I was ready for it.

They could overlook the aspects of my father's problematic person and consider him a hero.

I knew they wouldn't do the same for me.

That was okay, I never pretended to be something I wasn't. I wasn't anyone's hero except perhaps my own. I touched up my make-up, put on the jewelry of my late mother to accentuate my features as she wouldn't need it any longer, and looked at my black wings. They looked so good with this dress.

My wings were feathers like those of everyone in my family had, they resembled crow or raven feathers just larger. Mine were the only ones that were black. My father had beautiful gold wings that all of my brothers had inherited, and my sister had the same dark purple that my mother had. Mine were black like the mother of my mother that she said had dismissed her concerns when she hadn't wanted to marry my father.

As I looked in the mirror, I liked what I saw. It was the promise of someone I had never been, the promise of something new. A queen whose power or authority no one would question.

"It's time, Queen Amalia," one of my advisors said to me.

They were non-binary, and someone my father had once put down regularly. I thought they were lovely, and they were all too happy to assist me. They had been the ones that had the connections to marry off my brothers to this obscure kingdoms I wanted to forge alliances with.

"Thank you, darling," I said, as they offered me their arm.

Together, we walked down the stairs. They then left me at the top of the stairs as I heard my name being announced.

It wasn't nearly as quiet as I thought it would be. There were gasps, and oohs and aahs as I walked down the stairs, there were also whispers and gossiping emerging all around me.

Next came the announcement of my brothers and who they would be married to.

Now there was the silence I knew would come, and I smiled. "Now," I responded, my voice magically magnified. "I will say let us forget these unpleasantries and take to celebrating. My brothers will be married to princesses that care for them, and you have yourself a brilliant new queen that will shine brighter than any star you've ever seen in the galaxy."

"What happened to your father?" shouted an angry nobleman.

"He had a terrible accident," I said, baring my fangs.

He seemed to understand my meaning, and immediately backed off. Good! I wanted them to fear me, to be intimidated of me, to never question a single thing I advised or demanded of them. This was my kingdom now, and I would not be merciful to any who questioned me or my authority.

"What of your mother to be?" asked a noble woman.

"I had a mother and she died. I'm assuming you mean my step mother to be? She died. Heartbreak or so I heard. What a terrible tragedy," I said.

"Oh, she must've loved your father so."

"Must have," I answered, not really liking this conversation. I snapped my fingers in impatience, and one of my advisors came rushing over to take care of the plethora of irritating questions these people were bound to ask me about my parents that I simply wasn't in the mood for.

A woman was watching me, looking amused. I looked at her, knowing immediately what she was. She was a vampire, nearly as tall as me but not quite. I will admit it was a hard feat as I was six foot seven.

Faeries were tall, but I was tall even by our standards. The tallest faerie woman before me had been six foot four. Most averaged to be six feet. With these heels I was probably standing at a healthy seven feet.

"Queen Amalia, what a pleasure to make your acquaintance," the woman said, as she glided over to me.

She was attractive with long raven hair and dark eyes. She was wearing a black gown with red accents.

"Who may you be?" I asked, looking at her.

"Princess Dal," she answered. "At least, I was a princess before my brother became king and forced me out of his kingdom. Now he refuses to admit the evils of what he did. I know what you did, and I can sense you have a strong power. Will you help me take my kingdom back?"

"I must admit I am sympathetic to your plight, but I don't quite know you Princess Dal," I sighed. "Also, how am I to profit from a venture such as this? To sacrifice my knights and my soldiers, there must be something of interest for me, hm?"

"I thought you might ask that," Dal nodded. "I offer you my kingdom and my hand in marriage, should you be so inclined."

I looked over this displaced princess. She must've been desperate to offer herself. Then again, I was a queen…so it wasn't completely a selfless sacrifice, was it?

She grinned at me. "You've seen through me, but please don't hold it against me. We are two peas in a pod, and I will be the most loyal person on your side."

"Fine, I will take you up on both of your offers," I agreed. "But you should be advised that if you betray me, I will rip you to pieces. I will give you no mercy."

"I would expect nothing less," Dal told me, with a slight bow. "So when can I see you out of that dress?"

"That's a little forward for our first night together," I smirked. "But, perhaps, you shall see something soon," I promised, with a mischievous wink. "Now I happen to know a little of vampire lore. To ensure your loyalty, you make blood pacts, yes?"

"Yes," she nodded.

"Well, faeries enjoy the blood of vampires as much as vampires enjoy the blood of the fae. So if what you mean is true, let me leave my mark on that beautiful neck of yours," I responded.

I think I expected her to chicken out at this point or simply decline.

However, she pulled her long hair from her neck, twisting her head to the side. "Make your mark then, faerie queen."

Mm. She was really a strange one, promising me not only a kingdom but herself in but a moment, but I wouldn't question the gift horse that looked me in the mouth. There was nothing for me to lose here. Even if the kingdom wasn't rich or good enough for my standards, it could become a lesser faerie kingdom and I could ship every one of my rivals or war criminals there. We would have to see what that land yielded me.

I bent down, biting deeply into her throat, knowing full well it would leave a horrible scar. But the thought of her blood on my tongue gave me such euphoria that I forgot to be polite.

I drank enough of her blood that she swayed where she stood, and I pulled her into my arms as I walked over to one of my advisors. "Take her to a healer and make sure they take good care of dear Princess Dal here, won't you?"

"Who is she?"

"My future wife, and someone who made an alliance to me and our country," I responded. "We even get to kill her brother who forced her out of his country, too."

"That sounds delicious. You certainly move fast, Amalia."

"Well, we can't leave the saving of the world to the men of our kingdoms, can we? We have to be our own heroes and save ourselves," I told her with a smirk.

"Yes, that's true," she grinned. "Your grandmother would be proud."

I smiled, trying to pretend that would matter to me so as not to be rude. As she walked away with my passed out bride-to-be I gazed out into the sea of faces. I'm sure that there would be more that would pledge their loyalty to me, even only eventually. It only made me hungrier to start making big changes in this country.

I would not be a queen that would ever be forgotten.

This ball was the start of my new kingdom.

I couldn't wait to expand and broaden my horizons. My brothers would be out of my hair come tomorrow, and I would begin my new life very soon. It made me giddy to think that in just two nights I had changed my entire fate.

I was no damsel in distress married off to some man so that her father could look good, I was a queen who was going to rule with an iron fist and destroy any who thought they might destroy her.

Not bad for my first public outing, I thought. I felt some blood on the corner of my mouth, and gently wiped it off; careful as not to smudge my lipstick.

"Like the taste of the blood, eh?" I heard a male voice ask.

"Why wouldn't I? I've got a bit of a sweet tooth," I answered.

He laughed, glancing at me. "You're very lovely."

"That I am," I agreed. "I hope you understand that I will never be beneath a man," I told him. "I have no interest in being your queen. I have a kingdom to run, and historically queens are more powerful without kings."

"This is true, but couldn't you allow me to look upon those beautiful features of yours?" he asked.

"I don't easily trust men," I frowned. "So you'll have to prove your worth."

"I will," he promised.

That was yet to be seen. I didn't like the way he was looking at me, but I simply smiled. "We'll see," I said, before walking away.

"May I have this dance?" a man asked me.

I bit back my disgust. "I suppose just this once," I said, with a playful giggle. I knew I would have to play nice for now.

Linda M. Crate's works have been published in numerous magazines and anthologies both online and in print. She is the author of ten published chapbooks, four full-lengths, and three micro-chaps. She has a novella, also, called *Mates* (Alien Buddha Publishing, March 2022).

Hell-Bound

by Nicole Walsh

I'm seated at a shabby table, on a tiny chair, in a tiny room, trying to look like I'm listening. It's harder than you realise. Makes all the muscles in my face jump and twitch, like they want out of the room. I don't blame them.

"There's hope, Alliot," Megan is cooing.

"Not in this," Alliot moans, head in his hands. "It's too late."

"It's never too late."

"Eight offers. Eight contracts. Eight women. They *laughed* at me!"

I snort. Glares snap my direction.

"Susan," Belle growls. "We talked about this."

"Oh, ah yes, sorry." I rub my fingers over my smirk, trying to erase it. "Alliot…"

Everyone waits expectantly. Alliot's gaze cuts to me.

"Better luck… next time?" I hazard.

"Next time?" Alliot explodes.

"Yes." I'm pretty sure I have the expression right. I've been working really, really hard on 'worried/thoughtful'. It's very similar to the expression you get when you take a big dump.

"Why is she here?" Alliot whines. His hands lock around the notebook in which he compulsively scribbles, picks, twists and clutches.

"Susan apologised."

"She was banned!"

"For a fortnight."

"She should have been evicted." Alliot's voice has a whiney edge that makes me want to slap his head off. "She never says anything kind or supportive."

Megan reaches out comfortingly. She doesn't touch Alliot. Megan's learning to keep her hands to herself. Megan's a Churchie, one of a vast wash of idiots who believe their light will shine brightest in Hell. Five years into colonisation and Hell is full of Churchies. Most skip down here as voluntary colonists. The vast majority die in the first three days. That works for the rest of us. They bring in fresh supplies and the jaws of the local beasties get crammed full of soft Churchie meat, leaving our battle-scarred hides unmolested.

I clear my throat. Everyone looks at me warily.

"Go on, Alliot." I nod in a supportive, encouraging manner. I've been practicing that move. Erin had me carry a mirror around for a week to check my expression. I do glower a lot. Resting-glower-face, Erin reckons.

People exchange looks. I'm perilously close to being axed from Circle. Since this is my eighth Circle and friends are an essential part of the Healthy Relationships domain of our colony contracts, staying in this group is life or death for me.

"We're here for you, Alliot," Megan soothes.

Alliot scrunches his leather-clad notebook.

"She's not."

"Susan's here every week."

"She does everything she can to antagonise me!" Alliot wrings his notebook like it's my neck. "To make me feel vulnerable and unsafe. Last week she brought me a cake!"

Even Belle blinked.

"It was his birthday," I explain. "I baked it myself."

I hadn't. Erin had made it for me and I had repurposed it for Alliot, because me knocking at his door never failed to pitch him into a fit. Watching an arrogant and once highly-respected ward-mage collapse in his mouldy hallway, shaking and weeping hysterically, is as funny as Hell.

"She… it… I…" Alliot collapses into his scarred hands and notebook.

I open my eyes wide, lean forward and try for 'concern':

"Deep breath."

"Shut up," Alliot wails.

"Alliot," Belle snarls.

Megan reaches out, setting a hand on Belle's leg. We're sitting in a room that looks like an explosion of lace and photos and flowers. In the last few weeks Belle and Megan added a baby. I have no idea where the baby came from. In Hell, it's best not to ask.

"We evicted her," Alliot whines.

"Then she petitioned for a Second Chance." Belle's a huge, hulking ex-death-mage. "On account of the…" She twirls a finger at her own shaved, tattooed head.

I scratch the side of my skull, conveniently shaved to display the scars and caved in areas. That had been Erin's idea too.

"Brain injury," I explain helpfully.

"Alliot is trying very hard," Megan summarises. "He wants a family. A wife. Children."

I snort, then cover my mouth and nose.

"Sorry. Sneezing."

"Family is important. We're all…" Megan's voice wobbles. "Lonely." She looks at her wife. Belle's scowl collapses. The women clasp hands and share a long, soppy, ridiculous look.

"You don't need to do this alone," Megan says, to Alliot. "You'll find your family."

I manage not to snort. Pretty sure my grin says it all.

#

Circle ends soon after that. Nervous nellies like Alliot insist we disband before mid-afternoon, even though the streets are reasonably safe for any semi-bad-ass right up to an hour before sunset.

I head to Erin's place. We have dinner after Circle because Erin likes to hear how it went. I'm trying really, really hard to use my words and not shrug and grunt. Erin and I have a lot of fights over me shrugging and grunting.

"Crazy mess!" I conclude brightly. "Flowers and pictures. Pictures of other people! Unrelated people, lined on the walls, like they're… family and stuff."

"And a baby," Erin whispers.

I wave my hand dismissively.

"And Alliot?"

My brows fold in a thunderous clash:

"What about him?"

Erin has her back to me. She's slim and young and so far out of my league I've no idea why she even pretends to be dating me.

"He's one of your friends."

"Registered Friends," I growl. "All arrogance and soap and 'look, I write, I'm edja-ma-cated'."

"Susan." I can hear the frown in Erin's voice. "Circle is important."

"Didn't you hear me?" I explode. "I said it went well!"

There's an uncomfortable silence. I stroke circles on the scoured top of Erin's table. It smells like the herbs she cuts for her potions. Erin's a Healer. She patches me up and I break the skulls of any thug causing her trouble.

I pull in a slow, deep breath like Erin taught me and focus on my surroundings. Erin went all out with dinner. There's something in the oven as well as on the pot. There's a pie cooling on a bench and she wasted good money on purple flowers that clash marvellously with her pink dress.

"Don't like dating after Circle, Erin," I whine.

"It makes this look authentic." Erin sounds flat and sad.

"All Hell knows this is fake, Erin." It comes out harsher than I'd intended. I squirm and keep talking: "To give you a rest from dating after your crazy ex. To give me a chance to become more social and stuff."

There's a long, awkward silence.

"Ah…" I fumble. "Dinner smells good?"

Erin lets her breath out in a sigh. I hate it when she sighs. Makes me want to put my fist through something.

"I need to talk to you about something."

"Talk!" When Erin's talking, I can practice my smile and nod.

"I need you to be calm. Maybe after dinner."

"Sure."

Never did a lot of talking before Hell. You know when a hero is facing down a grim and glowering spell-caster and his small army of mindless thugs? I used to be thug number eight — the one waaaay up the back, smirking. There's a reason I hate spell-casters. I spent a lifetime taking fireballs for them, only to have them dump my ass when I was too old, ugly and damaged.

"Susan?"

I realise I'm glowering up a storm.

"Sorry. Went elsewhere."

Erin's standing over me, saucepan in hand. I fell in love the moment I saw Erin, sobbing into her hands, begging me to save her from her crazy-stalker-ex. That bitch was dead in hours. Erin had been eager to patch me up and we bonked like rabbits three days straight. On paper we are married. In reality she is the only friend I've ever had.

"Where?"

"What?"

"Where did you go?"

"Oh." I shrug. "Some battlefield or something."

"I was talking. Did you hear any of it?"

"Some?" I wince. Erin can always tell when I'm lying.

"I *said* this is really important to me."

I freeze, casting desperately through all the things Erin told me were important this last week alone:

"Making Circle work?"

"No. Well, yes."

"Being nice to Alliot?"

"That too." Erin's frowning now.

"Eating with my mouth closed? Not scowling at people? Taking different jobs?" I brighten as her expression clears: "Rescue jobs. Not thump and torture jobs!"

I flex my hands. My knuckles are bruised and bloody from pounding people. Erin follows my gaze. Her expression crunches. She drops the bottom of saucepan on the table like its suddenly too heavy.

"Did you beat someone up?"

"He deserved it." I hide my hands under the table. "Rapist…"

"Really?"

I hesitate, wanting so badly to lie.

"He owed money. That's bad too. Erin!" I whine, as she turns away. "Everyone down here is bad."

"Everyone down here is trying." Erin slams the pot back on the stove. "Everyone but you. You told me you were changing."

"I am! I checked for other work!"

"You just lied." I hear the wobble in Erin's voice. She hunches over the stove, shoulder bones as delicate as a bird's, ends of her long hair brushing her butt.

"Susan. Are you listening?"

"Sure," I lie. Her butt is a perfect upside down love-heart. She isn't wearing undies.

"This isn't working," Erin says. "I need more than this."

"You want…" I wave a hand at her kitchen — at the pie, herbs, flowers. "You want…"

What? I flounder.

Anger surges. I shoot to my feet, grab the edge of the table and flip it over with a crash.

"You want a functioning wife, right?" I shout. "You want someone who has a real job, not a hired fucking thug? You want someone who brings you flowers and doesn't shout at you and likes your vegan fucking cooking?"

I love the fact Erin is never scared, not even when I pull shit like this. She blazes back in my face:

"You have no idea what I want!" she screams back. "No fucking idea, *Susan*."

She shouts the last word. It feels like a slap.

"What's that supposed to mean?"

Erin yanks the ring off her finger.

"This," she says, dead calm. She sets the ring on the table beside the stove.

"You're giving up?"

"Giving what up?" Erin demanded. "I can't make this work with…" she hesitates.

"Broken pieces?" I snarl. "'Cause I'm not relationship material, right? Not family material?"

Erin tilts a shrug, face white with anger.

"Fuck you, little girl!" I roar. "You have no fucking idea what I am!"

I storm out of the house, slamming out past the doors and grills I helped her put up that first week, past the wards I bullied a local mage into putting around her house, past the fence I painted and down the street.

People jump out of my way. I'm shaking like a noob with post-battle jitters. The sky flames that streaky yellow it gets when it's working its way up to a Hellstorm. My boots crunch bones from some ravenous swarm that got itself de-fleshed by someone's wards in the night. Drunks are streaming home around me, singing and staggering and scowling. I go against the flow, heading into Pub Street.

Erin loves that card, the 'you're-not-functioning' card. It's a load of bull-fucking-shit. I've been here three years. I'm thriving!

I slam into the pub - the one Erin hates, 'cause it's all ex-dark-mages weeping into their cups and whining about better days. I can get a steak down here, something big and fatty and riddled with worms. Who needs soup, anyway?

I hurl myself onto a stool, nearly breaking it with my weight. I'm getting fat in Hell, the lean crags of my body rounding into softer curves. In my head, replayed over and over, was the click of the ring on the bench. I bury my face in my hands so no one sees my expression. Erin was ending it? Fine. It was bullshit, anyway. No one would believe we were compatible: a soft pretty Healer with a love-heart-shaped butt and a burly, ugly, scarred-to-shit ex-mercenary.

"I'm not a thug," I whine. "She doesn't know me at all."

I wipe snot on the back of my hand.

"She means the fake marriage, right?" I whine at the bartender, three beers in. "Meant that was over, right? Not, like, our friendship?"

"Depends how bad you pissed her off."

#

I walk home through shadows and monsters. Winged beasts circle. Things rattle and creep. I make it home minutes before the grills come crashing down.

"Susan…" the lobby-mage scowls.

"Fuck off."

Worry whirls in my head like a flail, making it impossible to sleep. When the sun is high enough to be mostly safe for anyone halfway competent with a battle-hammer I stagger out, climbing over the ravaged bodies of folk who hadn't been able to pay their rent last night. I rent a room in a hostel close to the pub strip, preferring to channel my earnings into my axe and hammer collection… and beer. Mostly beer.

I wash into Match-n-Punch with a wicked hangover and a mother of all glowers. I don't usually work Fridays, but I'm itching to hit someone. Match-n-Punch is a cheap-as-shit mercenary contract centre.

"Nope," I scowl. "I want different jobs."

The reeking, legless brute behind the counter gives me a baffled look.

"We work loan-sharks, drunks and junkies. What sorta work you talkin' about, Bruiser?"

"Susan," I remind him.

He forces his gaze North. Normally I wear layers of stained and filthy leathers. Today I'm wearing the thin lace-up shirt Erin brought me. My nipples poke through hard and perky. Erin reckons I don't need to be girlie to be sexy.

I squint, trying to recall Erin's exact words: "Something noble and heroic."

"At Match-n-Punch?"

"Harry…"

"Bogs."

"Bogs." I'm seriously bad with names, on account of the fact I don't fucking care. "Look, my wife's pissed. I need a better story then breaking some fella's leg or dropping a debtor down a Hell-hole. I need something grand."

"At Match-n-Punch?"

I was about ready to match and punch him.

I brace my hands on the counter and breathe deep and slow. He watches my nipple in confusion. Just as I'm easing through the count of six, his gaze snaps sideways. A kid just drifted in, like one of those weird ghost butterflies you get drifting through walls in the hours after a Hellstorm.

In a scrum of huge, battered thugs and sinister mages the kid looked pale and tiny. She's dressed in an academy uniform and walks straight up to Monster, the security thug by the register.

"I want to hire you," she announces.

Every thug in the place snaps to attention. Monster's face buckles in confusion.

"She's mine!" I shout. "Mine! No one touch her!"

#

I get the girl out in record time.

"Don't wave money around like that," I growl, to explain all the snatching and yanking.

"I'm hiring someone."

"You have me."

The girl squints at me. Her hair is sleek and blonde. There's a big dirty handprint on her shoulder where I grabbed her. No one saw the pouch of her money in her hand 'cause I folded my larger hand around it.

"I want a man."

"I'm better than a man." I strike a pose. "Safer than a man, too."

"I need someone big."

"I'm plenty big."

The girl, who came up to my nipple, flicks her hair sassily.

"Okay. Fine. Whatever. I need an escort to Black Circuit."

That makes sense. A cute little kid in a posh Academy uniform would need some ugly local muscle to go somewhere like that.

"Visiting who?"

"Morvan Grandtoxin, Black Sorcerer of Hellsgrove."

"Know him. Worked for him, actually, 'fore we all moved to Hell." I hold out my hand. She's working the pouch between her tiny fingers. Her nails are shaped like Erin's — small, clean and short.

"You'll take me there and help me get this spell?"

"Yep."

"Today?"

"Yep."

The girl sets the pouch in my hand without haggling. She cringes back. I realise I'm grinning.

"Sorry. Thinking about someone else." I check the pouch. "What the… splog?" I'm trying really hard to break a life-time habit of cussing.

"My mother's jewels." The girl sounds defensive. "They're real."

I manage to get my mouth closed.

"Where's your mother?"

"Dead."

"She was rich?"

"She was stupid. My father's rich."

Alarm bells begin clanging in my head like city bells.

"This spell you're getting," I glower. "Is it an assassination spell? An abortion spell? A malice spell?"

"What?" the kid blinks.

Erin gives me a *lot* of shit for taking jobs like that. I fold my arms and glare. The kid gropes for a charm hanging about her neck.

"I need a protection spell," she frowns. "It took every coin I had to make this charm a week ago." She displays the pendant. "It's not enough. I need a Marris ward."

A Marris ward is set into your breastbone. It tangles with your soul, making it Hellishly hard to break. The job sounds good: pretty, imperilled child; terrifying spell-caster; noble cause. I tuck the jewels away.

"Morvan's a busy man. You gotta make an appointment a year in advance. You'll need a lot more twinkles than this."

"I have enough." Dumb kid touches her bra, drawing my attention to the rest of her loot. I grin evilly:

"Follow me, little miss."

#

Kid and I stand beside a vast hole, staring into the crater. A hot, foul wind that reeks of charred stone and black magic lifts the ends of the kid's skirt and hair.

"Okay." I scratch my shaved scalp. "This is getting weird. Morvan, I get. He's prime-grade douche. Everyone hates him. But Glitch is rabid crazy and Blenda here was, like, old as the hills. How can all three of 'em be dead?"

"They're at war." The girl's fingers are white-knuckled around her charm. "All the battle-mages in Hell are at war. I need this done. Now. Today."

Unease chews at me, like rats at my vitals. The whole block is gone. That's a hard-core spell.

"Did you hear me?" The girl's rabbitting on. "I said, what now?"

Now I get a beer. I have a Hellish hangover and I'm too old and too smart to involve myself in high-level mage business, especially when it involves giant smoking craters and mass murder.

"Ain't much more I can do for you, kid. Taken this as far as it goes."

"What? No. I hired you."

"Hired me to find Morvan. We found him. What's left of him."

"What's your name?"

It takes me a moment to realise the kid's talking to me.

"Susan."

"You don't look like a Susan."

I give her a dirty look and snatch the paper out of her hand. I squint at the writing.

"My name's Cassie," the girl announces.

Erin would've asked that first up, back at the centre. She would have shaken the kid's hand, too. Maybe got down on her knee to gaze into the kid's eyes and assure her everything was gonna be okay. Thinking about Erin makes me feel squirmy, like ice-cold snakes sliding over one another in my belly.

"It's gonna be okay," I growl. I shove the paper at her. "Read the other names."

"These aren't battle-mages." Cassie strokes creases off the mangled paper. "They're Hell-mages. A Hell-mage should be able to cast this as well. With the right ingredients."

"Would they *have* the right ingredients?"

Cassie swings her cute satchel to the front. It rattles.

"I brought them. Just in case. There was a chance the war-mages would say no." She studies the paper. "Newton the Nightmare?"

"Nope."

"Why?"

"He'll use your bones. And mine. Who else?"

"Filthy Florence?"

"Mad as a hatter."

"Meaty Malicious?"

"Not even on a bad day. Keep going."

"Fracton the Fractious?"

Fracton was an arrogant slop who'd inherited his master's store and business when his master unexpectedly keeled over. Fracton advertised as a Hell-mage, but he'd been raised academy and was squeaky clean, despite the greasy hair and nasty robes.

"Perfect. Come on."

#

"Damn it!"

I jerk awake with a snort, rocking upright in my chair and floundering for my hammer.

"Wha the… fudge?"

Both kids glare, light and dark. Fracton the Fractuous answered the door in a deeply shadowed hood and a whispery voice. With the hood tossed back he's too soft and too clean, even with the eyeliner and greasy hair.

His ex-master, an infamous bone-boiler, lured the kid away from his school with the promise of an apprenticeship. The grotty old bastard had keeled over dead mid-grooming and Fracton had unexpectedly inherited the store and business.

That was three weeks ago. The door was covered with 'rent-overdue' and 'final warning' wards, which meant I'd been able to force my way in easily.

"What happened?"

"It failed." Cassie looks disgusted. "Again. You said you knew how to do this, Fracton. That's all the black spike I had!"

"Black spike?" I jolt upright. "That's dangerous."

Cassie shoots me a look. She isn't a Hell-mage, but she's well-educated and bossy and has attitude up to the gills. Fracton displays a shaking hand, pierced through with a black spike. I shoot to my feet, cross the room in one step and snatch hold of Fracton before the kid has time to react.

Fracton looks sixteen, several years older than my client. I yank the spike out. Fracton shrieks like a girl.

Cassie sucks in a breath, rummaging through the upended, trampled mess of the store.

"That's all we had! You used it all?"

I gawk around in horror, holding Fracton upright by a grip on his wrist, tight enough to ease the bloodflow. The spell must have exploded. Thin deadly shards of black spike are imbedded in the walls, table and chair.

"Cassie, are you hit?"

"No."

"Check," I growl.

"I'm hit," Fracton whines, sinking toward a chair. I yanked him upright.

"It's everywhere, idiot."

"Burned." Cassie's checking the spikes. "You need intact black spike to cast a Marris spell."

Fracton hangs in my grip, breath fast and panicked.

"How long do I have?"

Kid was dripping blood on my boots. Was tempted to say, fuck would I know, but he was so grey he looked pitched to faint. I fish a cloth out of his robes. Despite his filthy robes and greasy hair, his handkerchief is clean and ironed.

"Seven or eight hours." I've been pricked with black spike more times than I can count.

"Less," Cassie frowns. "That's arterial blood."

I study the mess coming out of the kid. He's a mage. Not my problem. 'Sides, it was obvious he couldn't pay me. Fracton had sold what he could and debtors had taken the rest. I'm holding his hand above the level of his heart. A thin silver ring shines on my finger, glinting through the blood. My heart gives an ugly little yank.

"I know someone who can fix this."

#

"Don't feel well," Fracton whines.

"Whose fault's that?"

"You *said* you could do this." Cassie's hugging herself like she's cold.

The air tastes thin and nasty. The sky's staining a fierce chemical orange. All around us, folk are slamming grills or hammering out repairs. A Hell-storm's brewing. Kids are nervy as cats, jumping at every growl and sneak. Ain't no call for alarm. Hell-Storm is hours away and the threat of one has chased all the beasties to lair.

I walk fast, eager to win my way in Erin's door with this pretty imperilled child and woefully injured mage. I snap my fingers, trying to remember the kid's backstory.

"Your Daddy's trying to kill you," I prompt.

Erin would ask questions like this, and be pissed I hadn't.

"I'm a sacrifice," Cassie agreed, voice flat. "He bred me specifically for a spell. He needs me trained as a spell-caster to add value to the spell. He started ordering the ingredients."

"And he'll kill you…?"

"On my fourteenth birthday. In six months. Are you sure your friend has black spike?"

"Yep."

"A Healer with black spike?"

"I'm dying," Fracton whines. "If anyone cares."

We arrive at Erin's gate. I hand Cassie my hammer. She gives me a sassy look. I glower. She lets out a long-suffering sigh and takes it, nearly pitching sideways with the weight. I grab the swaying Hell-mage and hook his arm across my shoulder. Since I grabbed his injured arm, he half-faints, which means I can drag his limp ass up the stairs.

"Erin!" I roar dramatically.

#

I haul the bleeding Hell-mage down Erin's hall. Cassie's trying to get my hammer up the stairs. Erin, bless her gentle helpful soul, ducks out to help.

"Dying kid," I roar. "Where do you want him?"

"Black spike." Cassie dumps her bag and my hammer in the middle of the kitchen. "I need black spike."

"Artery?" Erin gasps.

"Yep."

I scoop up the half-conscious Hell-mage. Erin flutters around, barefoot and wide-eyed. She has a hammer in her hands. I'm not sure if that's in preparation for the Hell-Storm or whether she always answers the door with a hammer.

"What happened?"

"Marris spell exploded."

I love the way Erin smells. I love the way her soft body bumps against me as I carry the Hell-mage into the store. After three weeks the kid's mostly bone. I dump him on the mixing bench where he rolls and retches and sweats.

"You can fix this, right?"

Erin hesitates, chewing at her lip. I love it when she does that. Makes me imagine sucking her soft trembling lips into my mouth, devouring her.

"Susan?" Erin was talking.

I snap to attention.

"Huh?"

"Is he your client?"

"She is. He got hurt helping her."

Erin gives me a startled look. I snap my fingers.

"Wait. I saved his bacon. He owes me now. You hear that, kid?"

Erin folds her arms. Behind her, Cassie is rummaging through cupboards, slamming about in a very competent way.

"Why bring him here?" Erin frowns.

My words stick.

"Cause… you're a Healer?"

Hurt flashes across her face.

"Three credits."

"What?" I blink. "Kid's bleeding out."

"No, he's poisoned. I'm a Healer. I don't work for free."

"Yeah, but I'm your…" I hesitate awkwardly.

Erin arches a brow.

"Your friend," I growl, at last.

Her blue eyes turn cold and nasty.

"Fine. Then, as my *friend* Susan, you know I'm about to lose the store."

"You have plenty of money."

"Grams' money. Which will run out in a month."

"You…" I flap my hand. "Sell shit."

"Healing supplies?" She arches a brow. "In a suburb filled with spell-casters and death-mages who heal themselves with magic?"

"You're doing that thing with the candles…"

"Comfort candles? In *Hell*? The store's haemorrhaging money."

"Since when?" I bleat.

"Since always."

"You never told me that."

"I have!" Erin shouts. "You never listen!"

"Well." I flounder. "I'll help you pay the rent."

"Do you *know* what it costs to rent on this street?"

"No."

"Because you don't listen! You're not here. You're not *with* me." She storms into her room. I follow, feeling shaky and out of my depth.

"Erin…"

She whirls into my face — never frightened, just furious.

"What?"

I hesitate. Shit-fest, I don't know. I rock my weight and wish I had my hammer. I always think clearer with a hammer in my hand.

"Maybe…" I stall. That's all I have.

Erin shakes her head with disgust.

"Forget it," she huffs. "It's none of your business, is it, *Susan*."

Hate it when she uses my new name like that, like a sharp narrow dagger 'tween the ribs.

"I'm your wife!" I roar.

"Fake wife!" Erin shrieks back, then burst into tears.

It's like an ogre grabs my heart and grinds it to moosh. I close the door, cross the room and grab her. She pulls a bit, then melts into my chest.

"What the fuck?" I whisper.

"You don't get it," she whimpers.

"That you want a family?" I growl, into the softness of her hair. "I get it, Erin."

"You never listen."

"I do," I whisper, eyes burning like we're standing in a dragon's den. "I'm trying so hard, Erin."

"Are you?" Erin's hands curl to tiny fists under my breasts. I love it when she sinks into me like that, when I feel the huff of her breath against my chest.

"No," I admit. "But I will. I swear. Did you see the girl? Proper, noble jobs. And the boy? Coulda left him there to die."

"Why come here?" she whimpered.

"Because…"

I teeter, more scared than I had ever been in my life. *Use your words*, my mind gibbers. It's that frantic, panicked part of my mind that I squelched down years ago, as a green noob taking blows on the field.

"Susan?" she begs.

"I love you," I say, simply. "I want to make this work."

She makes a sound. Not a sob, an eager noise. I'm on her in seconds, swallowing that sound, her breath, her mouth. She presses up on her tiptoes, tiny body melting into mine, hands pulling on my shoulders and arms. I devour her hungrily.

"We need to…"

"Soon."

Her fingers pluck at the laces of my shirt. She skims fingertips across the fabric, brushing my nipples, which jump to attention. I gasp. I love it when she touches me, so gentle, despite my size and scars.

She makes a soft, satisfied sound.

"I like your…"

"I know." I trap her hands, lifting her wrists back over her head so I can access the sweet, delicate flesh on the underside of her arms. She moans, arching. I can't get enough of her, sucking at the skin of her throat and her shoulder, bare under her dress. My palms skim her nipples, hard as tiny pebbles. She's bare under her dress, not a single thing on. I explore, my hand sliding down the flat slope of her belly up around her ribs, curving under the shape of her breast. I lift her so she's kneeling on the ridiculously high bed and I have a better angle. Her breasts look like round little apples but are so soft. I suck them through the fabric of her dress, getting most of each into my mouth. I love how she smells when she's aroused. She squeaks and squirms and sighs.

"I-I need to…"

"When I'm done," I growl.

She grabs me, pulling at my shoulders. I lean into the game, letting her flip me over her hip so my back and shoulders are flat on the bed. She pulls her dress over her head. Loose clean hair tumbles down her back, the air sweet with the perfume of her skin. She poises like a Goddess astride me, staring down into my eyes, fierce and wild.

"After I'm done," she corrects.

#

I walk out an hour later, knees a tad shaky.

Cassie's banging and clattering, making a Hellish mess in Erin's beautifully tidy store. There's bowls and crap everywhere. Fracton's on the floor, back to the bench, still breathing.

He gives me a filthy look.

"Do you even care?" he whines.

"Nope."

I'm grinning like a fool. Erin is more relaxing than a barrel of beer. I pad over to see what Cassie's doing, wrinkling my nose at the two bowls.

"You fixing him?"

"No," Fracton growls.

"Yes." Cassie flashes me a defiant look. "Only when he helps me with mine." The girl drops down onto her heel to glare at the Hell-mage.

"What next?"

"Mutwood," Fracton gasps. He doesn't look well. He's grey and dripping sweat, holding his injured hand like it was hurting.

Cassie shoots upright, banging about in Erin's neatly labelled herbs. I peer over her shoulder, pretending to check the book and bottles.

"Thought you needed black spike?"

"He knows a way around it."

"He's lying. Can't make a Marris ward without black spike."

Cassie froze. She looked down at the mage.

"Are you lying?"

Fracton glared up at us.

"Fix me," he growls. "And I'll fix that."

Cassie's face hardens. She upends the bowl into the sink, then tips the smelly mess on top of it.

"Fix that," she suggests.

I snigger.

"Oh crap!" Erin came pattering over on bare feet. "I… damn it. Did…?" she blinks at the mess in the sink. "Did you make the poultice?"

Cassie ignored her, stalking about the place with a lot of hair flicking. She crouches to rummage through her bag, tucking a few of Erin's books out of sight.

"Do you have black spike?" she asks.

"No!" Erin was flying around, grabbing a clean bowl and things off the shelves. She doesn't need to look at the book. I get jabbed by black spike at least once a week.

Cassie gives me a filthy look, grabs her bag and storms down the hall.

"Hellstorm!" I shout, amused as Hell.

The door bangs.

"Susan!" Erin whirls.

I roll my eyes.

"Cassie!" I roar, louder. "Hellstorm."

"Doesn't matter," Fracton pants. "Her father… Edmord Blackstaff…"

Erin froze.

"She's Blackstaff's daughter?"

"Was." Fracton pants. "Dead."

Erin crouched beside the mage, bowl of ground herbs on her knee.

"What?"

"Blackstaff's dead," Fracton whispers. "All of them, dead. Saw Blackstaff's mansion this morning. A smoking crater."

I scrunch my face, trying to make sense of that.

"You're playing her? She doesn't need a Marris spell?"

"It's true," Erin whispered, chewing her lip. "I saw the crater too."

Does she know what she does to me, sucking her lip like that?

"Susan?"

"Dead. Yep. Got it."

"The girl!" Erin's frowning, like I've fucked something up.

I snap to attention.

"Yes!" I bolt out the door. Shit-balls and ash - I'm somehow halfway down the path under a flame-coloured sky, on a darkening street without my war-hammer or boots.

"Cassie!" I roar. "Hellstorm." I pointed at the violently-coloured sky. The air is trembling and vibrating. Reality is about to rip like paper. Things are about to come tumbling out.

"So!" The girl turns, standing in the middle of the street. She's bawling her eyes out and she looks terrified.

I freeze. If she runs, I can't chase her, not without shoes. If she runs there'll be no point: the Hellstorm is almost here. *Use your words*, my mind growls. I mince out Erin's gate, careful of Hellish weeds.

"Cassie, I don't have shoes." I keep my voice calm, despite the slam of my heart. The sky yawns above us. My shoulders itch without my war-hammer. "I'm not chasing you. It's dark. 'Storms about to break."

"I don't care. I'd rather die than…than…"

She doesn't have the words. I get that.

"Erin needs to talk to you about your Dad," I hesitate, then modify that: "I need to talk to you about your Dad."

"He's going to kill me!" The bag slips from her shoulders and clanks to the ground at her feet. She's gripping the amulet with both hands now. "No one cares!"

"I care." I reached out awkwardly, even though there's a street between us. There's bones and glass everywhere. "Erin and I care. You hired me, right? Let me fix this."

"Fix this how?"

"Let me show you."

"You'll sell me back to him. I know what you are!"

"I chased you onto the street without shoes, in the middle of a Hellstorm. Pretty sure you have no idea what I am, Cassie. Come inside. We'll figure this out. Together."

I gesture with my hand. Erin reckons not everything can be solved with a fist. Maybe she's right. The kid's not bolting. I fumble for words, yanking out a piece of my own truth:

"You don't have to do this alone."

The kid scrubs at her face.

"The school won't help me. I asked."

"We'll help. *I'll* help. Come on."

The kid's shoulders slump. She picks up her bag and scuffs back down the street toward me. As she gets level with me, I set a hand on her back, like I'm patting her. I can feel Erin watching. As I turn, Erin's smile is radiant.

"Really?" she whispers.

Use your words, my brain instructs.

"Yes."

Nicole Walsh is a cat enthusiast from the east coast of Australia who loves fern gardens and long dresses. She writes short stories and novel-length speculative fiction and urban fantasy that spans from a little bit dark, a little bit amusing through to a little bit steamy:

https://nicolewalshauthor.com/ and www.facebook.com/nicole
walshauthor

Chimera Station

by Alex Minns

The monitor flickered. Like most things in this place, it was worn out and in need of replacing. Just like me. I'd been here four years and was still waiting for news of when my tour would be over. Picturing home was getting harder. Memories of my apartment felt more like images from a magazine. What colour were my carpets? I couldn't remember. But this room, even when I closed my eyes, I still saw it. Four years and it was starting to feel like a cage. A wall of screens flickered in front of me. Some were camera feeds, others monitoring displays giving me key data on atmosphere, planetary weather etc. A bank of dials and buttons spanned the width of the room. When I'd first seen it, I couldn't fathom how I would learn how it all worked. Now I could operate most of it without looking where my hands were. Movement on the screen distracted me from my malaise. He was prowling around again. I turned my attention back to my book. At least they managed to ship in some things fairly regularly. I now had the starts of my own library down here. Along the wall behind sat piles of novels; there was no decent shelving to put them on but that could be the next person's problem.

Crackling on the subspace made me instantly drop the book on the desk in front of me and spring into action. I wheeled my chair down to the end of the worktop and picked up the receiver.

"Chimera Station receiving." I held my breath; afraid the response would not come. Every time the fear of being forgotten, being left behind, got that little bit stronger.

"Chimera Station, this is Control. How's it going up there?"

I sighed and let the receiver tap against my forehead as I calmed down. "Peachy. This time of year, it's all sun. Been getting my tan on." I glanced over to the window. I'd already pulled the shade down, the reflection of the sun off the snow made it too blinding to see. So while it was almost eternal daytime outside, I hid in the dark like some cave dwelling creature. I couldn't help but glance across at the monitor.

"I'm almost jealous." Craven chuckled, causing more static to burst through the radio. I preferred it when he was on the other end; Taylor was a crushing bore and when that was your only human conversation over a week, it made it quite depressing.

"You want to come swap with me?" I tried to not sound quite so desperate. I failed.

"We're working on a replacement, don't you worry. We haven't forgotten you up there."

I bit my tongue. I was only supposed to have been here three years. Technical difficulties. Getting the unmanned interstellar supply shuttles up here was one thing but humans was not so easy. I barely remember my journey. It had been such a horrific experience I was in and out of consciousness for most of it. Just bright lights and flashing dials was all I could really piece together.

"How's you-know-who?" Craven changed the subject swiftly and I gladly went along with it.

"Usual. Prowls around for hours, stares at the camera for a while." I paused, looking back at the monitor. The creature was sitting on his bed, tracing lines into the walls with its nail. "Although."

"What?"

"You know he broke the camera a month back? Well, I think it must have hidden some parts of it in his cell because he's been playing with something. Not sure what. Don't fancy having to sedate him again and go in there." I shuddered, the thought of going back in there, weighed down by the hazmat suit while he lay on the ground, *hopefully* unconscious, did not fill me with joy.

"I wouldn't worry Mina, it's probably just using it to play noughts and crosses on the wall again."

I chuckled. "Wonder if he wins. How do you think he knows what noughts and crosses is? I mean how did he learn it?"

"Mina, don't go down that road, you can't start personifying him. He's a monster, remember that."

"I know." The creature was watching the camera again. I turned away but I could still feel the eyes on me. "Look can you send me up a new monitor on the next supply run. The one you sent last month got broken when was ejected from the shuttle."

"I'll see what I can do. Look I gotta go, we've got some crazy stuff going on back here. I'll try and radio in again tomorrow, talk a bit longer."

"Crazy stuff?" But he was already gone. I found myself wondering what could have been going on back home. Had they found more creatures? Would I have a few more detainees sent up to the Station?

"Who was that?" A harsh hiss echoed around the control room. Startled, I flew out of my chair and landed on the floor, the concrete floor sending reverberations up my spine. I crawled forward, back towards the desk. When I got close enough, my hands curled round the edge of the worktop and I started to pull myself up, very slowly.

My eyes rose above the desk and saw him staring back at me. He had moved right up to the camera again so his face filled the monitor. My breath caught in my throat as I was drawn into the electric blue thin circles that ringed his inhumanly wide pupils. His lips twitched and the hiss came across through my radio again.

"What shuttle were you talking about?"

I reached up and turned my microphone back on. "How are you doing that?"

He cocked his head at the camera. He couldn't see me but still he smiled. It tugged at his jagged cheekbones, pulling his paper-thin skin almost to ripping point. Everything about his was reminiscent of human but just a little bit wrong. His jaw was a touch too long, a few too many teeth in his mouth. Each movement seemed jerky as if he was recorded in stop motion. It had taken me some time to realise it was because he moved so fast, I couldn't perceive each change in position. But it was his eyes that were both the most fascinating thing and terrifying thing about him. The monitors didn't show it to their true depth, but he had two irises, two rings of colour around his pupil. The outer blue contrasted to the grey ring within, more so when he seemed to be in an heightened emotional state. Not that I had seen him in one of those for a while, months, if not a year. He seemed to have resigned himself to his situation.

But now, as I sat on the floor, listening to his voice, I wondered if he was just waiting.

He moved his hand in front of the monitor screen and dangled some wires. "It had all the capacity for two-way speech, it just took a bit of rewiring." The broken equipment. I hadn't gotten it all. "I've been wanting to talk to you."

"I'm not talking. I'm reporting this and then turning off the radio until we can fix whatever you've done."

"Reporting to who? Our gaolers?"

My hand hovered over the microphone switch.

"Seems to me, we are both trapped in our cells."

I flicked the switch off, silently cursing myself for ever engaging. In four years, I had never spoken with him. Every time

I had entered his room he had been sedated. Yes, I'd issued commands over the microphone but they had never done any good so eventually I had given up on that too. Although, I couldn't deny the urge to talk to another person was strong. Not that he was a person. I shook my head and slid back down to the floor, my hands rubbing at my tired face. I'd been here so long, so alone. But he was a monster.

"Mina?"

I froze. How did he know my name?

"Mina? Why won't you talk to me? Just for a little while?" His voice sounded like a wounded animal, pleading with me. I swallowed, my brain suddenly unable to process anything. He was so close, I could hear him breathe down the microphone. He was toying with me; I knew he didn't need to breathe. Spurred on, I got to my feet and got out of that room, the heavy metal door resisting my exit. It finally yielded and as it shut closed behind, cutting off his voice calling out to me again.

#

I was dreaming. I knew it. And yet, still I didn't wake up. I was on the shuttle, flashes of light and voices assaulting my senses. I could make nothing out, as my eyes tried to grab on to a detail it was gone, always changing, morphing. There was a growl, no, a roar. The engines? It felt wrong, it wasn't a machine. I felt pulled towards it, I needed to help. I reached out but my hands only grabbed thin air. Was I floating? The lights were becoming too much; I screwed my eyes shut against them. A whimper reached my ears and it took a few moments for me to realise it was me. Pins and needles washed through my limbs, what was doing that?

Something was forcing me to open my eyes. I shook my head, tried to resist but it was no good. My treacherous eyes opened and there he was, the monster looming over me, his mouth torn into some hideous imitation of a smile. He laughed, the sound was deafening. His frame jerked before me as he moved in his unnatural way; his head creaking to one side as he grew closer. I could trace the feint lines that traced over his neck and down beyond his collar, like distant memories of scars. His hand flashed up, holding something sharp. I yelled out but he was no longer there.

I was standing now. The lights had steadied and he was by the wall, carving. I didn't want to, but my feet were carrying me closer. He was carving noughts and crosses again just like I had seen him do over and over again in his cell. His head bent round to look at me. His wrist flicked and the object turned in his grip. He held it out to me, the pointed end digging into his palm, cutting the fragile skin. Another flick of the wrist and it was gone, concealed out of sight. He smiled again and waved his hand in the air like a magician. His gaze travelled to the door and I instinctively moved between him and it.

His head tilted, the light dulling in his eyes as sorrow coloured his features. "Mina."

The sound of my name acted like a slap to the face and I sat bolt upright on my bunk. My fingers dug into the thin mattress beneath me, nearly tearing holes into the thin sheet above it.

My breath came in ragged gasps and despite the low temperature that cursed this hell-hole I was drenched in sweat. Nightmares had been becoming more regular of late but that had been a particularly vivid one. A small voice in my head kept needling at me, telling me I should be reporting it back to Control. Was the isolation starting to mess with my head, or was it him? Perhaps he was stronger than we thought, still able to affect my mind. The reports I'd been given when I first took the post detailed all kinds of anecdotes about what he could do, what he did to survive. Bodies had been left in his wake, but it was the living victims that I pitied more. He'd gotten inside their heads and they'd been torn apart from the inside. Giving him any advantage was a mistake.

My blood ran cold. Flashes from my dream came back to me, his penchant for sleight of hand. If he had managed to secrete enough to rewire the speaker system, did he have enough to work the door?

I was on my feet in an instant. My running footsteps reverberating down the halls as I rebounded off walls around corners, desperate to get there quicker. I only slowed as I came to the hallway the led to his cell and nothing else. At the end of the corridor, the outer door remained shut. Probably it was all safe, I could just turn back to the observation room. My feet, however, were still carrying me forwards. At this end of the complex, there were no other nearby rooms, or hallways. The creature was isolated, as if they were terrified his proximity to anything would taint it. The only thing that surrounded him was the icy wasteland of this planet. They were so scared of his influence, they had discarded him to the far reaches of space and still they feared him.

I reached the gunmetal grey door and tapped the code into the lock. The mechanism released, echoing around the whole space as the metal slid out of place. It still took a lot of effort to push the door. It could be hermetically sealed if needed. I was vaguely aware of the protocol for venting the oxygen out of this area but I had never felt the urge to know how to enact it, even for the creature.

I had to wait for the door to close behind me before the lights would switch on: a safety protocol to make sure you sealed off the creature's exit. There was no way the inner door would open if that was still unlocked. The sound of the locks sliding back into place made my heart thump a little harder. Along the wall to my side was all the equipment you needed to sedate the creature. I could adjust the dials and pump a neutralising agent into his room. Of course to do that, I would have to be wearing my hazmat suit, which was in my room. Other objects sat in the racks that would do a little more permanent damage to him, at least in theory. I had only heard tales of when he had been captured and the thing I was sure of, was that they had filled him full of lead and he was still walking.

"Mina?"

Recoiling, I moved back to the outer door. The cold of the metal cut through my clothes and froze me instantly.

"You are there aren't you Mina? Are you worried I'm going to break out?" He paused, as if I might actually answer him. "I'm not breaking out Mina. I'm not leaving until you let me out."

The ridiculousness of his statement made me break my silence as I laughed out loud. I clamped my hand over my mouth but it was too late.

"I've missed that sound."

"You miss laughter? You hear much of that when you kill people?"

"I only killed those who threatened us."

Us? There had been more like him? I shuddered. I wasn't really sure where he had come from, but I'd always assumed he was the only one, otherwise I'd have more houseguests up here.

"What have they made you believe about me exactly? That I am a monster? A thing of nightmares?" Even through the door I could hear a hint of sorrow in his voice. Was he trying to warp my brain already? Perhaps the door wasn't enough to shield me.

"You are a monster. You're a killer, who takes the lifeforce of others to survive. An abomination of nature." The words fell out of my mouth dripping with a hatred I didn't know I had for him.

"Like your mythic vampires I see. I suppose I rip out throats just for thrills." I heard a sigh and a faint tap on the door, as if he was leaning his head against it. "Tell me. Why are you here?"

"Someone has to watch over you, make sure you don't get out."

"But why you?"

"Why not me?" I folded my arms over my chest, not sure why I was feeling so defensive. He didn't speak. The silence dragged on as he waited. I could have stayed quiet, should have done probably. "Some of us have to have jobs, okay? We need to earn money to buy food rather than just killing for it."

"Hmm." The one sound seemed to be filled with a whole raft of levels of meaning, but I had no idea what. "Where I was born, I would go and hunt for food. Not humans, before you call me a murderer again. I would hunt animals for us. We were fairly self-sufficient."

"Where you were born?" I dropped my arms and pushed myself off the cold door.

"Created then. Where my existence started, why not strip all humanity from it shall we?"

I said nothing as I stared down at the floor. It was covered in dirt and grime. Had anyone ever cleaned down here? My jaw twitched uncomfortably as I tried to ignore the feeling of guilt at my insensitivity. How dare he make me feel guilty? He wanted his humanity? He had killed countless. A pressure started to grow behind my right eye, a migraine on its way no doubt. How many had he killed? The files had stated all kinds of facts and figures but I couldn't remember.

"I apologise for my abruptness." His voice seemed to leak through the door like a mist towards me. "Please keep talking to me, it has been so long since we talked."

"We haven't spoken before. You're getting me muddled up with your last babysitter."

Silence hung in the air for a few moments. I fought the urge to check the hatch, suddenly finding myself convinced he'd somehow managed to disappear into thin air like the vampires of old.

"I suppose I must. How long have you been here Mina?"

"Four years." Four very long years.

"That is a long time to stay from home."

"Like I said, someone has to."

"Of course." I could hear him chuckle to himself. "What is your home like?"

"Nuh-uh, we're not going there. Why don't you tell me about your home?"

"My home? Ahh, it was far from anywhere. A farm where we could live away from prying eyes. It was quite perfect. I would source food, I even managed to start keeping some animals on the farm to save me hunting in the woods, and my creator would work in the barn. It had been converted into a workshop and laboratory. It was very impressive, alas I did not know what most of it was for."

"Why…" I trailed off. I shouldn't be here.

"Why what Mina?"

I sighed; he wasn't getting out of the door and no-one was here to tell me off for speaking to him. I'd not spent this long talking to another living creature in four years. "Why were you created?"

"Scientists," he laughed. "Why do they do half the things they do? Questions mostly. What sparked the original idea, I do not know. I believe her motives were pure, if I could be created, parts of me grown from existing tissue, then the applications for treatments were endless. Not only that but perhaps humans could be adapted outside of natural selection. They could be engineered to survive in different environments. She often talked about colonising other planets and that humans would not be suited to it as they were, and not the transportation either."

My eyebrows raised. He wasn't wrong there. Perhaps if humans were a bit more robust they could get my replacement up here quicker.

"What are you then?"

"I thought I was a monster?"

"You know what I mean. You are made of human tissue but you're not human."

"What is human?"

"That's enough. I shouldn't be here." I turned but could hear sudden movement on the other side of the door.

"Please Mina, do not go. I haven't seen another face for years, I'm not even sure I remember what faces look like." I paused; there wasn't even a mirror in his room. His hair never grew, nor did any stubble. Whatever he was, he had been made in the form he was now and never changed. I rarely heard another voice, but not to see a person at all would be torture. I at least got to watch him.

"We can talk later." The words were out of my mouth before I knew what I was doing. I typed the release code and listened for the click. I was half-way through opening the door when I paused. "What's with the noughts and crosses?"

"It was one of the ways she taught me motor control."

I gave a snort of laughter before heading back out into the corridor. As the heavy door closed behind me, I felt a strange sense of melancholy descend over me.

#

It was early the next morning when I found myself in the observation room surrounded by files. The light on this planet was so disorientating that without the clocks I would have no idea of the time; at this time of year, it was barely ever dark. The clock in here had the date on it too. When had it gotten to November again?

Sleep had been hard to come by through the night and when I had managed some, I was plagued by random images and dreams again. Hence why at six in the morning, I had pulled out all the files on the prisoner and laid them out on the floor around me. The internet didn't reach outer space so everything was paper based. I didn't mind, I was better at paper anyway. I was vaguely reminded of my university days. The pressure behind my eye surged again. The migraine hadn't broken yet but trying to sleep hadn't done anything to alleviate it either.

I turned my attention back to the files. I'd avoided the reports on the killings and went through the files on his origins. They were minimalist to say the best. There was no mention of the farm he'd spoke of yesterday, nor of the woman. There was nothing about his creator at all. The files seemed to start with reports of sightings of him in towns and cities, police reports of incidents he had gotten into before he had started to kill.

The files on his capture and initial years of incarceration had a bit more but nothing that went into his physiology. Surely, they had examined him. Yes, he was a monster. Yes, he was evil. But he didn't age, he'd been created from tissue samples and modified. Perhaps it was as step too far, but some of what his existence could tell us must have practical applications. And yet there were no medical records here of any kind, only reports on his abilities and what made him dangerous.

"Mina? Are you awake already?"

I looked up at the monitor. He was standing a little way back from the camera this time, gazing upwards with his hands behind his back, waiting expectantly. Reaching up and across, I found the microphone switch and turned it on.

"What's wrong? Your food should have been delivered already." There was a complicated system at the opposite end of his cell to the door but it worked on a very simple concept of a dumb waiter. I prepared his rations when I made my food and I took them to the delivery hatch. It then went through system of locked hatches, just like the one outside his cell; one wouldn't open until the previous one was locked. There was also no oxygen in the tubes. Whoever deigned it made sure he would never be able to try and get out that way.

"The food is here, thank you. It is early though, isn't it? Is everything okay?"

"Everything's fine. How do you know it's early?" I looked up from my papers again, my neck protesting. I'd been sat down here too long.

"I have a very accurate internal clock. I believe it has been eleven hours since we last spoke."

I checked the clock again before doing a quick check in my head. He was right. There were no timepieces in his room, or any windows. The only thing he could measure time by was his meals, which he only got twice a day because that was all he needed.

"That is…"

"Impressive?"

"Creepy," I lied. "You know, you really are very like a vampire. Speed, tissue regeneration, no aging, levitation…"

"I am not as strong as they were."

"Well, you can't do the whole blood sucking thing here."

"I never took blood." His image jerked forward towards the camera. I couldn't help but recoil. His head jerked to the side, looking down to the ground. "I only found that taking a bit of a person's life force would enhance my abilities by accident."

I was still a little hazy on how he did it. The reports were fairly light on those details too. There were plenty of reports about the husks of humans that had been sucked dry of their life. Whether it was blood or their soul, I didn't know or care, but he sucked the life out of them.

"Why do you hate me so much?"

The question caught me off guard. "You're a monster who killed people."

"Did I kill someone close to you?"

My mouth opened to speak but I waivered. He had killed decades ago. I wasn't even born then. And yet, I did hate him. So very much. And there was another feeling buried deep under all of it. An acute sense of loss. "It's because of you I have to live up here away from everyone."

"Away from who? Who did you leave behind?"

"I'm not telling you." I shook my head and started gathering the piles of paper together.

"It's been a long four years hasn't it." He sounded incredibly sad. When I looked up, he was no longer standing but was sat on his bed, facing away.

"Yes. But I suppose everyone you knew is gone."

His head turned, slowly this time so the movement actually appeared fluid. "How long do you think I've been here?"

"Why do you answer me with so many questions?"

"Why do you?"

I laughed. I couldn't help myself. He stayed on the bed, but I could see he was smiling. I knew it should chill me, the thought of making him happy. I really had been here too long.

A crackle on the longwave broke my thoughts. I stared at the unit in horror.

"Control is calling me. I have to turn off the microphone now."

"Don't answer it, tell them you went out." I rolled my eyes at the screen, forgetting it was pointless.

"Look, I'll turn it back on after, just please, please don't say anything from your end. If they hear you…"

He held his hands up in submission. "I shall be the proverbial mouse."

Somehow that didn't reassure me entirely. Frowning, I turned the microphone off and picked up the receiver. "Chimera Station receiving."

"Chimera Station, you're up early." It was Craven again.

"Why are you calling if you thought it was early?" I lumped down into the chair and rolled it closer to the desk so I wasn't stretching.

"I saw your lights were on. What's up, can't sleep?" I glanced at the desk in front of me. Each morning, I have to check the log for while I was asleep and then switch the monitoring back over to manual. I forgot they could watch everything I did from down there. Sometimes, I felt like a prisoner myself.

"Doesn't exactly get dark much round here this time of year."

"That it?"

I hesitated while turning to look back at the monitor. He was still sitting on his bed, staring at the wall he'd been carving on the day before. "Yep. Other than the endless repetitive boredom and loneliness of course." I reached forward and ran my fingers across the array of trinkets that sat on the shelf above the receiver. A couple of tools sat there, a puzzle cube, a small figure of a bear and a coin. I plucked the coin up and sat back in the chair.

"That old chestnut huh? Well, they seem to think they might be making headway on the transport."

"Oh yeah?" I'd heard that one before.

"Something about the stabilisation. The orbit of the planet isn't quite what they thought and it's taking longer to pass behind the asteroid belt but with the new modifications they are making, they think a person could manage a trip through it."

"Great. Hopefully they can get testing pretty quick."

"You sure you're okay?"

"It's just annoying they didn't check the orbit thoroughly before they sent me up. And typical it happens on my stint you know? I mean how many years has he been up here with different guards?"

"Twenty-seven years."

"Just odd they didn't see it coming."

"It's in another solar system Mina. They projected what they could, but they had the centre of the planet's orbit all wrong. The second star pulled everything out."

"I know, I know." I sighed and watched as the coin tumbled over my fingers, rolling from one knuckle to the next and back again. I smirked, amusing myself.

"Look, I'll talk to the doctor down here. I'm pretty sure we can send something to you to help you sleep. Then maybe you won't be so grumpy with me, eh?"

I took a deep breath and closed my eyes. It was a good job Craven was on another planet or I might have hit him. "Hey, I've been reading through the files again..."

"Why? What's happened?"

"Nothing. I just read all the books. Anyway, there's nothing in there about medical examinations. They must have done some after they captured him right?"

"I guess."

"So why isn't it in the files? I thought this was supposed to be everything?"

"Why does it matter Mina?"

"I'm just intrigued. I mean he can heal himself. Surely someone tested him to try and see how so we could maybe, I dunno, use as treatments."

"He's a monster Mina, an abomination. Toying with the mechanics of him will not end well. No-one would want to use anything that came from him would they?"

"Yeah but..."

"The scientist who made him thought they were doing the right thing and look how that turned out. A trail of dead people."

"Surely that's all the more reason for something good to come of it?"

"Where's this coming from? Is he getting to you?"

"What? No." My eyes moved back to the screen. His head turned; it was as if he knew I was looking at him. "Forget it."

"Mina..."

"Just if we aren't going to do anything productive from this, then why do we keep him alive?" I slammed the coin down on the desk and leaned forward. Craven went quiet. "Craven?"

"Because how would that make us any better, if we killed the monster that sucked the life out of people?"

I stayed quiet. A question popped into my head but I knew there was no way I could voice it.

"You're right." The static on the connection dragged on for several seconds. "Look, I'm getting a migraine, lack of sleep. I think I'm going to try and get some rest."

"Good idea." He didn't sound convinced. I suddenly wanted to hang up as soon as I could. He was beginning to doubt my sanity, and if they thought I'd been compromised, that the monster had gotten in my head? Well, they'd probably get someone up here a lot quicker. "Get some sleep. Stop looking at the files for a bit yeah? They're not doing you any good. He's a monster, you watch over him so he can't hurt anyone again. It's that simple."

I made the right agreeing noises and hung up but the question was still there in my head. But what if he couldn't help what he did? I stood up, left the observation room, went past my bedroom and headed straight for the corridor at the end of the complex.

#

I slid the viewing hatch across and peered inside. His head snapped up in an instant his face a vision of shock and confusion.

"Mina." He stood up hesitantly as if unsure if he should approach. I said nothing. I was breaking so many rules. He moved slowly as if he was closing in on an animal that might bolt at any moment. I suddenly registered the tension in my legs and realised he might be right. His eyes widened as he got closer. The blue ring seemed to pulse as the lights danced. There was bulletproof glass between us still but it did nothing to obscure the view. I frowned and looked closer. He was beginning to tear up.

He looked away for a split second, blinking away the tears. "It has been a long time," he said by way of explanation.

"I have questions."

"Could Control not answer them?"

"Not these ones."

"In which case, ask away."

Faced with the prospect of answers, I found myself not knowing where to start. "How long have you been here?"

"How long did they tell you I'd been here?"

"Again with the question as an answer."

"I'm afraid Mina, the only way to get to the bottom of this is with questions."

"No, answers do that. Why did they send you here anyway? How are you so dangerous they couldn't contain you on Earth?"

"I can manipulate minds remember."

"Are you manipulating mine?"

"Never you." He was so close to the hatch, I could almost trace the lines of light in his irises. He looked so sincere.

"This is a mistake. They're going to send a replacement for me soon." I reached up to close the hatch.

"Mina." The urgency in his voice made me stop. "Where are we?"

"What?"

"Where are we?"

"You're in a cell and I'm leaving."

"I'm so dangerous they have to send me to this faraway planet. What is it even called?"

"Demeter." The answer fell out of my mouth but it felt all wrong. He nodded, pleased with something he'd seen.

"And where are you from?"

"Earth." I snapped, the pressure behind my eye was pulsing again. Why was he throwing all these stupid questions at me? He was supposed to be answering me.

"Where on Earth?"

"I'm from…" The pressure was pulsing now, sending shockwaves of pain through my skull that was enough to make me nearly retch. I tried to focus through the pain, to find the words in my brain but the lights flashing in my vision were too much.

"Mina? Mina stop, stop trying to think of it. Tell me something else, tell me about your nightmares." His voice was hurried, frantic. I tried to blink away the lights, they began to settle enough for me to realise I was holding myself up against the wall.

"My dreams?" My voice was slurring. "How do you know?"

"Everyone dreams don't they? Even me. Tell me about them?"

It seemed like a reasonable question. "I might just sit for a second." I slid down to the floor and leaned against the wall. I could still see the hatch and his face peering out at me. "I dream of coming here. I dream of watching you. Noughts and crosses. And machines. You laughing. No." I frowned, there was more. Bits I didn't normally remember. "I'm laughing too. And there are trees. I haven't seen a tree in so long." My eyes fluttered closed as I pictured the woods in front of me. "And there's a song. A little tune but I can't hear it." Sadness washed over me. I knew there was a tune there but I couldn't remember any of it, not a single note. But it was important, so very important. Heat flashed on my cheeks as the tears began to roll down. Then there was a note, the first note. Then the next. The tune was from my childhood, my mother had whistled it every day. My eyes snapped open. I wasn't remembering it.

"How do you know that tune?" I stared up at him, humming through the window to me. He kept humming. "How do you know it?" I stood up again; the pain behind my eye forgotten. "I never told you my name either. Did the last guard tell you?"

"You are the only guard I've ever known Mina."

"No, you've been here twenty-seven years." I was shaking my head repeatedly as everything around me felt like it was unravelling. The tune, kept playing in my head. My mother's tune. I remembered her, her face, for the first time in so long I saw her face.

"How do you know my name?"

"I'm afraid I must answer with another question. How do you stop something from trying to escape?"

I stood closer to the glass. Feint lines traced through, showing the reinforcement. They looked like the bars that held him in. Then there was my face, a ghostly reflection superimposed onto his. The lines lay over my image, trapping it. "You make it so they don't realise they are a prisoner."

"Exactly."

"They aren't coming to replace me are they. I'm a prisoner too. Why? Why would they keep me here?"

"Because there is only one thing they fear more than a monster." He started to hum again,

More images flashed into my head. My parents, me, our home. My workshop, my project that no-one understood. I was ridiculed, ostracised. Until I was proven right, then I was shunned. I was humming, singing my lullaby as I moved round my workshop, working on my greatest breakthrough. The pain behind my eye flared like a supernova and I was brought to my knees as the walls that had been put in my head fell away.

"The monster's maker." My voice was barely more than a whisper. Memories of the farm came flooding back, how we lived there while I carried out my tests, until that night where he had been drawn into a fight in the village. It really had been an accident. But humans were not very forgiving or very understanding. I reached up and touched the glass. "Nathaniel?"

In the blink of eye, his hand reached up to mine. "You're back." His head dropped in relief.

"They made me hate you." Anger was the only thing keeping me on my feet. The sudden rush of memories was making me sway.

"They only made you think you did. Humans are very prone to fear. They used that to warp your mind."

Rage was still roiling within me but now it had a different target. Those narrow-minded humans always hate what is different, never seeing the potential. We could have done so much good but instead they twisted my own mind against me. "All of it was lies. Demeter? How stupid can I be? We've never been out of this solar system. We're still on Earth?"

"Somewhere in the Antarctic I believe."

"Well." I looked down at the controls and keyed in the release code to Nathaniel's cell. "We have two weeks until the next supply run, plenty of time to come up with a plan. They want something to fear, they'll get it."

Alex Minns is a self-professed Jack of all trades (and still a master of none). She writes a range of scifi, steampunk and urban paranormal fiction and inflicts all of it on her poor mother. You can find her work on https://lexikon.home.blog/ or on twitter under @Lexikonical

Publishing credits include: Spring Into Sci-fi 2022, Meteor Falls, Punk (Black Hare Press) and Harvey Duckman Presents Volume 8.

The Ballad of Black Rook

by MR Wells

"No electronics allowed near the prisoner. Do not hand him anything, at all, under any circumstances. If you cross the yellow line you will receive a verbal warning. If you cross the red line we can, and will, physically restrain you. Do you understand?"

The stony faced guard glared down at her, and Ms Sophia Chandler, ace reporter for the Daily Globe, nodded. "Yes, Mr Sinclair- and, as agreed, I have only bought a pencil and loose paper. No staples, no binder, no pen. All of which, I might remind you, you have checked 3 times since I arrived. Now, do I *finally* get my interview?"

Sinclair shook his head. "Ms Chandler- you are the first visitor the prisoner has agreed to see in 15 years. We get hundreds of requests, every year, for visits, and he has turned down every. Single. One. Until now. Until a reporter from a paper whose circulation numbers are, frankly, spiralling. You understand why we might be suspicious."

Sophia shrugged. "I can't comment on that, Mr Sinclair. I asked, he agreed. That's all I know."

The old guard frowned at her before, with a slightly helpless shake of his head, he gestured to the door. The nervous looking guard next to it leant in to the retinal scanner, which beeped an affirmative as a series of clunks indicated a large number of bars retracting. Finally, a green light, and Sinclair pulled the heavy door open.

Sinclair had time for a final warning. "I have two armed response teams right outside. The Liberty League are on standby. Just shout, and we will be there in a flash."

#

The door slammed shut behind her. Sophia wasn't quite sure what she was expecting in the presence of the most dangerous prisoner in the world, but this wasn't- quite- it. A barred box, lined with clear glass, in the middle of a large gym hall. Thick lines, one red, one yellow, surrounding this unusual prison cell and, of course, she counted half a dozen alert guards lining the walls of the room. Squinting against the bright lights illuminating the cell, Sophia also noted the armed guards on the raised platforms in each corner of the room.

With all of this security, the man they were guarding, sitting placidly in his cell, seemed almost an afterthought. Taking a deep breath, Sophia walked over to the yellow line. "Um. Mr… Mr Rook?" The worlds most infamous supervillain just looked at her for a moment, and then chuckled. "Mr Rook, oh, now that I like. Sit down, my dear, please. Before my friends have a fit." He gestured towards the armed guards, pointing their weapons menacingly at both her and the prisoner. Looking round, Sophia spotted the chair bolted to the floor behind her.

She cautiously moved back, sitting, and noting the weapon toting guards relaxing- slightly.

"Mr Rook, may I…?" Sophia waved her stack of papers. He smiled disarmingly. "By all means, Ms Chandler. My apologies for the inconvenience- I'm afraid they don't let me near pens any more." Sophia quickly snuck a glance at the cell, her shorthand noting- bed, chair, toilet, sink, a stack of books, making a mental note to try and get close enough before she left to see the titles.

"I have some questions, Mr Rook, but-" "I'm afraid that wasn't in the agreement, Ms Chandler. You signed the relevant legal papers; I am still allowed contact with my legal advisors and they have assured me all is in order. I talk, you listen. My story is published unedited, in full, every word, or it is not published at all. If you have questions while I talk…" He shrugged expansively. "I may choose to answer. I may not. Now, shall I begin?" Despite the distance, and the barriers between them his deep voice still carried clearly to her.

Sophia stared at him, openly curious. It had been 15 years since anyone had seen photos of the Black Rook, Scourge of the West Coast, Slayer of Red Justice, self proclaimed Emperor of the Earth. Even then it was a somewhat iconic photo- Pullitzer Prize winning in fact- of Black Rook, in his scorched powered armour and torn cape, locked in a grapple with a bruised and bleeding Ultimate Man, with two wounded members of the Liberty League lying prone in the rubble behind them.

That seemed a far cry from the simply dressed, well mannered man sat before her. He was younger than she'd imagined- no one had ever been able to establish his real identity but he didn't look older than his early 40's. A hint of grey in his slightly ruffled beard and at his temples, perhaps, but not a wrinkle in sight. Sophia wasn't sure what she had expected, but this certainly wasn't it.

After a few more notes, Sophia nodded. "I'm ready, Mr Rook."

#

"Well, firstly, Ms Chandler, might I say how delighted I am to grant you my first interview. I have no doubt your readers will find it most enlightening. I shall start, as they say, at the beginning. It may surprise you to learn that my upbringing was rather dully uneventful- loving parents of an only child, of moderate wealth, in a quiet settlement. Pillars of the community, you might call them. You see, there is no tragic backstory for me. No sibling cruelly taken from the family, no creepy relative, no abject poverty, no torturing small animals. Just a loving, normal- if rather boring- environment. But me- I was far from normal.

And no, I won't tell you who my parents were, or where I grew up. There's nothing to be gained by knowing that at this point and besides- it was a long time ago.

All you need to know is that I excelled in my studies, and great things were predicted for me. I read widely, and I learned- oh, how I learned. When I was 17, I left home, and I didn't look back. I was very fond of my parents, and bore them no ill will, but they were part of my past. Even then, I knew I had a glorious future ahead of me.

And so I travelled, and I kept learning. I worked odd jobs, mopped floors, served drinks, even travelled with a circus for a while. I helped build roads, and railways. I spent a rather productive period as night security at a library- spending hours reading by torchlight, and being paid for it! Remarkable.

And it might have continued- I sensed I had a great destiny ahead of me, but no idea exactly what it was, no idea exactly how I would gain the power I knew I deserved. And then, one day in the library, it all changed when I saw the photo on the front page of the newspaper. The gloriously coloured costumes, the proud headlines. The 'Age of the Superheroes'."

"The Age of the Superheroes? Mr Rook, wh-"

"No questions!" The voice snapped out, imperiously, and for a moment the air was thick with tension. Then Rook smiled graciously. "Please." He waited a beat, checking the reporter was still paying attention, before he continued.

"Yes, the Age of the Superheroes. That was the moment I realised how I would achieve my destiny. I didn't *become* a supervillain- I already was one. It was simply that I didn't realise it until I saw that first headline.

Oh, those early days were amazing. There must have been hundreds of us all across the country, thousands of us across the world, who suddenly realised all you needed was a costume, and a gimmick, and anyone could be a hero- or a villain. Oh, there were the superpowers of course, plenty of them- really, the number of crazy lab accidents back then would have made a health and safety inspector wince.

I had more than one name, of course, before I settled on the Black Rook. That name had gravitas- it's important to have a bit of class. I mean, Red Ravager and the Rampagers, Doctor Deathman- I heard there's now a new Scarlet Screamer, as if *that* name needed to make a comeback! Ahem. My apologies, I tend to get a little frustrated with the lack of creativity of some of the modern set.

So- the early days. Back then I was still learning the trade- a few art thefts, bank robberies, the odd tussle with superheroes here and there… and of course the deathtraps were entertaining nonsense, and really part of the tradition. It was all a bit of a game to most of them, you know- heroes and villains alike. They were all about the wealth and fame, and having fun doing the right (or wrong) thing. Amateurs.

It didn't take long before things got more serious, of course. Darker. I think it was the Krellian invasion back in '71 that did it- after they wiped out most of New York, suddenly, it was no longer fun. Whereas before I had, on occasion, teamed up with the odd villain with an obsessive need to leave clues or who only talked in rhymes, I was suddenly teaming up with alien warlords, time travelling despots and cold blooded murderers. All to further my own goals, of course. I was playing a very long game.

Joining the Revenge Squadron for the first time? All so I could gain access to the Liberty League's headquarters, and steal a sliver of Roxonite from their trophy hall. Kidnapping the Presidents son? That was only so I could get a full scan of Ultimate Man when he came to the rescue.

And it worked. I might have had to hold my nose and work with rather unsavoury characters, but when I formed my new Revenge Squadron 20 years ago, I was ready to make my move. I was finally ready to rule. I had laid my plans, analysed my foes weaknesses, and I was *ready*."

Sophia blurted, "But you failed! That's why you're *here*!" Gritting her teeth she flexed her cramping hand, before taking up her pencil again. Given the way Rook had snapped at her when she had interrupted before, Sophia was surprised to see him smiling almost fondly at her.

"Quite right, Ms Chandler. Indeed I did. For reasons, as you will understand, quite beyond my control. My defeat was irritating, true, but I had made certain contingency plans. I didn't plan to fail, of course, but I did take steps in case the worst happened.

But I imagine your readers will want to hear how it all went down, hm? How I put together the most formidable army of villains the world has ever seen, and came within a whisker of defeating the entire Liberty League?"

Some of the story was well known- the other members of the Revenge Squad hadn't exactly kept their silence as well as Black Rook- but Sophia nodded. "Yes, please."

Rook gave her another charming smile. "Well, as you asked so nicely… I spent two years vetting each of those I intended to invite to join my new organisation. A dozen supervillains, all powerful, all smart- well, smart enough, I didn't want anyone *too* clever after all- and no loose cannons. I assessed their weaknesses, and desires. And from there, it was easy. Silver Fog wanted funding for his experiments- I gave it to him. Kraark the Unstoppable wanted to test himself in combat against the best there was- I promised him first chance at the Ultimate Man, one on one, no distractions. Megara the Sorceress wanted power, recognition, and revenge on Levitating Lass- again, easy to provide. And so it went. I had spent two years carefully vetting them, reaching out, quietly drawing them in. And each of them swore their service to me- when the time came.

I was careful, of course. We each continued our own plots- museum robberies, opening portals to other dimensions, trying to alter the timestream, whatever. If a large group of supervillains suddenly dropped out of sight, sooner or later the Liberty League, or Hell Force, or one of the other do gooder teams would have noticed. No, this way everything was kept nice and quiet. Meanwhile, I tinkered away behind the scenes, bribed, blackmailed and cajoled politicians, businessmen, media moguls- and honestly, it was depressing how much of it was technically quite legal. Turns out 'lobbying' covers a whole range of sins.

So we waited, we prepared- and then, on the appointed day, we struck. I actually had to break that idiot Kraark out of jail the day before- he'd got himself arrested on a bail violation, of all things. And it worked. A few villains I'd recruited- anonymously, of course- to kick up a fuss did exactly that to draw the local heroes away, as did a number of terrorist groups, organised criminals and general lowlifes I'd cultivated.

Megara and the others she had recruited for her Circle cast their spell just outside Topeka, exactly as planned. They spent a week preparing. And then- 3.12 seconds, that's all it took. That was the time it took for a dome of mystical energy to cover 8 states, with areas of another dozen within the dome. And it was completely impenetrable after 30 seconds- nothing in, nothing out."

Black Rook arched an eyebrow at Sophia. "What did the media call it? Black Thursday? A little cliché perhaps, and hardly accurate, but suitably dramatic I suppose. For me- it was the day we showed the world what true supervillainy was all about. I understand that outside the dome, everyone was in rather a flap for weeks afterwards. Inside? Within 24 hours, we had the situation under control. The media were all on message, the politicians were saying the right things, and everyone considered it a little worrying, but nothing more. No power cuts, no civil disobedience, no chaos. Just a nice, quiet reordering where the Revenge Squad and I took over.

And you know what? We were good, hell, we were *great.* Afterwards, the rest of the world called it the '97 Dark Days.' But no one starved. Everyone got the help they needed. In those 3 months, the crime rate dropped 17%, GPA's were up by a whole point across the whole region, the unemployment rate went down, state benefits went up… and that was exactly the point. Sure, the Revenge Squad and I were the rulers, and we absolutely were not democratically elected, but by the 3rd month my approval ratings were better than the President!"

Rook shook his head. "The power of Megara's Circle should have kept the dome up for at least a year. By the time it came down, the rest of the States would have been *begging* to join my new, ordered society! Then that idiot Red Justice ruined it all. I don't know whether he was inside the dome by chance, or whether he'd somehow worked out what we were doing, but he was trapped in there with us. He actually tried to start a resistance movement, but underestimated our popularity. At the end, it was just him. The fool murdered Megara, in cold blood, and tried to do the same to me. And the kid was powerful, no doubt about that. He had to be, to take Megara. You've seen the video, I'm sure- it was clear self defence. Red Justice tried to kill me, and paid the price for it. But the sanctimonius idiot had already derailed my plans. Without Megara the rest of the mages in her Circle could only hold the dome in place a matter of days.

So we knew the dome would fall, and the Liberty League would no doubt come steaming in to overthrow the lot of us. No matter; I simply altered my plans again. My preference has always been the long game.

And they did, of course. The dome fell, the Liberty League came- and my Revenge Squad fought them, and we fought hard. We were close, we were very close, to beating them once and for all. But we lost. You might have been a little young to remember it but I'm sure you remember the Trial of the Century- the entire Revenge Squad captured and tried by a jury of the people." Rook gave Sophia a little smile.

"And you know, we were so popular they were terrified a jury might actually acquit us. Then, as now, people respected *style*. So we fought our way through the courts and eventually the justice system spat out a deal- the other members of the Revenge Squad would get minimal sentences, they would drop the death penalty request for the murder of Red Justice (which was always going to fail) and in return I accept a 110 year sentence, no possibility of parole. I've no doubt the Liberty League realised I was the true architect of the entire thing, and happily settled for locking me away forever.

Which brings me to the here, and now. And the questions." Rook stared at Sophia earnestly with his dark eyes. "You ask a question, I ask a question. We both answer truthfully. Until I get bored. I suggest you think carefully, and not waste this opportunity. Deal?" Sophia gaped, then hurriedly nodded.

"Um, yes, sure." She racked her brains, skimming through her notes- trying desperately to think of the right question to ask. Sophia noted a point she had underlined on the first page, and said, "Mr Rook- how old are you?"

"Older than I look." He stopped his pacing, looking a little too casually at the books in his cell, carefully not looking at her as he spoke. "I noted in one of your articles last year you ran the marathon as part of the team your newspaper put together. Got a very good time, in fact. Yet in another article you had mentioned breaking both legs in a riding accident when you were a teenager. Were you telling the truth in both articles?"

Sophia stared at him. "You read my articles?" She shook her head. "Yes, I broke my legs when I was 15, yes I ran the marathon. Now-" "-Yes, I do read your articles- they do still allow me newspapers, albeit a little late. My question." Sophia grimaced. She hadn't meant to blurt that out!

Rook had resumed his slow, steady pacing. "Does your mother still work at that little college outside Boston?" The question threw Sophia. "What? How the bloody hell did you know… no, she doesn't. My turn. In what year, *exactly*, were you born?"

A chuckle. "Oh, very good, Ms Chandler. Very good indeed. Well, I suppose at this point it really doesn't matter. I'm not entirely sure, in truth, but I believe 1622 or 1623."

"But that would make you almost 400 years old- you don't look a day over 45! That's a lie, right?"

"No. I said I would tell the truth, so there it is. My question again- what is your mother doing nowadays?" Sophia glared, trying to work out whether he was toying with her, despite his earnest tone, half wondering if she should terminate the interview there and then. But her journalistic desire won out. "No. She passed away 2 years ago."

Rook had continued pacing as they talked but, just for a moment, his step faltered, and as he turned at one end of his cell it was to turn away from her. Then his pacing resumed. "You have my condolences." After a few moments of silence, Rook noted gently, "Your turn, Ms Chandler."

Sophia sat there, determined not to waste another question. So- he said he was 400 years old. Fine. Let's assume that's correct. She skimmed her notes again, and something he had said more than once jumped out at her. Casually, Sophia leant back in her chair. "Mr Rook, what, exactly, is your long game?" Again, the supervillain's pacing slowed for a moment. "Oh, Ms Chandler, you are truly a treasure. That is very much the right question. Well, you answered my question, so I suppose I must answer yours- although you will forgive me for being a little… non specific, shall we say."

Rook's deep voice took on an academic, lecturing tone. "Hypothetically, a man given a prison sentence of 110 years is expected to die in prison. However, if such a man were, somehow, to survive that sentence then the authorities would be unable to prevent such a man walking free at the end of that period- his crimes paid for. Now, if such a man had briefly ruled, quite competently, several US states, and was a natural born US citizen with no active criminal record, a certain legendary status and a large amount of good old nostalgia about the good old days… along, of course, with a considerable fortune behind him- well, such a man would have little difficulty in securing whatever he wanted. Why, it might even be that the people would be urging such a wise, benevolent and venerable figure to… take charge, shall we say."

Sophia's immediate urge was to laugh in his face- what, did this maniac expect people to be begging him to run for the presidency if, somehow, he was still alive a century from now? Except… he claimed to be 400 years old now. If that was true, what was another century? And despite being in prison, he had an unerringly keen sense of how people worked- the Globe had run a survey to celebrate the 10th anniversary of the dropping of the dome which had nearly 40% of those in the dome actually stating they thought they had been better off under the dome, especially with the latest series of presidential scandals. Another century of distance to blur the Black Rooks' actual crimes? He might actually stand a chance of running for office successfully. Heck, half the current Senate had backgrounds nearly as shady as any supervillain!

Still, now she knew, and could warn people- urge the Globe to run a series focusing on his crimes, perhaps, especially the murder of Red Justice…

As Sophia finished scribbling her notes, she could feel Rook's eyes on her. "No more questions?" Sophia paused. She had enough already- of course she did. This story would make her world famous- the first interview given by Black Rook since his capture, his terrifying plans for the future, and yet…

"How did you know about my mother? I'm… I'm pretty sure I've never written about her in my column."

Rook was no longer pacing, simply stood there, dark eyes watching her. "I have had many lovers in my life, Ms Chandler. Men and women alike. I have travelled widely, to countries that no longer exist and are barely remembered. Occasionally, I meet someone with… a spark about them. A little under 30 years ago I was travelling, using one of my aliases, of course, across the states. I was in the very early stages of my master plan, and was making a few contacts at a political shindig in the area. At that party your mother… she stood out. She used the most inventive insult I've ever heard when she turned down a particularly boorish suitor- she caught me laughing, and stormed over, obviously under the impression I had been laughing at her. I was polite, courteous, and she was kind enough to let me buy her a drink.

For the next few weeks, I enjoyed her company immensely. I laughed more than I had for decades. She was a true gem. In truth, for a moment… for a moment I considered putting my plans on hold. What was another few decades to a man like me? I could enjoy a life with her and after she passed, well, my plans would still be there."

Black Rook was looking through Sophia now, his gaze fixed far in the past. The silence stretched on uncomfortably until Sophia ventured quietly, "Mr Rook?"

"Hm? Oh." Rook flashed her an apologetic smile. "Sometimes I get lost in my memories- and I have so very many of them." He sighed, shaking his head. "It was just a moment, but it was a dangerous one. I had grown too close to your mother, and so I left. Abandoned that identity entirely. As I say, your mother was a most unique woman.

But I am not by nature a cruel man, nor am I vindictive. I left a note, full of all the right platitudes and apologies- it isn't you, it's me… and I arranged a generous research grant for her, pulled a few strings here and there to ensure her life could run as smoothly as possible. And I kept an eye on her, just for my own peace of mind."

Rook was staring intensely at Sophia now. "You never saw her again?" Sophia half whispered this, suddenly angry at this man for entirely personal reasons. Her entire childhood, her mother had never dated, not once. Had always laughed off any suggestion of the matter. This supervillain had broken her heart and walked away- it was idiotic but right now Sophia was more furious at Black Rook for this than for any of the numerous crimes he had committed.

"Not once. Not even when she gave birth a little under 9 months later."

Sophia snapped, "You're lying! I don't have any siblings, mom would have mentioned it!"

And Black Rook smiled. Afterwards, Sophia would remember that smile. Proud, a little apologetic, and very self satisfied. "That's right, Ms Chandler. You don't."

Even then, it took her a moment. Maybe it was her own sense of denial, maybe she was being purposefully dense, maybe she just wanted to pretend a little longer that all those little mental alarm bells hadn't been screaming at her for the last few minutes. "No… that's… you can't be…"

"I'm very much afraid I can… my daughter." Again, that infuriating smile of his.

"Of course, I checked. It was remarkably easy to obtain a DNA sample- local doctors offices have rather woeful security, you know. Still, it might have all meant nothing. Until your marathon efforts anyway. That speed, after the extensive injuries you suffered when so young? That, my dear, is not normal. It is, in fact, rather extraordinary. And do you know, for all the woman I have slept with, you are the only child born of such a union. I find that quite… fascinating."

Sophia tried and failed to blink away her tears. "What… what are you saying?"

"I am saying, Ms Chandler, that I rather suspect that in, let's see, 94 years and 301 days… well, I wouldn't be at all surprised to find you at the prison gates, waiting for me, looking very much as you do now. I didn't have a grey hair until I was well past 300, after all."

Black Rook gave a rather expansive shrug. "I could be wrong, of course. I very much doubt it, but it has been known to happen. And so, you have a decision to make, my dear. You remember the terms of our agreement- every word is published, or none of it. So you can publish- earn yourself the fame you wanted when you started this interview, expose my plans for the world to see- and who knows? It might even make a difference. But you would expose yourself as the daughter of the infamous Black Rook. How many of my old allies- or old enemies- would start watching for you to become the next threat, I wonder? How many relatives of those I have hurt would seek you out?

You could, of course, keep quiet. My plans stay concealed, your secret is safe. And you can wait. Wait and see. Perhaps I am wrong- perhaps you will grow old, have a family, live an entirely normal life and eventually pass away in a few decades. Or perhaps I'll see you at those prison gates after all."

Sophia hadn't realised she had moved until the shout knocked her out of her shock. Glancing down, Sophia noticed her foot was already on the yellow line. The guard repeated on his loudhailer, "STEP! BACK!" Reluctantly, Sophia took a stumbling half step back. Her hands shook as she looked at the papers in her hand, torn between her desire to type up her story and to burn every single word.

Even as she tried to ignore him, he continued calmly. "Once you have seen the lives of those around you age and flicker out, so very, very quickly… I assure you, there is a certain longing for permanence. For someone who you won't have to mourn for a long time to come." His eyes gazed sadly at her, suspiciously bright, and for just a moment Sophia found herself wondering how many friends and lovers Black Rook had outlived and buried.

Then he half turned away, and as Black Rook turned to face her once again the supervillain was back- chillingly calm, superior, and quite in control.

Black Rook nodded fondly at her. "If you want to enjoy some more daddy-daughter time, if you have any more questions- well, I've asked you to be added to my visitor list permanently." And then, again, that damn smug little smile, which Sophia suspected she might learn to hate. "But next time, Ms Chandler, let's make it off the record."

Matt Wells, born in Wiltshire in the UK, currently lives in South Wales with a cat, Sooty, and spends most of his time reading, writing and playing a large variety of board games!

Tall Tales, or I Was a Teenage Superhero

by Eve Morton

Abigail was watering her plants when she first heard the children's voices. Several, at least three of them, by the cadence. They were around the front of her house, trampling dead grass. She tilted her hat up towards the desert sun and basked in its glow for several long seconds before she pulled herself away from her tasks. If there were three kids, that meant there would soon be four and five and then six—unless she set them right.

"Hello," she greeted, her voice as bombastic as it had once needed to be. She was happy to still have the skill, that her vocal chords had not gone soft in their disuse. She unlatched the back gate and slipped on her flip-flops again. The grass was sharper on the front porch area, since she didn't keep it watered and cared for like she did in the back area. "I hear you all. It's okay. I don't bite."

One of the three, a boy, laughed. He slapped a hand against his mouth as if he had done something horrible, sworn or taken someone's name in vain. The other two were girls. Same age as the boy, but head and shoulders above him. So they were probably thirteen or fourteen, around the same age when Abigail had transitioned from citizen to superhero. She noticed a curled up magazine behind one of the girl's back.

"Hello," Abigail said again. "It's polite to greet people. Even nowadays."

"I'm sorry," the boy said. He nudged one of the girls, the one not holding the magazine, and they apologized in unison. It was then that Abigail noticed all of them were dressed the same. Not like superheroes—though maybe that was what they pretended to be every morning as they got dressed for their Catholic school and went to mass while everyone was still asleep—but in dark jackets and plaid skirts. She figured it was for St. Paul's, a large school that had been built on former land owned by the indigenous population but sold off to a higher bidder. Like many of the other lots around this desert town had been. At least it wasn't a mall.

She smiled at the kids who were still staring at her as if she'd bite them. As if she was wearing her tights and her former uniform, not the simple sundress she had on now. She took off her large hat so her hair could fall out from its pin. Long dark locks fell over her shoulders and made the other girl gasp.

"You're so pretty."

The boy nudged her. "What were you expecting? Her picture's in the magazine."

"I don't bite and I'm not a witch," Abigail said. "But I don't appreciate trespassers. So how about you come inside for a drink, and that way, we can get all of this nonsense out into the open."

She opened her front door with a simple flick of her wrist. It was done so fast that the girl holding the magazine gasped. In all the write-ups Abigail had read about her life, always altered and always so much more dramatic than it really was, they had listed her powers of telekinesis, the ability to move things with her mind. She never had that. She was just really fast and really good at things. Would these kids believe her over the black and white lies printed about her? Maybe. Lemonade always helped.

"I'll put ice in the glasses," she said as she stepped inside, hoping the kids would follow. "It's going to be a hot day."

She'd cracked four ice cubes into as many glasses when she heard the steps of the children enter her small adobe house. She'd lived here for the past seven years, ever since her superhero team disbandment and retirement in the larger city of Austin had become too arduous to conceal. Austin's logo may have been to keep things weird, but she was too weird for them. A former superhero according to all the tabloids, or a fantastic gymnast and dancer according to her Olympic records, or some sort of witch and fairy and any number of different other ghoulies-of-the-week according to the online conspiracy mill. The truth was a mix of everything in between, plus one event that she really didn't like to think about.

Maybe it's time, though, she told herself. She didn't like the fact that the kids had shown up with a magazine. It meant the tabloids had found something to print, rather than just publish online and blog and blog and blog. Anything in print was serious—which usually meant there was at least a grain of truth to it—or maybe a small prick of the truth, like her cacti that she never needed to water in her backyard.

The kids' chatter brought her out of her worries. They'd gone into her living room, painted pink and green like the desert hotel she'd first stayed at when she arrived in the south, and wanted to emulate. A cattle skull hung on the wall, some framed pieces of Georgia O'Keeffe that no one but her had ever seen and knew were real, and then some other desert pieces that she'd found on her long walks around her home. She noticed one of the girls eyeing some of the skulls and bones she'd found.

"I didn't kill them," she said. "Don't worry."

"We're not worried," the girl said, dismissive. "You're retired, anyway."

"So I've heard. If you're not worried, then why don't you give me your names? You surely know mine already."

"Lazy Susan," the boy said. He swallowed. "I'm Tyler."

"Cara," the girl with the magazine said. "And that's Jenny."

The girl struck her friend in the arm. "Dammit. You could have said Jennifer. Now she knows my nickname and has more power."

Abigail set the lemonade she'd readied on a tray in front of them on the sky blue coffee table. She then fixed her best adult-gaze at Jenny. "Don't strike people."

"What?" Her mouth hung open and braces graced her teeth.

"Don't strike people," Abigail repeated. "It's not polite."

"Coming from you—"

"I never hit people," Abigail said. "Remember, I was Lazy Susan. I just appeared and reappeared. An acrobat at most, a thief in the worst lens. But ultimately, rather lazy when compared to my counterparts."

The three of them looked at her with wide eyes. *So it's true,* their faces seemed to say. Abigail sat across from them on a wicker chair while they remained on the couch. "It is true, yes, that I used to be Lazy Susan. But I doubt that most of what's in that magazine or what you read online is true. Those are tall tales slanted to sell you things. Never forget that. Advertising dollars run those places. Not the truth."

"So you haven't killed anyone?" Tyler asked. He sipped his drink but still stared at her through the glass. "Not even injured anyone?"

"No and no," she said, confident she was not lying. No murders to her name, and those who hurt themselves, well, they hurt themselves. Brought it on themselves. "And no telekinesis either, I'm afraid."

"Shoot," Cara said. "That was really cool."

"So you didn't steal the jewel, then?" Jenny sipped her drink as if it wasn't lemonade, but something stronger. "Is that a bunch of lies, too?"

Abigail smiled warmly. Oh, the jewel. Oh, her last job amongst the group of so-called superheroes and crime fighters. So-called because they were really just kids, just like these guys, looking to spend an afternoon doing something other than virtual reality or social media or even just hanging out at the mall. They wanted adventures, not advertising. They wanted excitement, not dull entertainment. And when they went around a circle in someone's basement, sitting on a cross-stitched rug that Abigail still remembered the texture of, they each listed off what they were good at.

Robbie: painting things and making stuff look just like an original. The Cardmaker became his name.

Julie: making potions and special chemicals that could make smoke bombs and glitter bombs. Whirl-Girl, her name.

Addison: fighting in all the best ways, all the best styles, having a dozen belts from so many different types of martial arts. She went by DUNK, simply because it sounded like the movement of her fists.

And her, Abigail: good at dancing, gymnastics, and otherwise contorting her body. Lazy, lazy, Susan, like those spinny things her mother had on the table for potatoes and dishes to be passed around.

By themselves, they were a bunch of nerds. In another era, they would have played Dungeons and Dragons and created characters to fight out mock battles. They would have started a club and said No Boys allowed (Robbie was only one boy, so they could have one) and maybe babysat and pooled their money. Something banal, ordinary.

But in the era of superheroes, of course, they assembled a team. And got pretty famous for it all.

"You *did* steal the jewel," Cara said, sensing something in Abigail's wistful expression. "I knew it."

"Where is it?" Tyler asked. "Is it here? They never found it."

Jenny held up the magazine, peering into its middle contents while displaying the old photograph of Abigail and her team on the cover along with a bold title *I Was A Teenage Superhero!* written in comic-styled letters. It was a nice touch, only made that much more garish by their tacky costumes. So much neon and gold and glitter. It had been the style at the time—no one wanted to blend into the night back then—and it had been a heck of a lot of fun making those pieces. They'd gone to so many different thrift stores and visited half a dozen seamstresses before settling on two main people to make their costumes. One, an old retired theater teacher who lived alone and also like Georgia O'Keeffe, and then Robbie's mom. She never told anyone a thing about their antics. She was the only one, truly Abigail understood now, who they could trust. A better Alfred than Alfred.

"Wow," Abigail sighed. "I miss Dana so much."

"Who is Dana?" Jenny asked, peering over the magazine. "Does she have the jewel now?"

"It's here," Tyler said. He looked around at the paintings on her wall, as if they could lead back to a secret safe, then he peered from the couch into her kitchen. "I can sense it."

"Let's not get too far ahead of ourselves." Abigail remained utterly cool and collected in her wicker seat, though her tone belied her authority. "I don't think you've come here to ask about the jewel."

"No?" Jenny said, dismissing her with a roll of her eyes.

"Don't do that either, Jenny," Abigail warned. "Rolling your eyes is a very violent gesture. Not to mention rude. And I can't stand either."

"Are you joking?" Cara asked. She nudged Tyler. "I think she's joking."

"No, I'm serious about manners. About trespassing and property damage and defamation. I may have been a teenage superhero, but that does not mean I didn't respect the law. I respect the order that my retirement has given me. And I would appreciate you sharing your magazine, young lady. I would like to see my CV according to the public."

After stern looks from her friends, Jenny handed over the tabloid. Abigail combed through it with an affected ease. Her blood pounded in her temples, her nonchalance a perfected act. She may have been in retirement, and she truly may have respected the laws now that she was on the other side of them, but she was also a woman with memories. Feelings. Excitement.

And speaking about the past was a delight. Even when the press often got it wrong.

"It's been ten years since the jewel of the city went missing," Cara said. "We read about it online and in the magazine and that's how we found you. Said you were out here, in Desert Son, when we thought only… you know…"

"Weirdoes live in this community," Tyler said. Cara nudged him. "What?"

"This is an intentional community," Abigail said, repeating the story she'd given people many times before. Like her own mother who understood her superhero dalliance even more than she understood her living amongst the hippies and dead-heads as she saw them. "Which means that we have all gathered together to share similar goals and similar outcomes in life. We grow our own food, we build a lot of our own appliances—or at least, I find other people who can. We're sort of like another crime fighting crew. Only the crime we're fighting is capitalism."

"What?" Tyler asked.

"It's okay," Abigail said. "Nothing to worry about in the abstract or in the practical. Desert Son can be a weird place from the outside, but I assure you that no one here bites like I don't bite. And," she added thinking of her former superhero team, "none of the others live here with me, unfortunately."

"Yeah, we know. They're all dead."

Abigail put down the magazine. She'd been skimming the retrospective piece on the jewel theft—so many details wrong, yet a surprising amount were also correct—but now she was no longer interested. "Dead? Are you sure?"

Jenny pointed to the magazine again. "It's all in there. After the main story, there's a Where Are They Now section. Robbie died in jail…"

Jenny continued to list the outcomes of her former crew and friends while Abigail also found the written words. Robbie had been arrested on another charge for something petty after they'd broken up their team. Something like shoplifting, which was so dumb it made Abigail wanted to scream. But he'd been a kingpin in jail, ordering people around and having yet another crew—until someone got him in the showers.

Julie, too, had died by her own folly and arrogance. She'd spent too much time in her lab, breathed too many fumes, and like Marie Curie, died before her brilliant discoveries on climate change could truly be implemented in her lifetime. At least she was still living on in her science, Abigail thought, though it was a cold comfort—much like Julie's hands were always cold.

Then there was Addison. *Oh, Addy. Dear little lamb.* She simply knew too much on how people fought. She wanted to be a peace worker after so much violence and bloodshed, as if to atone for all the bad guys she'd given bloody noses and broken fingers to. *As if they hadn't deserved it.* Abigail had written Addy a letter when she'd found this intentional community, trying to get her to join, so she could atone as she planted trees, not dodged bombs in a warzone or translated the AA serenity prayer into a dozen languages for former hit men. Addy had not answered.

Abigail knew why now.

Dead. All dead. How disappointing.

One day, Abigail had wanted a reunion. She'd wanted to see them again before old age truly got them. It had only been ten years, and they had all been teenagers. She wasn't even in her thirties now. It had seemed possible to reunite.

But all the dreams, and hopes with them, fell away.

"Shoot." Abigail set down the magazine on her coffee table. "This just sucks."

"We're sorry to bring bad news," Cara said. Her face was kind. She looked to her friends with a stern gaze until they nodded and also provided their condolences. Abigail appreciated it. She didn't mind these kids. She didn't mind the tabloids, either. It sucked that there would now be an uptick in people visiting her, now that her whereabouts had been reported again, but at least she was prepared.

And she was the only one. A smile lingered on her face before she shoved it away for sadness again. It was true sadness. She loved those guys. She would miss them—even if she would now prosper in the wake of their deaths.

"So you probably don't want to talk about the jewel theft," Tyler said slowly. Cara nudged him, but she also looked to Abigail with deep blue eyes filled with promise.

"It's in the magazine," Abigail said. "They mostly got it right."

"Well, what did they get wrong?" Jenny asked. "Can we at least ask about that?"

Abigail normally said no to requests like this, for any and all interviews from civilians or reporters alike, and especially on the jewel theft. It had been the last act that they had done together, before they realized they had gone too far. Fighting crime was one thing, even using vigilante means, but the jewel theft had been done simply because they could. Not quite for justice, definitely not for peace—but because someone else had something shiny, and they wanted it.

It was, as the magazine had described, the last act of a truly rebellious crew, who had spent much of their time acting as Robin Hoods, stealing from the rich to give to the poor. They'd taken food from grocery stores to give it to food banks; they'd destroyed bulldozers and other such construction equipment to protect land; and they had broken into every single investment bankers' house who was cheating on his taxes to make him pay them in full. Good things, political things that were slanted towards their own personal leanings, but still good things.

Until the jewel. Their motives were less pure—so of course, the story of the event was also less pure. She noted that Robbie, out of all of them, had been quoted. He was a kingpin in jail at this point, so of course, he obfuscated his involvement and spoke in the language of the high and mighty, not in the language of truth. Julie had not commented—too deep in her work—and neither had Addison, since she wanted peace and nothing but.

Abigail looked at Robbie's quote now. "I was the mastermind of the whole thing. They needed me to pull it off."

She rolled her eyes, though it was rude. But he wasn't here to argue. She looked at the kids who were in front of her, her eager audience to the truth. Or at least, her version of it.

And she decided to tell-all. At least a little bit.

"Well, I was a teenage superhero," she began, "and this last act was the thing that made me an adult. That jewel theft—it wasn't Robbie's idea. It was mine. I'd been an intern in that museum a long time ago. I knew how big it was, but I also knew that the jewel didn't belong to the museum. They'd taken it from the indigenous people. Addison checked into that story—she was always about peacekeeping and international relations, even then—and she verified it. We could never find that community to give it back to, since they'd dispersed a long time ago, so our anger was never really truly righteous. We wanted it, and since they didn't own it, we figured we had a right to it. So then Robbie became involved. He wanted to plan it like the ultimate heist. It was his idea, in theory, that it would be our last job."

"Why?" Tyler asked. "You were doing so well."

"Yes. So you go out on top. It just makes sense, and we were all almost eighteen," Abigail said. There was more to it—a love triangle, an inheritance, and Abigail's growing impatience with working nights—but it didn't matter. "So we made the plan. Last job, better than prom in terms of a rite of passage. Julie was sort of dragged along, since she was the only person who could outsmart the safety mechanisms and drug the people who were supposed to be on night watch."

The kids nodded, these details too familiar to them from the magazine story while also being brand new from the hero's mouth. "We staked out the place for a week to learn the schedule. We went to the museum during the day," she said, and noted that some grainy security footage of them were in the magazine. "We picked the date of a gala to get this done, so Julie could go with a well-known professor in her lab and slip the chemicals into necessary drinks and rewire the security system. Robbie, of course, was going to be look-out. Addison was going to be there too, since Robbie looked tough but she was the one with all the skills."

"That leaves you," Tyler said. He grinned from ear to ear. "You took the jewel. That's what's missing in the magazine."

"I knew it," Cara said. "It's here, right?"

"You're getting ahead of her," Jenny said. She turned back to Abigail with true respect in her eyes. "Go on."

"Thank you. I did, yes, take the jewel. All that ballet and gymnastics and other such fun stuff came in handy." Abigail smiled. She still felt weightless whenever she remembered this night, descending from the ceiling on a series of pulleys and levers made by Julie (with some help from Robbie's mom and the theatre teacher), then back flipping as she nearly knocked a sensor but brought it all back. "It was like some strange Cirque du Soleil show, if you remember that event. I sort of wish we did have cameras so I could remember it better. Except that of course they were off, because we were breaking the law."

"For a good cause," Tyler said.

"For a good cause," Cara echoed.

Abigail nodded. "We got the jewel. We hid it in our lair for a long time, unsure what to do with it."

"And that lair," Jenny said, picking up the magazine. She read out the art gallery that had once been a factory, that had once been their secret home away from home. "Is it still there?"

"No," Abigail said, sighing. "it was stolen."

"Stolen?" Tyler said. "Are you serious?"

"'Fraid so." Abigail shrugged. "That's how these things go, kiddies. You steal and people steal from you. Even when you're doing it for a good reason, it's still theft. It's always been so clear to me, ever since that night when we all came back after some celebratory pizza and discovered a gaping hole in our hiding place, that it was an unfair world. That crime fighting and breaking the law were terms that had the same meaning, but different connotations based on who you were and where you ended up."

"I don't get it," Cara said.

"It means that stealing is bad," Jenny said. She sighed, but refrained from rolling her eyes. "That's it?"

"Pretty much." Abigail stood from her spot on the couch. The kids were done with their lemonade, and since the sun was starting to set, she figured this was as good a time as any to wish them well. "You shouldn't steal, yes. Always good advice. And as cool as being a superhero may seem, you'll still end up needing to own a house. Clean your house. And water the rest of the plants in your garden. Think about your future, kiddies. Don't become superheroes."

Abigail gestured to her front door. The kids, though saddened, listened to her. She noticed that they left the magazine behind.

She tapped Jenny on the shoulder as she was slipping on her shoes again, and asked if she still wanted it.

"What's the point? It's all fake."

"Not all of it," Abigail said.

"You keep it, then."

Abigail nodded with a wry smile. "Thank you very much, Jenny. I really appreciated this visit."

The kids nodded their agreement, but it was subdued. They would tell their friends at school the next day that the glory was gone here. Just a lady with flip-flops and a big hat who wants to garden. No jewel, and never a jewel to begin with. Stolen! Stolen from the superheroes. It was a true story, a sad story, but one that Abigail delighted telling for the first time.

Maybe now, she could have some peace.

Abigail watched as the kids left her driveway. They walked in a horizontal line of three, chatting hurried to one another, and walked through her gated community doors again. Her neighbor closed her blinds and went back to her own business. Abigail was sure at the next potluck she'd have some explaining to do. Again.

But at least she had the magazine to help.

Abigail grabbed her hat from the spot where she'd once left it. She tucked her hair back up under it and went into her backyard. The sun would set in an hour, and the chill would come in. She didn't need to water her garden anymore—if she did the plants would surely drown overnight—but she wandered all the way to the back where her prize cactus was. A bright violet had bloomed from the bud it had been just in the morning. She beamed as she smelled it, cupped the soft petals in her worn palms, and sighed contentedly.

"It's funny," she said aloud, speaking to her cactus like she normally did, since it had been proven—by Julie, years after disbandment—that plants responded to their owner's ministrations. They even sometimes took on the personality assigned to them by their owner's words and actions. "No one ever asks what color the jewel was."

Abigail ran her hands through the dirt. The jewel, when they'd first seen it in that museum enclave, had been the same shade of violet to all of them. Yet in the museum listing, it was stated to have no color, only something that radiated light like a diamond. The lore that the indigenous people had for the jewel also listed it as see-through, as a vector for other colors. The violet to them had been something special, something that it still had once it was in their warehouse, and something they waxed philosophic about when they ate pizza that night.

Then they'd returned and it had been gone. Once there, now gone. All four of them had been suspects, but since they'd all eaten pizza together that night, none of them could have done it.

"Luckily for me," Abigail said, "I had another set of skills I could fall back on."

Abigail ran her hands through the dirt in the base of the cactus. The pot that held this plant was large, much too large to hold a single cactus. No one in her Desert Son community—save for Beatrice, the woman who had opened the place—had ever asked about the cactus. And Beatrice only commented on the violet color of the bloom at the top. "So pretty, so much like that jewel."

And Abigail had known that all her hunting, all her searching, had led her to the right place. It had taken Abigail three years to track her down, but only three minutes to set everything right again. She moved into Beatrice's spot in the intentional community, a group of weirdoes who welcomed her eagerly, since she was a former crime fighter.

"And we never really liked Beatrice," some of them had confessed at the local meetings and BBQs. "You're a much better replacement."

Abigail sighed as she thought of her past sins. All done for a good cause, all done to keep her friends and their secret safe. It saddened her now that they were no longer present to bask in the glory of the jewel or their further fame.

Abigail's fingers hit the hard surface of the jewel under the dirt. She tapped it, knowing it was there, and would remain there as long as she tended to her garden, as long as she tended to the news stories about her crimes, and as long as that new group of kids could remember just enough details of the truth to keep telling tall tales that made everything a much better story, one that was almost happy, in the end.

Eve Morton is a writer living in Ontario, Canada. She teaches university and college classes on media studies, academic writing, and genre literature, among other topics. Her latest book is *The Serenity Nearby*, released in 2022 by Sapphire Books. Find more info on authormorton.wordpress.com

The Tithe Collectors

by Andrew P. McGregor

Another dignitary emerged through one of dozens of off-world portals, her entourage in tow. Guardsmen of the Eternal Lord quickly checked over the small party and cleared them to approach the long line of other dignitaries leading to the tithe collectors. Flowing blue and gold gowns and the smell of soft perfumes accompanied the five people whose planet was anything but pleasant to visit.

Bob would know as he'd helped conquer the world several years ago. He snorted at the dignitary's pompous display of wealth and wondered how much in taxes she'd had to take in order to afford such gowns and smells.

"Doug?" he said to his fellow tithe collector. Doug opened his golden power armour's visor and turned to give Bill a curious look.

"Yeah, Bill?"

"I never asked you, were you on Terracon Prime?" he said, nodding at the newcomers.

"Terracon? Yeah, bud, I was there. I'd say the Terrconians got what they deserved, but…" he leaned in a little closer while turning off his transmitter so he could whisper, "Mr Eternal might've gone too far on that one."

Bill turned off his transmitter as well and opened his visor. He smiled down at a black-cloaked man with a bald head, whose slim smile did a poor impression of positive cheer. He laid a small chest onto the magnetised tray the collectors were using to gather the tithes. "A tenth of a world's wealth, reduced to a small box of... superconductors?" The bald man nodded and turned to head into the adjoining Grand Hall, where dozens of other dignitaries and their entourages were already mingling under crystal chandeliers. Bill whispered to Doug, "I think the boss went a little too far on a lot of planets."

"And that laugh of his," Doug said and shuddered. "Like a jackal mixed with a kookaburra and an old-fashioned chainsaw, while killing prisoners at that."

"Makes you wonder, doesn't it?"

"What do you mean?"

"How'd we get into all this? Butchering worlds and taking tributes at gunpoint."

"You know how," Doug told Bill. "Earth and the colonies turned on Mr Eternal and his works. How would you feel if you were in charge of a hospital, trying to save the lives of children, when the Terrans tried to shut everything down? They were children he had to save."

"Were they children anymore, though?"

"You know what I mean." Doug sighed and looked over the cowed dignitaries, some of whom were mingling under the watchful gaze of the guardsmen. "But I know what you mean. How'd we become an interstellar Empire? I admit I don't know all the details, but when you have children in control of nuclear arsenals, it doesn't take a genius to see how things can escalate."

"But why did you choose this side? I was born and raised on New Jupiter, so when the Terrans threatened to blow us up, I joined right away."

"That's noble of you," Doug said with an effort to keep the sarcasm out of his voice.

"Well, I never thought I'd be bombing civilian cities, but how else were we to get them to stop?"

"And the rest?" Doug said, indicating the carnage that followed the initial stages of the war.

"Well, we had to keep going, didn't we? World after world, until they couldn't harm us anymore."

"We certainly got that."

Bill shrugged off Doug's comment. "Anyway, what about you? Why did you join?"

Doug thought back to that fateful night when he got the urge to take sides. "I guess I was just good at what I did. I smuggled neural spice applicators from Mars to New Jupiter."

"You were a psych-runner?"

He nodded, ashamed to admit his illegal past. "Got caught by Mr Eternal himself, but since I had all the right connections, instead of killing me, he offered me a job. Running drugs instead of psychs for his experiments. I saw those kids grow into the death machines we know and fear today, so when they went a little mad at being shot at and bombed, I have to admit to a certain sympathy for them, but then Mr Eternal set them upon Solaris Echo." His voice dropped as he remembered that campaign and the horrors that were unleashed on the stubborn inhabitants.

"Yeah, I liked the Solarans too," Bill said. He sounded like he wanted to pat Doug on the back, commiserating the loss of the stellar neighbourhood's friendliest citizens. "I had a great time there, gliding over the mountain-trees of the Five Archipelagos, meeting the pretty locals, and imbibing my fair share of beer and synths."

"Wonderfully profitable place, too," Doug said with a grin. "And great people. I heard my eighth-grade maths teacher settled down there. Lovely lady, she helped a lot, and I doubt I would've gotten so high in the cartels if it wasn't for her."

"All dead," Bill said with a sigh.

"Yep. If only they'd surrendered."

"Would you have surrendered to our Eternal Lord's maniacal killing spree?"

"Not while he was cackling over the sounds of his auto-guns," Doug admitted. "The boss certainly had his fun there, didn't he? Still, if it weren't for the boss, I'd probably be dead right now."

"You mean because of the war?"

Doug shook his head. "Nah. The cartel had a lot of enemies, and all my profits were eaten up paying off my muscle or local law enforcement. Mr Eternal paid better. Much better, well enough that I could send my kids to university on Terra."

Bill thanked the next dignitary's offer of miniature anti-matter storage units and waved them on into the mingling groups of other dignitaries. "I suppose I'm grateful too. Mr Eternal's mad for sure, but he looks after his troops. Back home, I could barely afford the rent or medical expenses for my partner's cancer treatments. When I joined the war effort, we got free medical care. Free! Imagine that. We were able to have children, and I was infertile. Just look at this." He angled his helmet so that Doug could see the shining whites of Bill's teeth. "New teeth. The dentists were hell on the gums, though." He smacked his lips together, remembering the horrifically painful procedures performed by Mr Eternal's spidery medical robots. Doug winced, knowing how painful those little critters could be, especially when they didn't bother with anaesthetics and just got stuck into their work.

"And when I saved Mr Eternal from a drone strike," Bill continued, "he gave me three tubes of premium vat meat from Mars. Boy, that was a fine feast when we got stuck into that." He looked down at his leg. "Of course, I lost the legs to the drones, and I can still feel the pain, even with these prosthetics. Small price to pay for a feast, right?"

"I suppose. Is it worth it, the good fortunes we've had, do you think?" He looked at the swirling grey-blue portals that connected much of the interstellar Empire into the tithe hub, trying to recall individual events that occurred on the other side of each of the portals. He pointed at them, causing some people in front of him to flinch. "I lost good friends there. That one I had to decide where to plant hydrogen bomb mines; a school or an orphanage, isn't that messed up? It wasn't like I had much of a choice, was it? And that one over there I had to perform one of Mr Eternal's 'Thin-the-Herd' operations. Not the actual execution part, just the choosing. Wasn't the best afternoon I've ever had. I had a few stiff drinks that night."

"Yeah, I can imagine. But look at it this way: those 'Thin-the-Herd' operations put a massive dent in the insurgents' morale. You had to face a few thousand who were sure to die anyway, save a few billion from the Childrens' wrath."

"One of them was Sarah Wei," Doug pointed out.

"*The* Sarah Wei?" Bill shook his head and closed his eyes, distraught at the revelation. "Are you telling me you had to put the greatest actor in the star systems to the thinnings? Oh, bud, I'm sorry. Was it quick?"

Doug shook his head. "I left the Children to their work and got out of there. You're right, though, it certainly had the desired effect on the locals, seeing their beloved Wei turned into… that." He couldn't bring himself to think of it, of what happened to those that were 'thinned,' to become the lobotomised human husks, doomed to an eternity of servitude under the guidance of their new cyborg overlords. "Tell me, honestly, hypothetically," he raised an eyebrow at Bill, who cocked his head to the side, as if he were a curious puppy. "If one of these poor saps that came to pay their tithes for the month were to, I dunno, somehow vaporise the Lord Eternal, would you be sad? Wait, better question… would you let them?"

Bill's mouth dropped open, and his eyes widened a little. He looked over the dignitaries at the head of the crowd, who no doubt had heard Doug's query, and then flicked his eyes back to his friend. "I… I can't say how I would feel." He whispered, "I think I'd help them do it."

"Yeah. Yeah," Doug replied. It comforted him to know that Bill thought the same way.

"Oh, what have we here?" Bill asked as a bent-backed dignitary approached their raised dais. Upon the man's purple-clothed back sat a large wicker-basket full of what appeared to be precious red stones. The man grunted as he took each step, then almost collapsed as he lowered the heavy basted to the metal tray. He stunk of sweat, smoke and wheat, and took several long seconds to pant and spit his way to recovery. He placed a hand on his back, and both tithe collectors heard bones crackling as he returned from his bent-backed position to an upright one. "Rubies?" Bill asked the dignitary with a heavy dose of skepticism. "What are we meant to do with a basket of rubies?"

"Where's your entourage?" Doug asked. The dignitary's purple robes were torn and dirty, presumably from a long journey while carrying the heavy basket.

"M-my lords, I-I offer all that my people could bring. My entourage died, protecting this offering from the machines your Children left on my world."

Doug and Bill looked at each other, understanding crossing each other's face. The Children had a high-propensity to leave behind all manner of dangerous obstacles when they vacated a planet. Doug sympathised with the old, bearded man, but kept his face carefully opaque to any emotions. The man's red-rimmed eyes and shuddering voice reminded him of the million grieving victims he'd passed in his long, successful career.

"I see, and what value do these rubies hold?" he asked the old man in a stern voice.

"They're not just rubies, my lords. They represent the combined wealth of my people!"

Bill slammed his visor shut, making the old man jump in fear. He turned on his transmitter and clicked it twice to tell Doug to do the same. Doug closed his visor and turned on his transmitter so they could talk privately.

"They're just rubies," Bill said. "Mr Eternal will give us a flogging if we accept it. Better to blast the poor wretch."

"Wait, hang on. Rubies can be useful for some tools. Medical devices, watches, some lasers."

"Our factories can synthesise ten times as many in a single hour."

"Well, maybe his planet could do the same before we blew it to pieces. Have a care, let's hear him out."

"All right, agreed, but only because you've been at this for longer than me."

Both men opened their visors again and Doug addressed the old man, whose smell had worsened somewhat. "Tell me, where do you hail from?"

"Shoal Minor, my lords," he wheezed.

Bill and Doug looked at each other. "Ever heard of Shoal Minor?"

Bill shrugged inside his armour. "Not a clue."

Doug checked his power armour's computer records. The place didn't exist, but that wasn't entirely unexpected, he supposed. There were hundreds of worlds the Children and Lord Eternal had conquered, and the war had lasted many years. The Children had likely wiped out dozens of colonies they'd never heard of in the great purges. Apparently, this one had survived.

"Well, thank you. Your gift is well received." He scrunched up his nose and waved the man on to the main auditorium.

"Bonus?" Bill grunted quietly while the old man left the dais.

Doug nodded. "Bonus." He shifted the basket off the metal tray and dropped it behind the dais, to be pored over later at the men's leisure. "Compensation," he amended when he returned to the front, "for our sacrifices in the wars."

"I understand… and approve." Mr Eternal's auditors would not miss the basket of rubies. Life may have taken a turn for the worse since they'd joined Lord Eternal's ranks, but being collectors had its perks.

"Yeah, but I doubt this bonus will get us off Terra."

"Oh? Where would you want to go? There aren't too many places left untouched, even if we could bribe our way there."

Doug waved the next dignitary onto the dais. "I've heard the Sky-Arches of Lincoln's World are quite nice, high above the radioactive dust clouds. The auroras are meant to be spectacular."

"Hmm, sounds nice."

"*What sounds nice?*" A buzz-saw-like voice speared through their conversation from behind and above them. Both men hunched involuntarily, and the handful of remaining dignitaries and their entourages wobbled backwards or shifted nervously, while their faces drained of colour. The collectors turned to face the newcomer and neatly genuflected when their worst fears were confirmed.

Standing a little over seven feet tall, encased in a translucent shell, the skeletal form of the Lord Eternal stood above them. Metal covered the Lord Eternal's frame, and crystalline thorns grew out of the metal. Where once there had been a nose, eyes, ears and skin, now a ghoulish, silvery approximation of a metal face crested the spiked neck of the cybernetic creature. Red laser-like eyes tracked every rustle and every breath the men made while he awaited their response.

"Lord Eternal, what an unexpected surprise," Doug said.

"Y-yes, entirely un-unexpected," Bill stuttered in agreement.

"*But not a pleasant one?*" the Lord Eternal pressed.

"That depends, Mr Eternal, old friend, on if you're going to slap me in the face with your bare hands, or with your gauntlet this time."

The Lord Eternal stood silent for a long moment, so quiet and so still that he could have been a statue. Doug felt his heart thunder as his anxiety levels spiked.

"*Ha!*" the Lord Eternal's deep, buzz-saw voice barked. "*Ahahaha.*" It wasn't a pleasant laugh, but nor was it unbearable. Doug relaxed while the dignitaries and guardsmen in the room all looked on in horror. "*I always did like your jokes, Douglas. Come, stand up.*" Their cybernetic lord motioned with spindly fingers to get off their knees.

"Yeah, heh, jokes."

"*But you haven't answered my question.*"

"Ah, you mean what sounds nice? Uh, Bill and I were discussing what would make a nice vacation. With all the leave we've both built up under your latest employee scheme, we were thinking of visiting the Sky-Arches of Lincoln's World. If that would be acceptable?"

The Lord Eternal scanned both men for a few seconds longer, making them sweat. The metal face shifted to form some sort of… smile? "*Yes, that sounds nice. What you do in your spare time is of no concern to me. I hope you enjoy your time there. Are your families well? I heard Jenny has progressed well in her xenobiology studies.*"

"She's top of her class, thanks to your generosity," Doug said, and meant it. There was no way he could have afforded to put Jenny through xenobiology at the prestigious Mars University without the Lord Eternal's endorsement.

"*And Bill, your daughter… Sharon, isn't it? Her football skills are impressive.*"

"Y-yes, she's doing w-well," Bill said, attempting not to recoil from the Lord Eternal's flickering red gaze and grinding voice.

"*Good, good. You still suffer from that stutter, Bill. Have you seen the med-bots about it?*"

"N-not yet. I'm practising, though. Getting better."

"*Well, the cost is on me. So, gentlemen, what have these downtrodden scum brought us today?*"

The Lord Eternal stepped around the men to inspect the tithes placed on the metal tray. He opened his armoured shell and poked through the contents of several boxes. He murmured to himself while the rest of the room watched, fearing his inevitable outbursts of rage. "*Top of the range superconductors, not bad… Fresh fruits? The seeds may hold some value if they're extinct elsewhere…*"

He showed no emotion. Nothing. Most people thought he really was a robot, a murder machine, but Doug and Bill knew better. He'd been a man once, and really cared for his Children and employees, but that only made him more terrifying when he decided you had wronged him.

At the corner of his eyes, Doug noticed movement in the line. A flash of blue and gold whipped from one side, then the other, as if a wind blew against a singular being's cloak as it dashed towards the dais. "What?" he said in a quiet voice.

Bill heard his friend's stunned tone and turned to look at the small crowd, but his left foot bumped into something soft and he shouted as he fell backwards, hitting hard against the white tiles, shattering them under his armoured bulk.

A woman screamed.

The dignitaries in the auditorium and in the Tithe Hub gasped, fainted and shouted in fear.

Doug moved to dispatch whatever the soft thing was that had tripped Bill…

It was the dignitary from Terracon Prime, writhing under Bill's armoured bulk while screaming obscenities at him. She scrabbled with a free hand, slapping at the white tiles, trying to reach a small glass water bottle she must've dropped while ascending the dais steps.

"Let me get it! Let me kill him!"

The old man, who had gone only a few steps from the dais after depositing his basket of rubies, appeared at Bill's side and stooped over to pick up the bottle.

Doug pinned the woman's hand down while Bill got off her.

"Here you go, my lords," the old man said as he offered the water bottle to Bill.

"Kill him now, before it's too late," the perfumed woman screeched.

Doug and Bill looked at the woman, then at the water bottle. She was going to kill the Lord Eternal with a bottle of water? Bill grabbed the bottle and scanned it with his golden power armour's sensors. "Nano-machines," he said once his armour's computer had presented him with a preliminary analysis.

"Do it, now!" the dignitary yelled.

The Lord Eternal's heavy footsteps clacked sharply on the tiles. All Bill would have to do to kill the most powerful being in the human colonies was throw the bottle at him and watch him melt into a puddle of grey goo. He hesitated; the bottle clenched tight.

Doug shook his head minutely. Despite all the trials they'd gone through for this monster's conquests, all the sacrifices they'd made, he couldn't bring himself to do it. "No," he whispered to his friend.

Bill nodded fractionally before closing his visor and turning to meet the Lord Eternal. "N-n-n-nano-machines," he told the Lord Eternal. "She was t-trying to a-assassinate you." He opened his trembling hand to reveal the water bottle.

The Lord Eternal froze in place, and his laser-like eyes zeroed-in on the bottle.

The woman continued screaming while Doug held her down, away from the Lord Eternal and the bottle.

"Why?" she asked him, tears falling down her cheeks.

Doug ignored her and closed his visor. A watery film clouded his vision, and he squeezed his eyes shut. *What have I done?* Possibly their one and only chance to throw off the shackles of a mad tyrant, and he'd been the one to stop it.

"Take. Her. Away," the Lord Eternal laboured. His shoulders fell ever so slightly, as if he were surprised and saddened that someone would try to kill him. Two guardsmen took the Terracon Prime dignitary by the arms and reefed her away, intending to take her through a portal to one of many hellish prison planets. No doubt there would be a scouring to come from this, after the med bots had extracted all the information they could from the unfortunate dignitary.

Doug and Bill faced their boss and waited for their punishments.

"*I…*" the sound came out so quietly both men had to lean forward to hear the grating, electronic voice. "*I am grateful.*"

Both men frowned behind their visors.

"You have saved me, and the Eternal Empire. I must reward you."

Doug gulped. Rewards could be as welcoming as the punishments.

The Lord Eternal's eyes buzzed spasmodically for a moment while he gave thought to the 'reward' owed to the men.

"A planet to rule. Yes, you will rule over a planet together. You fancied the Sky-Arches of Lincoln's world, didn't you? It's yours. I will increase your pay to match your new positions. Time off your normal duties, of course…" He raised a finger and his face attempted a grin. "*And families. Your families will live there too. Finish the tithes and then go. I have some paperwork to attend to.*"

He leaned forward, and both men involuntarily leaned backwards, but the Lord Eternal stretched his unnatural arms so that they wrapped around the two men. "*Thank you, my friends.*" He let go after a few long seconds, and headed to the back of the Tithe Hub, where a new swirling grey portal opened to admit him, then disappeared when he'd gone through.

"Lincoln's World?" Doug asked Bill. They opened their visors, and their mouths slowly curved upwards until their reconstructed white teeth appeared.

"We just got a pay rise."

"The Sky-Arches are ours?"

"Our own planet…"

A murmur grew within the Tithe Hub and Grand Hall. The guardsmen looked over the crowds with concern in their eyes, as if the dignitaries and their entourages were about to explode in outrage now that the Lord Eternal had left them.

"Why didn't you kill him?" someone in the hall shouted.

"You could have saved us all!" Another said.

"Yeah."

"Fools."

"Idiots."

Many others began shouting and nodding in agreement. A glass flute of wine whizzed over the collectors' heads and smashed behind the dais where the Lord Eternal had portalled out.

Bill and Doug sighed and reached for their pistols that were strapped to their waists. The pistols were as large as miniature rail guns, but looked normal-sized in the grip of the large power-armoured fists. The dignitaries and their followers quietened for a moment, but then shouted louder.

Bill stepped down from the dais and picked up one dignitary and planted his oversized pistol against the man's temple, then waited for Doug to act. Doug dialled his power armour's external speakers to their maximum. "SHUT UP YOU FILTHY

WORMS." He nodded to Bill, who dropped the dignitary in a heap. Both men returned to their place behind the metal plate.

"Our own damn planet," Bill whispered.

"That Mr Eternal is one heck of a guy," Doug replied. He looked down the line of silenced dignitaries. "Poor sods. I'm glad I never changed sides."

"Same. What a dumb idea that would've been. I'm going to get myself a mini-glider and go flying around the arches."

"Good idea. Do you think the radiation zones extend to the far side of Lincoln's World?"

"I think the bots are cleaning up the area around the Sky-Arches. I haven't heard about the far side. Bit of a dump from what I've heard, so the Children probably didn't bother to bomb it."

"You two are horrible," someone at the back of the line said.

"Nah, we just chose the right side."

"Evil scum."

"Evil?" Bill said and shook his head, "because our boss gave us a planet for saving his life? Nah, we're just well compensated."

"Shut up or die," Doug said in a cheery tone and a wide grin before anyone else could voice their opinion. He beckoned for the first in line to come forward. "That's better. Next!"

Andrew P. McGregor lives in the rural town of Inverell near the East coast of Australia, working as an accountant. When not playing games with the wife and kids, he obeys his fishy overlords and goes to war against the cat. He writes science fiction and dark fantasy short stories, most of which are included in the 'Tales of Starships & Apocalypse' series of collections. He is also working on the fifth book in his 'Shellworld Conflict' series, and has contributed to the 'Persolus Race' Anthology, among other projects.

A New Kind Of Hunger

by Melissa Ferguson

A rat flew past Crimson's shoulder and splattered on the brick wall behind her.

"Careful, Merce."

"My guts are churning. That one's gonna make me gush from both ends." Mercy wiped her bloody mouth with the back of her hand.

"You eating or what?" Letty chased a well-fed, adult rodent through piles of cardboard.

"I had a couple earlier," Crimson lied.

"I must've missed it." Mercy and Letty shared a suspicious look.

Crimson couldn't explain to her sisters that she liked it when her stomach was as small and numb as the rest of her. That she would rather be hungry than nauseated or feverish from tainted rat blood. She'd accepted that the three of them would never understand each other. They weren't even really sisters. They didn't have the same surrogate mother or genetic donors. She would barely even call them her friends. Yet, according to the professor, they were her support network.

Letty touched Crimson's hand gently. In contrast to Mercy's sharp features, she had a round face that infused her every word and action with innocence. "Aren't you hungry?"

Crimson shook her off. They were always hungry. City rats were the wily, aggressive cousins of the lab rats they'd grown up with.

"You need to keep up your strength, Crims."

"Fine."

Crimson pounced on a scrawny specimen with greasy-looking fur. She held it by the neck to prevent it biting her hand and pierced its back with her sharp canines.

Fleas jumped from the dying animal into her short black hair. Now they were the ones abandoning the sinking ship. Although the whole city was a sinking ship and the rats seemed to flock to it rather than the other way around.

She dropped the drained rodent onto the buckled and cracking asphalt and kicked it beneath the bin. They were supposed to collect the carcasses in yellow biohazard bags and drop them off at the city sanitation depot, but the bags had run out after six months and no one had come to replace them.

Since leaving the institute two years earlier, no one had come to them for anything at all.

#

On the morning of her last day at the institute Crimson and her sisters had joined the breakfast queue in the cafeteria. She'd opened her mouth to speak and then hesitated. Was it even worth bothering?

"So, how are you feeling about finally getting out of here?" she said in a single rush of breath.

Mercy ignored her and Letty had bent over to tie her shoe at the exact moment she'd spoken. It probably wasn't worth it, but she couldn't start this new stage of their life with Mercy winning a petty power game.

She stepped in front of Mercy and raised her voice. "I was just asking how you're feeling about finally getting out of here."

Mercy rolled her eyes. "It's the professor's decision. What can I do about it? No point moaning about how long it took or getting worked up or whatever."

"No, I'm not moaning…"

Yet again, Mercy had (purposefully?) twisted her words. Whenever they spoke it was as though two separate conversations were happening in different languages, and no adjustments on Crimson's part ever made any difference.

"What do you think the city will be like?" Letty asked.

She often asked questions Crimson didn't know how to answer. The city was vague and mysterious in her mind. All she'd ever known was the institute, which was like a cold, emotionless machine with many interconnected, moving parts. She expected the city would have many more moving parts, and, hopefully, more warmth and feeling. Letty would look at her blankly if she even tried to put all that into words.

"We'll soon find out," Crimson eventually said, and Letty lost interest in her once more.

At the cafeteria counter Mrs Darla aimed her scanner at Crimson's left retina. After a short rumble, a box appeared in the meal chute. For as long as she could remember, Mrs Darla, or Mr Bobby or Ms Jenna, had handed her a warm, jiggling box of food three times a day. This would be her last such meal. And perhaps the only meal she would remember distinctly. All the others blurred and melded into one composite memory.

"Wait a sec. I have a little something for you." Mrs Darla retrieved a small brown paper parcel from beneath the counter and slid it across. "Be careful out there. There are some real assholes in the city."

Crimson didn't ask what she meant by that. She preferred to hold onto her expectation that the city would welcome them and shuffle its goings on, like subjects at a cafeteria table, to make a place.

"Thanks. I'll miss seeing you every day."

"You too, love." Mrs Darla squeezed her hands and turned to scan Mercy.

Crimson took her breakfast to her usual table. Young greenfaces took up most of the seats. All of Crimson's friends had come of age and moved on a couple of years earlier. Maybe they would be out there; Joan who ate her own faeces to extract all the nutrition from her sparse diet, Denny who slept for sixteen hours a day to conserve energy, and Sybil who made her own vitamin C. They would introduce her to all their city friends and invite her into their personal dwellings.

The greenfaces picked at their earthy-smelling bowls of muesli. They were less chatty than usual. There'd been rumours of a breakthrough in their photosynthesizing project. Their skin was already a vibrant, almost pulsating hue. It wouldn't be long before they couldn't keep any food down and were whisked away for the next stage of their treatment.

Inside the parcel from Mrs Darla was a pair of knitted socks. Crimson really would miss some of the staff. She tucked the socks into her back pocket. She wouldn't have to hide them under her mattress like the other small items she'd kept for herself over the years. They would be displayed openly in her new home.

She peeled back the lid of her breakfast box and six rats raised their noses to sniff the air. One of them stretched towards her, whiskers quivering. She took that one first and shut the lid so the remaining animals wouldn't piss themselves in fear at what happened next. The rat sat tame and comfortable in her hand. It only squeaked a little when she fed from it.

After breakfast, technician Ross intercepted her in the hallway.

"You need to come with me. Professor's orders." He winked.

"Of course. Anything for the professor."

He locked the door of a consultation room behind them and pulled her shirt over her head.

"I love the salty taste of your skin. It's like bacon or something." His chapped lips left loose flakes of skin, as colourless as his slicked back hair, all over her.

Crimson helped him free his skinny arms from his lab coat. She'd never tasted bacon, but she made an educated guess. "That's probably the excess salt from the rat blood."

He put a hand over her mouth and manoeuvred her onto the top of the examination table. "Don't talk." Once he was moving inside her, he said, "Bite my neck. Drink me."

She pressed her teeth against his throat. Blood pulsed through him the way water gushed through the pipes behind her bed. So close but out of reach. She could tear through his skin and into his blood vessels more easily than she could tear through the walls and the pipes. Her teeth were designed for that very thing.

She didn't though. It was just a fantasy of his. Only part of him really wanted her to bite him and only part of her really didn't want to. The part that told her it could kill him. Leave him limp like the pile of rats that built up beside her meal boxes. And of course, there would be consequences.

They both had to be content with pretending.

Afterwards he pulled up his pants and flattened down his hair. "Apparently the professor had to guarantee you'd behave yourselves out there before city council would approve your release."

"What do the city council people think we're going to do?"

He raised his eyebrows. "They're worried you'll start eating something other than small animals."

She scoffed. They feared her and her sisters? They were three women, not particularly big or strong, who'd spent their whole lives sheltered in the institute and didn't know a thing about living in the city. She didn't want to hurt anyone. She didn't even like hurting the rats.

"Well, goodbye and good luck, I guess." Ross reached for the door.

She swung her legs over the edge of the examination table. "Maybe we can meet up. In the city. After you finish work, or on your days off. Where can I find you?" She wasn't going to miss him or anything like that, but they'd had some fun and it wouldn't hurt to have another source of support out there.

"Not sure that's such a good idea. Good luck though."

"Thanks."

Crimson returned to the dorm to find her bed had already been stripped. Stains on the mattress chronicled the times she'd wet the bed or sweated out a fever. The indentation in the middle had deepened, year after year, to accommodate her growing shape.

Letty bounced up and down on her own bed and Mercy stared out of the window.

The technician with the unfriendly eyes came for them at midmorning. Crimson had hoped for someone kinder to deliver them into their new life. They followed him through the familiar halls. Familiarity was the only comfort the institute had ever offered.

They boarded a van at the front of the building. Nobody came out to wave them goodbye. As the van glided through the manicured gardens of the institute, the technician handed each of them a backpack.

"In these packs you'll find basics to get you started. Biohazard bags, clothes, shoes, a sleeping bag, some first aid supplies, and detailed instructions from the professor." He continued. "City council has agreed to your presence as long as you perform the duties the professor negotiated with them."

"What duties?" Crimson asked.

"You're to hunt and exterminate the rats that infest the city. Pigeons too if you're able to catch them."

"Huh." Letty looked as confused as Crimson felt. It was hard to imagine the soft, white rats they were fed every day needing to be exterminated.

"How do we hunt rats exactly? We've only ever gotten them out of boxes," Mercy said.

The technician shrugged. "The professor's theory is that if you're hungry enough you'll work it out."

The metal gate loomed ahead. A trio of ruminant subjects, on their hands and knees, chewed the grass along the edge of the fence. A first glimpse beyond the grounds of the institute hijacked Crimson's attention. She would always remember this, the way a single beam of sunlight cut through the blanket of grey clouds overhead, the screech of the gate as it rolled open, Letty's canines pressing so hard into her lips that they drew a bead of blood, the jolt as the van lurched into motion, and the film of sweat between her hands and the plastic seat.

She swivelled her head in every direction. The scenery blurred. The institute was surrounded by unkempt fields. Her fear that she would miss something important waned, only to return when buildings, neat and segregated by wooden fences, appeared.

"Houses!" Mercy exclaimed.

"They're pretty. Which one's ours?" Letty pressed her nose against the window.

The technician didn't look up from his phone.

The van driver caught Crimson's eye in the rear-view mirror and said, "Long way to go yet."

Every time the van braked Crimson thought *this could be it*, and butterflies filled her stomach. But the van continued until the buildings became larger and taller. The colours of the houses and their gardens were steadily replaced by grimy concrete. People atop two-wheeled vehicles swarmed around them as the van crawled along with the traffic.

"Maybe we're staying in one of these tall houses." Letty twisted her neck to view the towering structures. "Right below the sky."

Soon they would be amongst the throngs of people who walked the footpaths with purpose and belonging. Some of them looked kind and smiling, others more distracted but not necessarily mean or unfriendly. They could make friends in the city.

The traffic thinned and the high-rises gave way to stooped, hulking buildings.

Mercy banged her forehead against the window. "How much longer?"

"Not far now, girls," the driver called over his shoulder.

This part of the city was dirty and ragged, with broken windows and haphazard looking facades. Crimson willed the van to keep driving to another stretch of pretty houses. They didn't even need to be pretty. Clean, comfortable, and safe would do.

The driver pulled the van to a stop beside a broken chain-link fence. Tangled shrubs obscured the building behind. "This is it." He didn't turn off the engine.

"You sure?" The technician squinted out the window.

"This is the address I was given."

"Okay then." He slid open the van door and waved them out.

"Here?" Crimson hugged her backpack to her chest.

"Looks like there's a building on the other side of the fence. I'm sure it'll be better inside."

Mercy huffed and climbed out of the van. Crimson and Letty followed.

"Good luck," the technician shouted as the van drove away.

"That bastard," Mercy said.

"What do we do now?" Letty peered through the chain-links.

"Come on." Crimson stooped through a hole in the fence.

It had to be better inside. There would be someone to greet them and provide rats for their dinner, a warm bed, and a place to wash up. The professor had trusted they would work it out. They had no other choice.

#

"Oi! Bite my dick," a young man with facial piercings that sparkled in the orange streetlights, yelled at them from the top of the alley where they were feeding.

"Shit-eating bitches," added his companion, a young woman in athleisurewear.

Crimson tensed and waited for the pair to turn off the main road and reveal knuckledusters or batons, but they kept walking.

"Assholes. I wonder how they'd like it if I ripped open their necks?" Mercy pushed her stringy blonde hair away from her face. She often spoke of revenge on those who'd wronged them. She'd once boasted that she remembered every cruel face and one day she'd break into their homes as they slept and lap up the blood from their slit throats.

Crimson had never wanted to hurt anyone, but even she had to admit that some people deserved to be hurt more than others.

"Evening church service must have ended already." Letty scratched an infected rat bite on her cheek.

"We should leave before they come back with friends and weapons," Crimson said.

The area around The Church of Plenty, especially after services, was one of the most dangerous places in the city for them. But the blows could come from anywhere — even the most well-dressed and beautiful citizens.

They avoided the crowds, and the repulsive waft of frying food around the food carts that lined the streets, as they trekked to what Mercy liked to call their lair, in an abandoned warehouse on the outskirts of the city.

When they'd been dumped there, the inside had been littered with trash, rusted metal, cracked concrete, shards of glass, and pigeon shit. A small group of squatters had soon moved on when the sisters had begun chasing down rats and biting into them.

She'd been angry in those first weeks after the professor had flicked them away in the same way you'd brush a fly from your arm, without caring what they did next only that they didn't return to bother you. Each passing week without any contact only further confirmed the professor had abandoned them. She'd probably expected them to fail. And she'd been right. The rat numbers never seemed to go down. For every rat they killed, two pups took its place.

By habit the sister's journey home took them past the Overflowing Prosperity Charity Shop. Every so often the manager left a pile of clothes in their approximate sizes beside the back door. They weren't allowed inside because of their stench and bad manners.

It wasn't their fault they couldn't wash properly and had no access to clean clothes. It was like hating a person with broken legs because they'd fallen in a hole in the road. The city had proven to be a much crueller place than Crimson had ever imagined.

The store was dark and shuttered. As usual someone had ignored the 'DO NOT leave donated items on the footpath' sign.

"Ooh look!" Letty held up a stuffed bunny. "This one's going straight into my nest. Rabbits are one of the few animals that aren't extinct yet."

"Yes, Lets. You've told us all about the animal extinctions."

Crimson rolled her eyes at Mercy, but Mercy wasn't paying attention. She was squealing with glee at a box stacked with clattering crockery. Crimson rummaged through the pile and found a plastic bag stretched almost to breaking with books.

The moon was high by the time they skirted around the tip. Two underfed guard dogs bared their teeth and growled through the fence. Security had promised to shoot the sisters on sight if they found them raiding the hard rubbish again. Mercy kicked at the fence and Crimson bared her own teeth, which only incited the dogs into an even greater frenzy.

Back at the warehouse their heater had been stolen, for the third time. Letty got to work lighting a barrel fire.

"I'll shoplift another heater tomorrow," Mercy said.

Crimson smirked. Mercy wasn't the best thief. Her attempts at pickpocketing had been disastrous. Stealing required an ability to blend into a crowd and people were always on the alert around the three of them.

Mercy took her new crockery to what Crimson had designated 'the smashing corner' and pulverized it to dust with her taped-together cricket bat.

Crimson settled on the tattered couch and examined her book haul by lamplight. Mostly crime and horror. Not her favourites. Too close to reality. She preferred the escapism and giddy feelings on the pages of romances and fantasies.

At the bottom of the pile was a square hardcover titled 'Vampire Heat- A Modern Gal's Guide to Sexy Bloodsuckers.' Beneath the title was an illustration of a man with a black cape obscuring half of his face. Blood beaded at the end of his long canine teeth. His muscled torso was unnaturally shiny, as were his black curls and piercing blue eyes.

"What's that?" Letty looked over her shoulder and reached out to run her fingers over the glossy cover.

Mercy wandered over, twirling her bat.

"He's . . . handsome," Letty said. "Read it to us."

She opened the book. "Introduction."

Mercy and Letty flopped down onto the couch on either side of her.

"The history of vampires is intricately entwined with the history of humankind. Over the centuries they have metamorphosed along with societal fears and preoccupations. From repulsive and brutish creatures with their origins in myth, ignorance, and superstition, they have become charismatic, seductive, and intelligent symbols of forbidden lust and desire. Regardless of their current incarnation they are always monsters obsessed with the horror, glory, and sensuality of blood."

"Like us," Mercy said.

"Not really," Letty replied.

Crimson closed the book. "If you want me to keep reading you have to stop interrupting."

"Fine." Mercy leaned over and flipped the book open. "Go on. Not a word, I promise."

Crimson cleared her throat and continued. She read late into the night. Their eyes drooped and they took turns infecting each other with yawns until they reached the final page, where the vampire from the cover, his overly contoured abdomen in full view, had a thumb hooked into the waistband of his jeans.

"Can you resist your desires, or will you too invite a sexy bloodsucker into your boudoir?"

"Is boudoir another word for vagina?" Letty asked.

"No, it's like a fancy bedroom."

Crimson ran her fingers over the closed book. She'd heard the word vampire before but hadn't known what it meant, only that it was the name of a fictional monster.

"Are we vampires?" She said, more to hear the words out loud than to get a sensible response from her sisters.

Letty was horrified. "No way. We're not like them. Their hearts don't beat, and they live forever and never get old."

Mercy was more excited by the idea. "They're so sexy. People actually want them to drink their blood. They get off on it."

Letty kept listing differences. "We can go out in the sun, and we have reflections, and we don't need to be invited in anywhere. Just because we drink blood doesn't make us like them."

"Food makes us sick the same way it makes them sick," Crimson said.

"We should live like them. In fancy houses and castles. With fancy black cloaks and dresses." Mercy bounced up and down on the balls of her feet.

"Crosses don't burn us, and we can go into the church if we really want to." Letty retreated to her toy nest and sucked on her thumb.

"Imagine we could hypnotise people! Maybe we can. I've never tried."

"Why would we even want to do that?" Crimson rubbed her eyes.

"So we can drink their blood. Duh. That's our destiny. That's what we're supposed to do. Maybe human blood will give us all those other powers, like superstrength and immortality and even the power to turn other people into vampires."

"I can see the similarities, but I don't think we're the exact same kind of vampires as the ones in the book. They're fictional. We're real, but almost as monstrous."

"We're not monsters," Letty called out from her nest. "We're girls who were genetically engineered to revolutionize human nutrition. The professor doesn't make monsters she does alimental research to fight climate-fuelled hunger," she said, directly quoting from the professor's frequent speeches. "So, we can't be monsters. And in that book, all the vampire women have big bosoms. None of us have big bosoms."

Mercy laughed. "Imagine we drank human blood and our tits grew."

Letty looked down at her chest. "Do you really think that would work?"

"Of course it wouldn't work," Crimson said. "I'm going to sleep." She pulled an enthusiastic bedbug from her ankle and burst it between her fingernails.

Mercy squatted before her. "Just think, Crims. We could have everything. We'd be strong. Everyone in the city would be so scared. They'd do whatever we wanted."

"Goodnight, Mercy." Crimson pulled a blanket over her head.

#

At dusk the next day they went out to hunt up some dinner. Like the vampires from the book, they avoided sunlight. Not because it burned them, but because dark meant less people, more shadows to hide in, and most importantly, more rat activity.

The next stop on their regular rotation of hunting grounds was a high school. Mercy strode through the front gates, bold and cocky. Crimson usually preferred to avoid drawing attention to their activities, but she liked to fantasize she had been a student at the school and had wandered these very grounds with books in a satchel slung over her shoulder. Over there, by the bubblers, she'd had a water fight with her friends on a hot day and they'd all ended up reprimanded by the school principal. And here by the entrance to the canteen was where she'd had her first kiss with the most popular boy in school. She called him Thomas, after the love interest from a young adult romance she'd recently read.

They passed a lit window with a solitary silhouette, head bent to a screen. Crimson could see herself as a teacher here too. Her office would be beside this one and the two of them would work late each evening marking assignments and gossiping while they made hot beverages in the tearoom.

"Come on." Mercy ran back and pulled her away from the window.

The bins were at the back of the school oval. Mercy did cartwheels across the soft grass and Letty skipped. Crimson pretended she was a teacher supervising her boisterous students.

The shadows around the bins were unusually still.

"Where are the little bastards?" Letty got on her hands and knees and peered under the bin. "Here's one." She pulled a rat out by its tail. "There's more under there, but they're not moving." She brought it to her mouth and Crimson slapped it out of her hand.

"You know we don't eat them if they're already dead."

"I was just smelling it."

Mercy stooped to retrieve the carcass. "Smells funny."

"Why are they all dead?" Letty looked to Crimson.

Mercy and Letty had come to rely on the information Crimson had gleaned from books. Sometimes she liked being thought of as knowledgeable and wise, but often she found it exasperating.

"How should I know?"

She caught them sharing an eye roll, as though she were the one being unreasonable.

"Come on. Let's keep moving."

It wasn't the first time one of their hunting grounds had failed to yield a feed. Diseases occasionally went through rat populations, but they always bounced back.

The next site on their rotation was an alley between two apartment blocks. The rats there were dead too. With the same funny smell.

"What the hell is going on? I'm hungry." Mercy picked up a small box on the ground, frayed with bite marks. "This smells a bit like the dead rats."

"What's that?" Letty looked at the letters as though she had any chance of reading them.

Mercy handed the box to Crimson.

"It says rat poison." She flipped the box over, and quickly flung it behind the bin.

"Rat poison? That doesn't make any sense. If they poison the rats, then we can't eat them. Read it again," Mercy said.

"I know how to read, Merce. It said poison. A new, extra-effective formulation, evidently. Let's try The Harvest." She had an idea about what was going on, but she didn't want to say until she was sure.

By the time they got to The Harvest Hotel it was full of patrons onto their third, fourth, or even fifth drinks for the evening. Loud, raucous, and sloppy voices spilled out of the open door.

Letty liked feeding behind pubs because sometimes she found half full glasses of spirits, or bottles of beer forgotten while patrons groped or fought each other in the alley. Alcohol was one of the only substances, other than blood, that their stomachs could tolerate. Crimson was more wary and preferred to get to the pubs early, before drunks infested the streets near closing time. Drinking establishments were almost as dangerous as churches. Almost. Drunks were easier to evade than religious zealots high on nothing but their own God-given prosperity.

The rats behind The Harvest had also been poisoned. Three out of three sites. All in different parts of the city.

"I think we can assume all the rats in the city have been poisoned." Crimson leaned against the grimy wall. The city council logo had been stamped on the back of the box they'd found.

"What are we going to do now?" Letty squished a rat skull beneath the heel of her oversized boot.

Crimson had no answers. They'd already wasted energy trekking kilometres for nothing. They barely survived on the rats they could find when they weren't all poisoned. She couldn't imagine their life getting any harder. She only ever imagined better lives.

"Hey, hey, hey, yeah. Baby all right." A man sang his way into the alley.

The sisters squatted behind a stack of empty kegs.

He fumbled with the zipper on his pants, unsteady on his feet and soft in the knees.

"This is a sign," Mercy hissed.

"What?"

"We're not supposed to feed on animals anymore."

"Shh. Lower your voice."

"He can't hear me over the sound of his own piss and shithouse singing." Mercy peered around the edge of a keg. "Like the book said, only the weak feed from animals. And we're no longer weak. It's time for us to feed from humans. We're ready."

"You mean one of these drunk people?" Letty asked.

"They'll be easy. The really drunk ones are so slow. They don't even know what's going on."

"We'd probably get drunk on their blood too!" That possibility was enough to convince Letty.

The man shook, zipped up his pants, and yodelled his way back into the pub.

Crimson wasn't completely against the idea of drinking human blood, even though it would go against everything she'd been brought up to believe was right. The thought of burying her canines into the pulsing veins at a person's neck made her mouth water. If technician Ross's throat was in her mouth now, she didn't know if she would be able to resist.

She was tempted to break the tenuous and unspoken contract they'd made with the people of the city. The contract that labelled them as the weak ones to be attacked, and not the other way around. The city had broken the contract first by killing off the rats they subsisted on. What did they expect them to do when their food source was cut off?

They probably hadn't thought about them at all.

Still, Crimson had her role to play as the mature voice of reason. "I don't think that's a good idea. They'll catch and punish us."

"Not if human blood gives us all the powers of vampires. Then they'll fear us."

Letty looked between them, unsure which side to take.

"You know that's not going to happen."

Mercy tutted. "Shit." Even she didn't fully believe in vampire superpowers.

"Come on. There are some pigeons at the warehouse."

"Gross." Letty hooked her arm through Mercy's, and they trudged back to their lair.

#

A little over a week after the council had begun their rat poisoning campaign, the sisters lay in wait behind a pallet of empty boxes in alley beside The Rising Oceans Hotel.

Crimson had been the last to give in to the idea. She'd waited until the hunger pangs kept her from the refuge of sleep. Until she was sure the professor wasn't coming to take them back to the institute. Until it could no longer be considered a choice. Until it was an inevitable extreme weather event, like a bushfire or a storm.

The city had cut off their food supply and the professor had closed the institute gates to them. They were being murdered through neglect. A little human blood was small compensation.

It didn't take long for a victim to emerge. A dark shape obscured by shadow and distance. They would only drink a little. It would be like taking blood for a medical test. Everyone could spare a little blood. Some people donated litres of it to be kept in banks.

The man's face resolved as he came closer. A large, hooked nose, thin lips, a lock of hair on the crown of his head that bounced with every step. He was as real as them. And he wasn't alone. A young woman in tight jeans and fluffy jacket emerged from his shadow.

They were too weak to overcome two people. It was for the best. Crimson wasn't ready. By the time the next person came out she would be. She wouldn't look at their face. They'd be someone who deserved it. Someone who'd beat them up if they had their friends with them.

"The car's waiting over there," the woman slurred.

"It's okay. We're just going to stop here for a minute." He put his arm around her and hustled her deeper into the alley.

Mercy's muscles were bunched as though ready to strike. Crimson held her back and shook her head.

"What for? You said you'd see me to my lift."

The man's hand tightened on the woman's waist. "Just relax and let yourself have some fun."

If he was alone, he would have been perfect after all.

The woman batted his arms away and slipped out of reach. "Fucking pervert." She yelled over her shoulder as she ran.

"Cock-teasing bitch," he muttered and reached into his pants.

He was alone. It was going to happen. Crimson had already thought through all the alternatives and options and no matter how the wrongness of it nagged at her, the decision had been made. She'd promised her sisters.

"Let's get him while he's pissing," Mercy whispered.

Crimson froze as Mercy burst out from behind the pallet and, in seconds, had her teeth in the man's neck. He fumbled to stow his penis. The smell of blood activated Crimson and Letty and before he could zip up his pants, they were upon him too. He wore the same cologne as Ross.

There was so much more blood in him than a rat. Delicious and nourishing. It was like being thirsty your whole life and finally drinking clean water. He pleaded and whimpered, but in their bloodlust they had no self-control or empathy.

As the overwhelming pounding of his heart slowed and faded and the red cleared from her vision, Crimson pulled away. Letty wiped her mouth while Mercy pushed the man's limp body into the shadows. One of his shoes had fallen off. His socks were black with white tigers all over them.

"Tigers are extinct," Letty murmured.

Cheers came from inside the pub.

They ran. There had been more than just alcohol in his bloodstream. Or maybe it was the power of human blood itself. Soon they were skipping. Colours throbbed and shifted outside of the boundaries of objects and into some fourth dimension just out of Crimson's reach. Her aches and pains disappeared. Her body was no longer just the vehicle for her mind. No longer an endless source of turmoil with its relentless needs and ailments. It was hers and she would take better care of it. No more rat blood for her beautiful body. She emerged from the emotional suit of armour that had weighed her down all her life.

They roared like lions, the once kings of the jungle, through the nearly empty streets and danced from the orange glow of one streetlight to the next. An approaching man crossed the road to avoid them.

"Yes, be afraid. Be very afraid." Mercy bared her bloody canines at him.

The city was theirs. They would no longer hide.

"We're super vampires," Letty screamed.

A light sprinkling of rain glistened on every surface, like fairy dust. They smeared blood onto each other's foreheads and pinched each other's cheeks.

"Your skin is so soft."

"I love your face!"

Crimson had never felt so close to her sisters.

In the early hours of the morning the high of the drugs and blood faded. Crimson's muscles stiffened and her temples throbbed.

On the surface the streets looked deserted but from inside sleeping bags in darkened doorways, warm blood and beating hearts called to the sisters. They were now attuned to humans the way they'd once been to rats. They had changed.

Back at the warehouse they curled up on Letty's toy nest. Mercy stroked Crimson's hair, and Letty rested her head against Mercy's belly. Crimson had always thought she was better than her sisters. She could read and write and had been more respected by the institute staff. Now hunger had brought her down to their level. She hadn't lived up to her own expectations and instead of being disappointing, it was freeing.

Letty held a koala plushie above them and moved it as though it were talking. "I'm extinct, you know. Do you think that man's extinct now too?"

Mercy sat up. "We killed him, didn't we?"

"No . . . His heart was beating when we left." Crimson closed her eyes against a memory of his face in a pale, rictus of pain. "We're not killers."

There had been so much blood. All over them. Gushing down their chins. How much blood did a human hold? How much did they need to live? He couldn't have died. People didn't die as easily as rats. Someone would have found him and filled him up again with those plastic bags of blood.

"We need to leave the city," Mercy said.

She was right. They would come for them. Even if they hadn't killed him. They had attacked a citizen.

"I'm tired," Letty whined. "Let's go later."

Mercy slumped back down. "Just a little rest and then we'll go. We can travel from city to city and feed like proper vampires. We'll move on before they figure out what's going on. They'll never catch us." She gave a big yawn and curled into Crimson's side. "What do you think, Crims?"

"A nap can't hurt," Crimson lied.

By the time they napped, packed up, and decided where to go it might be too late. Part of her wanted to be caught. A homeless, roaming life, with no bed to return to sounded horrible and exhausting. It had taken months to work out how to live in the city and make the warehouse comfortable. Life on the road would mean never knowing what was going to happen next. Never feeling safe.

Back at the institute could be the best place for them. There wouldn't be the highs and ecstasy of drinking human blood. But they would never again be hungry, or cold, or sleep in a bed infested by insects. Never again be beaten by cruel strangers. She had thought of herself as a prisoner of the professor, but she was closer to a pampered pet. The freedoms of the city had proven overrated.

#

"Shit we overslept." Mercy woke them in the early evening.

Crimson stretched out her stiff limbs. The blood all over Mercy's face confirmed her memories of the previous night. She rubbed the edges of her own mouth and dark, dried flakes floated down like red dandruff.

"Nobody came." Mercy peered out one of the shattered windows. "I knew it. They're afraid."

"More likely they haven't worked out it was us." Crimson peeled off her bloody t-shirt and pulled a clean one out of a pile from the charity shop.

Letty uncurled and raised her head. "Maybe they couldn't find us."

"We haven't moved in two years. They know where we are," Mercy said. "They're too scared to enter our lair."

"Maybe the guy wasn't so badly hurt. Or . . . or . . . maybe he was so drunk and drugged up he can't remember what happened," Letty said.

Crimson didn't bother trying to argue with their faulty logic. She suspected the relief they felt was like that experienced after a painless injection. The side-effects were yet to hit. If the institute didn't come for them, the city police, or a lynch mob, would.

Letty opened her mouth to say something else and Mercy yelled over the top of her. "Whatever, Lets. We got away with it and now I'm starving."

Crimson felt it too. Hunger wasn't anything new, but this hunger was different. She'd assumed the man's blood would keep them satisfied for days. Instead, her stomach was stretched, hollow, and ravenous. It demanded backpay for all the years of substandard meals.

Mercy pulled on her runners. "Let's go and find someone to drink."

Letty looked at Crimson with her eyebrows raised.

Crimson could imagine and fantasize about a better life, but this was the reality. They'd been one step above the vermin until the city no longer needed them and they became vermin themselves. She let go of her hopes for the approval of society, or even a resumption of her life in the institute and let her sisters' optimism, and her own bloodlust sweep her along.

"All right." If she was to be a monster, she would experience the benefits as well as the shame. Her mouth watered at the silky, knee-weakening memory of human blood running down her throat. After everything they'd suffered that was their reward.

Letty jumped up and down and clapped.

"But—" She would also be the best, smartest monster possible.

Mercy groaned and Letty sank back down.

"We need to be more careful. We can't kill anyone. And the people we feed from should be people nobody is going to miss."

"Sure. Let's go." Mercy was already heading for the door.

"No!" Crimson yelled after her. "I'm serious. Let's think about this. We need to work out a strategy so we can't be identified. We don't want to get caught or beaten up."

Despite what Mercy imagined, they weren't physically stronger than they'd been before they'd tasted human blood.

"Wait." Mercy stopped by the door with her ear cocked. There was a clatter of footsteps on corrugated metal. "Someone's outside."

Letty turned off the lamp and Mercy scrambled back from the door. Occasionally strangers turned up at the warehouse to take drugs, vandalize, or explore. Sometimes they stole from the sisters. Most of the time they were harmless. But this could be someone come to avenge the man in the alley.

Mercy grabbed her cricket bat and Letty pulled a frying pan out from beside her toy nest. Crimson fetched the steel bar hidden down the side of the couch.

"Is this one of those food delivery services?" Mercy giggled.

"No! We can't feed from someone in our own home. What was I just saying before, about not being identifiable?"

"Jeez. It was a joke."

"Sh!" Letty clapped a hand over each of their mouths as the door creaked open.

The beam of a torch played over concrete, metal, graffiti, and debris before landing on the corner of the warehouse the sisters had made their own. Mercy laughed softly and leaned forward, poised to strike. There was a good chance this was a kid looking for somewhere to smoke a bong or do some graffiti. What would Crimson's sisters do to them? What would *she* do, once the scent of blood was in her nose?

"Hello? Crimson?"

She knew that voice.

"Ross?"

She'd almost forgotten about him. He belonged to another life.

"Technician Ross from the institute?" Mercy whispered.

"Uh huh. I think so."

Letty lit the lamp.

"Guess I don't need this." He lowered his torch and blushed, blotchy beneath his freckles.

He was smaller. Meeker than Crimson remembered.

"What are you doing here? Did the professor send you?" In two years, he'd never come to see her once.

"No. No, nothing like that. Wow, you're different. Glowing," he said.

She looked down at her shabby clothes and the dirt and dried blood in the creases of her hands. Maybe the man's blood had done something to them after all.

"Thanks."

She supposed she was different in other ways too. She was no longer that subservient girl who'd do whatever he asked, whenever he wanted, wherever he wanted. She'd been wrong to ever think she could go back to that life.

"You going to tell us why you're here?" Mercy swung her cricket bat around in lazy circles.

Ross held his hands up. "Okay, okay." He took a deep breath. "I um . . . I heard about a man. A man with his throat ripped out. They're saying it was a pack of wild dogs. All the abandoned pets are getting more desperate for food apparently, but I wondered . . ."

So, the man was dead. Crimson wasn't as shocked as she'd expected to be. His life should be on the consciences of the institute that had ill-prepared them, and the city that had left them starving. Not hers or her sisters'.

"What exactly do you want, Ross?"

"I've been thinking about you. Ever since you left the institute. I missed you, I guess."

"You gonna let him into your boudoir, Crims?" Mercy and Letty sniggered and whispered amongst themselves.

"Shut up, you two. I'm sure Technician Ross quickly found another naive, young institute subject to act out his fantasies with."

He moved closer and whispered in her ear. "I'm ready to let you drink from me. For real this time."

Blood rushed through him like distant floodwaters. Crimson licked her lips. She hadn't had sex since leaving the institute and the familiar smell of him sparked a throbbing between her legs. To combine sex and blood. That was what the vampire book had claimed the pinnacle of experience. She looked him up and down.

Mercy and Letty did an exaggerated tip-toe past them. "We'll leave you two alone."

"Hold on. Where are you going?" It had never been advisable to let them out without her, and even more so now they'd broken the taboo of drinking human blood.

"Don't worry. We won't get into any trouble."

"Bullshit. It's not a good idea."

"We won't go far. Promise." Mercy winked.

"Yeah. We'll stay outside until you two have finished." Letty smirked. "We *do not* need those images seared onto our brains."

They weren't completely trustworthy, and they never took anything as seriously as she did, but Ross's presence was overpowering. It wasn't often that what Crimson wanted walked up and offered itself freely.

"Okay. Seriously though, don't go far. I'm trusting you."

"Of course."

The door slammed behind them. It was a mistake, but she was tired of taking responsibility for their mistakes. She was tired of everything. She deserved some pleasure.

"Are you sure about this?" Crimson put her hand on Ross's chest. His racing heartbeat vibrated through her body.

"I've always been sure. I just knew you weren't ready yet. When I saw the reports about the man, alongside the news of the city-wide rat poisoning campaign, I knew you'd finally embraced your true nature."

Crimson laughed. "Embraced my true nature? How poetic. I think you've been reading too many vampire books."

"Heh. Maybe. But I really do want this." He placed his hand over hers.

For the first time in their relationship, she was the powerful one. He was almost begging her.

"Take your clothes off," she said.

His hands shook as he undid the buttons on his shirt. Piece by piece, his clothes formed an untidy pile on the filthy concrete floor, until he stood naked before her. The blood vessels beneath his pale skin fluoresced and pulsated.

"Aren't you going to take yours off too?" He reached for the hem of her t-shirt.

"No." She slapped his hands away. "And no licking either. I'm not your bacon lollipop."

"Okay." He lowered his hands in front of his crotch.

"Lie on the couch."

She ran a sharp fingernail down the centre of his chest and his penis swelled.

"Don't kill me."

She suspected reassurances weren't really what he was after. He wanted the danger. "I'll try to control myself."

She straddled him. "Don't look at me. Turn your head to the side."

"Like this?"

"Yes." The artery in his neck loomed large in her vision.

She rode him until almost the point of her own climax, and then leaned over and gently pierced his neck. Blood rushed into her mouth, and she clutched him to her as she came. A fog of red descended.

Somewhere far away someone yelled, "Get off me!"

Slowly the red faded. She returned to find him punching her weakly in the back. She pulled away and he tumbled off the couch, pale and woozy.

"Are you okay. Was that not what you wanted?"

"Stay away from me." He crawled over to his clothes and pulled on his pants.

"You can barely walk. Let me help you."

"I said stay the fuck away." He staggered to the door.

Maybe it wasn't wise to let him go. But he'd asked her to do it. He had no reason to complain to anyone.

The blood washed through her like a wave sparkling in the sunlight. She melted onto the couch. Smug, satisfied, and content.

In the early hours of the morning the hunger that had been submerged by Ross's blood, rose to the surface. Along with all of Crimson's worries and doubts.

Mercy and Letty should have been back.

She paced the warehouse and pressed her face to each window to create a fractured picture of the grounds outside.

Where were they?

The four walls were like hands over her eyes. She needed to see into the distance and get a glimpse of her sisters returning.

She stepped over a puddle of vomit outside the door. Ross? She hoped he'd gotten home okay. He'd run from her in fear. The way she'd run from him after the first time he'd dragged her into an empty room at the institute. But was he afraid enough to tell? With any luck he'd be too ashamed.

She walked out to the fence and climbed through a gap. The world wasn't yet at full daytime colour. She stood in the middle of the empty road, the soles of her feet caked with dirt and mouldering leaves. This early the city was almost quiet. The cars on the nearby freeway were distinct packets of sound rather than a single, droning beast.

Everything would be okay. Any minute now Mercy and Letty would appear around the bend in the road. They would be full of excuses. And they would *not* have a homicidal amount of blood on them.

Her stomach grumbled. This new kind of hunger had made her stupid. What would it do to her sisters who were already too reckless? She knew the hunger would coerce her into making even more mistakes in the future. It would wield her like a tool. Instead of elevating her to the status of the vampires in the book, it had made her an out-of-control monster.

Maybe leaving the city was their best option. They could find an abandoned building in another, similar city. It would take a while to make it comfortable, but it wasn't impossible. They'd adjusted once, they could do it again. It would be easier than the first time. No one would know them or their history. They'd be careful about where they fed and who the fed from. They wouldn't make the same mistakes in revealing their nature. They might even make friends.

She heard the police cars before she saw the first one cruise around the bend. Its lights flashed like the glowing accessories on the youths who flitted between nightclubs in the early hours of the morning. Those youths always looked so carefree and joyous, even after they'd spat at the sisters' feet. Drinking human blood was the closest Crimson had ever come to that kind of euphoria.

Mercy and Letty's blood-smeared faces stared out of the back windows of the first car. Had they led the police back to the warehouse and to her? Those two had been more like the weeds that infiltrated every crack and crevice in the warehouse and slowly pulled it down, than a support network.

She backed towards the fence.

"Halt! On the ground. Hands behind your head."

The gun was small. Just a piece of metal, like so many pieces lying around on the dirt. Still, Crimson froze.

It would be okay. They would take her back to the institute. Back to clean, climate-controlled rooms, and warm showers. She would be safe. There would be three boxes of clean, docile, disease-free rats per day. She wouldn't miss going wherever she wanted, waking and sleeping whenever she wanted. She wouldn't miss moments of privacy and the absence of painful tests and procedures. And she wouldn't miss human blood.

She swallowed the saliva that had pooled in her mouth at the thought. It wouldn't be okay. Now she had tasted something better, she could never go back. She couldn't let that indentation in her mattress deepen until it swallowed her completely. She couldn't be polite and subservient to those she wanted to feed from. They had created her, but they couldn't have her. She had evolved beyond their alimental research program. They were food for her now. They were the rats.

Let them try to destroy her like all the species they'd forced into extinction. Let them come with their blunt teeth. Or let them set sharp-toothed dogs onto her scent. At least that would be a fairer fight.

In the back of the police car her sisters nodded and smiled. She couldn't be sure what that meant. They'd never really understood each other. She memorized their faces and mouthed goodbye. She fled into the labyrinth of abandoned warehouses and piles of refuse until the sound of bullets faded. The people of the city would no longer only fear their own hunger. They would fear hers too.

Melissa Ferguson is a medical research scientist who likes to explore scientific possibilities through fiction. Her debut novel, The Shining Wall, is available now.

Misdemeanor Murders

by Glenda Thompson

Ava Dodkins waddled through the office, weaving between closely packed desks. She turned sideways to keep her colossal baby bump from colliding with her coworkers. Eight months pregnant and five-foot-nothing, she was almost as wide as she was tall. Despite the air conditioning, sweat trickled down her spine, soaking into the waistband of her stretchy maternity pants. *Freaking hormones.*

Panting, she reached her desk and dropped her bag next to the computer. She leaned against the desk to catch her breath. *Awfully hard to breathe when you have feet digging into your diaphragm.* A low level hum of voices and clacking keyboards filled the air.

The decibel level rose as more employees arrived, chattering about this and that as they clocked in. The scent of fresh coffee flooded the room. Her best friend, Savvie Nelson, handed her a cup topped with heavy whipping cream.

"Savvie, you're my hero." She took a sip of the coffee and wrinkled her nose at the sour taste. *Decaf. Yuck. Maybe not such a hero after all.* She placed the cup on the corner of her desk as she plopped into her chair.

"I saw that face. You know what the doctor said. No caffeine until the pumpkin makes her appearance. You only have to hold out two more weeks."

Ava pouted. "I know. Two more weeks of indigestion, cankles, and no caffeine." She placed a hand on her abdomen. The baby kicked—hard. She smiled. "After all these years of trying, it's hard to believe our dreams are about to come true."

Savvie held her hand above the baby bump and tilted her head to the side, asking permission.

"Go ahead."

Savvie pulled back with a laugh as the baby pushed against her hand. "I could see her move across your belly."

Flipping on her computer, Ava asked, "When are we sending them today?"

"This group is studying the second American Civil War. We're dropping them in 2026."

Tongue peeking from the corner of her mouth as she concentrated, Ava did a quick calculation in her head. "A hundred and sixty-seven years back? Just a hop, skip, and a jump, right? That shouldn't be too hard a trip." She grimaced. "I need to make a quick trip to the ladies'. She's tap dancing on my bladder today. Let me know when they are ready."

Halfway to the restroom, a torrent of warm fluid gushed down her thighs. "Savvie? Can you call Ron, please? It's time. Now."

#

Ava fought her way through the darkness, swimming toward the light. Her muscles cramped and trembled. She heard muffled voices, tried to peel open eyes that felt cemented shut. *How many drugs did they give me?*

Sorrow and empathy filled the doctor's voice. "So sorry… didn't survive. Nothing we could do… seeing a lot of this… seems to be a genetic defect, most likely from exposure to a defective version of the Lrdx1 vaccine."

"The one they forced on us?"

The angry voice belonged to her husband. She tried to reach for him, but her limbs wouldn't move. She tried harder to open her eyes. Her empty arms ached. She wanted her baby. *Where's my baby girl?* The words would not come. *Nightmare… I must be having a horrific nightmare.* As her husband's sobs filled the room, she drifted back into the darkness.

#

Ava curled her hands into fists. Her ragged fingernails cut into her palms, raising crimson welts. The baby's wails pierced the inside of her skull. *No wonder Ron left us.* The cries sliced into her brain, giving her a splitting headache. Or maybe, just maybe, her headache came from the pungent fumes of boiling bleach. The fumes coated her tongue with a plastic taste while burning her nose and the back of her throat like spending too much time in an over-chlorinated swimming pool.

Silver flashed as Ava stabbed her scissors into the belly of the fuzzy brown teddy bear she held and placed them both—the bear and the scissors—on the rickety formica table. Ava walked to the baby swing.

Drab gray paint peeled from the walls. Spots of mold lingered in the corners. She took a deep, cleansing breath but choked on the pale green-yellow gas slowly filling the one-room apartment.

She plucked her little girl from the swing and cuddled her close. "Shh, angel, it's okay. Mama's got you."

Juggling the infant in one arm, she pried open the kitchen window with the other and positioned a box fan to draw the fumes outdoors. The rattle of the old fan almost overpowered the baby's shrieks.

Swaddled in a unicorn-covered receiving blanket, the baby lay still, not wriggling or fighting the wrappings. Yet the shrill cries grew stronger in Ava's mind. Ava paced from one side of the bleak efficiency apartment to the next. She bounced the baby in her arms as she walked.

Back and forth she went, rocking and crooning nonsensical phrases. Still the baby's cries echoed in her head, an icepick jabbing at her tired brain.

Laying the baby in her crib, she crossed to the kitchenette and mixed a bottle of formula, warming it in the microwave. She hated using formula, but she failed at breastfeeding. The baby wouldn't latch. She sprinkled a few drops of the liquid on the inside of her wrist, checking for temperature.

Satisfied, she scooped the baby from the crib and sat in the only quality piece of furniture in the place—a hand-carved maple rocking chair. She liked to pretend her grandfather had built the rocker for her mother when her mother carried her. In reality, she splurged and purchased it at a second-hand store. Since she didn't know her family, her grandfather could have made it. Who knew?

The child refused to eat. Formula ran down her chin and pooled around her neck, but the wailing ceased. Rhythmically rocking and tunelessly humming, Ava tried again to get the baby to eat. No dice.

"It's okay, Baby Doll. If you're not hungry, you don't have to eat. Let's get you cleaned up. We'll try again later." She washed the baby's face and changed her, efficiently snapping the snaps up the leg and front of the one-piece footed pajamas. Silence drifted through the apartment.

Rubbing her temples to relieve the pain, Ava stepped over to the crib. Sweeping away a stack of stuffed animals, she placed the infant on her back on the thin mattress. The child lay silently, not squirming, not kicking. She stroked the baby's tummy.

Tip-toeing back to the kitchenette, Ava checked the boiling bleach. *Good.* Crystals were forming. She removed the pan from the heat to allow it to cool. In a chipped glass bowl, she stirred salt substitute into water until no more would dissolve. Careful not to spill any, she poured both liquids together and placed the resulting mixture into the freezer to continue cooling.

Sitting back down at the table, she picked up the teddy bear and continued pulling stuffing from its belly. She whispered a lullaby as she worked.

An alarm on her phone beeped. She set aside the bear she was working on and rose, brushing away stuffing and threads. Walking swiftly to the tiny bathroom in a corner of the efficiency, she changed into her work uniform and grabbed her badge where it hung off a corner of the aluminum-rimmed mirror on the medicine cabinet. *First day back to work.* She sighed heavily. *If only maternity leave lasted longer.*

She checked on the sleeping infant once more, whispering, "Be a good girl. Mama's going to work."

On her way to the stairwell, she tapped on the door to 3C.

The door opened a crack. Watery blue eyes framed by wire-rimmed glasses peered out beneath the security chain. "Ava, girl, is that you?"

"Yes, ma'am. I'm headed to work. Will you keep an ear open for Loretta? She should sleep until I get home."

"I'll be happy to, child. She's just a doll, never makes a sound. Don't you worry 'bout a thing. Your young'un's safe with me."

#

The clatter of a busy office screeched to a stop as Ava walked in the door. A hundred pairs of eyes focused on her. Heat flushed her face and chest. Savvie reached to meet her. Puzzled, she turned to Savvie. "What's up around here? Haven't they ever seen someone come back from maternity leave?"

"Ava, what are you doing here? Did the doctor release you?"

Whispers circled the room, buzzing from cubicle to cubicle.

Biting her lip, Ava rubbed her hands together as if washing them. "I'm here to work. Maternity leave only lasts so long."

Savvie guided Ava to an empty conference room. She pulled the blinds closed, blocking them from curious eyes. "Girl, are you still taking your medications? Are you sure you are supposed to be back?"

"Medications?" Ava fiddled with the charm on her necklace. "My prenatal vitamins? I stopped those after Loretta was born. Speaking of Loretta, why haven't you come to see her? She wants to meet Aunt Savvie. Please tell me you didn't take that jerk's side in the divorce. I miss you."

Savvie hugged herself, rubbing her hands up and down her upper arms as if cold. Her mouth opened and closed. She cleared her throat. When she finally spoke, her voice trembled. "Ava, you know the baby didn't survive. We've been over this. I'm not sure you should be back at work yet."

"That's not funny. How can you even joke about such a thing?" Ava grabbed her bag, clutched it to her chest, and backed away from Savvie. "Why would you say something like that? What is wrong with you? Loretta is at home in her crib. Mrs. Simmons is watching her."

"Ava…" Savvie reached for her.

Ava whirled around and headed out the door. "I need to go to the ladies' room. I'll be ready to work when I come back." She darted out of the conference room and down the hallway to the archive room. With a quick look around, she slipped into the computer room. *Empty. Excellent.*

Opening her bag, she grabbed her pad and pen. She looked through the notepad for her supervisor's password. Gabriel always jotted them on a sticky note beneath his keyboard. *Great security, huh?* Logging in, she began searching for the inventors and manufacturers of the Lrdx1 vaccine. She wasn't sure why it was so important, but she knew deep in her bones she needed the information. Jotting down the names and locations, she made a special note of the date—April 7, 2173. Shutting down the computer, she tucked the pad safely into the depths of her bag just as Savvie rounded the corner into the room.

"Ava, what the hell are you doing in here? You know we don't have the authorization to access these machines."

Ava clutched her bag. "You're right, Savvie. I shouldn't be here. I need to go home. Tomorrow I'll be back at work."

Savvie placed her hands on Ava's shoulders, looked into her eyes. "Ava, please call the doctor. I'm worried about you."

#

Walking in the door, Ava headed straight to the crib where her daughter slept soundly. *Hasn't even moved. Such a good girl.* She kicked off her shoes and stretched. The popping noise in her back and neck reminded her she had sat too long hovering over the keyboard when she snuck back into the office after everyone else left. *What is wrong with Savvie?* She caressed Loretta's cheek. *How could she say my sweet baby didn't make it?*

Swallowing a handful of pain relievers, she rolled her neck on her shoulders. *Worth every bit of the pain.* She pulled out her research and began making plans for a trip of her own back to the past. *Probably have to wait until this weekend for the easiest access to the machine. Can I do it alone? Would Ron help me?* She snorted at the thought. *Ron won't help feed his daughter. Why would he help me break the law?*

She glanced at the stack of unfinished teddy bears. Changing out of her uniform, she slipped into her coveralls and added a mask.

She retrieved the potassium chlorate concoction from the freezer. Setting it on the rickety kitchen table, she pulled out a bag of sugar. Digging under the kitchen sink, she pulled out four or five empty cardboard toilet tissue rolls. She placed these on the counter next to the sugar. That done, she mixed a fresh bottle of formula for the baby.

Once again, the little one refused to eat. Formula spilled down her front and pooled again around her neck. Sadness swamped Ava. *Why won't you eat?* She rocked and cried. *Suck it up, buttercup. You have work to do.*

Rising to her feet, she once again bathed and changed the baby before placing her back into her crib. After rubbing the infant's back, she tucked a llama-covered blanket around her and her tiny, unmodified teddy bear.

Ava gathered four or five of the larger teddy bears with their bellies cut open and stuffing removed and stacked them haphazardly on the table. She grabbed a bag of sugar along with the toilet paper rolls. With the tip of her tongue sticking out in concentration, she meticulously measured three parts of her homemade potassium chlorate to one part sugar into five separate containers. She grabbed the duct tape and closed off the bottoms of each of the empty paper rolls before filling them with the new mixture. She taped off the top of the containers and then cut a three-quarter-inch hole in the tape.

Hands trembling, she tucked one each inside the belly of a teddy bear and set it aside. *Murderer. That's what they will call me. History will despise me.* She focused on the crib—no cooing, no gurgling, no baby babble. Her heart hardened. *So be it.*

Ava walked to the bathroom and opened the medicine cabinet. Rows of glass vials filled with sulfuric acid lined the top shelf. She counted them. *Plenty to do the job.*

#

Savvie walked up behind Ava at her desk. "Whatcha' doing? Planning a vacation?"

Ava slammed her notebook closed and shoved it out of sight. A shrill giggle escaped her like birdsong under the overpass. "Yeah. Just a dream, though. No one can travel safely with an infant these days."

A concerned look crossed Savvie's face. "Ava," she spoke gently, "are you okay?"

Before Ava could respond, their supervisor walked up. "Ava, great to have you back, but if you ladies don't mind, I need you to get to work. We have an impatient group of anthropologists waiting in the launch room to get to 1859. Let's send them when they want to go PDQ."

#

Ava went over her plans one more time as she packed her backpack. *Teddy bears - check. Acid vials - check. Diapers and formula - check. Dang it, Mrs. Simmons, why did you have to go visit your granddaughter this Sunday?* She hated taking Loretta with her, but at least 2173 would be a short hop back in time. The trip shouldn't be too rough on the little one. She scrubbed a hand across her face. Maybe she could leave the baby in the launch room. Yeah, that would work. No one should be in the office on a Sunday morning and if she timed the jump right, she could go and be back before Loretta even realized she had left. She just needed to be gone long enough to right a wrong.

She moved back to the kitchen table and finished disassembling her rifle, tucking each component into the shock-absorbing foam cutout inside the custom case shaped like a guitar case.

#

Arriving in 2173, Ava took a moment to orient herself. She hated the way time travel ripped you apart, dissolved you into tiny particles, and then reassembled you when it dumped you out of the time stream. The church should be half a block up on the right. According to her research, Dr. Varicella never missed a Sunday service.

Wearing her backpack and carrying her disguised rifle case, she strolled along the sidewalk looking as if she hadn't a care in the world. She scouted the area, looking for an appropriate place to build her nest. *There.*

She climbed the shaky fire escape ladder on the outside of the building to the roof directly across and above St. Brendan's Cathedral. Pulling a spotting scope from her bag, she checked distance and range. Flags fluttering in the warm breeze helped her gauge windage. Content that she'd found a suitable spot, Ava climbed down the fire escape carrying one of her modified teddy bears. A vial of sulfuric acid nestled in her front jeans pocket.

She paused at the base of the ladder. Voices raised in song drifted toward her from the church. Seeing no one watching, she darted across the street to the cathedral's parking lot. She searched until she found the vintage luxury sedan bearing the vanity plates DOC V1, plates she had memorized when doing her research.

Ava opened up the teddy bear she was carrying and secured the vial of sulfuric acid upside down on the toilet paper roll inside so the cork filled the hole cut in the duct tape. She opened the vehicle's gas cap to allow fumes to escape and tucked the bear against the rear driver's side tire. Glancing at her watch, she calculated how long it would take the acid to eat through the cork. *Plenty of time.*

Returning to her sniper's nest, Ava assembled her rifle and double-checked the bolt action. She settled deeper into her hide. *Patience is a virtue.* She pursed her lips and fiddled with the charm on her necklace. Her internal temperature crept upward. Music from the Sunday service continued to float on the breeze. She blew out a breath and waited. If she had timed it, ignition would occur just as services ended.

In a rare and fleeting moment of clarity, Ava remembered why she was here. Her obstetrician's voice echoed in her head. *Genetic defect. Vaccine Lrxd1. Her sweet baby girl never drew her first breath.* She had to stop the vaccine. *Murderer. Who do you think you are? Who gave you the right to play God?*

She chewed on her lower lip. Yes, murder was wrong, but what was the weight of one life against many? She had to stop the death it brought with it. Pain stabbed through her chest. Her empty arms ached for the feel of a squirming infant she had never held. The agony was too much. Her mind escaped back into her fantasy world. In her world, Loretta napped in her stroller in the launch room, patiently awaiting her mother's return.

Grinding her molars, Ava's lips flattened against her teeth. The muscle in her cheek jumped. She placed the rifle in her lap and shook out her hands. The sun sank beneath the horizon, washing the world in blood-red light. Across the street, halogen lights flared to life, flooding the parking lot with bright white light and dancing shadows. *Soon.*

She picked up her weapon, the composite stock of the rifle rested cool against her cheek. She snugged the butt tighter to her shoulder and waited. Adrenaline cascaded through her body, swamping her limbs with a low-voltage electrical hum.

The door to the church swung open and children rushed down the steps, followed more sedately by their parents and grandparents. As the crowd reached the parking lot, a flash of green fire exploded from the stuffed bear. Gas fumes flashed. The targeted vehicle caught fire. Dr. Varicella, the man responsible for the creation of Lrdx1, rushed to his car.

Lining the scope up on the temple of the silver-haired man, Ava inhaled deeply. She exhaled and gently squeezed the trigger. She watched through the scope as the man's head exploded.

Chaos erupted in the parking lot. Screams of panic accompanied people running—a few toward the doctor, the majority away from him. Mothers grabbed children and pulled them away. Everyone pulled out a cellphone. Some called 9-1-1 while others filmed the dead man.

Hands calm, Ava efficiently broke down her service weapon, stowing it away as she had done many times during her mandatory military service. On autopilot, she gathered her backpack and made sure no sign of her presence existed before she decamped. Inside, her brain screamed, racked with guilt. Her throat thickened as she choked back nausea. *It had to be done. It had to be done.* She repeated that mantra on a loop. Pressing her return button, she felt the time stream suck her in.

#

Tiredness sank into Ava's bones, but it was a good tired. A lightness filled her chest. Dr. Varicella was gone. *Success!* She leaned back against the elevator wall, at ease, and in control for the first time in months. The elevator doors opened, and she stepped into her office.

"Ava! It's so good to see you." Savvie rolled up to Ava in a wheelchair and held out her arms for a hug. She lowered her voice to a sympathetic tone. "We heard about Ron. I'm so sorry. Asshole. I can't believe he left after you lost the baby. How are you doing?"

Ava stumbled to a stop. Folding an arm across her stomach, she stepped back. Her mind didn't even process what her friend was saying. "Savvie? What happened? Why are you in a wheelchair?"

Savvie's nostrils flared. She glared at Ava. "What the hell, girl? You trying to be funny?" She gripped the armrest of her chair so tightly her knuckles turned white. "Because it's not—not one little bit."

"Savvie, I—"

Savvie cut her off. "I've been in this chair since I was fourteen years old. Mandatory vaccine? Remember?" She made a sweeping gesture encompassing the entire office. "Side effects. Just like nearly everyone else here. Just because you are one of the very few who didn't react to the vaccine doesn't give you the right to make fun of the rest of us." She spun her chair and headed away from Ava.

Ava looked around. Her previous feelings of triumph turned to horror. Her new reality included an office of desks modified for easier access, braille markings on every sign, wider aisles, and bright colored vests draped on service dogs. Men, women, and children were all victims of this new reality she had created. *No. I helped. I HELPED.*

"But... but... Dr. Varicella couldn't create the vaccine. I stopped him. Savvie, wait. What vaccine are you talking about?"

Savvie looked back over her shoulder. "Doctor who? Never mind. You know the vaccine. Lrdx1. The one Viscount Maitor forced everyone to take at age fourteen."

#

Ava dragged herself up the stairs to her tiny apartment, trailing fumes of disappointment and depression. *How could I have failed? All that research. I was so sure getting rid of the scientist would stop the vaccine. How could I have been so stupid? It was never just one man.* Her eyes grew hot. A feeling of heaviness crashed over her. She dropped her keys as she tried to unlock her door. Tears filled her eyes. Finally, fitting the key into the lock, her door rattled as she turned the key. The door stuck. She slammed her shoulder against the door, accepting the pain as her due punishment.

She dashed the tears from her cheeks with balled-up fists. *You can only cry so much before your soul is dead.* Exhaustion flagged her steps. Across the room, no noise came from the crib.

I can't wait until the weekend to go back. I have to fix this now. Today. Tomorrow at the latest. It would be harder sneaking in while people were working, but she had no choice. Ava stuffed three teddy bear fire starters into a large, black vinyl garbage bag. She shoved three vials of acid into her pocket and grabbed a red ten-gallon gas can. She would stop and fill it with diesel on the way back to the office. One lonely teddy bear remained in the apartment's corner.

#

Retching, Ava threw up her lunch, meager as it had been. Traveling through time twice in one day was not recommended, and now she knew why. The world spun. The sidewalk beneath her feet wobbled like the deck of a ship caught in a storm. *What I wouldn't give for a meclizine tablet…*

She wiped her mouth on the back of her sleeve before reaching into her backpack for a lukewarm bottle of water. She rinsed her mouth. Spit. Took a small sip of water and waited to see if it would stay in her stomach. When it did, she drank deeply. Grabbing the trash bag and diesel container at her feet, she checked the GPS unit on her wrist and took off walking to the east.

Within an hour, she faced a multistory building clad in reflective mirrors. The sun danced on the glass, brilliant beams flashing into her eyes. A cloud slid across the sun. Ava blinked rapidly, resetting her vision. She had timed it right. All the employees, except for an elderly security guard, had left the premises.

Ava tucked her supplies behind the base of a tree across the street from the laboratory. She mussed her hair and tugged on her clothing to make it look as if someone had assaulted her. She rubbed dirt on her arms and the side of her face. Rushing inside the building to the guard, she screamed hysterically. "My baby." She pointed outside. "He grabbed my baby." Tugging the guard by the arm, she dragged him outside the building. "Help me. Please help me." She pointed down the sidewalk. "He's getting away. Please."

The guard raced down the sidewalk, chasing shadows.

Ava darted back behind the tree and grabbed her things. She tugged on latex gloves and covered them with leather work gloves as she wound through the building, looking for the laboratories.

Hands sweating inside the gloves, Ava poured accelerant on the interior walls of the building. She soaked the computer towers and pulled open file cabinets. Careful not to let the diesel splash on her clothing, she drenched the paperwork in the cabinets.

Unsure which projects pertained to Lrdx1, she opened glass boxes and smashed Petri dishes and vaccine samples to the ground, and drowned them in diesel. Humming Loretta's favorite lullaby beneath her breath, she placed the three specially altered teddy bears in a triangular pattern around the room. As she sat the third bear in a puddle of fuel, she glanced at her watch. Diesel fumes caused her eyes to tear up. Ava blinked rapidly to clear her vision and checked the time again. She calculated how much time she had left to get out of the building. She needed to pick up her pace. After a last look around the room, she felt confident everything would be destroyed. *This time I'm doing it right.* She placed a gentle pat on the teddy bear's head before she gathered her supplies and dashed from the building. The security guard was nowhere in sight.

Once she cleared the building, she pressed her return button, knowing she was taking an enormous risk. Her arrival back in time would be right in the middle of the workday. The office would be packed to the brim, but she couldn't help it. Her stomach clenched as the time stream once more ripped her apart.

She landed on her knees in the middle of the launching room. Silence closed in on her. A musty odor warned her something was dreadfully wrong. As the room stopped spinning, she stood. Unsteady on her feet, she lurched from the room. The gratefulness she felt upon arrival faded, replaced with an uneasy fear.

Where is everyone? At this time of day, there should be at least eighty-five people scrambling about. And that didn't include the anthropologists and archaeologists who should be impatiently waiting to be transported to whenever their research demanded.

Ava wandered from empty room to empty room. Fluorescent lights flickered overhead. A layer of dust covered everything. The whoosh of the air conditioner kicking on sent chills across her skin. Cotton filled her mouth. She craved a drink of anything wet. Her chest tightened. The echo of her footsteps haunted her.

In the building's foyer, answers waited. There, in the middle of the smoke-veined white marble wall, a copper plaque proclaimed "A man's body dies, but his deeds live forever." Beneath the plaque hung row after row of photographs of former employees, along with labels listing their name, date of birth, achievements, date and cause of death. Nearly eighty-five of her coworkers stared at her from the wall. Running her fingers across the photos, she scanned the causes of death—tuberculosis, Zika, Nipah, Lassa, Middle East Respiratory Syndrome. The list went on: all diseases that vaccines had eliminated through the years. *How could this have happened?*

Ava screamed and dropped to her knees in anguish as she found her best friend's photograph. Her fingers traced the outlines of Savvie's face. Savvie, her sister of the heart, her mentor, the one person who never gave up on her, is dead. *And I killed her.*

Darkness swirled around Ava, threatening to pull her under. The warmth of unconsciousness hid the pain. If she was asleep, she couldn't feel, but the guilt wouldn't allow her to give in so easily. *One more trip back.*

No one had ever taken three trips through time in the same day successfully—ever. Not even three trips in one week. At best, it could shatter her mind. At worst, death waited. It didn't matter. Sanity flooded Ava's mind, confirming the realization that she had to fix her screw-ups, no matter what. This wasn't the scientist's fault. The lab created more good than bad. She had to stop herself from destroying the future by jacking with the past.

Her mind whirled. Thoughts chased each other until logic settled into her bones. She saw things clearly for the first time in months. If she had never taken the vaccine, Loretta would have been healthy. If her baby girl had survived, she never would have gone off the deep end and murdered Dr. Varicella or destroyed his lab. She knew what she needed to do and if the third trip killed her, so bit it. *It's not like I have anything to live for anyway.*

Ava raced home and grabbed the final teddy bear. She couldn't take any chances with this one. Opening the bear, she removed more stuffing and replaced it with fertilizer. The fire from the potassium chlorate-sugar mixture should trigger an explosion. She just needed to get it close enough and hope it was big enough to do some good. If not, she always had her rifle.

She didn't look in the crib. She knew she would just find a plastic baby doll she had convinced herself was her daughter. A tear escaped and slipped down her cheek. *If I look, if I give in to the pain, I will never stop what I started. I'll live forever in a world that doesn't exist.* She scooped up the rifle case and a box of match-made 7.62 rounds.

Returning to the office, she entered the launch room once again. Lights flickered off and on above her. Hands shaking, she dialed the setting to 2172. If she went back before she made the first changes, this trip should erase them all. Praying it would work, she punched the launch button.

Excruciating pain ripped her skull open, blinding her. Cold water splashed against her face. She inhaled and choked on muddy water. She had landed face-first on the edge of a small pond surrounded by royal empress trees with gigantic leaves. The vanilla scent of the lavender flowers exacerbated her nausea. Rolling over, she spewed out a steady stream of bile. The previous trips had already emptied her stomach of what little food she had consumed. A thin stream of blood trickled from her right ear. An echo of her trainer saying the dorsolateral prefrontal right cortex of the brain is considered the region most involved in time perception rattled in her head. *No wonder the veins inside the right side of my skull feel like fire is blasting through them.*

The faint scuffle of feet and barking dogs alerted her to approaching trouble. Ava scrambled into the trees, searching for a place to hide. She clutched the teddy bear to her chest and dragged the rifle case after her. She didn't have the strength to lift it. Once sheltered by the trees, Ava pulled the acid from her pocket and secured the vial upside down into the tissue tube. She knew she wouldn't get another chance. *Tick-tock.* The time had started.

She tucked the rifle case beneath the two-foot-wide leaves as the rustling of the approaching enemy grew louder. Tucking her head into her knees, she rolled into the smallest ball she could.

Scenting her, the guard dogs bounded toward her. The Doberman in front of the pack skidded to a stop and growled. She peeked around the tree. The scruff on his neck stood straight up. Sharp incisors glowed as he snarled.

A man garbed in black tactical gear with a Sig Sauer 9 mm strapped to his hip and an HK-94 submachine weapon slung over his shoulder followed the dogs. "I know you're in there. Come on out and I won't set the dogs on you."

Ava held her breath. She curled in on herself and pressed harder against the tree trunk. Squeezing her eyes closed, she prayed he wouldn't see her.

The guard stepped around the tree. "Just because you can't see me doesn't mean I can't see you." He nudged her with the rifle. "On your feet, missy. Let's go."

Reluctantly, she stood. Clinging to the teddy bear, she projected a calm—if a little lost—exterior. Inside, her heart raced. If it didn't slow, she just knew it would explode. Knees weak, she leaned against the tree. She left the rifle case hidden beneath the leaves. *There goes Plan B.*

"Come on out. Keep your hands where I can see them. Don't even twitch. If you do, I'll shoot your ears off."

Ava stumbled out of the patch of trees. The sunlight intensified the pain in her brain.

The Doberman bared his teeth and stepped closer. A low growl vibrated in his throat.

Ava stepped back. The dog stepped closer.

"Zeus, heel." The dog returned to the guard. "Who are you, and what are you doing here?"

Her calm facade shattered. "I - I - um -"

"Spit it out, missy."

Holding the stuffed bear tighter to her chest, Ava slurred. "I need to see Viscount Maitor. Important. Very importa…" She collapsed to the ground.

Deciding Ava was no threat, the man lowered his weapons and approached her. Tenderly, he helped her to her feet. "Here now. You're bleeding. Are you okay?" He pulled a freshly laundered handkerchief from his shirt pocket and wiped the blood from her ear.

Ava wavered on her feet. "Need… Maitor… please."

"Ever hear of making an appointment? And why do you have a stuffed animal?" He shook his head and turned on his heel. "Never mind. Follow me."

Surreptitiously, Ava slipped her hand into her jeans pocket. She clutched her return button with a silent sigh. "Where are we going?"

"To meet Viscount Maitor as you wished. God have mercy on your soul."

A shiver of fear ran down Ava's spine. The hair on the back of her neck rose. Swallowing audibly, she brushed the dirt from her jeans and followed her captor.

The guard's heels clicked against the marble floor as he led her down a long hallway. Oil paintings of dour faces glared down at her from where they hung on the walls. Her apprehension grew with each closed door they passed. Finally, they came to a stop in front of double doors of carved mahogany. Twice her height, the doors, and what waited behind them, caused her to tighten her hands into fists and then relax them repeatedly. Her breath quickened. Her knees weakened. *This was it. My last chance.*

"What?" a voice growled in response to the guard's knock.

He took a deep breath as if steeling himself and pushed open one door. He gestured for her to enter before him. "Sir, I discovered this… visitor… looking for you on the grounds."

The man sitting behind the desk did not measure up to the monster Ava had created in her head. Thinning hair topped a pale face. Coke-bottle thick glasses covered rheumy eyes. The liver-spotted hand that motioned her closer trembled with age.

"Well, girl. Who are you and what do you want?" Only his voice contained the ferocity she imagined.

"Sir, please. Don't make us take the vaccine. The side effects…" She choked on her emotions. Clearing her throat, she tried again. "The Lrxd1… it kills people. It kills babies. It killed my baby. Please, sir, you can stop this. You can prevent it."

"Bah, what do I care of side effects? I'm not taking the shot. Do you know how much money I stand to make from the sale of those things? Well? Do you, girl?"

"But sir, the babies…"

"Why should I care about the babies of the riff-raff? One less mouth to feed, I say." He laughed.

How dare he? A roaring noise filled her ears. She lunged at him.

The guard stepped between them. He grabbed her by the shoulder and turned her to the door. "Time to go, missy."

No! Her mind raced. She needed more time. She had to keep Viscount Maitor talking, and she had to get closer. Ava no longer felt like a murderer. He deserved to die. Turning back to face him and easing forward a few steps, she changed tactics. With a fake smile plastered to her face, she asked, "How much money will you make from the vaccine?"

The old man chuckled. He looked at the guard. "Women. They're all alike. Mention money and everything else goes out the window."

While they were distracted, Ava slipped closer. She dropped the teddy bear at the base of his desk, hidden in the shadows. She hoped it was close enough. As the men laughed and taunted her, she kept her eyes turned downward. The timer in her mind counted down. *Now!*

A flash of green fire ignited inside the teddy bear. She jammed her thumb down on her return button, hard. A massive explosion ruptured her ears. A flash of heat raced over her just as the time stream sucked her in.

She landed in a collapsed heap on the launch room floor. The scent of singed hair and burned clothing filled the room. She lay there, trembling, unable to rise.

Savvie raced into the room. She kneeled beside Ava. "Sweetie! Are you alright? What happened?" She helped her friend to her feet. With an arm around her waist, she helped Ava limp to her desk. Savvie shoved an iced-cold bottle of water into her hands. "Drink this. I'm calling a medic."

Pain wracked every inch of Ava's body. Even her hair hurt. Fighting to keep her eyes open, she noticed a bright yellow sticky note on her computer screen. Laughter, tinted with pure joy, bubbled from her lips.

The note said, "Ron called. The daycare said Loretta is out of diapers. He will pick some up on the way home so you can send them with her tomorrow."

Glenda Thompson, a sixth-generation Texan, can 'bless your heart' with the best. A former EMT married to a Texas Lawman, she's used insider information to build her Broken world of Texas Rangers with dark secrets.

When not embarrassing family dancing on a country road, she's huddled in her writing cave.

Under The Fig Tree

by Lyra Meurer

Finally, with the efforts of their vast and tireless numbers, the skeletons chained down Rrendurra, the lost Great Dragon Queen of the West. She writhed her enormity against the bonds, her blue scales flashing like the ocean's heave, desperate spurts of flame shooting from her jaws. The struggle, the muddying haze of dust, roiled in the long shadow of a broad-shouldered mesa, a solitary stander in that blank red desert.

Reynauld Gerontiaux watched this last show from an opposing hill, sitting upon the throne he had reclaimed from the Kerum, the legislative body over which he had once presided as Royal Minister. The throne served no practical purpose, for he was dead. No heat nor need for water troubled his magically-preserved body, and his knees, held together more by his magical framework than muscle and cartilage, never ached for relief. He merely thought it unbefitting of his stature to witness history standing about on a hillside like some bumpkin. He wore a crown, did he not? A golden crown deserved the dignity of a throne, even if the throne's paint was faded.

Rrendurra gasped a final gout of flame, a vivid flag against dawn's dour twilight. Many fleshless hands took many weapons to her long neck, slaking the red sand with her steaming blood. With a final shudder and without much ceremony, Rrendura, that disgraced and forgotten tyrant, died.

With her death came silence. The skeletons fell still, brainlessly awaiting their next order, the wind whistling through their hollow ranks. Reynauld Gerontiaux rose, surveying the fallen dragon with pride. Rrendurra had long been presumed dead after her overthrow by her human subjects, but no — the threads of fate intertwined, surprising even him with the outcome. He, Reynauld Gerontiaux, the Terror of Ghabur, had the honor of discovering her location and killing her.

She wouldn't be the only titan he killed today.

Reynauld flexed his focus inward, making an adjustment to his reanimation frame so his voice emerged in enormous, rich tones, echoing across the desert and up towards the heights of the mesa. "Your last defense has fallen, Salsdmir. After years of hiding you must face my inevitable return. So comes the day of your death. Prepare yourself. You don't have long."

As the echoes bounced off the mesa walls, Reynauld imagined the final battle between him and his lifelong rival: the grappling of their minds, the whips of fire, the zoomantic oddities Salsdmir had cooked up in their years apart. Then, at last, Salsdmir's fall, the humiliations performed upon his corpse. Finally, Reynauld would prove the supremacy of his abilities beyond a doubt.

At Reynauld's mental gesture, the skeleton army leapt into action, mustering at the foot of the mesa. They folded themselves and stacked, limbs interlinking, a choreographed dance of clattering bone constructing a staircase to the top of the mesa.

Reynauld left his throne and ascended the stairs with the rising of the sun. Skulls, ribs, spines, shoulder blades creaked under his feet. He mounted the caprock and laid sight on the little castle built there: modestly walled, a single tower pointing like a finger accusing the sky. Advancing with a majestic gait, he drew magic along the leylines of his reanimation frame like pearls on strings, ready to unleash it on the gates to blast them down.

But the gates stood open. Reynauld faltered. "So, Salsdmir welcomes me," he said. "He welcomes his end."

Beyond the gates he found no danger, only a courtyard so explosive with greenery it shocked his sight. More surprising was that he recognized many of these plants. Some stirring deep within him insisted that was a willow weeping over the enchanted brook bordering the courtyard, that those were poets' narcissi eyeing him from the shade, and those drooping red inflorescences, gruesome as dangling guts, were called tassel flowers by some, love-lies-a-bleeding by others. And all over the crowding crocuses, the violets, the heavy-headed yellow roses, were the familiar markings of Salsdmir's magic: a neat, painstaking crosshatch, gentler than Reynauld had ever seen it, as if Salsdmir had dabbed it in with his fingertips.

Reynauld scoffed. "Well, Salsdmir picked up floramancy while he waited. A worthy pursuit for a coward. I'm sure his flower arrangements are beautiful."

Yet he stopped again, rolling his insensate foot bones into the pea gravel. He found himself feeling elsewhere-ish — but where? His sight landed on a congregation of ghostly snowdrops in the shade of a fig tree and a memory burst into his mind. Thought transmitted into words: "Emberneath."

That had been the name of the estate he'd been raised on in the rainy south, where the air reeked of dewdrops and flowers. Reynauld tutted to himself. That ancient memory hardly bore on the current situation, namely that this garden irritated him. Beads of magic became a liquid rush; fire gushed into his grasping hand. He imagined smiling, formulated words of triumph — only to be interrupted by a polite, peeping voice.

"Salsdmir will see you now."

A bird-like creature, resplendent in plum-coloured plumage, strutted through the pea gravel and stopped before him. It stood no taller than his pelvis and tilted its head, staring at him with eyes as large and unblinking as saucers, tiny, uncanny human hands knotted together in front of its chest.

"You're one of Salsdmir's creations," said Reynauld, flames fizzling out.

"Yes," it said from its thin yellow beak, throat feathers flashing and fluttering with the reedy efforts of its syrinx. "A birding. Salsdmir will— "

"Take me to him."

Unfazed, the birding turned around and strutted down the path, head bobbing with every step. It took a path to the left, leading Reynauld past a thriving vegetable garden in raised beds, over an arched wooden bridge, to the shade under a narrow portico. Without much effort, the birding opened a set of doors three times its height. Reynauld followed it inside.

Stalking behind the birding, Reynauld gathered himself, magic rippling through his leylines, uncertain which door or atrium might hold his enemy. In a similar way, he gathered together their whole sordid history, which began with a chess game when they were students at the Ghabur Academy of Arts and Magics.

It had happened in their first year, when the Academy buildings and the streets of Ghabur felt new, beautiful, promising. One of Reynauld's friends — Reynauld couldn't remember his name — had procured a keg of cloudwine on the cheap. Reynauld led the group in humorous toasts and drinking songs to general acclaim. They tumbled through the streets, loud and merry, to the coffeehouse near the Academy.

This was Reynauld's idea: there would be pretty girls at the coffeehouse, deluded into desiring the affections of some dour poet. Reynauld and his friends would show them that what they wanted was strapping, broad-chested masculinity. Reynauld's success was certain, for he was the handsomest of the bunch: carefully preened, fair-haired, with eyes like sparkling sapphires and the Gerontiaux family fortune tied to his name.

When they arrived, they found a few girls, who evaporated like water in the desert when the boys tested their charms. Clearly, they were fatally indoctrinated into the cult of poetic manhood. As Reynauld and his friends questioned this phenomenon, Salsdmir, who sat in a corner, looked up from his chessboard and challenged Reynauld to a match.

Reynauld didn't know Salsdmir well yet. They were just in the same zoomancy class, which Reynauld had to admit Salsdmir excelled at, in his own quiet way. He had no flair, though, and was terribly ugly compared to Reynauld, big-nosed and glum.

Reynauld accepted, though Salsdmir barely warranted his attention. Reynauld's friends and the coffeehouse layabouts gathered around to watch Reynauld gambit with flashy ingenuity while Salsdmir scratched his head in perplexity.

Reynauld won, of course. Then, for some reason, there was a fight. All Reynauld remembered was Salsdmir spawning a flock of monstrous bats, the coffeehouse owner yelling, fireballs flying. The coffeehouse burnt to the ground, and Reynauld and Salsdmir became Academy legends.

The story ran laps around the school, effacing even talk of the overthrow of Rrendura, the monstrous Dragon Queen who had oppressed and massacred her human subjects in the west. Nobody realized then that while the old guard of great leaders died off, a new generation was being born.

After years of schoolboy sniping, spells shot under desks, and elaborate pranks, the rivals graduated at the top of their class, Salsdmir with honors in zoomancy, and Reynauld with honors in pyromancy. From school, they branched into politics, ascending from governorships to the Kerum, where they could battle for supremacy in the field of legislation.

Before long, Salsdmir and Reynauld led opposing parties, bouncing the throne of Royal Minister back and forth according to the nation's political whims. They fought each other on every issue, from handouts during a famine to trifling laws regulating the uses of graphomancy. All along, they nipped each others' ankles — Salsdmir stealing and marrying Reynauld's fiancée, Reynauld assassinating her, Salsdmir assassinating Reynauld's wife, and so on.

Their rivalry, their fiery eloquence, widened a rift in Ghaburan society. When fighting erupted in the streets, devotees gathered outside Reynauld's mansion, chanting demands that he lead his followers in war against Salsdmir's heathens.

Salsdmir's and Reynauld's armies met in many glorious battles, leaving mountains of dead and swathes of magical destruction. The end result of the war didn't matter; the people turned on their former leaders and outlawed them both. Salsdmir disappeared into the desert on the back of the tortoise-like creature that carried his howdah, and Reynauld died.

It was the most obvious solution. He'd already created his phylactery and practiced necromancy on the corpses of the fallen during the war. The poisoning and actual dying were uncomfortable but went over without a hitch. He awoke in his phylactery, a mere grain of a soul, and swam from the bedside table to reinhabit his body. Enough people saw his corpse to think he'd committed suicide and truly died. He crept away while they celebrated in the streets.

He returned to the sites of the battles he and Salsdmir had fought, and raised the dead from their hasty graves with vast symphonies of magic. When he returned to show the populace what he thought of their celebrations, his death had only made him more beautiful — pale and terrible, the dread lich who would be forever remembered by the cowering masses of Ghabur.

It had taken Reynauld many years to track down Salsdmir's location in the vast, empty desert and many more to penetrate his defenses. Reynauld had faced hungry sands, magic-eating spells, illusions that soliloquized on the temptations of death, villages of zoomanced creations which fought valiantly, only to die and swell the ranks of Reynauld's undead army. Patiently, he had fought and puzzled through it all. Patiently, until now, the moment of his victory.

Stalking behind the birding, Reynauld flexed his magic and his abstracted, gutless rage. The birding stopped before a door and, grasping a low doorknob, pushed it open, leading the way inside. Reynauld burst through, knocking the birding off its feet and eliciting a startled chirp. He searched the room for Salsdmir, flames flickering up his arms.

He'd expected his rival to be standing, ready, spell in hand. Instead, he found an old man lying in a bed under a window. "Birding," said Reynauld, "I told you to take me to Salsdmir, not some random man."

"I am Salsdmir," said the old man.

Reynauld stared at him. He had aged, his face slouching off his bones, but that nut-brown skin, the strong eyebrows grown white and unruly, that pendulous nose — Reynauld had to admit he was Salsdmir.

"Come, sit with me," said Salsdmir. Seeing the renewed inferno in Reynauld's hands, he said, "Why bother destroying me? I'm not long for this world anyways. We might as well talk for a bit."

Stupefied, Reynauld let his flames die and shuffled to a chair beside the bed. He settled down with the clicking of exposed bones against the wood.

"You're old," said Reynauld.

"So I am," said Salsdmir. "I wouldn't recommend it. Aging isn't for the faint-hearted, though many must suffer it. I view it as my penance. I still prefer my choice to yours, though. That can't be comfortable either."

"You are a fool. I feel no pain. My body and powers do not wane. I will be indestructible forever."

"But can you feel comfort? Have you had any companionship in these long years?"

"I will be comforted when you are dead."

"Then what?"

"I can do whatever I please with the world."

"And what would that be?"

A squirming deep in Reynauld's soul. He hadn't thought beyond his moment of triumph, but he would rather have his bones crushed to dust than admit that to Salsdmir. He snapped, "I have as much time as I desire to decide that."

Silence fell. Reynauld stared at Salsdmir's cascading wrinkles, reaching for magic and the right thing to say before ending it all. Nothing came. He had a question anyway. "Rrendura," he said, "The world thought she was dead. She flew into the sea after she was overthrown."

"Ah, it's an interesting story. She faked her death, like you did. Though I suppose you didn't fake it because you did die, technically.

"In any case, it's a myth that dragons will die in seawater. She planned to start her empire anew, but, as she bided her time, her conscience erupted and wouldn't be silenced. I found her starving herself in the desert, saying it was punishment for the evils of her reign. I told her to come with me, to learn to better herself in the community I served.

"She knew she'd fight you someday. She said that when she inevitably died in battle, she would have cleansed her soul of guilt. I suppose she is free now, though I'd rather she were alive.

"I wish we could've done more but we've been hampered by circumstance and location. I fear my redemption will be incomplete. At least we have watched over what life is here."

Shut up, just shut up, thought Reynauld, flexing his creaky hands in an attempt to dispel the tension of his feelings. He said the first, most devastating thing he could concoct. "You've done a poor job of protecting your creations. Those creatures on the outskirts died and are part of my army now. The rest are soon to join."

Salsdmir's eyes had grown wet, though he didn't cry. "A mistake of youth. I thought there was no moral harm in creating people for my defense. I was wrong. Once they existed, I couldn't rob them of life. If you could at least spare the birdings, I'd die happy. I once thought I was their master simply because I created them, but they rebelled and taught me that I must serve their common good, as they do for each other. I have tried to learn from them. I would hate for them to be destroyed on my account. They are their own people, not my possessions. "

Reynauld scoffed, his emulated voice a hollow echo.

Salsdmir sighed and went on, "Before you do what you must, I want to say: I'm sorry we fought all these years. I regret it deeply. We could've been friends, and as friends we would've done good — for the world, perhaps, but also for each other. I dream of what could've been if I'd been less prideful. If I'd let you win the chess match — "

"I did win the chess match."

"You misremember. I did. You were angry to lose. That's how the fight started."

"No, *you* misremember, old man. You've gone senile in that flesh prison. My memory is as clear as ever."

"More phenomena than age can cloud memory, but perhaps you're right. Does it really matter who won?"

Reynauld didn't know what to say. That squirming in his soul, that tendril of doubt tickling the notion that maybe he hadn't won the chess match after all, hadn't won the war for Ghabur either.

His arm itched. He scratched at it, peeling up shreds of frail flesh.

Salsdmir, wet eyes overflowing, said, "Phantom body syndrome? I hear it's a nuisance."

Reynauld stood, the chair toppling behind him. "Why are you crying, old man?"

"I am sad, Reynauld, for many things. But also — I hope it isn't rude to say — though I have no sense of smell— " (Reynauld had never realized this. He remembered Salsdmir as a schoolboy, splashing him with a pot full of rancid leftovers without even wincing. So that explained it.), "—the eyes still react to a strong exudation."

Reynauld reached for the source of his fire, shoveling deep into his small collection of inwards sensations. He flicked his arm out to immolate Salsdmir, but nothing came, save for a glimpse of his flesh through his tattered sleeve.

Reynauld's gaze fastened on his wizened arm. When had he last spared a thought for the state of his body? He pulled up his sleeve and reeled back in shock. Under the desert sun, which persisted against every attempt to preserve his beautiful body, his remaining flesh had become a mottled mess of unpleasant colors, from moldering black and brown to green to sickly white.

Reynauld turned and ran. Shoving the birding away from the door, he fumbled his way through the halls until he spilled into the courtyard. He fell to his knees beside the enchanted stream, under the broad frills of the fig tree. His wavering reflection met him in the water.

Reynauld hadn't seen himself since he'd entered the desert; he hadn't taken any mirrors. Now he realized he'd left them behind because his reflection had begun to displease him. It'd been bad enough when his flesh went from pale to mottled, a perch for flies. Now, the face that wavered up from the water made him wish he could vomit. When had he lost his eyes and lips? How had so many of his teeth fallen out without him noticing? When had his crown sunk into congealed flesh, tangling with his last strands of hair?

Reynauld's sight jolted away from his upsetting visage, catching again on the phantom flock of snowdrops at the base of the fig tree. A plume of memory rose from his unexplored depths, sparkling with detail.

He had been a child, playing in the hedged gardens of Emberneath with his younger sister. She loved the snowdrops, so he pulled them up. She cried, so he threw a rock at her. The governess took his sister away, scolding him, leaving him to think on his actions.

It had been early spring, stinking of tulips — how had he forgotten this? How had he remembered it? He'd stayed outside and sulked amid the torn snowdrops, certain he was right, that he'd been wronged. Wasn't that the way the world worked? He was father's favorite, heir of the illustrious Gerontiaux lineage, a boy around whom the world revolved, before whom women knelt to wash his feet.

He tried to suppress the thought, but — what had been his sister's name? He'd forgotten she even existed. It didn't matter — but he wondered what had become of her. Had she heard of her brother climbing the ladder of a foreign government, leaving the rungs covered in blood? What might she have thought? Whatever she thought, Reynauld doubted she was surprised. Certainly she wouldn't be proud or impressed to see him now: a corpse, revolting to all who perceived him, too pathetic to figure out how to enact his pointless revenge or what to do afterwards.

Convulsively, Reynauld tore at the snowdrops. Up came a handful, white bulbs and all, their frayed roots still reaching for the damp earth. White, like bloated bloodless bodies with grasping, desperate fingers. He thrust the snowdrops back into the soil. The damage was done: their fronds were bent and drooping, their flowers bruised.

How many had fallen? He'd seen the bodies mired in filth, had killed those still clinging to life. He'd heard the wailing in the streets, had almost felt something, but told himself he'd been wronged, that he was right. Always that fleeting terror when he saw an emaciated form crouched by a fire or men pitching bodies into graves, bodies which would soon rise, clawing the dirt with rotted fingers. That deep, swift terror, too dangerous to touch, lest it unfurl all its incisive barbs.

Later, he used to tell himself, *Let me worry about it some other day, when this is over, when I have won*, until he forgot uncertainty existed. Now that self-questioning lunged at him, threw open his robes to show him for what he was: decaying outside and within, his beauty and desirability rotted away to reveal his emptiness, his memory hated without reverence by thousands who were just happy he was gone.

Reynauld tried crying. Distorted wails flowed from his magical frame, but, with no throat to burn from the efforts of weeping, the sounds felt meaningless. He beat his fists against the soil, but he felt only the impact without pain. He tore his crown from his head, and the remnants of his scalp came with it. The tearing of his flesh was just a sound, without sensation.

He threw the crown in the brook and the splash felt distant. Everything felt distant. His remaining senses of sight and sound were mere emulations, unnecessary for his survival. Unless his phylactery were destroyed, he would always exist, even if his bones were pulverized to dust.

What to do with these thoughts of guilt, these memories of his sister, his wives, his children, shrinking into themselves in the face of his abuse? What to do with the blood soaking his name? If death and pain weren't available, there was only one option: accept the lonely punishment beckoning from the desert.

As Reynauld strode towards the gate, a birding called out, "Salsdmir offers his hospitality!" The offer went unheeded. Reynauld emerged into the full spearing of the sun and descended the sepulchral stairs he had created mere minutes ago, when he was a different lich. He walked into the desert and, since he did not tire or sleep, never stopped walking.

#

Long ago, when he was young in his lichdom, he buried his phylactery in the sand. He didn't know where, didn't intend to know. He thought he'd never want to die. He'd thought victory would bring him happiness, never would've guessed it only offered emptiness, an eternity without purpose. He'd made his phylactery immune to all harm except that from specific spells. The likelihood of anyone finding it and knowing what to do with it was devastatingly low. He was assured of his immortality.

Now, with all the time in the world, he wandered the desert, day and night, in no particular direction, hoping his foot might strike metal and he'd discover, with unknotting relief, that jeweled box that held his soul.

He tore off his tattered robes. He relinquished the futile spells that struggled to protect his flesh from damage. Whenever he remembered the battlefields littered with corpses, how he had walked among them, laughing at the tormented faces of the dead and dying, he kneeled in the sand and scooped it up, grating it into this flesh.

Reynauld knew not the passage of time. He only hoped it would pass faster, that he would find his phylactery sooner, that he would be freed from his past foolishness. His flesh fell from his bones until he was naught but a skeleton, denuded and bleached by the sun.

#

One day, he spied shapes on the horizon. He hurried away from them, thinking they were a traders' caravan, but the shapes followed him. For several days, even though he lost them past the horizon at night, they always reappeared.

Finally, he had to admit they were following him. The kindest action would be to allow them to catch up. As they approached through the shimmering heat, he discerned several birdings riding on the back of a camel-like zoomantic creation with a dangling belly and the long swift legs of a wolf.

The creature skidded to a stop before him. The three birdings hopped off its back, their scaly feet splashing in the sand. "Salsdmir sent us to find you," said a birding dusted with white speckles. "He requests your return to the mesa."

Reynauld stood in silence for an uncomfortably long time; he'd forgotten his thoughts needed an extra thrust to make a sound. When he did speak, his voice came out too loud: "Why?" The birdings jumped, feathers fluffing with surprise.

"To help," said the white-speckled one, "He's close to dying, and wants someone to tend the gardens after he is gone."

"What use would I be? I have done no good in my existence."

"Salsdmir said you would say that," muttered one of the other birdings.

"He told us to tell you that neither had he for most of his life," said white-speckle, "He told us— " and the voice that came out of the birding's beak was a reedy reproduction of Salsdmir's: "'Endless self-punishment benefits no one except oneself. Harder than any punishment is to relinquish the idea that you alone are eminently punishable and instead decide to see what happens if you do better next time.'"

Reynauld stood so still for so long that the birdings looked at each other nervously. One of them cheeped, "Hello?"

"I'm thinking," he said. Thinking felt unfamiliar. All the cogitation he'd managed while wandering the wastes had been circular. To think of anything but his own sin, his own worthlessness, the bodies on the battlefield, required unprecedented effort.

"Will you come?" prompted white-speckle.

"Yes." He realized that, though he no longer needed sleep, he was exhausted.

#

Reynauld wished he could feel his heart racing as they approached the mesa, mounted his skeleton stairs, and encroached on Salsdmir's bedroom. This purely mental distillation of anxiety rocketed around his brittle skull until he thought his cranium might crack from the pressure.

Salsdmir laid in bed as he had before, now sallower, more sunken into his wrinkles. This time, however, Reynauld didn't stink enough to make his eyes water. Salsdmir smiled at his old enemy, and said, "I'm glad you came back."

"I don't understand why," Reynauld muttered, "Why would you want *this* back?"

"Because now you have the means to change. Did you intend to wander the desert for eternity, meeting no one and hating yourself forever? Would it have made you feel better?"

Reynauld said nothing, hanging his skull and staring at the floor like a chastised child.

Salsdmir spoke gently, "You carry a great evil, Reynauld, an evil as great as mine. I understand the impulse to punish yourself forever, but it's selfish. You must do better, even if it's the last thing you want to do, even if it's easier and feels more righteous to wallow."

"Is that what you did?"

"It was my intent. I wanted to help the world, but I had to wait until I had been forgotten so I'd be able to re-enter society without being cast out or killed. I waited too long. I got too sick to go back. I regret it. I've had to expiate my sins on what was at hand — helping the birdings thrive, learning to be their assistant and not their master. I hope it is enough.

"That's the advantage to your immortality, Reynauld. You have all the time you need to practice morality, to learn to serve others. When you have learned enough, you can return to the world and see what it needs, what oppressed beings need your help. You have an eternity to make up for your wrongs with deeds big and small."

Reynauld tentatively brought his gaze up to Salsdmir's kind face. "How am I supposed to practice?"

"The way I did. With help. The birdings aren't here to practice on. They have their own society, their own lives. Nonetheless, they've said they're willing to teach you and welcome your help. I haven't much time left. Soon, I'll be of no use to anyone except the worms in the garden. I ask that you remain in my place, watch over the birdings, protect them."

"You really think I can do this? You think I'm worthy?"

"If I could, you can."

#

For a long time, Reynauld thought Salsdmir had been mistaken about him. Only in retrospect, years later, did Reynauld believe Salsdmir had been right all along, even about the tempestuous and forceful Reynauld of those early days.

Reynauld was tasked with stewardship of the garden and the birdings' farms, which Salsdmir said would teach him about the ordering of living things, the value of providing the best care for each unique being, and cherishing all stages of life. Reynauld read the gardening books inattentively and slowly. He planted zinnias in the shade and set the potted fuchsias in the sun. He overwatered grape vines and pruned apple trees to death. When

Reynauld brought news of dead plants to Salsdmir, the old man diagnosed them from his bed and laughed, saying "There is a cost to mistakes. Be glad this cost is so small, and learn."

He was to study the birdings' ways and culture, to spend time in their village, which was on the mesa outside the castle, but he often missed his lessons to stand at the edge of the caprock, looking out into the desert and fantasizing about spells that might uncover the location of his phylactery. When asked to mediate the birdings' arguments, he succumbed to the drama, picked sides, made threats, flew into rages.

Slowly, he changed. He remembered what happened when he didn't water the flowers and learned to associate their wilting with guilt. He tired of imagining his death and learned to tell the birdings apart and call them by their names. Next came compassion for their experiences, a desire to help, and, with that, the desire to maintain a level head and care for everyone equally.

Salsdmir died a year after Reynauld's return. To Reynauld's surprise, he cried when it happened, to what extent he could. It was not a lamentation of his own immortality. No, Salsdmir had been his friend, he realized, a master of the strange alchemy that had turned their entrenched hatred into affection. "He believed in me," Reynauld muttered, while the birdings patted at his bones, sending comforting tremors through his reanimation frame. "He offered me forgiveness. No one else would've."

They buried him in the courtyard, and Reynauld grew flowers on his grave, a riot of colors, for sight was one of the last senses he could enjoy. Under the careful tending of Reynauld's magic, they bloomed year round.

The years after Salsdmir's death passed uncounted, and Reynauld grew into his routines, tending to the living by day and looking over the desolate land by night. The crown laid forever at the bottom of the brook in the shade of the fig tree, a reminder of what he'd left behind.

Generations of birdings rose and broke like waves. Each generation had something new to teach him. Surprising how, no matter how much time passed, he still had so much to learn.

Reynauld slowed down. Slow to anger, deliberate in his considerations, meticulous in his pruning and trussing, always aware of his infinite time. He knew he would have to re-enter the world some day, find his role in it, but the time never felt right. With the slow wisdom of endless years, he realized the time would come on its own. He couldn't force it.

#

Reynauld wove water through the air, turning it into a localized rain shower over the base of the rose bushes. He noted, with approval, that not a single leaf got wet — until the apparent shine of a droplet made him look closer. No, not water, but honeydew and aphids. His fingerbones combed through the leaves. Aphids everywhere, a mealy encrustation on the undersides of the stippled leaves.

Even a few years ago, he would've *tsk*ed, just for the performance of it, but lately even small affectations had dropped away, as his flesh had once left his bones.

He crouched there, thinking about how to improve his usual method of shooting the aphids off with concentrated jets of water, until the sound of someone stepping through the pea gravel roused him.

He looked up, wondering which birding had come to see him, only to jump in surprise when he saw a human standing above him. How shocking he found the human form! So tall, so naked of feathers, that tuft of yellow hair swooping from a head perched on a spindly neck. This human's shape was further distorted by a suit of chunky black armor, made of a material unfamiliar to Reynauld: matte, like painted ceramic.

The human pointed something at Reynauld, a long metal object with a glass barrel full of glowing magic, blue as cloudwine. "Don't move, foul beast! I have come to face your master, the evil Zazimir! Take me to him and you won't be harmed."

Reynauld cocked his head at the human. *Zazimir…Zazimir. Oh!* He laughed. "Do you mean Salsdmir? You're too late. He's been dead since…since I don't know. There's nothing evil here for you to kill, I'm sorry. Unless you wanted me?"

The human squinted at him, his heroic face falling into a frown. "Who are you?"

"Reynauld Gerontiaux."

"Who?"

"Reynauld Gerontiaux? Does that name appear in your legends and history books? Scourge of the…whatever? Slaughterer of thousands? Zazimir's enemy?"

The human shrugged. "Never heard of him. I know the legend of the immortal Zazimir, the sorcerer who came out to the desert with his riches, never to be found again."

Reynauld laughed. "Trust me, there's no riches to be found here. Unless you like fruits?"

"Stop laughing!" shouted the human, brandishing his weapon. "Do you know what this gun could do to you?"

"Whatever this 'gun' is, it won't kill me. I'm a lich. Unless you know where my phylactery is?"

The human grimaced his way through these thoughts, his weapon drooping.

Reynauld convinced him to come in and eat some food. After that, the human insisted on being shown everything to prove there was no treasure. He gawped at the birdings he met along the way, then called off the tour halfway through, conceding that yes, there was no treasure. Only then did they properly exchange introductions. The human's name was Pedredez, and he was from

Haboor, which Reynauld guessed was the modern name for Ghabur.

Sitting with Pedredez in the kitchen, Reynauld asked, "What is the outside world like these days?"

Pedredez described terrible and wonderful things — weapons that could shoot magic farther than any person, towers that touched the sky, levitating vehicles, the wealthy waging wars with their armies of mind-controlled servants, poor folks subsisting on nutrient pills. He had come on this quest because his family was on the verge of losing their housing. He imagined returning home with riches to buy them a new house and a grand feast of real food.

When Pedredez lapsed into silence, his cheek slouched into his hand, Reynauld said, "Well. I've heard enough."

"Oh," said Pedredez.

"I mean — for now. Enough to know."

"Know what?"

"It's time for me to leave. You have brought me a sign. Take me to your world and I'll see how I can help."

Lyra Meurer is a sentient muscle spasm with a restless hunger for writing. They live in Colorado with their husband, pet rats, and stacks of journals and books. They have short fiction published in Night Terror Novels' anthology *This is Not a Horror Story, Twenty-two Twenty-eight, Tree & Stone*, and *Cosmic Horror Monthly*.

The Family Legacy

by Sarah Lapalme

Viktoria threw open the door to her father's office, causing it to bang against the wall. She narrowed her eyes as she stalked into the room and glared at the man seated calmly behind the desk. He didn't even look up as she stomped forward. Viktoria was surprised he was up at all. She couldn't remember the last time her father woke before noon.

She slapped the note on the gleaming cherry wood desk and crossed her arms. She wouldn't be the first to break the silence. But her father kept scribbling in his ledger as if she wasn't there at all. She pursed her lips and continued to wait.

After several tense seconds, he sighed. He rested his pen on top of the leather-bound book that took up half his desk and removed his glasses. He pinched the bridge of his nose and closed his eyes.

"What do you want?" Disdain dripped off every word as he turned his bloodshot gaze on her.

Not for the first time Viktoria wondered why she stuck around. She could've moved into her own place by now. She surveyed the man before her, from his thinning hair to his skeletal cheeks. Her father was a disgrace. Before her mother died giving birth to her brother, Viktoria's father had been fierce. Not only had he been full of life, he'd been a force to be reckoned with.

Now, he was a pathetic old drunk. Her nose wrinkled in disgust as she held his gaze. Finally, she decided to speak.

"So, you've decided to play the coward. What, couldn't bear to tell your own daughter she wasn't going to run the family business she'd worked herself to the bone to be worthy of?"

Octavius crossed his arms, leaned back in his chair and grinned. "More like I couldn't be bothered."

Viktoria shouldn't have been surprised. Her father had shown her nothing but hatred for as long as she could remember. So, when his note was slipped under her door, she shouldn't have let it bother her.

Octavius's grin widened the longer she let the silence stretch between them. But for once, she was at a loss for words. Her father chuckled as he rose from his seat and strode around the desk. He took his time crossing the room to the door.

"Hunter doesn't even want the business! But I do. I'm more than qualified to run it!" Her heart sank as the words were ripped from her throat. She should've stayed quiet. Vulnerability was exploited in this family.

Octavius paused on the threshold, hand gripping the doorknob. He glanced over his shoulder and grinned. "I know he doesn't want it. He's not capable of running his own life, let alone this company."

Viktoria's pulse quickened as Octavius swiveled to face her. He studied her for a long moment and Viktoria dared to hope he might reconsider…until his lips twitched, one corner lifting into a smirk.

"You're not getting this company for the simple fact you want it."

Viktoria's heart plummeted into her stomach as Octavius sauntered from the room cackling. Tears stung the corners of her eyes. She clenched her fists and ground her teeth, willing them to recede. She was done crying because of him.

Her chest heaved as she let her despair turn to anger. She scanned the room, eyes unfocused until she spotted light seeping from underneath one of her father's bookcases behind the desk.

Viktoria cocked her head toward the open door, straining to listen for any indication her father would return. She figured he was probably a third of the way into whatever bottle he was currently favoring and would be passed out on the bathroom floor within the hour. But the silence pressed in, suffocating her in isolation. So, she swiftly crossed the room and closed the door with a soft click before returning her focus to the shelf. Not sure what to expect, she approached it with caution.

At first glance, it appeared to be an ordinary shelf full of her father's business ledgers, save for the light emanating from behind it. Tapping a manicured finger against her chin, she surveyed the piece of furniture carefully. She wondered if she'd have to tilt the spine of a particular book or pull a lever to get it to open.

She plopped into her father's leather chair to consider her next course of action when her eyes alighted on a small red button. Invisible when standing, it was painfully apparent from her current vantage point.

Eyes gleaming in triumph, she tucked a stray strand of her shoulder-length blonde hair behind her ear and leaned forward. She took a deep breath then pressed her fingertip to the button. With a gentle pop, the bookcase swung forward. Viktoria caught it and peered around the edge.

Her shoulders drooped as her eyes landed on yet another bookshelf. The longer she stared at the shelf before her, her brows furrowed deeper. Why was her father concealing these books?

Viktoria ran her hand over the spines of the closest tomes. There was no writing, nothing to identify their contents from the outside. She pulled one out and flipped it open. The musty scent of old paper wafted to her nostrils and the pages crinkled with age as she skimmed the words.

Viktoria's eyes narrowed the farther she scanned the page. She flipped through several more before slamming the volume shut with a snap. She let it fall at her feet with a thud before snatching another off the shelf.

Her lips curled back in a sneer. Her father must've finally lost his mind. Dropping the book from her hands, she pulled down another. They were all journals that belonged to her ancestors. Each one belonging to a different, and exclusively male, Payne, going back hundreds of years. And they all centered around some place called the Veiled Isle. The earliest one belonged to Judd Payne nearly 500 years ago.

They would've been fascinating if they weren't filled with ramblings about magic and some kind of power source on the island. Apparently, her family had been trying to fulfill some quest started by Judd to get their hands on this magical item. Supposedly it boosted one's magical abilities and allowed whoever possessed it to control people and thus the world.

"What a load of rubbish." Viktoria slammed the cover shut.

"What the hell are you doing?"

The book fell from Viktoria's hand as she whipped to face her snarling father. Octavius stood in the doorway, bottle in hand, gripping the frame, knuckles turning white. His lips were pulled back from his bared teeth and his eyes shot daggers at her. He dropped the bottle with a crash as he stomped toward her.

Grateful for the desk between them, Viktoria smoothed her face into disinterest and shrugged. She bent to retrieve the book and opened her mouth to ask him why he was hiding the ridiculous journals, but before she could say anything, he stalked around the desk and lunged for her. She stumbled, but he caught her wrist in his hand and dug his nails into her skin, causing the journal to tumble from her grip once more and land on her foot. Grimacing, Viktoria fought to free herself but her father's grip only tightened. She cried out as his nails drew blood. His eyes crazed like a rabid animal.

"I asked you a question," he gritted out as he continued to claw her flesh. Viktoria tried to pull away, but that only caused her more pain. She felt her skin start to prickle as stars danced in front of her eyes. She followed them as they flowed down her arm and over the skin of her wrist before bouncing to her father's hand. She ground her teeth together and met his gaze.

"Let go of me." To her surprise her father's eyes glazed over milky white. They unfocused as he released his grip on her and took a step back. He stood, arms at his sides, staring off at nothing and not moving.

Viktoria snatched the book from the floor, clutching it to her chest as a shield. Her eyes widening at the sight of her father. He was so still. What just happened? She couldn't wrap her mind around the conflicting images of her father trying to rip her skin off, and the one of him as a statue with clouded eyes.

She peered at her father's still form and contemplated how she had gotten him to listen to her when the phrase "mind control" invaded her thoughts. Judd's Journal. She pried open the book in her arms, remembering seeing those written on the page and quickly flipped through until she found the entry. She scanned the writing until she found what she was looking for.

I have found that I have come into the peculiar ability of mind control. With one

thought, I am able to get others to bend to my will.

Her head snapped up to scrutinize her father. Could she really have controlled him with magic? Was that even possible?

"Father, leave this room." Viktoria held her breath watching Octavius. Not even a muscle twitch. Her brows furrowed. How did it work the first time? She opened her mouth to issue another command but noticed his eyes clearing of their milkiness and coming back into focus. Her breath hitched as her pulse sped up.

If she didn't figure out something soon, he was going to tear her to pieces. Viktoria chewed her lip as she scanned the journal but she couldn't find any instructions on how to control someone.

"That's not yours!"

A small squeak escaped her lips as her father roared and made a grab for the book. He missed, his hand closing on her injured wrist again.

"Stop!" She winced as the pain in her arm intensified from the pressure of his grip, but his hand didn't tighten or loosen. She looked up to find him in the same state as before. Eyes misted and total obedience. She looked at his hand clamped on her skin and then back at the book. Near the bottom she found what she'd been looking for. Judd *had* left instructions.

It appears that my gift has its limits. In order to override the free will of another

I must first make contact with them by touch. They will follow every direction,

every command, so long as my hand is touching them as I give instruction.

Meeting her father's unfocused gaze, Viktoria squared her shoulders ready to try again.

"Sit down." Viktoria shifted as Octavius dropped into his desk chair. Her eyes widened. She did it. She had given him an order and he'd obeyed.

"Don't make a sound or get up, but release me." Octavius let her go before going still. Viktoria set Judd's journal down and began pacing in front of the desk, one idea after another whirling through her head, until she saw the note. That heinous note. Her lips perked into a smile.

She got out the necessary paperwork and laid it in front of Octavius before rounding the desk and placed a pen in his hand. She rested her hand on his shoulder.

"You're going to sign over the company solely to me. Full control over everything. Then you're going to return to your room and not come out until I tell you to."

Octavius tightened his grip on the pen before pressing it to the last line of the contract. Viktoria flipped through the pages for him as he signed everything over to her. Once he was done, he pushed up from the desk and exited the office. Viktoria stood in the doorway and watched him until he closed himself in his room.

Now that she'd put her father in an indefinite comatose state, she'd go through the journals in his office and find out more about this Veiled Isle and the power it contained. If she was able to control someone as stubborn as her father with her power, then she'd be able to get anyone and everyone to do whatever she wanted, especially if she had the immense power the island boasted of.

#

After several weeks, Viktoria finished combing through all of the journals in her father's possession as well as every piece of lore or literature on the island she could find. It wasn't much. It seemed there was some sort of secret organization that made sure the secrets and history of the island were heavily guarded. It took her several days but she had finally found someone who claimed to have an ancient map from the collection of the Queen that lived on the island when her ancestor Judd had been there. The man told her it contained labeled areas that weren't known to the general public. Viktoria hoped to uncover the location of the power source. She had learned only the Queen and her sister knew anything about it, and they'd been selective about who they shared the information with.

If this map was the true artifact, it would be well worth the trip to the godforsaken island she was on her way to in order to purchase it. The man had withheld his name, telling her he would only meet with her in person in the tavern he owned on some island she couldn't pronounce. She was instructed to ask to speak to the manager when she arrived and she'd be brought to him. She wasn't excited about brokering a backdoor deal with some creepy bar keep, but she had her power if anything went amiss so she wasn't worried.

She was uncomfortable in the broken-down pickup truck that was sent to meet her at the tiny airstrip. It rattled like someone had tossed marbles into the engine and there was no AC, so she had to have the window rolled down. She couldn't wait to get to her destination. Her sweaty companion was singing along to the radio at the top of his lungs in another language and shooting glances her way every five seconds. She debated making him drive himself off a cliff after he dropped her off, but thought better of it. While she'd grown dependent on her new abilities, she didn't want to do something so extreme. Controlling someone was one thing. But forcing them to hurt or kill themselves was a line she didn't want to cross.

Besides, she'd learned quickly that her power came with irritability and a low tolerance for disobedience. It was also a drain on her energy and left her feeling altered a little each time. However, using her abilities had become necessary in some cases. After she'd put her father into his comatose state, the staff began asking too many questions. She compelled them to forget everything they saw and seek employment elsewhere. She was now down to one loyal butler.

She'd have to start hiring and ensure their discretion and compliance once she returned, but for the moment, she let her mind wander to all the things she could accomplish once she acquired the island's power as the truck continued its bumpy journey through the dense jungle. She was just envisioning waking her father up to shove her success down his throat when the truck stopped outside a small building. Viktoria scrambled out of the vehicle and ignored the driver as she hurried through the door into a dimly lit bar.

She hitched her purse further up her shoulder and held her head high as she scanned the room. It was foggy as smoke curled toward the ceiling from several patrons' cigarettes. The whole place smelled smoky and stale. Viktoria's nose scrunched as she made her way to the bar and asked for the manager.

Twenty minutes later she was being led through the backroom and up a rickety staircase by a young man who looked barely old enough to shave, let alone work in a tavern. She frowned at the clothes hanging off his scrawny frame as she followed him up one step after another. Finally, they reached a scraped, wooden door. The kid knocked three times before pushing past her and heading back down the stairs. She debated calling him back and demanding he wait with her, but before she could do anything, the door was yanked open so forcefully she was surprised it didn't fly off its rusty hinges and slam to the floor.

Viktoria stifled a gasp at the behemoth standing in front of her. He looked to be about six four, and on top of that, he was built like a wrestler or bodybuilder. Any intimidation he could've had over her disappeared the minute he looked her up and down and licked his lips. Viktoria inwardly rolled her eyes. She was used to dealing with men like him, and this encounter wouldn't be a challenge at all. She'd have that map soon enough and she most likely wouldn't have to use her power.

The man gestured for her to enter and as she squeezed by, she caught a whiff of stale tobacco and sour body odor wafting off him. She resisted the urge to gag as she took a seat at the desk in the center of the room.

The door snapped shut and Viktoria tensed as the lock clicked into place. Her palms started to sweat as the manager lumbered across the room to take the seat opposite her. He leaned back in his chair and rested his hands behind his head as he surveyed her. His eyes twinkled with a menacing gleam as his lips pulled back revealing yellow teeth.

"So, tell me, what's a ritzy lady like yourself want with an outdated map of the Veiled Isle anyway?" He raised an eyebrow as Viktoria mentally kicked herself for the pantsuit she'd chosen for this meeting. She wanted to be taken seriously, but she could see now that this man wouldn't have respected her no matter what she wore and the suit was obviously making him question his decision to sell the map for the price they'd agreed on. She could practically see him weighing his options and mentally calculating a new amount to charge her.

"There's no treasure on the island, if that's what you're worried you'll lose out on. I'm interested in the map for purely ancestral history. It's for my family archives." She gave him a small smile hoping to appear meek, but he sneered at her. Viktoria edged back as he sat up straight and leaned over the desk. He jabbed his finger in her face.

"You expect me to believe that? I did my research, *Viktoria Payne.* Heiress to the most successful artifact recovery company out there." He spit on the floor to his right and crossed his arms over his chest. "You and your family are treasure hunters. You're quite famous on the black market."

Viktoria had to give him credit. He was smarter than he looked. She should've known better than to give him her real name when they spoke over the phone. She let the smile fall from her lips as she crossed her arms mirroring him.

"It doesn't matter who I am. You agreed to sell me that map and that's exactly what you're going to do." The seconds ticked by as her words hung in the air. The silence grew thick between them. Until the man dropped his arms and began to chuckle. He gripped his stomach as his whole body shook. Viktoria watched him for a full minute before he gasped for breath and wiped a tear from his cheek and met her glare.

"That's a good one. Tell you what, I'll be keeping the map and as payment for wasting my time, you're going to pay me the price we agreed on and then get lost." She watched as he pushed to his feet and strode around the desk to tower over her.

Tired of the charade, she reached out to snag his wrist in her hand. He jerked his arm trying to break free, but the familiar sparks were already bouncing along her skin and darting to him. His eyes slid out of focus.

"When I release you, you're going to give me the map of the Veiled Isle. You're not going to take payment and once I leave, you'll forget I was ever here." She pushed more of her will into her words as his eyes glazed over white.

A wave of exhaustion came over her and she released him. Viktoria watched as he did what she ordered. A weight settled in her chest as she rose from the chair and exited the office, map in hand.

Once the door closed behind her, she unrolled the map to make sure it was the right one and after confirming it, she rolled it back up and headed down the stairs. She couldn't wait to get the hell out of this place.

The tavern was heavily packed when she emerged from the back room. She glowered at all the people clamoring at the bar before sliding the map into her purse and elbowed her way through the crowd toward the exit. She was getting angrier with each foot she had to fight to gain when a young man slammed into her.

He apologized profusely but backed off when Viktoria growled under her breath. She shoved past him and the last couple of people between her and the door, marched outside and let it slam behind her. She gulped down the fresh air and peered at the star filled sky. Finally, the piece of the puzzle she needed to find the island's power source was in her grasp.

Feeling giddy, she reached into her purse to pull out the map, but her hand closed around her wallet instead. She pulled her bag around and grappled inside to no avail. Panicking, she dumped the contents in the dirt at her feet, giving the handbag a firm shake, but the map was gone.

Viktoria's teeth ground together as she scooped her belongings back into her bag, turned around, and tore the door to the tavern open. She stepped through and quickly scanned the crowd, looking for the young man that had collided with her. He must've stolen the map from her bag during impact. That was the only reasonable explanation for its disappearance. Glancing around the bar, however, revealed the young man was nowhere to be seen.

Her hands clenched at her sides as she tried to remember every detail she could about him as she pushed her way to the bar. The gawky man from earlier was gone. Replaced by a striking dark skinned woman with unruly curly hair hanging down her back. She gave Viktoria a cursory nod from down the counter before sidling in front of her.

"What can I get you, gorgeous?" She flashed a sparkling smile at Viktoria who under different circumstances may have flirted back, but instead she smoothed her face into a grimace and widened her eyes.

"I think someone stole my wallet. Have you seen a young man, maybe in his early twenties, light skin, spiky blonde hair, green eyes, come through here? He bumped into me earlier, but I don't see him now." Viktoria chewed on her bottom lip and forced her eyes to water.

The young woman shook her head, eyes downcast and swore under her breath. "That sounds a lot like Spencer. He's a frequent visitor. Always getting into trouble, that one. I'm so sorry, but I think he was on his way to the airstrip. Last I heard, he was heading back to New York. But you won't make it there before the plane takes off." The woman pouted at her and looked truly sorry but Viktoria was in no mood for pity. She thanked her before stalking outside, whipping out her cell and calling for her company's private jet. She might not be able to catch him en route, but he was heading to her city and she'd make damn sure she'd catch him there.

A week later and Viktoria still hadn't located the thief. He was a slippery one. He didn't leave much of a paper trail or digital footprint. There was plenty about his navy hero brother, Owen though. She'd just have to keep looking and if worse came to worst, she'd use Owen to lure Spencer out. Surely, he'd come to her if his brother was in trouble. That's what she would do if the situations were reversed, and it was her brother that needed saving.

As if summoned by this thought, Hunter appeared in the doorway of their father's former office. He leaned against the frame, arms crossed, smirk on his face.

"You look like hell, sis. How long have you been holed up in here? It's starting to smell like the dumpster outside of a coffee shop." He crossed the room in two long strides and plopped into the leather armchair across from her.

She couldn't help the smile that spread across her face. Her brother looked every bit the spoiled bachelor. Dark designer jeans, black boots, white t-shirt, topped with a leather jacket, coupled with his blonde hair tousled from the ride over on that damn bike she wished he'd never purchased. If it wasn't for his complete lack of a work ethic, he could've been a model.

"Nice to see you too, little brother. What are you doing here?" She cocked her head as she watched a dark look come over his face. It was gone before she could even open her mouth, replaced by a lazy smile.

"Can't a brother just pay his sister a friendly visit?" He ran a hand through his disheveled hair as she scoffed.

"He can. But there's more to your visit. Last I checked, you were shacked up with some red-head in the Bahamas. What's brought you back? Out with it." She tapped her red lacquered nails against the desk as he squirmed in his chair.

"Jameson called me. Now, before you get angry and fire him, remember he's been our butler since we were kids. He's been more of a father to us than our own. He was worried about you. Want to tell me what's up?"

Viktoria's fingers stilled as each word tumbled from her brother's mouth. She wanted to be angry that Jameson called Hunter, but she couldn't. Hunter was right. He was the closest thing they had to a family.

She exhaled, threw her hands in the air and began pacing. She wasn't sure how much she wanted Hunter to know. She'd wanted to keep him out of this, but unfortunately he was involved now. So, she told him everything, about the journals, the magic, what she'd done to their father, and what she planned to do once she retrieved the map.

Hunter hung on her every word and waited until she had resumed her seat to comment. "How can I help?"

Viktoria's eyebrows rose.

#

At first, Viktoria turned down her brother's offer, but when he suggested they lure Spencer out with an opportunity to steal a fabled treasure map, she relented. It was a good plan. Put the word out the Payne's were in negotiations to loan a priceless map to the Metropolitan Museum for a limited display run, leak the time and date of the delivery to the museum and ensure minimal security on the pretense of secrecy.

Viktoria had to hand it to Hunter. His ingenious plan worked. She had Spencer tied to a chair in her basement. Her thugs had brought him in late last night and she'd been stuck in meetings all day, so she hadn't had the chance to interrogate him yet. But the time had come. Viktoria would finally get her hands on that map.

She made her way to the elevator and pressed the button with her thumb. She rifled through the folder the client she'd just left had given her. He wanted her to locate some long-lost vase or jar or something in the Amazon. She hadn't been paying attention, her mind on the current occupant of the basement. She snapped the folder closed, unable to focus, and tapped her foot as the elevator finally arrived. The doors slid open but instead of being empty, a woman stood in the middle. A woman Viktoria hadn't seen since she was ten years old. Her beloved nanny, Amanda.

Viktoria sucked in a breath as she was immediately transported to her childhood. Amanda had raised her. She'd been her surrogate mother when Viktoria's mom had rejected her. She'd been her everything. Until she wasn't. Her father fired the woman when Viktoria was only ten. He claimed incompetence but Viktoria knew better. It was out of spite for the children he hated. The daughter he never wanted, and the son he blamed for his wife's death. But the worst part was, Amanda had let him. She'd left without putting up a fight. Viktoria had believed she loved her like a daughter. But she'd been wrong.

Now the woman stood in front of her, smiling gently, and all Viktoria wanted to do was grab her by her hair, drag her to the basement and use her thoughts to manipulate Amanda's mind into believing she was being electrocuted until she was breathless and unconscious, before tossing her out on the street with no memory at all.

Instead Viktoria pursed her lips and stepped into the elevator ignoring the woman who'd once been her entire world. The silence grew heavy as the doors closed and the car descended. It pressed in on her until she wanted to claw at her throat for air. The seconds ticked by as they made their way to the bottom floor. Viktoria wished the elevator would move faster. She wished she could bore a hole in the cool metal and hide there. But she said nothing. She forced herself to inhale deeply.

After another moment, Amanda cleared her throat and laid a hand on Viktoria's shoulder. Every muscle in her arm tensed. She sucked in a breath and waited.

"Viktoria. I'm worried about you." She gave her shoulder a gentle squeeze.

Viktoria whipped to face her, fire in her eyes and venom in her throat as she sneered. "*You're* worried about me? What a joke. You weren't concerned about me when you walked out of my life. Why bother now?" Viktoria jerked away, letting Amanda's hand fall to her side. She watched as the woman flinched.

"You don't know the whole story, but that's not why I'm here. I came because you're making a mistake in chasing down your ancestor's legacy."

Viktoria held up her hand. "How do you...Jameson." She pinched the bridge of her nose and closed her eyes vowing to deal with him later. First, she had to get rid of Amanda. The elevator finally stopped, the red light illuminating the button marked for the basement. She took a deep breath as the doors scraped open and strode out. To her dismay Amanda trailed on her heels.

"Viktoria, will you listen to me? You've become obsessed. This path you're on will lead you to nothing but ruin. I don't want to see that happen to you." Halting her steps, Viktoria faced her former nanny and glowered. She reached for Amanda's arm and wrapped her slender fingers around her wrist, letting her nails dig into the woman's flesh. To her credit, she didn't flinch as Viktoria squeezed harder. She clenched her jaw and ground her teeth together as she willed all of the pain, and all of the suffering she felt at Amanda's departure to the surface and let it seep into her arm. Sparks danced along her skin making a beeline for her hand, her fingertips, and finally sinking into the older woman's flesh. She watched Amanda's gentle blue eyes cloud over until they were nothing but white. A void, like the one Amanda left in Viktoria's chest when she left and never returned.

She let those feelings surface until she couldn't bear them any longer, until the hollow emptiness threatened to consume her. She steeled herself and forced them into Amanda. She watched as the blood drained from the woman's skin, as her jaw fell open, and her face crumpled. Amanda sagged under Viktoria's grip, her knees buckled, as if being crushed by an enormous weight that slowly pushed her to the ground. Her kneecaps cracked as they pressed into the concrete, but still Viktoria bore down on her. Not satisfied until the woman was curled into a ball, unmoving.

Under her grasp she felt Amanda's pulse slow to an uneven rhythm until it stopped altogether. Her eyes cleared of their milkiness but remained hollow and unseeing. Viktoria released her arm and watched as it dropped like a stone. She nudged Amanda over with the toe of her boot and knelt down to check for a pulse. There wasn't one. She knew there wouldn't be. She'd felt the life drain from her former caretaker.

She cocked her head to the side, her own pulse slowing as she peered down at the woman who'd once meant so much to her. She dug through her feelings and memories but couldn't for the life of her figure out why. What she did know was that she no longer felt empty. Where the void in her chest used to be, it now felt full like someone had taken a spackle and filled in the cracks.

Viktoria rose to her feet and pulled out her phone. She instructed the grunt on the other line to come get the body and toss it in an alleyway on the other side of town. When she hung up, she crossed the basement to the intercom on the far war. She called for Jameson and asked him to meet her downstairs. She exhaled as she waited for him. It was time to hire a new butler. Questioning Spencer would have to wait.

#

It wasn't until much later after the police and the coroner removed Jameson's body, convinced it was a suicide, that it all came crashing down on Viktoria. She slumped to the floor in the shower, warm water raining down on her, pelting her with the prickling truth. She gasped, her breaths coming in quick succession, unable to fill her lungs. Hot tears welled in her eyes and streamed down her cheeks, mingling with the spray from the shower. *I used my powers to murder. Two people are dead because of me.* She pressed her palms to her eyes until it hurt and stars flashed across her vision. She stayed like that, huddled into herself as the water beat down on her and turned cold. She wanted to stay there until the numbness overtook her. She felt it creeping along her skin and through her veins. She thought it would bring relief. But all it did was carry the pain away until she was a shell of herself, an inner voice telling her they deserved it. That they were interfering and would've stopped her. Besides, it reasoned, if anyone was to blame for their deaths, it was her father. He was ultimately the cause for everything and he should be punished.

The voice told her to get up and hold her head high. She had a job to finish. Her eyes slid out of focus as her heart hardened. She took slow, even breaths until her vision cleared. Viktoria got to her feet, turned off the water, and stepped out, ready to do whatever it took to fulfill her family legacy. But first, she'd pay Octavius a little visit.

#

Viktoria perched on the edge of the four-poster bed in her parents' room. She watched Octavius's chest rise and fall with each breath as he blindly stared at the ceiling. He looked so helpless. Her father, the man she spent her life trying so hard to please. To make him proud.

Her chest constricted as she reached out to place her hand in his. Tiny sparks illuminated the room as they danced between them. Viktoria closed her eyes as memories swam through her thoughts. The one responsible for every ounce of pain she'd ever felt.

"Wake up, father. Mother's home."

She opened her eyes in time to watch her father shoot up in bed. A smile that lit up his entire face appeared as he glanced toward the doorway. His eyes moved as he slowly turned his head as if tracking the progress of someone making their way across the room to his side. Tears streamed from his eyes as he extended his hand to cup the invisible cheek of the woman he loved above all others.

Viktoria concentrated on her memories of her mother. The more accurately she could picture her, the more real she'd appear in Octavius's mind. She must've succeeded since he appeared to believe she was truly present with them.

She allowed her father to drink in her mother's image a moment longer before altering it. Her mother's brow wrinkled as she pulled away from Octavius.

"You killed them, Octavius. How could you?" Tears leaked down her cheeks as she turned away from him.

His eyes widened. "What are you talking about? I didn't kill Amanda or Jameson. I've never killed anyone."

He reached for the ghost of his wife he saw in his mind's eye, but she moved farther away.

"Amanda and Jameson are dead. Because of you. You pushed Viktoria too far this time. You're a monster."

Octavius recoiled as if slapped. His color drained and his face fell.

"I didn't mean to make Viktoria kill them."

Before he could say anything more, Viktoria made the image in his mind shift again. A dark stain appeared on her mother's dress where her heart should be and the moisture on her face morphed into viscous trails of blood. Her eyes rolled back in her head. Octavius pulled at their joined hands trying to get to his wife, but Viktoria held him firmly in place as she made the image of her mother grip her chest and roil in pain as she sank to the floor.

"Your fault. Your fault…murderer. Monster. Can't love a monster."

Viktoria allowed that image to linger as her father slumped against the headboard, sobbing and reaching for his wife. His mouth opened but no sound came out. Viktoria smirked as she forced the thought into his head that he'd lost his wife's love as well as caused her death, instead of dying in childbirth. His hand shook in her grip as she watched the guilt and pain flit across his features.

Finally satisfied, she returned him to his comatose state, released his hand and stood up. She turned to leave but stopped short as she caught sight of Hunter lingering over the threshold. She took a step forward, but halted when Hunter flinched. *How much had he heard?* she wondered as she appraised him. He squeezed his eyes shut, inhaled and exhaled before meeting her gaze.

"Amanda and Jameson are dead?" He crossed his arms over his chest and cocked his head.

Viktoria remained silent.

"You killed them?"

Viktoria nodded slowly. She stared at her shoes, unwilling to meet his eyes. The voice was unusually quiet in her mind as she waited for Hunter to say something.

She heard him let out a low whistle and raised her head to explain. She watched him run a hand through his hair and for a moment, worried he'd run. She feared that she'd gone too far and this was the point she'd lose the last remaining family she had. The only family she cared about.

He peered at her without a word before letting out a shaky breath and striding toward her. Viktoria's eyes widened as he took her hands in his. She forced herself to meet his eyes, scared of what would be reflected in them. But there was no fear. No disgust or pity. And no hatred. They were warm and held no judgment. His expression was open as he squeezed her hands.

"Whatever happened, I'm sure it was necessary. I trust you and I'm here for you no matter what."

Viktoria's heart leapt. At this moment, she didn't feel so weighed down. She let Hunter wrap his arms around her and draw her in for a hug. They stayed like that for several minutes before he pulled back to grin at her.

"I love you, sis. Now, what do you say we finally go down and interrogate our guest?"

#

Spencer had confessed a week ago to stowing the map at his brother's place. He'd told Viktoria voluntarily. His brother was out on some job and wouldn't be back for a while, so he knew the map would be safe. She'd decided to let him stew since the map wasn't going anywhere and she needed time to prepare for her trip to the Veiled Isle. Besides, he deserved it for putting her through all the trouble. She'd considered disposing of him, but thought better of it. His thieving might benefit her someday.

Viktoria powered down her laptop for the day with the intention of returning to her room for a hot bath before dinner, when the sounds of a struggle reached her in her study. She pinched the bridge of her nose and pushed back from the desk, but before she could get to her feet, two men burst through the door, knocking it askew on its hinges and leveled their weapons at her.

"Where's my brother?" It was Spencer's brother, scowling as he took a step toward her. Viktoria settled back in her seat and laid her hands flat on the desk. She watched as he sized her up before lowering his weapon.

"I'll get right to the point, Owen." Viktoria steepled her fingers and peered at him through slanted eyes. "You have something I want, whether you know that or not. Your brother took my map and hid it at your place. Retrieve it, and I'll let him go. Unharmed. Refuse and I'll have his neck snapped by one of my men before you can even pull the trigger."

Viktoria watched the dark-haired man clench and unclench his jaw. A vein pulsed at his temple. He turned to the other man and gave a slight nod. His companion lowered his weapon but didn't relax. Owen turned his gaze on Viktoria.

"I'll get it. But my buddy Jake is going to stay and keep an eye on you." He stepped toward Viktoria and pointed a finger at her. "If you harm either of them, I'll make sure it's the last thing you do." With that, he turned and stomped out. Viktoria shifted her attention to Jake, who remained stoically by the door, and smirked.

#

Viktoria waited in the basement when Owen returned a couple hours later. She stood behind the chair Spencer was tied to. Her hand rested on his shoulder. His gun was trained on her again, but this time he was surrounded by her security team. She watched Owen scan the room. "Where's Jake?"

A smile played over her lips as she gave a small nod to one of her guys. He exited the room and returned a moment later with Jake's limp body over his shoulder. He unceremoniously tossed him at Owen's feet where he stared up at him with unfocused eyes. Owen knelt to check for a pulse. His eyes never left Viktoria,widening when he didn't find one. Owen stood tall and aimed the weapon at her. She squeezed Spencer's shoulder and he cried out as sparks trailed down her arm to his. Her lips curled as Owen took a step forward but halted when she squeezed again and elicited a scream from Spencer.

"Place the gun on the floor and slide it over here. Or, if you'd prefer, I can continue hurting your brother." Without a word, Owen did as she asked. She loosened her grip and gestured for the map. "Give that to me." She watched warring expressions cross his features. She rolled her eyes and dug her nails into Spencer. He wailed, causing Owen to jump forward and hand her the map. She passed it to the guard standing to her right and watched him unroll it. She snarled as she took in the smudged ink from water damage and the large tears running through it. But it was the message scrawled across it in large black letters that caused her to see red.

Better Luck Next Time, Ms. Payne!

She whipped her head in Owen's direction and clawed at Spencer's shoulder. "What is this?" She wrenched the map from her guy's hand and tossed it across the room at Owen. He retrieved it, careful not to disturb Jake's body and took a look.

"This wasn't me and it's not Spencer's writing either." Spencer shook his head as Owen turned the map in his direction.

"It wasn't like that when I left it." He could barely choke out the words through his sobs. Annoyed by the sound, Viktoria eased the pressure on his shoulder so he'd shut up and let her think.

The map was still intact for the most part. She could recreate it while on the island. But that would take time. And whoever ruined it and left her that message knew what she was up to. She tapped her chin in thought and then looked at Owen.

"Looks like we're going to be stuck with each other for a little longer. You're going to recreate the map for me." She laid both hands on Spencer's shoulders. Owen crossed his arms over his chest as he returned her stare.

"Why the hell would I help you? You tortured my brother, and murdered my friend." Viktoria grinned as she squeezed Spencer's shoulders. Sparks trailed down her arms, and his eyes misted. Viktoria forced her will on him and within seconds he was screaming and fighting against the rope that held him to the chair. Viktoria stepped aside as Spencer continued to struggle. Owen lunged forward but two of her thugs held him back. He sank to his knees watching his brother.

"What did you do to him?" His eyes widened and he pulled against the hands holding him.

"Right now, your brother believes he's on fire. Believes it so much that his mind has convinced itself and his body that he feels actual flames burning through his flesh." Owen's jaw dropped as he peered up at her through narrowed eyes. She saw the argument form on his lips but anything he could've said was drowned out by the frantic screams of Spencer. His wrists bled from being rubbed raw as he struggled to free himself.

"Make it stop!"

Viktoria smirked. "Swear your allegiance to me." She watched as his face fell.

"Fine. I'll do what you want. Just stop his suffering." He continued to struggle against his captors, but it was no use.

Satisfied, Viktoria strode over to Spencer, put a hand on his cheek and all at once he lay still, panting as he tried to catch his breath. His pained eyes slid to Owen's. Viktoria watched relief flood Owen's face before his head dropped and he stopped struggling, defeated. She clapped her hands as she looked from one brother to the other. Her eyes sparkled in delight.

"Pack your bags, boys. We're off to the Veiled Isle."

Sarah Lapalme currently lives in Las Vegas, Nevada with her ten-year-old daughter. She's working toward a BA in Creative Writing with a concentration in Fiction and a minor in English Language and Literature. An avid reader, she enjoys Fantasy and Science Fiction and is currently working on her first novel.

The Alien I Shot

by Helen Obermeier

The Protector of Protectorate 117 lounged at the meeting table, boots propped up on the seat next to him, and daydreamed of a high-frequency laser beam hitting the alien mountainside. Orange-yellow lava bled down the steep slope next to the pathetic homestead. Aliens swarmed out with their barbarian weaponry at the ready.

And one alien had even dared to shoot at him, her peach-colored face wild with hatred. He could still taste blood in his mouth—

"Zee-On! Are you *listening*?"

"Yes, sister." He deliberately didn't look up from the table. He already knew what her face looked like right now, regal calmness suffused with a hint of anger—a sight he was sick of by now. "I will look at my delegates' reports." The table's reflecting surface made everything black-and-white, appropriate for his black hair and aristocratic Core complexion of leaden grey. "As soon as I find the time—"

Her voice cut in. "Pulse weapon Four wasn't dismantled. The rebels have gotten hold of it."

His head flipped up. "What?"

The Head of Coalition's white-eyed, galaxy-reigning stare bore into his eyes. "Be *silent* and read the data package."

He skimmed it in seconds. "That's the rebel cell I just dismantled. They're all dead or will be soon. And …" He trailed off. The alien was in there, apparently female, her face smooth and calm. She had raised her gun and shot him right in the face. To no avail, of course.

Sure, he should have zapped her like the other stupid aliens who had tried to run. Somehow he had gotten distracted. "She knows something. Interrogate her."

"Your proposals are enlightening as always, brother." His sister's voice dripped with corrosive sarcasm. "She has a brain bug."

What a surprise. No interrogations then, unless they wanted to risk activation of a nano-sized explosive in her head. The upside was, she couldn't control it, or she wouldn't have been taken captive.

"She might know everything about the Pulse," his sister continued, "or she might not. In any case, we can't pry it out of her."

He shrugged. "So what? I'll turn the rock upside down—"

"Zee-On!" Her voice boomed across twenty-six thousand light years. "While you were playing with your toys, the rebels acquired a weapon of mass destruction. They will ruin this planet, this rare, resourceful hab planet, way worse than you ever could!" She leaned forward with her royal tunic flowing around her, a rare display of emotion that almost made him cower back in turn. "I will say this only once. *I will replace you.* You will go back to the Core, and Protectorate 117 will be governed by someone suited for the job."

He put his feet down on the floor. In his mind, the beam burned into the jagged mountainside with a full, vibrating, singing sound—just like the Pulse, a thousand times stronger. "You wouldn't."

"Try me, brother." Her teeth shone brilliantly between her lips. "They will have it ready in five weeks. You will prevent a strike, or your successor's first task will be to clean up the mess you made."

He stared. His fingers twitched, ready to make fists. The alien's face was back in his mind, the pure hate in that split-second when she had been sure of her imminent death, the two of them staring at each other as the sulphuric breeze wafted over them. *Should have killed you*, he thought clearly, *and fuck the planet.*

As soon as his sister's projection snapped away, he jumped up from his seat, turned up spherical hardcore in his ears and went straight to the shooting range.

#

He sat in his armchair on Command station, let the cat drag her small white paws across his naked hand and stared out the space-facing window into blackness. The station rotating around Protectorate 117 was tiny, the interior design atrocious. And there was nothing of the electric liveliness of the Core, the glowing sky and the huge young star discs hovering everywhere, the billions of habitats and spaceways.

The crampedness, the bland fabricated food, the fights, the unending mazes of the military asteroids—he surely didn't miss those. Not that a man of his standing would have to deal with that anyway. He was only going to be sent back home in shame. That was all. And it was too much.

The cat's triangular ears peaked up. She jumped from the chair in a long, low-gravity arc just as the door slid open. The alien stepped into the room, the soldiers behind her retreating on his silent command.

The last time he had seen it—her—, she'd had her useless gun trained at him, her soft light skin smeared with dark patches. Now, she had been cleaned up and dressed in a green low-quality overall. Her facial structure was typical 117—hardly any drift from the main stock, except for the thickness of her limbs compared to his, a tell-tale sign of a gravity species. The hair on her head was cut shorter than his own.

And she looked at him as if she had never seen him before. Or as if she didn't care. The only reaction he could identify: a rapid fluttering of her eyelids.

He made a step towards her and saw her flinch, more reflex than anything. He realized he hadn't looked up her name. No matter.

"Where is the Pulse weapon?" he asked, experimentally.

The pathetic bit of color in her skin seemed to drain away. Her face was impassive. A synthetic reaction, a warning from the brain bug. Dangerous territory.

Less than five weeks. No time for a careful psychological evaluation, no time for elaborate plans. No, he would have to do this himself. It couldn't be that hard to talk something out of an alien, could it? After five years as Protector, he surely knew how to handle them.

"Who has it?"

A tremor ran through her body. Her face twisted. She stayed silent.

The stubborn kind, then. He folded his arms. "You know, I can read your face anyway."

Her eyes narrowed. The unmodified irises were a yellowish, washed-out green. "Oh? Read me, then."

Insolence. "You know who I am, right?" He looked down on her. She wasn't tall for her species.

Unbelievably, one corner of her pale mouth turned upwards. "The alien I shot."

A hot bolt of rage ran through him. He imagined torturing her, scraping her brains clean, that impertinent face smiling dully at the masses as he paraded her around the Protectorate as a good example. It would be the last thing he did on this rock.

He grit his teeth and commanded another door to open. "This was Leisure Room 2, originally. Enjoy while you can."

She turned without another look. The cat sniffed at the door closing behind her and gave a tiny whine.

#

Leisure Room 2 was three by four meters, luxurious—he had shared the same space with five others, back in his cadet days. The alien didn't seem to appreciate it. She lounged away on the couch, used the chemical shower and toilet, stared out the tiny window, all with a blank, calm expression on her face.

He tried to approach her. He *really* tried. All he got was fierce stares. He mentioned her friends, mentioned he could up her rations or give her entertainment. No reaction at all. He had even, grudgingly, wasted time trying to look into her past. There was nothing. Contact, and the years since then, had been a chaotic time.

Well, who needed information anyway? He had put terror in a billion aliens before. They cowered before him, barbarians that they were, before his impassive face and his gun and the crimson-red Protector's insignia.

I will replace you, his sister's voice reminded him. He imagined some new Protector stalking around the planet, maybe some slimy upstart from a provincial hab planet nearby. After all he had done to get this far. And now he wasn't good enough. Fine. *Fine.*

On the fifth day, a mission came in. He walked over to Leisure Room 2. The alien lay flat on the floor, exercising. At the sight of him, her face slipped.

"Still alive?" he asked.

A soft touch on his shin. The cat streamlined into the room, her little nose vibrating. She hopped on the bunk and started to lick her paws in front of the window, her slim shape a spot of starlight white against the sad emptiness of galaxy-edge space.

The alien glanced at her, skepticism furrowing her brow. "She should be on Earth."

"She has everything she needs in here. Instead of starving down on the planet."

The alien stared back at him, impassively. He felt anger rise in his throat. "And anyway, she's just a stray. She should be glad to be alive."

Now the hatred was back on her face. This was going wrong. If his sister pinged him now, he would have only failure to show her.

"Get up," he said. There was the chance that this was going to trigger the bug. He was ready to risk it. "We're going planetside."

For once, disbelief covered up the hatred on her face.

#

The pilots exchanged a glance when the alien stepped on board, but didn't comment. Outside, the dock tumbled away and the planet appeared, fat and colorful above them. The alien was staring.

They curved towards the rock in an arc, easily picking a path between satellites and solar collectors. The nose of the shuttle dipped low. Wide brown-orange deserts turned into narrow greenish bands in the North and South. Vast oceans of deep hydrogen blue gleamed in the local sun's yellow-white light. All very fragile, as planet-restricted living was.

The locals, the entire half billion of them, called it—how creative—Earth. Like a thousand other rocks in the galaxy.

The shuttle touched down on the landing field in the green belt on a Southern continent. The field was cheaply built, the surface already dented and even melted in some places. Above, the piercing blue sky loomed eerily empty—safe for the yellow-white local sun and the hazy white sphere of the planet's single pockmarked moon.

Behind Zee, the alien gingerly stepped down the ramp. The restrainer tags on her wrists blinked in the sun's light. In his head, he had started to call her the stray.

"How does it feel to be back?"

The stray's expression showed, over the ever-present current of dislike, a mild curiosity. "I've missed the smell of real air."

For a split-second he thought of the cat, left alone in the quarters, sneaking around his ankles and trying to scurry out the main door as he opened it. Well, he only smelled dryness and fecund traces of decaying alien flora. "It's even better since we cleared out all the toxic waste your ancestors left you."

She didn't answer.

At the farm, the strike was in full force. Peaceful, they said. A congregation of a few hundred aliens, sitting around on the concrete wasting their own and their supervisors' time. Their skin tones varied, strangely vivid tones of soft brown and red-tinted black. No leaders in sight, which was smart. Drones hovered above them, soldiers were posted around the mass. Behind them, the semi-transparent dome of the farm towered, where edible greens jutted up into the sky in hundreds of stories.

The work could have been done by bots, but those aliens were immature. Like this so-called strike showed, they still didn't know what was good for them. He noticed the shift in the flock as they saw him approach with the soft breeze stretching out his cape behind him, an effect of planetary climate he had always liked. A low rush of whispers, heads turning, fearful glances. All as it should be.

Only, if his sister got proven right, it wouldn't be that way any longer, would it?

The factory's security delegate took a second to recover from seeing an alien in the Protector's wake, but still managed to inform Zee about the strike. The delegate himself, of course, had done nothing to stop this nonsense. Zee liked to think of himself as the ultima ratio. His sister would say that this wasn't exactly the most important part of his job—but it was the best part.

He glanced at the alien standing next to them, her face closed off. In the warm light of the sun, reddish strands glinted in her short hair. "What are they protesting?" he asked loudly.

"The working hours, sir. Some cultural issue. They ask to be home before sundown to perform rituals."

Which sounded just typical. "How many meals will they miss because of this?"

"So far, there will be no evening supper for them, their families and the surrounding villages, sir."

Single-minded creatures. Next to him, the alien let her gaze sweep across the mass, trying to look uninterested. Well, he would show her.

He gave the command. The drones flurried around and singled out aliens for his attention—popular ones, ones the aliens around them looked up to. His soldiers marched right into the flock of sitting aliens and dragged out a bunch of them. The rest looked uncomfortable, but still it sat. Zee waited until they had brought him the first alien.

It stared at him in open defiance. Zee unholstered his gun and fired.

The herd inhaled with a soft whoosh. Scattered shouts rose up. The body scraped across the concrete as it was dragged away.

The next alien twitched and jerked in the soldier's grip. "I didn't want to strike! I just did what they told me! They would have taken away my rations—"

Zee fired. Murmurs and shouts filled the air. A quick glance at his involuntary companion. She had stepped back, well behind him and the delegate. Her face remained—calm.

Another alien was dragged up. The herd started to vibrate. Aliens rose up, raised their hands. On a corner, a regular fight broke out. The soldiers didn't intervene. The alien, a wrinkled and small specimen, had its gaze fixed at the concrete floor. But then it looked up, to the stray. Its expression changed.

Anger. Disgust. Why disgust? Zee hadn't yet come to a conclusion when the alien, her eyes still on the stray, suddenly spat on the ground. "You rebels," it snarled. "Damn troublemakers—"

Zee fired. The alien crumpled to the ground. He turned, saw the stray stare at the body. Was it contempt on her face, or confusion? "So what did that mean?"

"Seems that she didn't like me." The stray looked up to him, her eyes hard. Was she angry? Sad? It couldn't be that difficult to read an alien's face. "Protector, this show you're putting on will not make me talk."

Well, he could see that. "It's not for *you*."

She raised one brown eyebrow. "So it is for fun, then? Playing with your toys?"

His sister's words. He felt his face slip for a nanosecond. A sudden urge: activate the punishment mode on her tags. Or zap her outright. The alien must have seen the slip, because she reacted — with a rapid flutter of eyelids, nothing more.

He turned. The flock was already disbanding. It would be easy to separate them and herd them back to work. He holstered the gun, ignoring the next alien still trembling in the soldier's grip, ignoring the delegate, and grabbed his alien's arm. She flinched, but didn't resist.

He made for the shuttle. Halfway, he remembered the weakness of her alien flesh and let her go. From the corner of his eye, he saw her rubbing her arm. Pain showed up alright on her face, just no other emotion he had been trying to coax out of her.

"This is just the Protector doing his job," he said slowly, emphasizing every word. Behind them, the shuttle's hatch opened. "And the Protector decides to keep you around."

She was silent, but her green eyes fixed his. No, they were nothing like his sister's—but somehow, he felt judged.

Three weeks left. Plenty of time, right?

#

His administrative staff took good care to act as if nothing out of the ordinary was happening while he kept taking the shuttle for leisure trips, with an alien as his sole companion. He wondered if they were thinking what he thought they were thinking. The idea made him shudder. Civilized people didn't mate with aliens.

And not with this one, surely. There were no funny reactions with her, no drama. So far, no conversation they'd had—as crazy as it seemed, there had been conversations—had gotten him anything but lifted eyebrows or disgusted looks. Not even real anger.

Thirteen days left. No progress. None at all.

He had brought the shuttle down right in the middle of the Contact ruins, a perfectly round circle of deep black surrounded by yellow desert. His boots stepped down on the hard surface, the thermal radiation emitting from the sky-black surface palpable on his naked face. Behind him, the alien took a tentative step, hands hovering on waist level as if to assess the heat.

She looked discontent. A lot of aliens had been discontent after the Pulse had burned through five hundred clicks of atmosphere, phase-shifting the solid ground thirteen meters deep. But after, ninety-six percent of the population had been ready to accept the Coalition.

"This is what you get with a Pulse weapon," he said, his voice the only sound in the ruins' hundred-and-twenty-click diameter. "You want that happening to a city?"

She frowned, smoothed her face down again.

He was prepared. From his outstretched wrist, a holo sprung up, a dark brown sphere crisscrossed with bright red veins. "You see the impact craters? The Coalition arrived too late. Intraspecies war, no life remaining. We're probably going to strip-mine it. Waste of a perfectly good terraformable planet."

Her face showed disinterest. "With this kind of power, we would have done greater things." Her voice sounded flat, as if sucked up by the space-black ground.

She really thought they were special. Maybe they had been, once. There were ancient digging sites on the neighboring planets, probes decaying in orbit. But there were also other remains. "Then take a look around. Your fossil resources are almost depleted. The atmosphere was tampered with. We stopped you from ruining your planet."

Her eyes narrowed, her voice rose slightly. "Oh, that story again?" It seemed he had hit a nerve, finally. "The selfless invaders. Ruling us from your oh-so-civilized Core, drinking Ambrosia—"

"What's Ambrosia?"

She stared at him, wondering if to answer. "The gods drink it."

Funny. Of course, that was what she would think. When the Coalition had arrived, their leaders had been living in luxury, letting the low people starve. "Not likely. We're all working hard."

Her eyes wandered across his body. *You don't look the part*, he read on her face.

Fine. He pointed to the sky, into the rough direction of the galaxy center, invisible through the thick atmosphere. "In the Core, there are no hab planets like this one. Most people live and die on stations and asteroids. You have to work for your bed, for your ration of protein bars, for your free shift once a month. Every single of us invaders has gone through this."

"Your sister is the queen of the galaxy—"

"And she earned it." This alien didn't need to know about the long, hard way they had gone, he and his sister both. Some of it might have been considered barbarians' behavior. "You, down here on the planet, you've got everything. You're the gods here. Be grateful for once."

The wind stroked their faces. Then the cold contempt returned to her expression. "Just a few days ago, you were shooting people in the open. Should we be grateful for that, too?"

She couldn't be that naive. "Sometimes you got to make sacrifices."

She laughed. He had never heard her laugh before. It was a soft sound, a bit mocking. "Sacrificing others, you mean. Protector. What are you even protecting? Your own pathetic existence?"

The blood rushed to his face. His hands twitched. He could snap her neck before she knew it. Right now. And her eyes, that pale green, told him she knew. Do it, they said. I dare you.

"Think what you want," he said, his voice so calm that he wondered, for a bizarre moment, if his sister had inhabited his body. "You want to tell me about that weapon now?"

She didn't.

#

The celebrations for the fifteenth anniversary of Contact day would take place in a cold, rainy city named Lund in the Northern hemisphere. He mentioned this to the stray, who asked: "Aren't you supposed to give a speech or something?"

"That's what my administrators are for." He wasn't in a good mood anyway. His sister had called and asked for progress. *You need to take responsibility, Zee. You can't solve all your problems with your gun, Zee.* Always the same.

"So you won't go at all?" Interest slipped across her face, shut away as soon as it had come.

He decided he would after all, and she would come with him. He felt jittery anyway, had wondered if to take some suppressants. It had to be the alien's annoying, abrasive presence.

Or the fact that he had seven days left to secure the weapon, and no idea how to do it.

The celebrations coincided with a local cultural festival the aliens held every year. Lund's brand-new grey buildings were alight in glaring tones of pulsing red and green. People, humans and aliens alike, wore colorful clothing sparkled with gold and red-and-white headdresses, remnants of a barbaric tradition. With just Zee and the alien, no soldiers, no delegates, some of the aliens didn't even realize who he was, until they made sense of his low-gravity height and grey skin.

He had never been this close to them, except in fights. He couldn't decide if he liked it.

They crossed an old-fashioned concrete-and-metal bridge spanning a river. "Lund is one of Earth's oldest cities," the stray said. She had been throwing in quips and bits for the whole walk. "I was born here."

Interesting. Surprising. He said nothing. An unpleasant organic smell rose up to them, probably aquatic animals.

"My family has always worked the plants," she continued. She had to mean the combustion plants, inefficient atmosphere-killers. "It was hard work. They're both gone by now. I would have followed them in their jobs—barbarian social order, as you would call it." Her face, turned towards the slow-flowing water, was calm. "Then you came along."

A group of aliens made to cross the bridge, thought better of it when they saw him. "And we ruined your awesome life?"

Her face closed off. This conversation was over, then. He turned away from the railing and walked down the bridge. Ten steps later, he suddenly heard her. "My life gained a purpose—"

He turned around to face her, which saved her life and his face.

The bridge exploded.

Pressure and heat pushed against his back, singed his hair. Close. He stumbled forward, not entirely voluntary. *She'll burn up.* He shoved her down to the ground. No matter now if some bones broke. The protective cape flared out across both of them. He wasn't fast enough. His left arm was still exposed, and *holy heat death*, that hurt. He lost all feeling in the arm. Probably for the best.

The heat subsided. She didn't move under him. Maybe the impact had killed her. Maybe the bug had activated. His cape was burnt to a crisp, but his body was intact. Except for that arm.

"Stay down," he hissed, hoping she could hear him. In the fastest motion he could manage, he jumped up into a crouch and scanned the area for the nearest target.

Nothing moved. Festival music droned on a few streets away. The scene was a painting of blackened greys and browns and burning patches of red. A gaping, blackened hole in one building—not the bridge had exploded, but a trash collector. Between rubble and patches of fire, he counted twenty-three twisted alien-sized lumps of coal.

Aliens and their weak physique. The heat had been generated by Core technology. Just a taste of what was to come if they activated the Pulse.

It had been meant for him.

He got to his feet just as he saw the movement right next to him, under the bridge. An ambush. He was off-balance with his unfeeling, unmoving arm, and almost fell down on his ass as he whirled around. Over the barrel of his gun, he saw three wide-faced aliens, their heads not even reaching his hip, in ridiculous red festival gear.

They were small. Two of them were crying. The third one's gaze shifted to something behind Zee.

He spun around. A split-second to spare at the stray. She still lay flat on the bridge, unmoving. He saw the real threat. An alien, barely able to stand, burn marks all over its skin, but still able to walk. And in his hands—

"Get behind me! Down!" He had no idea if the small aliens would understand. The alien raised his hand. Zee brought the gun up, aimed at the explosive flying in mid-air, shot.

Just a fraction too early.

The second, much smaller explosion was only a mild breeze on his face. He wasn't even pushed backwards. But the attacker was thrown back against the bridge's railing and hung limp.

Analyses ran down in his vision. No threats left. The hum of drones reached his ears, seconds before they appeared above. "Took you long enough," he murmured. Then he saw motion on the bridge. The stray raised her head, pushed herself up on her elbows. He hurried over to her, careful not to grab her arms too hard as he helped her stand. Her face was pale, her hands trembled. Her only injuries were some bruises and abrasions.

"That brain bug is pretty sturdy, I'd say," he said.

She looked at him, confusion and pain flitting over her face—then anger. "I want to talk to her." Her voice was raw.

Her. The alien crumpled on the bridge. Who should have been his first priority as well. Meanwhile, the small aliens were still huddled on the ground, all three faces turned up to him. He was tempted to shoo them off, but the stray had already freed herself from his grip and limped towards the attacker.

Who was done for. The ruined face twisted as it got a glance of Zee, but then it turned to the stray. "You work … with him now?" The words were slurred.

"This—this massacre." The stray's chest rose and fell in a rapid motion. She was trembling. An aftereffect, surely. "Are you mad? Are you completely mad?"

"You've seen … nothing yet. Wait until we … use the weapon." Then it escaped interrogation.

The stray stood up in a sudden, jerking motion, as if disgusted. Zee stared at the body. *You can't solve all your problems with a gun, Zee.* He should have preserved the attackers, not some random bystanders.

All energy drained out of him. He sat down in the street, left arm dangling. The stray looked down at him, frowning.

"Well." He shrugged with his good shoulder. It hurt. "Wasn't this fun? And now we wait until they melt a whole city down."

Her eyes narrowed. *You did this*, they said. *You invaders.*

They didn't talk all the way back to the station.

#

They were both patched up in his quarters, medics and bots swarming around them like flies. The arm would take eighteen hours to heal. He slept for exactly thirteen hours of programmed sleep, woke up groggy and confused, watched a summary of the day. The cat had puked on the smart carpet. Now it sat next to the alien in her room, content to be scratched behind the ears, while the alien read a Core magazine, her thoughtful face turned towards the window.

Six days were left. His chances of fulfilling his task had dropped to a fraction above zero. His guts coiled. He pressed a hand to his face. Where would it hit? Twenty-seven cities the size of Lund on the rock, and they couldn't evacuate them all, not without severe damage to the economy. Thousands and thousands of alien settlements littered the surface. Somewhere, the massacre would repeat, much worse.

And he was going to sit here, watching, and packing his things.

The door slid open. The stray hesitated before she stepped up to his lounge, her reflection perfect in the glassy surface. The cat followed, rubbing its head against her shin.

"Why didn't you shoot me on the mountain?"

"I have no idea." Not quite a lie. He couldn't well tell her: *Because I saw something in your face.*

"And now you saved my life."

"Because you're valuable."

Her face stayed blank. "The children weren't valuable."

It took him a second to remember the small aliens. „I'm just protecting the Coalition's investment. That's what my job description is, right?"

She stared at him. Then her lips curled into a thin, unhappy smile. It stayed on her face while she told him about the Pulse weapon—the location, the codes, the security measures.

The muscles of his face twitched with the effort to keep it still. "You're lying."

"You know I don't."

True. Her expression was calm, open.

"Then *why*?"

Her chest rose and fell in a slow breath. "Well, Zee-On." She had never said his name before. The translator made it sound natural, pronounced perfectly. "I have figured out who you are. Or at least I think I do. They …" Her eyes clouded over as she thought of her wannabe-successors. "I have no idea what they are."

People who were prepared to make sacrifices, he guessed. But he wouldn't be the one to tell her that.

She gestured at him. "And besides, if you get yourself fired, how will I know who will follow? You're the evil I know."

He nodded, slowly. Then he smiled.

"Aren't' we just the same, Alien."

She gave him a long look before she turned and left the room.

#

He put the recording into a high-priority message. Half an hour later, his sister called back. The sweetness in her voice told him she was surprised about his success. "I will confirm your posting again, to make sure the next promotion is already in line."

Well, this was great news. The best news he had received for months. So why did the triumph fall so flat? Well, because he hadn't solved the riddle. He had needed the stray to tell him.

"Oh, and I am authorizing her processing. You'll be free of her."

For some reason, he thought of his cat, curled up in the alien's lap right now, purring away while the alien scratched her head. There was a long pause. He imagined his sister sitting behind her desk, the blinding Core stars swirling behind her.

"The only one processing aliens from Protectorate 117 is me," he finally said.

A second of silence. "No spectacle. No witnesses. We don't need martyrs."

"You take me for a moron?"

She took too long to answer. He said his goodbyes and signed off.

#

They walked across snow and rock, the sky above space-black except for the small gleaming sliver of the moon. Gravity tugged on Zee's legs. He checked on the cat, curled up in his vacant seat on the shuttle, yawning and showing its sharp little predator's teeth. It had strayed around his ankles again as they had been about to leave. Just this once, he had obliged her.

No witnesses out here. A cat surely didn't count.

The lava on the mountainside had congealed into a twisted black mass. The homestead had already been processed, no trace left. The stray walked around the empty slope, her face closed off. Zee looked up at the sky with its two thousand points of weak, distant starlight, found the familiar white ribbon of the Great Street.

The Core was just a blurred spot of light, hidden behind gas and dust. "This sky is fucking empty."

No answer. He turned.

She was standing ten meters away, half-turned away from him, right on a drop. The sharp wind tugged at the hood of her jumpsuit as she glanced down into the abyss behind her.

He hadn't even surveyed the area beforehand. Coldness spread in his veins. His hand touched his gun. "I'll shoot your spine."

She returned his gaze. "I'll fall."

"I'm faster than gravity. I'll catch you."

"I've got an explosive in my head."

"It hasn't triggered up to now, so ..." He gaped at her like an idiot. "You can control it." No matter how fast his reflexes were, they wouldn't beat her neurons. "Why are you still alive, then? Why not do a martyr show down on the planet?"

She hesitated. Wondering if to tell the truth. Then a small shrug. "I wanted to get to know you. If you weren't worth it, I thought, I could stop any time."

Any other alien he would have just called a coward. But not her. He believed her.

She continued. "And now it turns out you got to know me." Bitterness slipped into her voice. "So well that you managed to interrogate me without even trying."

"You *chose* to tell me about the weapon. Which is kind of pathetic for us both."

She gave a brief laugh. "You are just messing with me again. You're good, Protector." Her body turned, towards the drop.

"Hey!" He almost shouted. Undignified.

Anger crossed her face for a second. "You need to get rid of me anyway, don't you?"

Silence. The wind had to bite into her soft skin. He barely felt it at all. His hand tightened around the gun.

Then he holstered it, made a step backwards, raised his hands. He had never raised his hands on this planet before.

"I've transferred you the rights to the shuttle." His voice echoed back from the mountainside. "Engage the AI. If you crash somewhere, it's not my fault. If you get yourself caught, it's not my fault."

Her eyes widened, her mouth hung open. A mad grin tugged at his lips. He wished he were closer to her, to savor the moment. "I'd like to remind you that the cat is still in the shuttle. Get it back where it belongs. And take care of it, or I'll find you and gut you slowly."

"Why?" For once, he could hear the suppressed tremble in her voice. And he knew that she wasn't asking about the cat.

He thought of the twenty-three burned lumps on the destroyed street. "The evil you know, remember?"

The last thing he saw was her confused face, a pale patch in the darkness. He turned away, cut communication to the shuttle, and marched down the slope. It would be a long walk to the surface, more than enough time to compose an elaborate lie for his sister. He would tell her that the sneaky alien had set a trap for him, and he, ever-stupid, ever-bumbling, head-through-the-wall Zee, had fallen for it.

The Head of the Coalition would believe it, he was sure of it.

Behind him, he heard the hissing of the shuttle's engines reflected from the rock, receding, vanishing. He turned on some spherical hardcore and started to climb down.

Helen Obermeier is an engineer, project manager and part-time writer who loves to write about space, bloody battles and questions of morality. Her work has been published in several short story anthologies. She lives in Southern Germany with her human and feline family.

For The Hunt

by Jordan Davidson

Sitting in the sun watching the execution carnival is giving me more freckles.

I used to hate the freckles. They came about my first year of hunting Ave-Witches for the kings. Ave-Witches prefer to live outside, another unnatural aspect of an already unnatural hybrid between human and bird. As such, my team and I rode under near constant sun, which dotted freckles on our skin with precise hands. At first, I was foolish enough to think that I could wash them off. That did nothing but irritate my skin and add more. Now they've grown on me; freckles come from being in the field. If you aren't in the field, you aren't catching Ave-Witches, so the freckles are something of a sign of a job well done. That doesn't mean I enjoy looking at them. Purely aesthetically, my face looks better sans spots. Especially when my quest company's healer, Carter, fixates on capturing them in his caricatures. We have a running joke where I tear his pictures out of the notebook, and he tolerates it. I employ the joke today, laughing; he stares grimly as I crumple it and hurl the paper ball across the muddy execution stage, past the gallows, and down to where the stables are. There, a horse grinds it to pieces with its hoof.

"Awww, poor Carter. When will you learn that Alexavier is a dick who thrives on crushing your hopes and dreams?" Kalina, our sword mason, slides in next to me, her sticky fingers leaving a film on all the benches they touch. I don't need to look to know that Nathalie and Enna are there as well.

Every month, all the Ave-Witch hunters gather in the capital with the people they've caught. We all have a monthly quota. Failing the monthly quota means joining the slave holdings. So more often than not, less successful witch hunters bring in mildly suspicious humans instead of the real thing. Hence the execution carnivals. The best—but not the only—way to tell a human from an Ave-Witch is hanging. When you hang an Ave-Witch, an Ave-Witch sprouts feathers, a beak, the likes. The most powerful even turn into birds.

Humans, on the other hand, just have their necks broken.

"What do you think of that one?" Kalina throws a bit of sugar-spun popcorn at the line. It hits one of the haggard figures in the forehead. Blindfolded, the old woman swings around several times before tripping over her chains and faceplanting in the dust.

I give her a quick once over. "Not a chance. They'll hang her and get nothing."

"You think we should save her, then?" Enna's quiet question makes Kalina double over with laughter, but they both wait for my answer.

"No." I take a piece of Kalina's popcorn. The sugar grits on my teeth. "Let whoever captured her take the fall. We've proven our worth here. And Enna? Be careful how you phrase things. I wouldn't want to have to accuse my best seer of being an Ave-Witch." I was—and still am—willing to take on people of questionable bloodlines in exchange for talent. But talent is always secondary to quotas.

Unconcerned, Enna hums a few lines of a song in the background, "the blood of a murderer…"

Kalina offers me another kernel. I take it. Throw it up to the Anythian Kestrel perched on my shoulder. Sarysi snatches it from the air with a satisfied caw. A few of the prisoners in line screw up their faces like Sarysi's voice causes them physical pain. Not the old woman. Too bird-dear to be an Ave-Witch.

And I'm right. The kings' soldiers lead the old woman up to the gallows. When her neck cracks, no feathers float down. No talons tear through her nails. Not even her bones break hollow. A useless catch. The soldiers throw her body in the burning pits.

My company and I draw handkerchiefs over our faces to ward off the haze of black smoke. While the old woman may have been a dud, several other prisoners show promise when they're led to their deaths. One man coughs up an owl pellet when the rope snaps his neck, another grows a beak. They go in the burning pits too. The only Ave-Witches that escape the flames are the ones powerful enough to make full transformations into Anythian Kestrels. That's how being an Ave-Witch works: as time goes on, the human part of an Ave-Witch withers. A bird grows in its place, a bird that can wield strange and horrifying magic in direct opposition to our gods, The Lords.

Hunters deal with the threat.

And my company's reputation speaks for us—we've never had one miss.

This month, we've brought in five. And all five turn into Anythian Kestrels when hanged. The soldiers capture them in rune-lined cages that will prevent them from transforming back. Later, a disciple of the Lords Magilyn will use their particular brand of magic to lock the Ave-Witches into their new forms. Anythian kestrels are then given to hunting companies as magical aids and gifts. I have one—a relic from my first assignment and my first freckles. Not many hunters can be said to have trapped their own sister.

Now Sarysi serves me.

I'm watching a soldier grip the neck of a particularly nice-looking white kestrel when a small girl appears at my shoulder.

The official crest of a kings' messenger—seven interlocking crowns—is stitched into her leather shirt.

I wave my hand at her. "Speak."

She points up to the balcony across from the execution stage. "A king wishes a word with you."

"Thank you." I press a coin into her hand, and she goes.

Kalina hands me the sword I have resting by my seat. "Aw. There goes our rest time."

"Good." Nathalie, sitting behind us, crushes a nut in her fingers. "Lolling around here makes us soft."

"For the last time, Nat, relaxing in the blood of our enemies isn't a crime," Kalina calls back.

I abandon the two to their bantering—playful on Kalina's end and irate for Nathalie's part. When a king calls, you don't leave them waiting.

Unfortunately, waiting the king already is by the time I navigate the crowds vying for bits of burnt bone.

"You're late." This particular king has knots upon knots of white hair piled on her head.

I bend at the knees, pressing my lips to her hand. "Yes, your majesty."

A swift jerk of her wrist sends me scrambling back. We walk from the execution carnival to the gardens. Here the crowds have thinned out. No one wants to walk here this late in the fall—all the trees look skeletal, and the carpet of leaves that squishes under my boots lets out a faintly unpleasant smell.

"I've heard your company is the best." The king stops at a fountain, fixing her hair in the water's reflections.

"We do our best to serve you and the Lords Magilyn."

The king makes the sigil of the Lords across her forehead, the proper honor to our gods. "The highest sacrifice to Them."

"The highest sacrifice to Them," I mimic, making her same hand gesture.

After I'm finished, the king continues. "You haven't had one missed witch, have you?"

"No, your highness."

"Excellent. I told the council you were right for this. Your compatriot Enna sensed her. One of the most formidable foes we've faced in a long time. Needless to say, I expect results. You know the fall that comes with failure."

In my mind's eye, I can see the line of bowed slaves scrubbing away blood on the execution stage—the price for missing a quota or failing a king's assignment. The severity of the action determines whether you end up the blood or the slave.

I take the scroll she produces from her robes, and she makes her way back down the garden path, leaving me no indication that she wants me to follow.

I roll open the scroll. The name listed at the top makes me pause. Swallow. Pause again.

Capture Starling Mercium alive to stand judgement before the Lords or execute her in their name by the ninth of winter.

Starling.

Her last known location hints at it, but I check every fact in the scroll one more time. All of it falls in line.

It is Starling.

My Starling.

My company and I have quite the work cut out for us.

A journey this long into the center of Akasal takes not only tremendous skill but tremendous preparation. Despite being dragged from the festivities early, my company shows no resistance to packing specially bred horses with hundreds of pounds worth of supplies. Some of what we need takes days to travel in from different parts of Akasal, but by the end of the week, we're ready to saddle up and ride towards the mountains cresting the center of our country.

The night before we leave, my memory wraps me in strange dreams of Starling: she and I are fifteen again, pacing back and forth in her mother's house. Above us, the ceiling is carved in whorls of feathers and leaves. Smoked thyme and hemlock thicken the air. Starling stands on a bed, stretching up her long, white fingers to the carving. She has her blonde hair tied back in a braid with bits of feathers just poking through.

I can tell she's unsettled by the way the skin on her shoulder blades writhes with wings waiting to come out. "Are you going?" She asks me.

A scroll appears in my hand, the wax seal stamped with the crest of the kings. I memorized the words as soon as I got it, so even in a dream I don't have to look at it to say: "I don't have a choice, Star. If the Lords command it of me—"

"The Lords." Bones snap through her shoulders, and her face tightens in pain. "The Lords whose priests want people like me to die? The Lords who you've never believed in until now? I'd never take a job where I had to kill people. Not even if they held a knife to my throat."

"I'm going." I stand, travel bag on my shoulder.

"Just know that if you go, I die." Blood begins to run from her eyes.

I back into the wall. This argument doesn't go like this. I've replayed it so many times that I know she should say: *be safe, remember me*, but instead, she advances closer and closer, silver shredding her pupil into her iris, all the while bleeding from her eyes, mouth, nose…

"Your sister will die." Her voice takes on different tones as the expression melts from her face, leaving a blank, white canvas crawling with feathery lines. Hundreds of voices press through her, some human, others not… "I will die. Eventually, you will die."

I throw open the door, but the mountainous plain I grew up in has vanished; in its place stretches a stone hallway, and from one of the rooms, my sister screams, "help me! Help me!"

Turning my back on Starling who isn't Starling, I run through the maze of corridors until I throw open a door marked with a feather, only to see a copy of my decaying body strapped to a table, the Anythian Kestrel that was my sister feasting on its stomach. But the kestrel has Enna's human eyes.

Normally, I manage dreams well. But this one haunts me through the first two days of fighting winds and incoming storms.

A journey this long gives me quite a lot of time to think. The chatter among my quest mates dies out after the first few days with our fresh fruit. The extended periods of silence that follow let me ruminate on Starling:

She hasn't seen me with freckles yet. I have to laugh at the ridiculousness of it all—there's quite a lot of me she hasn't seen: my height, the new cut of my hair, the scars on the sides of my face. The boy who left her has vanished somewhere under the armor and his duties. Eight years does that to a person, especially eight years serving the kings.

And yet. I'm fixating on the freckles. Counting them in the polished saddle of the horse. Lamenting about them even…why couldn't they have made up their mind about whether or not they wanted to cover my skin? A patch above my left eyebrow darkens my forehead entirely, while around my chin one could connect every single one and still not form a constellation. In between, there's a dot for every snowflake that hits my face as my company and I cut through the storm.

It's snowing today. Sarysi digs her talons into my shoulder, reflecting the displeasure I'm sure radiates off our entire party. She's hungry and slakes that hunger by biting off small chunks of my ear. Blood runs in a steady, red line down my neck.

"The bird unhappy?" Nathalie, her face contorted, pulls up beside me. "Bad omen. That and the snow…" Her body ripples with muscle; I've seen three people riding on each other's shoulders smaller than Nathalie, and she weighs more than all three of those people combined.

"We'll retrieve the prize." I spur my horse forward, less to end the conversation and more to make sure my horse's feet don't freeze to the ground. Plumes of frost already curl across my eyelashes and through the lining of my gloves.

Nathalie joins me in the quicker movement, her gigantic stallion steaming and chomping underneath her brutal hand. "Oh, I'm not worried about the prize, Lordling. I'm worried about what you'll do once we find it."

It.

The it has never bothered me before. But Starling as an it…that doesn't settle well with me. I know how I should feel. On missions before, I've scanned Nathalie's eyes to see if she regrets what we do, and every time I've found nothing but unblinking, unremorseful red. So I wouldn't trade her for a hundred more soldiers. No prize can escape Nathalie.

No prize can escape any of us.

Adjusting to the faster pace, my company fans around me. Our shape mimics the flock of frost geese that we soon overtake; I have point, leading the way with Sarysi and the undulating lines of the topography map.

Nathalie relents back to my left while sharing a disapproving eye with Kalina. Behind them, Carter—pale as death and as quiet as it too—leers and lulls at the reigns. Across from him, Enna fixes a stray strand of blue hair that's fallen from the crest of her bun. Her spear drags behind her in the snow.

It must be my imagination that a curl of feather floats down with her fingers. She's a seeress, not an Ave-Witch, although I have heard stories of one masquerading as the other—no. To uproot the small voice in my head, a montage of images play in between my eyelids: Enna slitting throats, Enna writing the rune lines to capture kestrels, Enna divining every place an Ave-Witch has been.

I shake my head to clear it all.

In front of us, the storm seethes. Tendrils and teeth of ice slit back the exposed skin at the edges of my gloves and the side of my face. Sarysi, deciding she's had enough, spreads her iridescent wings and gives a great cry, the kind that paralyzes a brave soul and kills a cowardly one, displaying one of the unique abilities of a properly trained Anythian Kestrel. Snow explodes out from us, giving momentary relief that's crushed—quite literally—in mountains of sleet cascading back in retaliation.

This kind of mist makes it impossible to see the ridge lines and landmarks. Even if the topography map wasn't sodden, there'd be no proper way to read it here. Just like Starling, to make her new home in a place so well guarded that people with friendly intentions couldn't make it up the peaks, let alone us. If it wasn't such a damn nightmare for my company and me, I might laugh.

As is, I pull up my hand. There's no more ground we're making today. The muffled footsteps of the horses stop. When I swing down, I sink up to my knees in ice. Nathalie crashes through a great deal more, but Enna, Enna takes the cake, sliding so far under the snow's outer skin that I can't help but wonder if she touches the earth.

We leave her there; she'll reappear at some point during the night. Instead, we concentrate our energy on the usual that comes with stopping for the day. Deer hide tarps. Digging snow holds for ties. Boiling down ice. Cooking enough to get us through the night, which turns against us quickly, the sky so filled with white that I can barely see my hand when I raise it in front of my face, almost as if the air itself has been filled with Sarysi's feathers.

The plague of white sends me into a troubled sleep when I retire to my tent. I'm met with two dreams, one concerning the fulfillment of my task, and another concerning what will become of me if I fail.

In the first, I sit before the circle of the kings cross-legged, in the center of their ring of thrones. Each one looks me over with cruel eyes—none of them speak. I know this means I'm to present, but my tongue fasts itself tightly to my lips, and the only sound I can make is the harsh kri-kri-kri- of an Anythian Kestrel. Blood leaks into my tastebuds. Staining my mouth copper.

The king who gave me the mission ties her white braid around my throat, lifting my chin. "Collect her for us, boy. Collect her by the ninth of winter."

Then her face blurs, and I wake in a bitter sweat, encased in the kind of cold that cuts through the skin to the joints, making opening and closing your hands difficult. Darkness has settled over the mists. I listen but can make out only the rustles of my company in their tents.

Their breathing lulls me into sleep again.

I wish I hadn't closed my eyes. As the waking world falls away, a stream of feathers encases me, drawing me higher, higher from the mountain peaks until the sun stretches over spindly plains trees with their bows shaking in a bitter wind—on the top of the tallest of one, an Anythian Kestrel spreads its wings. The wind forces me to bow. The kestrel sheds its feathers until it walks towards me on two human feet, and its face is one I used to know well—

A cold hand draws my hair back from my forehead. "Why, my brother, won't you just die?"

I take the hand in my own. The years as a bird have changed it. Scaly skin hardens what used to be soft, and the ends of her talons tear stars along my knuckles. "Oh, Sarysi. You know why."

She lets go, retreating back to the tree and giving me a good look at her. Red feathers entwine her night-black hair. "I wish you would. I wish you would fail. I want you to be afraid."

Failure. Even the thought of it makes my tongue taste like copper coins. Yes. I'm afraid. I've always been afraid; that's why I gave her up, and she knows this, she *should* know all of it, but before I can tell her again, Sarysi's caught in a stream of feathers and swirls back into a bird that bites my ear, pulling me from sleep.

The harsh light of morning barley penetrates the sodden clouds. Pain prickles my temple; while I was dreaming, Sarysi tore a chunk of flesh away from my head.

My team rises early with me. Nathalie has already disassembled the tent over Kalina's head. She nods to me with a dull sort of resignation and deep sleep marks under her eyes. "Alexavier. You look terrible. Dreams?"

"Another threat from the Lords and words with my sister."

Scanning my head, Nathalie almost smiles at the horrifying irony of it all. "Was that before or after she decided to disfigure you?"

"During."

On my shoulder, Sarysi screeches. I've always wondered how much she can understand in this form. It doesn't seem like I'll get an answer any time soon.

A cool touch soothes the ache. Carter, with his fingers so thin the points are almost entirely bone, presses against my head; in his wake, the cut seals itself. He mumbles a prayer to The Lords, then returns to the quiet vigil that he must have kept all night judging by the amount of snow coating his eyelashes.

"Are we off?" Kalina's bright, dimpled smile doesn't match the surroundings. But then again, I've never seen Kalina not smile, even when dismembering crowds at a time with her short sword, all pursuant to the Lords' orders, of course.

With a derisive snort, Kalina pushes past, already on the way to her horse. I mount my own creature before the telltale scratches of Enna's nails against ice send Sarysi into a flapping fit, but I listen for them. When our company is whole, we ride again.

Overnight, the snow had lessened and altogether stopped. For the first time on our journey, I can fully see what spreads out ahead of us: jagged mountains rupture the thin membrane of tundra, their tops disappearing into the mirage of clouds. We're in one of the valleys between them, cradled in the hands of death by glacier fields and scree.

Nathalie pulls her horse next to mine. "Which way, Alexavier?"

Going forward? Steeper and more treacherous than climbing a solid face of smooth marble using only your fingertips. And that marble shakes. Violently. As we contemplate the trail, the ground around us whispers with the murmur of rockslides below the ice.

Turning back? Sarysi wheels high ahead. I won't consign my company to a fate of slavery at the execution pits.

"I'd rather die than go back empty-handed." I mean it as a joke, but the words tear out almost as if they're pressed under the weight of the great stones we now need to climb.

Around me, my company nods.

And onwards we go.

The farther up we climb, the more our chests tighten and our mouths taste like copper. Breaths come fewer and far between while cracks in the ice plague each unsuspecting step. Several times, Enna topples from her horse only to be caught by Kalina's or Nathalie's clever hands. Each time, the blue-haired girl stares further into the horizon, her eyes whirling with the reflection.

My horse shakes ice from its feet.

For three days—three miserably cold days blistered with wind—we go on like this, climbing when the wind gives us reprieve, carving ourselves shelter in the snow and glaciers when darkness slows our path. My feet burn, alternating with reperfusion and freezing. The second blood comes back to them, it's leached out again.

But we manage it. We always do, even with Enna falling through every fifth snow hole.

On the dawn of the fourth day in the valley, we crest the ridge to a clear sky, looking down at the plateau that blooms before us. Enna's face lights like a thousand candles. "Do you feel it?"

I do. All through my arms and the hollow of my throat rises a great fluttering. Life breathes from this valley, the earthy smell of moss campion and clear water springs heady and spinning around me in a cloud of pure air, so thin, so sweet. With a cry, Sarysi takes off from my shoulders, her red feathers molting to pure silver as she shines against the sun.

And there, nestled in between the legs of two wide drainages, the tiny specks of a village wink at us, inviting us in.

Even Carter manages a smile through his paper-thin lips. "Our goal?"

Only Kalina remains unimpressed. Her smile strains at the edges of her face. I can tell from the way she curls her hands around one of the blades at her hip that all she wants is to reach Starling and stick her through. "Let's just skin the bitch so we can get back to the warmth!"

That sends a shiver of disquiet through me. One that I desperately tamp down. I'll kill Starling if it comes to that. But I don't want it to, I don't, I—

My mouth tastes of blood and feathers.

Several moments go by, and eyes prickle my spine. My company looks to me for a response that rolls off my tongue faster than I want it to. "Only use violence as a last resort or if your life is in danger. The kings want her alive." True enough. A living Ave-Witch is more useful to the kings than a dead one.

Slowly, we start down the valley. Scree gives way beneath us, and several times, someone swings down from their horse with a rope to rescue another member of the company (usually Nathalie for Enna) or self arrests halfway down the mountainside, elbows buried in the snow.

That night, I dictate a camp nestled into the shoulder of a drainage, just close enough to a small stream to fill our water skins, but far enough away to avoid any unwanted animals snarfing through our dwindling foodstuffs.

When the rest of the company has gone to bed. Enna and I sit cross-legged in silence, watching Sarysi wheel over the moon. Enna's eyes have a strange rapture about them. They leach in color with their churning blue irises. She offers me a drink of scorching tea from a pouch around her neck. "What will you do when you find her?"

I accept the tea. Mint and a hint of a few other herbs roll around the crevasses of my tongue. Turning away from her so she can't see my hesitation, I say, "What The Lords want of me. Would you follow me if I gave you the order to kill?"

The mountains tremor, just a little. I must be too tired to see straight.

"I don't know if given the choice between serving the kings and dying if I wouldn't take dying." No, I'm not imagining it. A feather trails down from her head.

"But you're here." Bursts of color pop in and out of my vision.

"And sometimes I wish not to be." With that Enna stands, fading back into the mist by our tents, leaving me lost in a maze of footprints and mountains. Somehow, I stumble to my tent, the world wheeling—

And I dream again. Starling, grown into a woman as I have grown into a man, pulls back the deer hide flaps of the tent and mounts my hips, pulling me into sweet submission until just before the climax when her fingers grow to talons, and she comes away with clumps of my hair; the scream that lurches in my throat withers as she braids pleasure with agony by ripping out each one of my teeth with her now curved beak—

"Alexavier!" Nathalie hits the side of my tent. She sounds strangled, desperate. The air explodes with the sound of beating wings—

I need to sit up. Sit up. But my arms shake underneath me. My stomach heaves. Everything gives way, I collapse against the seam where leather meets snow, I vomit clots through my clenched teeth and the world undulates, undulates with hazy forms, each breaking off into bird cries and feathers and I'm crashing, crashing through snow with blackness closing in and the smell of blood wind-whipped around me—

Lords, if I'm going to die here, at least let me die under the stars. Don't send my company to death with me.

Black invades.

For the moment, I am lost, suspended.

Brightness invades again. "Where are they?" The words come out crooked with a swollen tongue. I fight against strips of cloth tying me to a makeshift bed frame.

"Shh." Enna holds one of my hands, her eyes clouded with worry.

Enna. She's alive. Enna!

All the lights shine too brightly, and sweat drips from my eyebrows into the corner of my eyes. The ceiling has a familiar pattern, but one I can't place. Interlocked spirals, the edges tranced with feathers. The air too smells familiar—where have I breathed in roasted thyme and hemlock?

"Will he live?" Enna asks.

"I don't know." The voice—

"He can't die now. He can't. It has to—" The floor creaks as Enna paces, paces.

"He'll make it to the ceremony. The spell *will* work."

I—

She—

She hadn't seen me with my freckles. Now she has. I wonder what she thinks of them as I fade away again.

"I can't thank you enough for this. Bringing him to me." Starling.

"I had to. For all of us. If they can all be human again—"

"That doesn't make it any less brave."

It takes gargantuan effort to crack my eyelids open.

In the dim, candle corpses send smoke curling through an open window. Two women, one slight with blue hair, the other several inches taller and *strong*. Even in the dim, I can see the stark lines of her white dress. Where—where has the rest of my company gone? I remember the screaming.

If I was a better hunter, I'd stay quiet. Get as much information as I could. Starling's the enemy. But I can't hold it in any longer. It all cracks out of me: "Starling. Starling!"

The woman in white turns. My heart catches.

Starling's changed from the last time I saw her. Then I curse myself: of course she has. We were fifteen years old, me hanging out of one of the king's carriages, her running behind, arms outstretched. I've imagined her changed too, only none of the imaginings came out like this.

She's more beautiful than I thought she would be, more solid. She stands like she owns the world.

"Alexavier." Her voice sounds different too.

Closing my eyes for a moment, I try to reconcile the image I made of her with the Starling in front of me now. Nothing works.

As she draws closer, I see that she carries a knife strapped to her belt. When she gets within six inches of me she draws it. The old panic in me jolts away—she puts her hands up. Silver glints. "Your hands are bound. I'm going to cut you free."

It takes me a moment to place the pain around my wrists. Bloody rags tie me to the bed. Like she says she would, Starling slits the fabric. Every brush of her skin on mine sends my breath heaving.

I know she can feel it.

But she doesn't show it. She just offers me her hand.

"Thank Ave." Now Enna's dropped to her knees next to my face, checking my pulse and how my pupils dilate. Something about the phrase strikes me as odd: shouldn't she be thanking The Lords and all Their power?"

"Thank Ave when the mission is complete." Starling pulls me up. "Ave will want your full prayer, and we still have work to do."

Traitorously, my legs shiver under me, so Enna starts to wedge her shoulder under mine. Together, they guide me out the door.

The snow fell hard while I slept. The entire mountainous valley I gazed down on earlier is covered with the stuff; I sink knee-deep while Starling walks on the surface. We stop just on the border of a forest.

Starling carries me through the thickets. In the dark, the alien mixes with the familiar; we pass a knotted clump of pines, and I swear that's where Starling and I used to play castle as children, and after that, we swerve into a clearing where the dark waters of a lake I don't know lap unfamiliarly jagged shores.

My hands hurt, even though I can't move them. They're taking on a strange color, something that hovers between blue and purple.

Then we break through the lines of trees. Bonfires, each so much brighter than the fires the kings use at the executions stages burn at the base of colossal poles. Tied to each pole is a member of my company, but there's nothing they can do; their hands are bound with ropes of feathers, and their heads are slumped with drug.

And in the sky, hundreds of thousands of Anythian Kestrels spiral through clouds of smoke.

"What is this?" I try to stumble forward, to help them, but with one flick of Starling's hand, the birds descend to block me. The force of their wings knocks me back. One in particular cries out—Sarysi regards me with disdainful eyes before alighting on Starling's shoulder.

"You know what to do," Starling whispers to my sister.

Sarysi cuts through the mass of birds. Through the channel of them, I just get a clear view of Kalina, and then the body that used to be Kalina as Sarysi tears open Kalina's throat with her beak.

Kalina doesn't even have the chance to cry.

I force myself to watch the blood pound from her body. A hunter's goodbye. All the while, Starling paces back and forth with her back to the mass of birds and slaughter. I find myself not able to recognize a single thing about her.

"You…you said you would never…"

Something like pity fills her face. "People change. You changed." This just increases the urge to sink my fingernails into her face…after what she's done to my company…my family…

My fingers twitch, but don't move. Starling kneels next to me, cupping my face in some kind of perverted embrace. "What did you do to Sarysi? What would you have done to Enna if you realized what she was? What were you planning to do to me?"

"I know what he did." It can't be. I haven't heard that voice since—

Starling angles my face back to the mock execution stage. There, emerging from a cloud of feathers with black wings angling from her back, my sister walks away from Kalina's body. Blood crusts the edges of her mouth. One of Kalina's hands dangles from a set of talons protruding from her fingers.

How…HOW…

"On a task from his new king," Sarysi sidles closer and closer, "He stole his own sister from her bed and gave her to this wretched sword-girl thing , just so that he'd win favor when an Ave-Witch from his own family stumbled up on the execution stage, already marred with scars. Her wings unfurl, revealing the myriad scars from Kalina's sword crisscrossing her chest.

"How did you reverse the…" The Lords grace us so that the magic is irreversible. That's the tenant of the kings' rule…

A sigh from Starling. "The blood of the murderer, killed and eaten fresh, shall reverse the kings' magic and their behest. You have to be ended and devoured by an Ave-Witch you trapped. It's the only way we've found to reverse the binding spell. Of course, it can't bring back all the witches you've burned."

"Or the humans you've burned in their place." My heart drops. Enna's wings beat around her shoulder, blowing ash-filled air up my nose and mouth. Enna. Enna. And when she speaks it feels like the corners of my heart are being torn away from the rest of my chest: "You've gone on to kill, or maim, or torture everyone you could to get where you want to go."

"Can I do it now?" Sarysi bears her teeth. "The number of birds that want to strip him of his flesh…"

"Give us a moment." Enna and Starling exchange a glance, and Starling puts her hand on my forehead.

"He doesn't deserve to die painlessly!" Sarysi screams.

"I don't do this for the torture." Starling cuts her off firmly. All the while, Enna's been rifling around in her pockets. From the depths of one, she pulls out a small, green pill.

I've heard it before. That when people are about to die, they slowly become unmoored. Their life flickers around them. Starling's face flickers around me. All the people I'd imagined she had become wink out. Enna slides the pill into my mouth: mint and other herbs I can't identify.

And as the lights go out, as Enna and Starling pull me towards my pyre, I catch a glimpse of myself in Starling's mirrored eyes. Seventeen thousand freckles all spread across my face.

It must be the freckles she doesn't like.

Jordan Davidson is a student at Yale University majoring in Humanities and Applied Physics. These two disparate subjects produce incredibly disparate homework which is fortunately somehow unified in fantasy writing, maybe because some people think that neither degrees exist. Her work has been previously published in Class Collective, The Common Tongue, and is upcoming in Troublemaker Firestarter.

The Fourth Source

by Steven E. Scribner

1

Ras-Ero repeated the words to himself again, as if they were one of the lorematers' litanies against fear and hardship, "The quest is noble. The goal is virtuous. I set my heart upon the duty. It is of no consequence that some get hurt along the way. The quest is noble. The goal is virtuous…"

The sky was gray and the air was hot and moist. Ras-Ero's footfalls and the clack of his walking staff clattered against the gray shale shards strewn along the high path. His backpack bounced on his shoulders. On either side of him, the rocky ground sloped away, down into patchy green forests and meadows, and farther on, the sea. Even from this high vantage, the roar of the waves reached his ears, though diminished to a whispered rumble. His nose could still sense the salt smell. The sea was all around, after all; this island was not large enough to hold areas hidden from the ocean.

"The quest is noble. The goal is virtuous. I set my heart upon the duty…"

It was obvious that Skorak knew he was approaching. The island knew no hiding places just as it knew no respite from the sea. Even if Skorak hadn't been able to use the Fiery Eye, he would have been watching Ras-Ero. He would have also seen Ras-Ero speak with the Prisoner, though Skorak's Keep and the Prison of Trees were on opposite sides of the island. Not the way Ras-Ero would have designed it. But, he reminded himself, he was there to remove Skorak; it did not matter how Skorak planned the layout of his small realm.

"I set my heart upon the duty. It is of no consequence that some get hurt..."

Ras-Ero turned his eyes to his destination. The Keep rose out of the rocks like a lava plug thrust from the earth itself. Most of it was rough-hewn and slate-gray, though here and there were sparkles of brighter crimson and green and yellow — shards of color that indicated what would be seen from the inside as stained glass.

Ras-Ero trudged forward, and reached the front door. The customary door-gong hung beside it, a shiny bronze disc as round as Ras-Ero was tall; but there was no reason to strike it. The wooden door had been slid to the side and the way within lay open. There was no sign of any guards. Ras-Ero proceeded in. He would defeat Skorak without much of a fuss.

"Welcome to the Keep, Wanderer." The commanding voice surprised Ras-Ero, though he could not say later what was so surprising about it. He stood still and observed his surroundings.

Skorak himself was seated on a metal throne against the far wall. He wore a formal robe, though bedecked with brown and blonde fur and colored gems. His face was squarish, ruggedly handsome and far younger than Ras-Ero had expected for an elder loremaster; his tan skin, blonde-brown hair and scruffy beard was of the same folk as Ras-Ero himself — not a Southlander like his name would have indicated. Behind him stood, rising to thirty feet or more, a riot of color and light: a stained-glass wall arranged in three arched tableaux separated by thin traceries of white stone. The central held, against a blue field, an irregular patch of brown and green that was probably supposed to be the shape of the island seen from the air. The four-pointed star of the loremasters hovered in its own space above it. The four colors shown out: topmost, fiery orange-red; then light blue and aqua-green for the central spikes, and earthy gray-brown for the lower: the colors of the elements, with earth as the foundation and fire seeking upwards. The left glass panel held images of grand towers of the Imperium with the outstretched wings of its eagle above; in front of this scene was the tiger of the Southlanders, facing inward and kneeling as if in submission to Skorak's throne. The right tableau held similar symbols of the East and Northlanders, all facing inward and in an attitude of deference.

"You seek unity of the peoples of Tond within this grand edifice," Ras-Ero observed. He did not mention that the four-pointed star, that of his own people, was clearly at the top.

There came a snorting laugh from Skorak's throat. "Indeed," was the reply, "On this island I can dream anything. The Keep itself was an easy construction; I merely transmuted a scaffold of *lornáalis* and gave it constructional aspects, then affected a translucent state to let *kullándu* image the scenes."

"Skip the false modesty and the fancy loremaster language." Ras-Ero's voice assumed the harsh intonation he had planned. He spat without regard for the other, "You have a *mechana* that solidified some of the air to appear as stone, and another that casts illusions to give the impression of stained glass. This will all crumble the second you leave. We both know that I seek something more permanent upon this island."

Skorak scratched at his beard stubble. "You want to forge your own *mechana*, so you seek the Fourth Source because the other three are guarded." He paused, then, "What makes you sure that it is on this island? And I'm assuming that you are aware of what happened the last time someone tried to make a *mechana*?"

"To answer your first question, I have seen it in the Fiery Eye, and I spoke with the Prisoner." Ras-Ero did not need to answer the second question. The statistics ran through his mind: thousands dead in the initial blast, possibly millions in the ensuing years of horror. The *mechanas* — seemingly "magic" items of the Ancients — were a well-guarded secret, as they should be; and any attempt to produce a "new" one could result in untold disaster. But, he affirmed to himself, the quest is noble. It is of no consequence if some are hurt along the way.

"You quote Ras-Tannino well," Skorak chided, "Do you really know what your 'noble' quest is, exactly?"

Ras-Ero's eyebrows furrowed; he was not aware that he had spoken the lines aloud. He answered, "My quest is freedom. I will release everyone from their prison."

Skorak sat back on his gleaming seat. "You would release *my* prisoner, then?"

"Him, and you. From the prison of your own self. To quote Ras-Tannino again: there need be no prisons when all is perfected."

There was a moment of silence. Ras-Ero frowned; perhaps he had disclosed too much. But Skorak merely leaned forward again and smiled (was there a hint of malice in that expression?) and changed the subject. "You say you have spoken to my prisoner. You may speak with him more, but you may find it hard to release him. It was easy to trap him, of course; I merely altered the living aspects of *tandáalis* and surrounded him with a growing wall of timber. It may be more difficult for you to reverse the causation." Skorak sat back on his throne, then added, "He is of the Merfolk, not so?"

Ras-Ero spat his words again, "Enough of the fancy loremasters' language and the false ignorance. He is not of the Merfolk; he is a Shindo-Layon; the People of the Moon are fishlike when they are young, before their feathers grow and they take on the appearance of swans. As for how you trapped him: you have a *mechana* that draws wood from the earth and you ensnared him in an unnatural tree. May I ask, though, why you imprisoned him?"

"Now I must ask you to stop the false ignorance. You know as well as I do that he is imprisoned because he knows the whereabouts of the Fourth Source. He must never use it." Skorak pointed his finger at Ras-Ero, "*You* also must never use it, now that you have spoken your purpose."

"I seek merely the perfection of life."

But the man on the throne mumbled a cluster of nonsense syllables — one of the Ancients' formulas — and jumped from his seat. He lunged at Ras-Ero brandishing a shiny sword that he had pulled from the air itself. Ras-Ero dodged, knocking his walking-staff on the floor so the wooden casing fell off and exposed the hidden blade. Now it was a pike. Ras-Ero grabbed it with both hands and held it up to deflect Skorak's blade. Metal bashed onto strong wood with a sharp crack. Both men spun around at the impact, and assumed the guarded stance from the warfare of their people. Skorak lunged again, flailing the sword. Ras-Ero met it with his own blade, drew it aside. Ras-Ero swung his weapon, Skorak dodged and thrust his blade again. Ras-Ero stepped to the side and resumed the guarded stance.

Ras-Ero's mind continued to work. Obviously Skorak had the *mechana* with him, that had built this throne room, and had used it to make his sword. He might be able to materialize something even more deadly if given a chance. But Ras-Ero also had a *mechana* in his pocket, the one that had brought him to this island in the first place. Skorak would be removed.

As Skorak charged again, Ras-Ero spoke his own formula and stepped aside. A bluish glimmer of light appeared in the room, behind Skorak: a flame with azure tongues. In a second it had assumed a regular, quadrangular form, somewhat translucent, as tall as a man. Its near and far ends exchanged places and it opened as a door into a dark blue void.

"So, you plan to escape and not use the Fourth Source?" Skorak mocked. His back was to the blue Passage, but obviously he could sense its presence.

"I have no plan to escape." Ras-Ero lunged, twirling his weapon. Skorak's sword met the wood with another crack. Ras-Ero dodged aside and grabbed onto Skorak's left arm. Skorak brought his sword around from the other direction, but Ras-Ero's own blade knocked it aside. Ras-Ero pulled. Both stepped into the blue hole. Skorak thrust his sword again. Ras-Ero stepped to his right, near to the gleaming walls of the void, and pulled Skorak farther in. Skorak swung the weapon one last time. Ras-Ero ducked and dived out of the open door, muttering another formula as he impacted upon the floor of the Keep. A snapping, ripping noise, a scream from Skorak, and the opening folded in upon itself and was gone.

Ras-Ero chuckled. The dark blue void — the Passage, as it was called — had brought him to this island when it was open at both ends. But this time he had not specified the locations of the ends, and a Passage with no ends was nowhere. Skorak did not have a *mechana* to re-open it from the inside. He would be sealed in until he starved, or until Ras-Ero decided to release him.

...It is of no consequence that some are hurt along the way...

Ras-Ero replaced the wooden tip of the walking staff, covering the blade. He exited the Keep, trudging back along the high path. He was going to speak with the Prisoner at the other end of the island, and the Prisoner would rejoice that his captor was gone. Ras-Ero did not watch as, behind him, the Keep withered into a thin and insubstantial mist, and disappeared into the hot afternoon light.

2

Either the evening was far cooler than Ras-Ero expected, or this part of the island was sheltered from the midday sun. Either way, Ras-Ero shivered as he entered the grove of trees. The air was still and moist, and not even the aspen leaves quivered. Ras-Ero passed a cluster of rough-barked fir trees and a towering maple (all trees that should have been in more temperate climes, confirming that this part of the island was indeed cooler than the exposed high path). He strode up to that strange tree that had first caught his attention, seen in the Fiery Eye.

The trunk was cylindrical but vaguely bulged halfway between the soil and where the first boughs protruded. The branches, likewise, swelled ever so slightly between where they attached to the trunk and the sprouting of leaves. The leaves were round and flat, coin shaped, and about the size of Ras-Ero's palm. The bark, most obviously on the trunk, sported an array of fish-like scales, arranged in an overlapping grid. Clusters of grapelike fruit sprouted, seemingly at random, from all over the tree, from the trunk as well as the branches — but the fruit was not edible. It was whitish, stony gray, the only color difference on the entire tree; the rest of it, bark as well as leaves, was a darker gray that was almost imperceptibly greenish as if moss had grown on it and then fallen off. The whole impression was not of a living tree, but of a detailed sculpture, a statue of a tree: this was in fact the tree that Skorak had brought out of the stone in the ground.

But one part of it was clearly alive. Ras-Ero's eyes scanned it up and down until he recognized it: about the level of Ras-Ero's head, a corrugation in the scales of the bark had assembled themselves into a rough approximation of a human face. Its eyes were closed.

Ras-Ero tapped on the truck with his staff, and the eyes opened. The fading light caught their gray-green sparkle. The mouth, a lump of smaller scales, spoke. "You have returned. What is the fate of Skorak?" The voice was whispery, whooshing, like wind in branches.

"Skorak is no more. I have kept my part of the promise," Ras-Ero replied. "Now you must keep yours. I will attempt to set you free, though Skorak did not believe I can do so. But then you must show me to the Fourth Source."

"It shall be so," affirmed the man in the tree.

Ras-Ero stood for a moment, pondering if there might be any alternative to his plan. He had not managed to take anything from Skorak before sealing him away, and the *mechana* he had with him would be of no use to free the Prisoner from his stone tree. It could open a portal to another part of the world of Tond, but it could not smash stonewood. Very well then, his original plan would have to work. It chanced harming the Prisoner. But, he told himself, in that case there would merely be another casualty, and it is of no consequence that some get hurt along the way. He might even be able to find the Fourth Source by himself.

He took his staff and knocked off the end again. This time he grabbed the detached end in his hand, and began to beat a rhythm with it, hitting the tree again and again, in one place just above the face of the captive. The tree began to vibrate. If Ras-Ero was correct, the stonewood was weaker than natural stone; though strong enough to hold and immobilize a captive, it should shatter when the vibrations reinforced each other and grew strong enough. He sped up and slowed down, listening for maximum resonance. There it was. The tree rang out with a gonglike clang.

The sounds grew louder, clink clink. Almost musical. A grape-sized shard cracked off, but he did not alter his rhythm. Another piece, smaller than the first, flew off and landed next to his foot. Clink clink clink. A shallow hairline crack appeared and spread up the trunk. He continued to hammer. A larger stone, perhaps the size of an apple, thudded down from the branches above. He dodged aside, causing a pause in his tempo. The tree stopped ringing; his next blow was a dull thud. He swore to himself, and began his incessant pounding again. The tree sounded its gong reverberation again. Then, clink clink clink clink. Pain of fatigue shot through his arm. Ras-Ero clenched his teeth and continued to bang. As a plum-sized irregular chunk dislodged from the other side of the trunk and thudded to the ground, a wave of agony spread from his hand through his arm. Perhaps he should change hands? But that might interrupt the rhythm and he'd have to start again. Clink clink clink. Globules of sweat began to form on his forehead; he could feel them (despite the air which was still growing cooler) and then one ran into his eye and blurred his vision. He wiped it with his other hand and continued to hammer. A final piece the size of a ripe orange fractured near the impact site, and then:

"Jump aside!" Ras-Ero yelled as the entire tree cracked and splintered, tumbling onto the ground in a loose pile of sharp-edged stones. Dust billowed up. The Prisoner, suddenly appearing manlike, yelped and leapt to the side and fell upon the ground. A chuck of rock impacted the dirt near his right leg as he dodged the bulk of the collapse. The rock rolled a few feet toward a nearby maple tree.

The dust began to settle to the ground. The Prisoner rolled onto his back and sat up, staring at Ras-Ero, then screeched and flopped back onto the ground. "Move slowly," Ras-Ero stated, "You haven't been able to budge since you were trapped, so it'll be difficult at first."

3

The former prisoner's name was Kalavan. It was an odd name for someone in the world of Tond, he admitted, though it was common among the People of the Moon. He was similar to a human, but he was not a human. He had a head and a torso and two arms and two legs like a man, but there was something fishlike about him. His shape was wrong; bulging at the middle with no discernable waist, though not soft and fat. His head seemed somewhat too large, and it was joined directly onto his body as if he had no neck. His skin was a network of fine overlapping scales. He was wearing a woven shirt and trousers, torn and puckered up and caked with dirt; all difficult to distinguish from his skin because it too was mottled and patched with encrustations of soil. These were the result of his long imprisonment (he needed a bath and a thorough scrubbing) but something else lingered from the confinement itself: if part fish, he was also part tree. Small branches sprouted from his shoulders, bedraggled with those gray-green coin-shaped leaves; and his legs did not end in well-formed feet but in unkempt tangles of roots.

He remained there lying on that patch of grass and soil in the grove of trees for five days while Ras-Ero tended him. He did not need to eat or drink, taking nourishment and water directly from the soil by digging with the roots that were his feet. On the fourth day, he spoke with Ras-Ero. "I was an orphan. There are often storms on this island; I was marooned here. Yes, my parents are People of the Moon; we came here on a sky-ship, but it was destroyed by a storm. But this island is full of voices, seen and unseen; in an hour or two Skorak had heard I was here and he rescued me. After several years here, he called me his son, since he had none of his own. But then I found the Fourth Source, and

Skorak imprisoned me lest I ever use it. He called me his son, but he became my enemy."

Then he asked Ras-Ero, "What of you? I know you came here to find the Fourth Source. How did you learn of it?"

Ras-Ero stared at the fish-man for a moment, decided to tell everything. The latter was not a loremaster, and would not be likely to understand all of Ras-Ero's words. And, if the fish-man knew too much, he could be removed later, in the same way as Skorak. So Ras-Ero chuckled. "Ras-Tannino was a pirate."

"What?"

"Ras-Raydo, Ras-Tumilo, Ras-Tannino. They were three brigands who haunted the seas two hundred years ago. Ras-Tannino wanted to plunder the Island of Silver and Gold. He never found it; I believe it does not exist. But he wrote his famous lines between two of his voyages: 'The quest is noble. The goal is virtuous. I set my heart upon the duty. It is of no consequence that some get hurt along the way.' Those words have always inspired me. But he also said, 'there need be no prisons when all is perfected.' I did not understand those words until after I saw a mordth."

"A mordth? There are none here. Did you see it on the mainland?"

"Yes, near the Blue River. Loremasters like myself wander, and I was living with the Southlanders at the time." He paused and slapped at a mosquito alighting on his arm. He continued, "Ras-Tannino was speaking of riches, I think; he assumed that if he had enough wealth he would buy his freedom from anyone who caught him. He thought that the ability to escape meant he was perfect. He was probably wrong. But his words had deeper meaning." He faced the fish-man, staring as if to bore a hole with his eyes. "Have you ever seen one, a mordth, I mean?"

"I have not. I know only that they appeared when someone tried to make a *mechana*. They wished to conquer the mainland. There was a war."

Ras-Ero's eyes grew moist. "It was on the banks of the river. The war was raging elsewhere on the mainland, but there in the Southlands it was peaceful, for the moment. I saw something gliding toward me, not really on the river, but above it, as if it was floating down a second river that was invisible and above the first. The sunlight reflected off of it; shards of silver light filled the air. As it drew nearer, I recognized it from what others had said: serpentine form, but with many jointed legs, and tentacles on its head like an octopus. When I describe it, it does not sound like a beautiful sight; but that is to ignore what it is. Mordths are artificial. They were made in that shape to be able to go anywhere, to slither into small spaces, to swim in water and in the upper air. Their shape and their form are perfect for their function. They are living *mechanas*, and they are perfect. They can only be killed by another *mechana*, or by a spear down their throat. I will make one of my own, without having to make another *mechana* first, when you take me to the Fourth Source."

Kalavan's eyes grew fierce. "They may be perfect, according to you, but they wished to destroy everything on the mainland!"

"Yes, destroy and start again. Remake everything in a better way."

The fish-man said nothing for a moment, gazing at the trees around him. At last he spoke, "I promised that I would lead you to the Fourth Source. I will not break a promise, but now that I know your purpose, I think I should not do it. Why can you not use one of the other Sources?"

"They are on the mainland. One is in the Tower of Kings; the mordths ruined it during the war. It is buried under a mile of stone. One is in the Halls of the Grimborn. It was blasted by fire and can no longer be used. The third is in Borrogg; it was crushed by a glacier soon after the war. None can be worked." He slapped another mosquito, then turned to the fish-man again. "Those are three of the elements: buried under stone; burned by fire; crushed by frozen water. So, I reasoned, there must be a Fourth Source, that no one had heard of. That is not common knowledge among the loremasters; I only deduced it from what I had learned about the others. I had the *mechana* to make the Fiery Eye, and I used it to search all the mainland, and then the islands in the sea. I finally found that it must be on this island." He chuckled, "One would think that, if it's on an island, it would be a source of the power of water, but apparently it is of the air."

"…And you could not see it with the Fiery Eye?"

"All of the Sources are shielded from sight, at least from sight by means of a *mechana*. I only thought it must be here because this island is a blank space that the Eye cannot penetrate. So I came here, and found you; and you confirmed that it is here."

Kalavan nodded. Whether or not he had originally intended to tell this to Ras-Ero, the secret was out. He sighed. "Tomorrow I will keep my promise. I will show you to it."

The two of them slept in the open in the grove of trees, as they had done the previous nights. Once during the night Ras-Ero awakened and thought that the did not sense the other's presence nearby; but he said to himself that the fish-man had merely gone elsewhere to urinate. He rolled over on the soft moss and went back to sleep. A mild rumble, like distant thunder, insinuated itself into his dreams later, but upon awakening again, he did not remember it.

4

The morning dawned with the chirping and chattering of birds. The sky was cloudy and threatened rain, but for now the air was hot and sticky again. Kalavan stood and stretched. "I am well enough. We may go now."

Ras-Ero ate a pear from one of the neighboring trees along with dried meat and oily cheese from the dwindling supplies in his backpack. Then he clutched his walking staff, shouldered his backpack, and signaled for Kalavan to begin the journey. A gentle rain had begun; Ras-Ero let it comfort him as it washed his gluey hair.

The path forked, one way leading to the high path and the vanished Keep; the other into the woods. Kalavan led along the second way. Fir and maple trees arched overhead, joined now by the occasional palm, and the ground beside the path was covered with ferns. The sound of the sea, never absent on the island, seemed louder, echoing among the tree trunks. Kalavan stopped after about twenty minutes and motioned for Ras-Ero to look around him. Ras-Ero could see nothing different; the dirt trail continued straight ahead into a denser and darker cluster of trees. On the left were four maple trees; on the right was the base of the rock cliff that, if climbed, would lead to the high path. Kalavan pointed to the stone. There seemed to be nothing unusual about it; gray slate and orangish sandstone, with a smooth but irregular surface. A patchwork of lichen clung to it here and there.

"Here I will wait," said Kalavan.

Ras-Ero stared at him. Surely this was a mistake? But then, as his eyes passed over the stone again, he noticed an indefinable darkness across a section, a slight diminution of its color. It seemed that something the size and shape of a doorway was casting a faint shadow on it. Ras-Ero glanced skyward. The clouds hung low, visible between the arching branches, but there was nothing there to cast such a shadow. Ras-Ero turned back to the stone wall, and chuckled to himself. Yes, now he understood. He had heard of such permanent illusions, made by alterations in the properties of the air. There would have been no way to detect it without the proper *mechana*, which he did not have. Kalavan must be able to see it because the eyes of the People of the Moon see different light than those of humans. Ras-Ero reached out to touch the obscure patch, and his hand went through. It was an invisible doorway. He put one foot in, testing if the ground was solid, and then stepped in.

He had entered a tunnel hewn from the rock. The walls and ceiling were of the same smooth gray and brownish orange as the outside; the floor was a continuation of the dirt path. There was perhaps enough space for two men to walk abreast. The passage was illuminated by yellow-white light that seemed to come from all directions. Ras-Ero smiled. He had not seen one of the Ancients' Sources, but from what he had gathered, this is exactly how one should appear. He walked forward.

He came to a second illusory wall: a rock slab that looked, if his memory was correct, an exact copy of the one outside. He reached out and put his hand through it. He tested the inside with his foot again, and then proceeded in.

He had entered the Innermost Secret Place, and its strangeness, now that he could begin to recognize it, forced him to his knees in awe. The far walls were perhaps a hundred feet away; not a huge cavern, but they were covered with *power.*

Lights. Strange lights that had been flashing and glittering for hundreds of years.

Metal. Flat surfaces wrought of unknown and unknowable metal, mined from the depths of the earth, and even stranger snaky shapes of metal and something black, curled or stretched across the floor and across the walls and hanging from the ceiling.

A pool of water, perhaps ten feet across, sapphire blue, glowing with a light from within. The walls that contained it were marble and carved in an octagonal shape; and it sat against the wall to his left.

The power-floor. An empty square, colored or painted in a pattern of bright hazy blue and white, beside the marble and sapphire pool. Above the empty square was another empty square on the ceiling, painted in the same pattern, and there was an energy pulsing between them: not visible, not a light, but something Ras-Ero could feel touching the edge of vision. He closed his eyes but still could feel its location. He opened them, and realized that, if he stared long enough, he could make out dim blue flashes arcing within that field of energy.

The four glass pillars. Standing against the wall on either side of the cavern were columns of glass that reached from the floor to the ceiling. They were several feet wide, and more of the invisible/visible energy pulsed between and through them.

The table of *mechanas*. Jutting towards the far wall from the center of the room, the table sat at an angle facing the pool and the pillars. Wrought of dark wood, its surface was covered with orderly rows of crystals, protruding knife-handles, and lights: square and rectangular lights, moving lights, lights that made patterns of lines and curves.

The power-swords; several strapped to the table with leathery ropes, and dangling towards the floor on the side closest to the pool.

The stone pillars, grey and white marble, eight of them; four on either side, arranged in rows angling in the opposite direction from the glass poles; they were twice as wide as a man and they reached from floor to ceiling as if to hold the massiveness of the earth overhead.

Ras-Ero went out onto the floor to the Innermost Secret Place, and came before the Table of *Mechanas*. He gazed across the surface of the table and found a hollow in the shape of a person's right hand. That was where to begin. He placed his palm in the indentation.

The Noise surprised him. A boom, echoing in the unknowable depths, and a quiet roar, the sound of the wind, but infinitely remote. It began low, increased in volume and pitch, and settled as a quiet, continuous rushing. The power had been reawakened from its hundred-year slumber.

A voice spoke: female, emotionless and without intonation. The words seemed to come from all directions. "Welcome to the Island of Storms. You stand before the power of Lornáalis. You are a stranger here. State your name and your purpose."

Ras-Ero smiled. This is exactly what he expected. "Grendul Ras-Ero, Loremaster from Eyuhand in Central Mainland Tond. I seek to create a mordth, in order to perfect life in Tond."

There was a sputtering noise, again from an uncertain direction. The voice said, "I do not understand. You stand before the power of Lornáalis. You are a stranger here. State your name and your purpose."

Ras-Ero stared at the table and into the space before him. He squinted for a second, then allowed himself another slight smile. Yes, of course; this was the power of the Ancients. The voice had been modified to speak the present language, but in order to use the power, one had to speak the Old Tongue. Only the loremasters still knew it. He spoke the words with the same meaning as his previous statement: "*An Gréndul Ras-Séro, an ahíinor Miaswa Tánd ni Eyuhand karáa. An mórdh teilándan-zúnggas, Tánd ni léyu zan ráisas.*"

Another sputtering sound, then the voice: "You may proceed."

"Thank you," Ras-Ero acknowledged, though unaware whether the voice could actually hear him now or not. He gazed at the surface of the Table and looked for the arrangement of the crystals… Yes, there. Four thumbnail-sized gems sat in a diamond shape: orange-red, light blue, gray-brown, deep aqua. He tapped the light blue one with his finger because this Source was associated with Lornáalis, the element Air.

The glass pillars lit up bright blue with white streaks through them, as if containing the sky far above the island. Lights in the room flashed blue and white.

"Wow," Ras-Ero mouthed the word to himself, then quoted from the Song of Origins, the very "fancy loremasters' language" he had chided Skorak for using:

Lornáalis is air and sky, wind and breath;
Now the gentle cool scent of the breath of evening,
Now the roar of storm winds untamed,
Now the swirling current under the feathered wings of birds.
But Lornáalis cannot fly by itself, for Teilyándal' is the Wind.

But to create a mordth, Ras-Ero would need more than the power of Air. He reached for the brown crystal.

Darkness fell. Only the crystal itself remained glowing a somber green and brown.

"Well, what did I expect?" he muttered. "Of course Earth and Stone have little in the way of lights." From the Song of Origins again:

Tandáalis is earth and mountain and stone;
Now the lichen-covered rocks of the sky-touching mountains,
Now the delicate sands of the desert,
Now the fixture of the earth, firm, monolithic, immovable.
But Tandáalis cannot stand by itself, for Teilyándal' is the Foundation.

"This should be more impressive," he muttered, and took ahold of the red crystal.

The glass pillars flickered and roared into life again. Brilliant, almost ghastly light shown out from them, and they reverberated with continuous thunder. Ras-Ero laughed aloud.

Kullándu is fire and energy, power and change;
Now a soft flicker of heat in the chill air,
Now the roar of crimson destruction,
Now the burning passion to father anew and forge beauty.
But Kullándu cannot make or unmake by itself, for Teilyándal' is the Maker.

Yes, the power of Fire. Only one more to see; Ras-Ero tapped on the deep blue-green crystal. The pillars of light responded; now they were water, a glowing aquamarine blue, a flowing of hues and reflections. The octagonal pool of water began to splash and gurgle.

Kewándii is rain and river and sea;
Now the life-giving diamond-drops on the sand,
Now the current of river water and all that flows,
Now the thunder of life and might at the edge of the sea.
But Kewándii cannot live by itself, for Teilyándal' is the life-giver.

Ras-Ero let out a chuckle. Yes, those were the powers of the Four. The Elements. He would need all four: air, for the creature's spirit; stone, for its metal skin; fire, for the spark to bring it to life, and water, for its lifeblood. He ran the Ancients' formulae through his mind one last time, and then stood still. Now he would take the part of Teilyándal' in the Song of Origins. He would be the Wind, the Foundation, the Maker, and the Life-Giver. He would make a mordth. "The quest is noble. The goal is virtuous. I set my heart upon the duty. It is of no consequence that some get hurt along the way." He grabbed the red crystal again. Thunder and power roared back into the room; he left the table for a moment and came before the pillars, almost to the edge of the Power Floor, which was glowing and shaking also. There was a rhythm and a flow to that cataclysm of noise; there was a throb to it, and for a moment he danced to its sound.

He wiped sweat from his eyes, went back to the lore-tables. Now his hands flicked across them, pulling knife-handles and grabbing crystals; no longer was he really aware of it all. He shouted the ancient formulae. The powers flashed and throbbed around him, growing more intense, thundering, spiraling, burning. This was his moment; all of his loremasters' training had gone into this. He pulled one of the flashing metal swords from its cord; it would be the raw metal from which his mordth would be forged. He walked out to the center again, and came before the Power Floor. He lay the sword down in front of it; the sword flashed and the Floor lit up with pulsations of power.

He went back to the Table. Touching crystals, pulling handles, and reciting formulae, he began to knead the power before him; all the flashing, burning power. First it became like a pillar itself, a glowing column of light; then he fashioned it into a smaller shape. The sword on the Floor began to sputter and crackle; it burst into flame and joined into the column of energy. He formed it into a yet smaller shape, and its light grew in intensity. He elongated it, stretched it out into a centipede shape, curled it up into itself. Suspended there between the floor and the ceiling, he formed it, a torus of pure light.

His fingers closed around the red crystal again. More power rushed into the room; he could feel his hair crackling and sparking. He fused that power into the torus, and its light increased; now it gave off the radiance of the sun.

A third time he took hold of the red crystal. The pillars themselves began to tremble. Now the power was even stronger. It tugged against him, trying to force his hands into different positions across the table; he wrestled with it and fought against it; in the end, it fused into the torus and the light increased yet again. Now it seared the air with a palpable fire.

He smiled to himself. This mordth was to be a living *fyer-yam mechana*. The fourth level of power, forged here in the Fourth Source. Did he dare? But he knew that he must. He reached out, hesitated, then grabbed hold of the red crystal one last time.

Fire and light and terror roared into the room from everywhere and nowhere. It caught him and he felt himself burning; it roared around him and thundered through him. He hands danced across the table, and he fought and wrestled again; he felt the world collapse into a burning cinder of pure light; he could not see, but he continued to feel and hold the crystals on the table. He wrestled and fought; the power hovered there in the center of the cavern, a gleaming sun but perhaps even brighter; he dared for a moment to look at his hands; he could see the bones through his flesh. He cried out and molded and shaped the power one last time, dancing and flashing his burning fingers across the table; then, with a deafening crack and boom, the power was confined in the shape of the suspended torus.

He watched it uncurl. For a second it remained there, a serpentine sun in the cavern; then it leapt into the octagonal pool and the water exploded into steam. All of the lights extinguished themselves, though Ras-Ero's eyes were still showing bright lights that were no longer there. He could see nothing of what he had made.

The roar had ceased as well. Ras-Ero stood there for a moment, dazzled, his hands and face still feeling heat and burning. Gradually his eyes readjusted. The pool came into his sight. The mordth was crawling from it; at first merely a twisting shape of dark metal. More details emerged; the octopus tentacles at its front end, feeling for its surroundings; the many-jointed body, the fifty legs for creeping across any surface. Ras-Ero's eyes could now see its color, and he rejoiced in its beauty: a gleaming, metallic, eight-foot-long, opalescent, crystal dragon. The creature pulled its last legs out from the marble octagon (there was no water there now), and it ambled across the floor and sat there facing Ras-Ero. He smiled.

The voice of the cavern spoke again, "Grendul Ras-Ero, you have completed your *mechana.* You have successfully made a mordth." Its next words came as a surprise: one of the Ancients' formulae.

Ras-Ero gasped and shielded himself with his hands. In that second, he knew that the fish-man *could* use the loremasters' power, and had betrayed him by coming here in the night and telling the Voice to command the mordth.

The glistening centipede hurdled at Ras-Ero, its tentacles flexing and curling. He fell under its impact, rolled on the floor and grabbed for his walking staff and knocked it on the floor of the cavern. He stabbed its exposed blade at the mordth, shoving it down the creature's open gullet, and he rolled aside. He said the formula to open the Passage, specifying both ends so that he would not meet the imprisoned Skorak, and slipped into its dark blueness.

The fish-man Kalavan entered the Innermost Secret Place and watched as the mordth writhed on the ground, its new life ebbing away. Far above his head and above the rocks, a heavy storm rain was pelting the island.

And so, Ras Sero escaped from the betrayal and slipped away in his Passage, a portal back to the Tondish mainland. There, he plotted his return to the island, and his capture of the Fourth Source.

Another tale is told about Ras-Ero on the island: one where he has a different name that means "One Who Prospers"; one where a shipwrecked crew comes ashore to find him living in uneasy peace with Kalavan; and one where Ras-Ero is a villain who torments the crew in revenge for a wrong committed against him some years earlier. That is indeed a later chapter of this same tale; but it is also a different tale from a different age and told by a different people. Tales from the Tondish Mainland and the surrounding islands leak into better-known (and lesser-known) tales of other worlds. Loremasters, the People of the Moon, and mordths may appear elsewhere, and readers of all worlds are left wondering at the brave new world that has such people (and creatures) in it.

Steven E. Scribner is a high school teacher, amateur musician, part-time blogger and full-time nerd, living in the tree-y suburbs north of Seattle. He is the author of the high-fantasy "Tond" series and the upcoming "MadStones Tetralogy" (also set in the word of Tond) as well as two other books. He enjoys reading sci-fi, fantasy, historical fiction, experimental fiction, and nonfiction.

A Necessary Sacrifice

by Erin Swann

Every tragedy should have a villain. Someone to blame, somewhere to place anguish and hatred. A name to curse when a loved one is lost.

Disease is not tangible enough. You can't shout at a cough, glare defiantly at a rash, or swear revenge on a fever.

The villain needs a face.

Queen Serenia gazed down from the tall parapets of her frozen fortress: an impassive porcelain vestige, the last image of perfection presiding over a dying world. Pearl pins pierced her grey locks, wrapped in tight curls and piled above her frigid face.

Swirling crystals of ice clinked against the iron railing, glossing over her domain. Below the fortress, clouds twisted at a lower elevation, forming an impervious mist to eyes without the gift of magic. But Serenia had plenty of magic and her supernatural sight swept across her realm, down the base of the mountain, and into the towns mottling the ground far below. Into the kingdoms of men.

How far could she reach?

How many could she ensnare before the end?

Flashes of white softer than snow reflected the sunlight bleeding through the winter storm—the wings of one of her angels.

Serenia outstretched her pale blue arm, stone-hard against the biting wind and sharp talons of her snow owl as it alighted on her limb. It didn't speak. Owls could do no such thing. But they could do far better than that: they were her voice to the outside world.

Her lure.

"One village at a time," she murmured. "Seek the strong, the untouched. The perfect. Bring them to me. Slowly."

#

"Is the Ice Queen beautiful?" Beth asked, nestled in her bed. Her great cow eyes clung to Brogan, as if he had all the answers in the world.

"Of course she is," Brogan said, smiling down at his daughter. He had no idea. But it was the right thing to say. In *his* version of the story, someone who could save others from the Burning Plague ought to be pretty.

"The Ice Queen sits above the world, sending her snowy angels to call the worthy to her castle. Ones untouched by the plague. Some say she is immortal, immune to the disease herself."

"If she's immune," Beth said, "why does she stay in the castle and only invite the healthy?"

Brogan bowed his head. "Why indeed? Others say her haven of ice is the last true place free of the plague and she keeps her distance to keep it pure."

Beth gave a nod, satisfied. "That makes more sense."

In reality, no one really knew.

The kingdoms of men avoided the Frozen Mountain until recently. There were too many tales of travelers gone missing, of bewitched minds, of a selfish sorceress who sought only the very best to inhabit her domain. She kept them to herself, whether or not the occupants wished to be there.

Once you stepped foot on the mountain, there was no return.

When the Burning Plague tore through the land, everything changed. There was no cure, no magic spell, no miracle potion. Only the inevitability of death.

"Is that why she uses owls? So she and her people won't get sick?" Beth breathed, covers rising and falling more rapidly than they should.

"Yes, the agents of the Snow Queen bear a 'gift' to certain individuals. A letter."

"What do the letters say?"

Brogan wasn't exactly sure, but he'd heard enough. "She promises a haven for the healthy. In exchange, they must leave everything behind." Not all accepted the offer, but those who didn't were eventually consumed by the plague. With the alternative being death, more were answering the call despite their fear.

There were other rumors Brogan didn't share with his daughter. Rumors that the distant queen herself started the plague, lonely and in want of company. She spread the sickness to make villagers desperate enough to brave the frozen mountain and come to her.

"Do you think she'll send an owl to you and mom?" Beth asked.

Brogan's throat swelled for a moment and he patted Beth's small hand to buy himself time to find his voice again. His fingers brushed her delicate skin, and he fought the instinct to flinch as her flesh burned beneath his touch. Her small hands used to be a beautiful shade of caramel, far lighter than his own. Now, splotches of red spread day by day, like spilt wine on a fine tablecloth.

"Maybe," he managed. "But I'm not going anywhere without you."

Brave far beyond her scant dozen years, Beth smiled. "I don't think you'll have to choose. You and mom should go."

Brogan heard a muffled whimper in the doorway, the old wood of their cottage creaking in protest beneath shifting weight. His wife, Myra, hid in the shadows of the narrow hall outside Beth's room. She'd been listening, of course, but she couldn't hide her sorrow like he could.

Brogan was the brave face.

#

The invitation came the day after Brogan buried his only child. A downy white owl perched on the splintered fence of his small vegetable patch. He'd gone out to weed, to do something aside from wallowing in despair, and found the hateful creature studying him with unblinking, unfeeling eyes.

So it wasn't just a rumor after all.

"Now you come," he said, voice hoarse, heart raw. "Where were you a month ago? Three weeks ago? How *dare* you come to us now."

It might have been terrifying, but he would have sent Beth to the queen if it meant saving her from the fate she suffered. But Beth was already gone.

Brogan's hands trembled as the owl stuck out its foot, unmoved by his impassioned words. Someone had tied a small scroll to its leg. Brogan almost ripped it off, leg still attached, but he wasn't certain how powerful the Ice Queen truly was. Would the plague consume him if he enraged her? Would it take Myra?

Myra.

Would she be in the letter?

Curiosity won out, and Brogan removed the scroll from the owl's leg. The great bird immediately took flight as if Brogan's answer didn't matter. Maybe it didn't.

A haven of health and a long life awaits. Come. Brogan.

Brogan stared down at the words, numb. He turned the small scroll over, hoping for more words on the back. Just one more word.

"Is that the invitation?" Myra's voice wavered from their back door. "Is the Ice Queen real?" His heart broke all over again at the hope in her tone. She'd despaired for so long, he had forgotten how lightly her voice used to ring.

Brogan turned to face his wife. Dark skin worn thin in more ways than one, crinkles webbing the edges of her deep eyes and forehead. She hadn't bothered to tie back her hair in weeks, the warm brown it used to be fading along with her smile. Now, her face looked flushed, her chest fluttering with quickened breath.

Why summon *him*? If this strange queen was looking for the best, Myra was far more worthy. Steadfast, loving, hard-working.

Perhaps he could strike a bargain.

"Yes," Brogan said, forcing the words out in a steady stream as he pocketed the scroll. "An invitation for both of us."

#

They came, of course. It was the way of humanity. Survival instincts won out in the end.

Queen Serenia didn't leave her towering perch as she watched frozen pilgrims trudge trails through the snow-crusted banks. Not all made it to her fortress; bodies of the dead who failed to make the journey blemished her pristine mountain.

It was a necessary culling. She would only accept the strong. Only the strong were worthy.

Some pilgrims came in pairs or trios, hoping to save their loved ones as well. But invitations rarely included more than one individual. Few remained untouched.

Another inevitability of humanity: refusal to accept an undesirable reality.

They would seek to negotiate with her, thinking they were an exception to her rule. Pathetic. But that wasn't why Serenia stayed in her lofty tower, watching the poor, desperate fools try to force their companions through the iron gates of her fortress.

She must remain untouched, pure.

Her bewitched guards wrangled the chosen away from their loved ones. If they made it this far, then these pilgrims were worthy; their compassion was misplaced, not unwanted. In their current world, there could be no compassion. Her attendants would ensure the pilgrims that their companions would be examined. If they were indeed pure, free of the Burning Plague symptoms, they would join the chosen later.

But that never happened. If they were worthy, they would have received an invitation.

The early signs of the plague were invisible to those who refused to accept the truth, blinded by love. Shortened breath, fading coloration, flushing of the skin. How easy that is to excuse.

She watched as the guards corralled the chosen, ushering them into her sanctum to await nightfall.

Queen Serenia turned away to prepare.

#

They took Myra.

Brogan paced the length of his small chamber. The extreme conditions of their journey had cracked his worn leather boots and he could feel cold spots where moisture had leaked in, but he didn't care. What was the point in caring if she was gone? He kept eyeing the door, waiting for it to open. The guards said Myra would be examined and then join him if she was worthy. She *was* worthy.

It couldn't end like this. It had taken so much to get here. There were a few times on the mountain where he thought they would freeze to death. Indeed, he and Myra had passed quite a few corpses on their way to this haven above the misty clouds. He had no idea how long the poor souls had been left preserved in the snowdrifts; it didn't seem like this mountain ever saw a season aside from deep winter.

He rubbed his chapped hands, split and bleeding, with a salve left by the attendants who brought him a set of clean, warm garments. The floral scent reminded him of the baths he gave Beth as a child. He told himself the water in his eyes was from the pungent ointment.

Brogan sat with tentative care on a brocaded ottoman by the door to pull off his boots and change. He was almost afraid to touch anything, the furnishings far finer than any he'd seen in his small village. The wooden legs of tables and chairs were stained dark and carved into intricate shapes of reindeer and owls, feathers and antlers detailed exquisitely. Candlesticks of fine silver stretched out from the walls, dripping beeswax that flavored the chilled air.

Myra would love it.

He darted another glance at the closed door.

Dressed in a fur-lined tunic and pants soft enough to whisper against his calloused skin, Brogan cautiously moved to the bed and nearly jumped back up, fearing he would sink right through the mattress. But no, it was simply stuffed with something far softer than the coarse straw packed into his own mattresses at home.

How Beth would have enjoyed this. He could hear her laughing as she burrowed under the crisp sheets, wrapping the thick fur throw around her like a cocoon. His heart throbbed and he turned over on the bed, but there was no Myra to mourn with.

He couldn't do this alone.

Brogan drew a calming breath. The queen offered haven to the healthy. Myra was healthy.

"She withstood the mountain's will. That was quite a feat," the guard had told him. Though he said it without emotion, not meeting Brogan's eyes.

All the queen's attendants were like that, as if she had sculpted them from ice as well, emotionless but polite. They *looked* human enough, but Brogan almost preferred a rude comment or a condescending look to the frosty demeanors of the castle's staff. He felt far more alone than he should. All those stories of bewitched travelers felt a lot more plausible now.

Perhaps the queen would bewitch him, too. Was that better or worse than contracting the Burning Plague? Could he stand to see Myra that way? *Would* he see Myra that way? It had been hours since they took her and no word.

Brogan shook his head. Myra would be fine.

She was just fatigued from the long journey, which had caused her labored breathing and pallid complexion. It wasn't the plague. They had said that about Beth too, of course, but this was different. It had to be. He couldn't lose them both.

Laying on his back, Brogan stared up at the lacy, white molding trimming the alabaster ceiling. He'd never seen so much white before the Frozen Mountain, mud and grass coloring his village in full. At first, he found the blankets of gleaming snow beautiful, the way it sparkled and glittered in the sunlight. His view soured the longer he and Myra spent out in the elements with little shelter and meager rations. Until it became terrifying.

The new color of death.

Now, as he looked out his small window at the expanse of white glazing every surface of the queen's expansive gardens, he felt…

Brogan wasn't certain how he felt, aside from fatigued. Exhausted. The guard that escorted him to this room told him to rest. An induction ceremony would begin at midnight, where he would have a brief audience with the Ice Queen herself. Once he swore fealty to his new monarch, he would be accepted into her domain officially.

Perhaps he would be saved. Perhaps he would lose his soul.

As he rested his head on a pillow far too soft to be real, Brogan closed his eyes and saw her again in his mind. A distant figure atop the parapets overseeing their arrival. He thought she was a sculpture at first, statuesque and grand, cut from crystal itself. Then, she lifted one graceful hand in a brief greeting, like a swan stretching its wing to the sky. Something that lithe and angelic would surely listen to his appeal. She couldn't be as monstrous as the stories depicted her.

Brogan would rest. And then he would ask after Myra.

#

Queen Serenia stood on a marble balcony the color of bleached bone, long elegant fingers straining against the railing. She only had enough strength for one more tonight. The others would have to wait until tomorrow.

Two of her guards led the next chosen through the courtyard, the dark stone below bathed in silver moonlight, suspiciously absent of snow to those that were more observant. This peasant seemed a little more well off than some of the others, but even from her perch above, she saw the telltale shadow of loss deepening rings below his sallow eyes.

But loss touched *all* souls at this point. The Burning Plague was taking their land and the lands beyond, rampant and unstoppable, even by magic.

Broken and sorrowful he may be, but this one was pure. Untouched by the plague itself. He would join the others in her new, pristine world. His violently red hair flapped in his eyes as they rose and narrowed to study her. Serenia leaned forward to let him take in her willowy form, enrobed in grey downy fur and soft leather skins.

"Your name, chosen," she breathed, her voice drifting among flakes of fresh snow.

"Brogan," he called, far louder than necessary.

He winced at the echo and nervously glanced around the square of stone festooned with shining icicles and grand fountains frozen in a moment of motion. Dark figures lined the walls, blending in with the velvet shadows cast by the moon. When his eyes found hers again, she didn't soften her expression, anticipating the words he would speak next.

"Your grace, please. My wife, Myra, is well. She made the journey with me. I assure you she is healthy."

"If she is, then you have nothing to fear," Serenia said indifferently. "The invitation was for you and you alone. It was rather impertinent to use my generosity to seek more. And ungrateful."

Brogan cast his eyes to the flagstone dusted with the newly fallen snow. "I wasn't asking you to accept her as well. I wanted her to take my place."

"That is not how my invitations work." Still, that caring quality was one to preserve. Her owls had chosen this one well. "Brogan, I am here tonight to induct *you*. There are few I can bestow this honor on. True safety from the plague."

"How?" His eyes shone with naivety.

Queen Serenia raised her hands, calling on the frigid winds, willing the clouds to lend her the moisture in the air, and lifting the layer of white from the ground. The snow ceased swirling around them, and Brogan's eyes widened, glancing from side to side.

It appeared as if she had frozen time itself, but she had only frozen the ice crystals. With a mere thought, she willed them to adhere to the young man's body, weaving in her glacial magic to preserve his beautiful vibrancy. An excellent addition indeed. The chosen barely had time for a gasp of surprise before he froze solid, encased in the deep sleep of winter.

"You are perfect. Now you will remain so."

It was the only way she had found to keep a body pure, free from the plague. He would live together with the others, forever untouched. If they were to scamper back among the living, the plague would reach them too. Here, frozen without breath, her subjects were safe; they were perfect. And her spell was as immortal as she was.

The guards lifted the chosen and moved him to the edges of the dark courtyard, lined with other statues. She would arrange her new statues at a later time, after she gathered more.

Serenia gave a single nod to the guards as they bowed to her, taking their leave for the night. They would eventually become infected as well, interacting with far too many of the chosen's loved ones. It was a pity.

But a necessary sacrifice.

#

In that moment, as Brogan's body grew abnormally rigid and his senses dulled, shock battled with a bitter sense of irony. He battled hypothermia, fought to bring Myra to a safe place, avoided becoming just another frozen corpse on the mountain. Now, he would be a frozen corpse decorating the castle of a cold-hearted sorceress instead. And Myra, if they deemed her worthy, would suffer the same fate.

#

Time passed at a glacial pace. Seasons labored by below Serenia's frozen paradise and the age of man guttered out as the Burning Plague consumed the living, reducing all to figurative ashes.

But time did not touch the Ice Queen.

Serenia paced around her garden of perfection, admiring her handiwork. Vibrant faces frozen in moments of surprise: the last remnants of humanity. She stroked a tender finger down the cheek of a stone cold child, steely like her own skin.

It was different seeing them up close now, her human garden. Serenia had descended from her solitary confinement above after her avian angels finally brought word that the last city of man exhaled its final breath.

The years had been long and arduous, staying pure, staying separate. She *had* to be the last. It was lonely, but it was necessary. Her perfect world wouldn't work otherwise.

The grounds outside her courtyard sanctuary of stone and ice were still. It was silent enough that she could hear the ice crystals hitting the snow banks around her fortress walls, tiny beads of tinkling glass pattering the pristine sheaths of land.

"Your grace," one of her guards rasped, struggling to bow. He was trembling, tender pink skin blotched with crimson. "We are ready."

Serenia dipped her head and extended a hand. "A new world awaits after you take the final step."

Her remaining staff shuffled out into the snow, dedicated to her every whim. They had given up their humanity long ago, swearing fealty to her when she promised to end the plague at all costs. Now, after years of ushering away loved ones of the chosen, they were spoilt too. She could see their glassy eyes and glazed expressions in minute detail now, after years of painstaking isolation. Red stained their skin in patches, steam wafting off their tainted skin in the arctic air.

The plague had reached her kingdom at last. Inevitable. She had made certain it was the final place to be purged.

Most of her staff succumbed to the disease weeks ago, and the remaining members formed a meager procession out of the courtyard. Their fiery skin burned a path across the frozen gardens to a marble archway carved in the shape of wings unfurling around each other.

Serenia took up the rear of her attendants and guards, who had stopped caring for their state of dress, threadbare and faded, clumps of their hair missing. She wasn't certain if it was her spell that made them stop caring or the reality of what they were undertaking.

They were dead the moment they agreed to serve her.

One by one, the infected attendants stepped past the marble archway and plummeted off the sheer cliff beyond, down the mountain where the rest of the infected that found their way to the fortress lay. They didn't look back, didn't whimper, their will no longer their own.

Soon, Queen Serenia was alone.

The last sentinel of a dead world.

The burning was hateful, warming Serenia's marble skin and tarnishing it with angry red patches that grew by the day. Neither the cooling kiss of snow nor the brittle embrace of the winter wind could tame the kindling in her very bones.

A burn victim without a fire.

It was cooking her from the inside. And she had no one to curse, no one to rage at. No one to blame. But it was as she planned. She had remained pure until the end. The last to suffer this fate. As it should be.

Plague-ridden bodies lay far below her toes, beneath the cloud cover: blemishes removed from a perfectly disease-free haven. Now, she had to remove herself as well. If she had a heart, perhaps it would be pounding. Her skin felt a slight tingle as she stretched a foot over the empty air, but that might be the plague burning her flesh.

Was she afraid?

She had cauterized her emotions when she began this journey, knowing foolish sentiments would leave this world with no chance in the end. Compassion was not unwelcome, but it wouldn't save the world. For life to continue, the absence of a heart was required.

No, Serenia wasn't afraid. She was savoring the moment, the silence. The sun crested the churning sea of clouds at this high elevation, tinting them with golden light. This mountain had been hers since men were a glimmer in the eye of their creator. And now, for the first time, it would be without a master.

A necessary sacrifice.

With one final breath, Serenia stepped off the edge.

The fall wouldn't kill her. She was immortal, immune to that kind of death, though the impact would be painful. The Burning Plague, however, would eventually burn away even her stony flesh. Her demise would be slow and painful, but it would be enough time to rid the world of the remnants of the plague.

When she breathed her last, taking her magic with her, Serenia's new world would begin.

A gust of wind blew snow off a plaque set on the top of her feathery archway, revealing words chipped into the stone.

Here we take the final leap, a sacrifice for a better world tomorrow.

#

His limbs tingled, and Brogan squeezed his eyes shut from the sudden noon sun high above. It had been midnight mere moments before. He had been staring at the Ice Queen as she froze his body solid.

But the willowy angel of death was gone.

Had she changed her mind? Was the spell broken? Had someone vanquished her?

Murmurs of shock drew his attention, and Brogan turned. He wasn't alone.

Bewildered eyes searched similarly to his own, all dressed in identical treated garments far grander than any of them could afford on their own. Brogan was surrounded by others chosen by the cold-blooded sorceress.

"Myra," he said, but there wasn't a single familiar face in the courtyard's clustered crowd. Maybe she was somewhere else. Maybe she was still being examined. How much time had passed?

A tiny whimper warbled to his right where a slight girl no older than eight stood shivering, soaked. Brogan realized he was soaked too, though the fur-lined tunic and pants were still keeping him warm.

This young girl was shivering from fear.

Instincts took over and Brogan knelt down. "Are you cold?" he asked, extending a hand.

The girl tensed, still shaking, eyes wide as if she thought it would help her understand. "My parents," she whispered. "The man took them away. He said they were coming later."

Brogan frowned. Had they all been told the same thing? Was it the truth or another lie?

He gave the girl the warmest smile he could manage, thinking of Beth. "I'm looking for someone, too. Maybe we can help each other."

Erin Swann is a lifelong lover of fantasy and space adventures. She holds an MFA in Education and works as an art teacher, feeding the imaginations of others while fueling her own creativity. She also enjoys cooking, working on her own art, and playing video games. She lives in Central Maryland with her husband and family.

Thank you…

Thank you for taking the time to read our collection. We enjoyed all the stories contained within and hope you found at least a few to enjoy yourself. If you did, we'd be honored if you would leave a review on Amazon, Goodreads, and anywhere else reviews are posted.

You can also subscribe to our email list via our website, Https://www.cloakedpress.com

Follow us on Facebook
http://www.facebook.com/Cloakedpress

Tweet to us https://twitter.com/CloakedPress

We are also on Instagram
http://www.instagram.com/Cloakedpress

If you'd like to check out our other publications, you can find them on our website above. Click the "Check Our Catalog" button on the homepage for more great collections and novels from the Cloaked Press Family.1

Made in United States
North Haven, CT
01 July 2022

20863174R00186